About the Author

Lori Connelly was born, and still lives in, Oregon. Despite being a good student, her teachers complained about her tendency to daydream. The tales dancing through her imagination were frequently far more entertaining than real life. As far back as she can remember Lori made up stories, to calm her sister after a nightmare, to entertain herself in boring classes, and wrote in countless notebooks, many never again to see the light of day. She earned a BS from Eastern Oregon State College and married her best friend almost twenty years ago. She has three brilliant, handsome sons, one amazing daughter-in-law, a beautiful granddaughter and two spoiled dogs. When not writing, she loves to read, hike, camp, rock hound, and take long walks with her husband just after it rains.

Find out more about Lori Connelly at www.loriconnelly.com, loriconnelly.blogspot.com or www.facebook.com/lorilconnelly, and if you'd like notices about new releases or future Written Fireside stories please sign up for my eNewletter, http://eepurl.com/

Also by Lori Connelly

The Outlaw of Cedar Ridge
The Lawman of Silver Creek

The Lone Cowboy of River Bend

Lori Connelly

A division of HarperCollins*Publishers*
www.harpercollins.co.uk

Harper*Impulse* an imprint of
HarperCollins*Publishers*
The News Building
1 London Bridge Street
London SE1 9GF

www.harpercollins.co.uk

This paperback edition 2017

First published in Great Britain in ebook format by
HarperCollins*Publishers* 2017

A catalogue record for this book
is available from the British Library

ISBN: 9780008263126

This novel is entirely a work of fiction.
The names, characters and incidents portrayed in it are
the work of the author's imagination. Any resemblance to
actual persons, living or dead, events or localities is
entirely coincidental.

Set in Birka by Palimpsest Book Production Limited,
Falkirk, Stirlingshire

Printed and bound in Great Britain

For my family

Prologue

At high noon, Nathaniel Rolfe looked up, away from the teeming town square to the clear blue sky. The sun blazed gold overhead. On this rare winter day, not a drop of rain, flake of snow or cloud above was present, only the pronounced chill in the air suggested it was nearing the end of November. The drone of countless conversations around him increased in volume and his breath frosted the air in an irritated huff.

Restless, Nate straightened away from the old, weathered post as Marshal Evans' voice cut through the din. He turned, giving his back to the gallows. He determined the best way to escape the crowd after the hanging while only half listening to the lawman's statement. With nothing left to do, he tugged the brim of his hat down, shielding his eyes from the sunlight's glare, and waited.

An expectant hush fell. The group surrounding him pressed in tighter. He tensed, eager to be gone. As soon as Nate heard the leaves of the trap door crash open, he started walking and didn't bother glancing back. People who usually stayed at home during this time of year, rarely socializing with those outside their immediate family,

1

stood young to old all around him, doing the exact opposite. He shook his head in disbelief, watching them crane their necks, straining to get a better view of the Nash brothers hanging at the ends of their ropes. Only the bonds of friendship and family brought him to this spectacle and he couldn't wait to leave.

It wasn't that he disagreed with the sentence. The two men convicted of the murder of Janet Payne and the abduction of his shirttail cousin, Claire, had been guilty beyond all doubt. They'd earned their fate. Still, Nate frowned when cheers echoed down the length of the street. He took in the excited crowd, hooting and hollering, celebrating death, and his scowl deepened. It was times like this he questioned taking part in society at all.

Nate quickened his stride, heading toward the Trail's End Saloon on the edge of Silver Falls City, where he'd arranged to meet his friend, Matthew Marston. People littering the streets and plank sidewalks hindered him, slowing his pace. After only a few yards' progress the sensation of someone staring at him prickled his skin, further souring his mood. Two possibilities sprang to mind. Occasionally a person took a less-than-polite interest in the scar a strand of barbed wire had left over his eye in childhood. He hoped that was it.

However, something odd had been happening lately. Women had been taking an undue interest in him. He pressed onward harder, somewhat faster, but hadn't made it ten steps before a young woman planted herself in his path.

"You're him, aren't you?" She matched his sidestep, stopping him cold when he tried to dodge her.

Nate stepped in the other direction. "Excuse me."

Again, she matched his movement, remaining directly in his way as she reached out, placing a hand on his arm. "I'm Nancy and you're the—"

"No," he broke in, hoping to stop her loud, high-pitched voice from cutting through the ruckus of the crowd and drawing more unwanted attention to him.

Her hands clapped together like an excited child. "Yes, you are."

How did she notice me in this mess of people?

It didn't make any sense. Nate gritted his teeth. He wasn't unusually handsome. His facial scar wasn't that remarkable. He wore the same basic clothing as most of the men on the street, sturdy leather boots with signs of wear, blue jeans, an oil- cloth duster over a wool-lined coat and a brown hat that had seen better days.

"I can't believe I spotted you."

Neither could he, but Nate managed, barely, not to speak the sentiment aloud. He didn't try to question her, though. Recent experiences led him to believe it'd be pointless, asking the others hadn't gained him any useful answers.

In the last several months while he'd been helping Matt, the Sheriff of Silver Creek County, and his cousin, Ben, track rustlers, someone had spread romanticized gossip about him. Only Heaven knew why. Now random women sought him out but how they'd known Nate on sight remained a mystery. At times like this, he could swear someone must have drawn up a sketch of him, then passed it around the county, woman to woman, like some sort of wanted poster.

"I need to go."

"You can't leave." A slender, gloved hand clamped onto him with surprising strength. "My sister would die to meet you." The cunning glee reflected in her eyes sent the sensation of being an albino deer, hunted for its rare hide, washing over him. "We brought a picnic and you must join us."

Revulsion knotted his stomach. Too many people were acting as if they were attending the summer county fair instead of a winter hanging. He'd never understand why a somber event excited some otherwise good citizens. Nate fought to respond with the manners his mother insisted on from all her children even as adults.

3

"No."

Her face fell into a crushed expression at the mere hint of harshness in his tone, reminding him of her youth. Nate ground his teeth again for a few seconds before drawing in a fortifying breath. He managed to tack on a muttered "thank you" before moving away from her as swiftly as possible.

The easy escape sent relief coursing through him, but before long he sensed someone was following him again. Hoping the young woman wasn't pursuing him, he glanced back and discovered Sheriff Marston, the man he sought, a few paces behind him. Nate grimaced even as he paused, waiting. The smirk on his friend's face gave him the distinct impression Matt had witnessed his encounter.

Nate shifted impatiently. His gaze swept the people near him, worrying Nancy, or another like-minded woman, would dart out to grab him. In seconds that seemed to take an eternity to pass, Matt stepped up next to him.

"Don't."

"Don't what?" His good friend sounded a shade too innocent.

Delivering a glare as his only answer, Nate resumed walking toward the edge of town.

"Don't ask you about the fine young woman who stopped to chat with you?"

Nate flicked a glance at the other man, holding his tongue with effort. He was pleased Matt and his cousin, Claire, had healed their relationship, truly, but ever since those two had gotten back together the man was insufferably cheerful. He found a positive take in almost every situation now.

It grated on his nerves.

"She looked sweet."

Ignoring the statement, Nate kept moving, weaving through the milling people.

"What was wrong with this one?"

Resisting the urge to roll his eyes, he snapped, "You already know."

"She dared speak to you?"

Nate didn't respond.

"Were you this rude to the poor child?"

"No."

"Really?"

The disbelief in Matt's tone made him reconsider his answer. "Maybe, a little."

"Shocking, your mother would be appalled."

"Then it's good she's in Ireland, where word of my poor manners won't reach her."

"Oh, you never know, it might. Stories about the Recluse of River's Bend have traveled throughout the wilds of Oregon."

Nate halted abruptly, scowling anew at his friend. "It's not funny." He and his brothers were responsible for the family ranch while their parents were overseas. "I don't want anything spoiling Ma's visit."

Still grinning, Matt raised an eyebrow. "Your mother hasn't seen her sisters in over twenty years. I doubt hearing you've been rude would surprise her, let alone *spoil* anything."

"You're not taking this seriously." Nate shook his head, moving forward again. "And I have to be rude. These women aren't discouraged by polite chit chat."

"You shouldn't let a little attention bother you."

"I don't like it."

"They're just flirting with you."

"Strangers? With no encouragement?" Nate shook his head. "They're making a laughing stock out of me."

"Those women were definitely not laughing at you."

Nate leveled a look at Matt. "Last week, out on the Double J, Judson's hired hands kept hanging back in the shadows of the barn, grinning and whispering."

"They could've been talking about Ben."

"They wouldn't have been smiling if the subject had been whether or not Ben is the rustler." Nate held his gaze steady.

"Good point." Matt paused for a moment, then advised in a more serious tone, "Don't let it get to you. Ignore it."

"I've tried. Hasn't helped."

The long-legged men covered a lot of distance in a short span of time. They passed three storefronts before Matt spoke again. "Gossip usually dies if it isn't fed."

"Then obviously someone is feeding it."

"Agreed, but you have to admit, it's fascinating how far the story has spread."

"I don't need every woman I run into trying to heal my imaginary *broken heart*."

"Don't exaggerate. It's only been a handful."

Matt smiled in the face of Nate's hard stare. "That's five too many."

"There has always been a woman or two seeking your attention, what's a few more?"

His friend's matter-of-fact tone frustrated him but a group of approaching women caused him to hold his tongue. Nate moved, putting Matt between himself and the group of seven. He bowed his head to hide his face until after they passed.

"No woman singled me out until the stupid story spread."

"Emmaline Porter."

"What about her?" Nate demanded. "She married a pig farmer from Corvallis."

"After she spent a year trying to get you to notice her."

"One misguided woman." He waved a hand in a dismissive gesture.

"And Agnes Gardner?"

"Moved to West Bend with her sister."

"Because you broke her heart."

"I never spoke a word to her."

A short bark of laughter burst out of Matt. "Exactly."

"Your point?"

"The basic story irritating you now has been whispered by the good women of Fir Mountain for years. Someone simply built on what was already floating around."

"You think I brought this on myself?" Indignation accented each word.

Matt shrugged. "Some women don't appreciate being ignored."

An increase in raised voices distracted Nate. He looked in the direction of the sound. A short distance ahead of them people had withdrawn, clearing a circle in the middle of the street around a handful of men who were shouting and shoving one another. A glance back at Matt revealed the somber shift in his companion's expression. His friend appeared to be on the verge of stepping in but then Marshal Evans arrived on the scene. The other lawman shoved his way through the onlookers and in minutes had the situation under control.

"I don't ignore people. I just enjoy spending most of my time alone. Nothing wrong with it." Nate indicated with a jerk of his head the sullen men facing the marshal as he and Matt walked past them. "Some people could benefit from doing the same."

"Or perhaps they need more time with others to reinforce proper behavior."

Nate shrugged. "With time and patience you can make a coyote a pet but it's still a coyote."

"So you fear certain women want to make you a pet?"

"Cute."

"My point is—"

"Silly."

"That being reclusive makes you-"

"I'm not a recluse."

"Oh? Other than when you're helping me? When do you ride into town?"

"How often I'm in Fir Mountain is immaterial."

"I beg to differ. The fact you're rarely seen makes you seem mysterious—"

"Mysterious," Nate scoffed.

"Mysterious," Matt repeated firmly. "Especially after you moved onto River's Bend. Ever since, you've come in for staples or to attend church only once in a blue moon. The women refer to you like some sort of tragic hero, finding you romantic—"

"I am not romantic."

"Plainly the young woman disagreed with you." Matt laid a hand on his chest, fluttered his eyelashes, then without missing a step continued in a high-pitched mockery of a woman's voice. "After losing the love of his life, the poor man moved out into the wilderness, all alone, to nurse his wounded heart."

"You don't need to repeat the whole ridiculous story."

"It's what I heard Nancy say to another young lady after you stomped off."

Nate shook his head. "So a twisted version of old gossip is being spread further. Great."

"That's the nature of gossip, twisting the truth."

"So you still believe this is harmless tongue-wagging?"

"Actually, I'm not sure." All hint of the good-humored teasing dropped from Matt's tone. "The rumor about Ben is a deliberate, directed act. Someone wants to pin the rustling on him. The sudden attention to, and spreading of, your heartbroken recluse story has a similar feel but—"

"Someone is making me into a laughing stock."

"If so, then why? You're one man living in a remote area of a sparsely populated county."

"Are you trying to say I'm not important?"

"In the grand scheme of things, no."

"But?"

"I don't like coincidences. Someone made certain to spread your story far and wide around the same time as the rumor about Ben cropped up. Perhaps, as a distraction."

"From what?"

"Good question."

8

"One you didn't answer," Nate muttered, stepping off the sidewalk onto the muddy road. "I need to get my gun."

Only lawmen had been allowed to carry firearms in Silver Falls City today. Nate couldn't have cared less whether he carried a weapon in town or not, but out on the range a gun was necessary for protection. Matt changed direction with him and they headed for a small stand, where a couple of the marshal's men guarded the confiscated guns. The inconvenience of having to reclaim his pistol deepened his impatience and, noticing a line forming, he hastened his pace. He couldn't wait to shake off the dust of this place and get clear of all these people.

"Because I don't know. My first assumption may be correct."

"Miss Collier?"

"Hell hath no fury like—"

Nate looked pointedly at his friend. "I did not scorn that woman."

"I'm sure it wasn't your intention."

"I turned down a single invitation."

"Publicly."

"She cornered me outside after church."

"Where half the town heard you say no."

"I was polite."

"I know."

"And for that you think she …" Nate shook his head. "It doesn't make sense."

"It's clever, making your refusal all about your broken heart instead of being personal."

"Seems like a great deal of trouble to go to over one man's no thank you."

"Miss Collier strikes me as someone who does not like being told no and if someone shared the old gossip about you with her, well, it's not that big of a leap."

"I'd think others would see her purpose, then."

"Not if what she said fit the narrative."

9

"Which is?"

"You don't socialize because Faith broke your heart."

"Oh for the love of … That isn't it."

"She did hurt you."

"So?"

"Well, now it seems only the right woman can heal you," Matt responded as they closed in on the men gathered in front of the stand.

"What? I don't need—" He broke off when more men approached from behind. Nate rushed forward, securing a place in line, then continued when his friend caught up with him. "We'll finish this later, on the road."

Matt raised one eyebrow at Nate's cross tone. "I look forward to it. I need a word with Gus before we go." He nodded to the left. "I see him over near the saloon. Come join us when you're done."

Troubled thoughts rolled through his mind as Nate watched the other man amble away. Coincidences disturbed him as much as they did Matt. How was the resurrection of old gossip connected to the rustling? The answer remained as elusive as the identity of the rustlers. Despite months of hard work, there was still no hard evidence, just suspects and suspicion.

Ranchers throughout the county were growing understandably furious. Yesterday a number of cattle had gone missing from the Crooked Rim Ranch, a few hours' ride from Silver Falls City. He'd met Matt there early this morning. The owner was certain he knew who was responsible. Frank Meyers had accused his friend of not doing his job because he refused to arrest Ben right then.

Nate reached up and rubbed the tense muscles on the back of his neck. If undisputable proof didn't turn up soon, he feared his cousin would take the fall. Distracted, he was slow to step forward when the person in front of him moved and a familiar, smug, voice attacked.

"What put a sour expression on your face, Rolfe? Was the sight of those lowlifes' necks getting stretched too much for a man like you?"

Great. Can this day get any worse?

Chapter 1

The man who had married Faith, the woman he'd once thought to spend his life with, stood behind him. What she'd seen in the short, balding man with a nasty attitude was beyond Nate. Randy Haze had always taken pleasure in cutting people down.

"Well, was it?"

His expression carefully blank, Nate didn't react. To him needless conflict was a waste of time and energy. He stepped up and handed his token to one of the men returning weapons, hoping Haze would lose interest if ignored. To speed up the process, he pointed to the revolver in his holster, hanging on a peg to the left. When the man reached up to match the tag on his gun belt to his token, Randy persisted.

"Are you deaf, Rolfe?"

"No." Nate kept his response brief and bland as he took his weapon from the deputy.

"Well then?"

When he stepped off to the side, allowing the line to move forward, Nate felt the other man follow him without pausing to collect his own firearm. He adjusted the belt around his hips before looking over, meeting the disagreeable man's gaze. For a moment he considered responding with a few choice words, then decided Haze wasn't worth his time. Without a word, he strode off to rejoin Matt.

"I guess what they say is true."

Nate kept walking, heading for the men standing near the corner of The Trail's End Saloon.

"You hide away because you're a lily-livered coward."

His jaw clenched, but he allowed the taunt to go unanswered, unwilling to show how the slur bothered him. The ugly charge had joined the gossip regarding him in recent weeks. His suspicion about the man's involvement deepened.

"Trouble?" Matt asked when Nate joined him and Marshal Evans.

"Just Randy being Randy."

The marshal studied Nate briefly then looked beyond him. "Personal issue?"

"Likely." Nate offered a measured response. He was slow to warm to people and had only met Gus on a handful of occasions.

Matt, on the other hand, knew the marshal well and was more forthcoming. "Randy Haze likes to stir things up. I suspect he's one of the people behind the rumors we talked about."

"Like the one saying you need to be kicked out of office?" Gus turned, facing Nate squarely. "Was he bad-mouthing the sheriff?"

"No."

"What was his beef?"

"Just trying to rile me."

"A troublemaker?"

"Doubt he'll cause you any headaches." Matt drew the other lawman's attention. "He probably came for the hanging and Nate had the bad luck to run into him."

"That's over." Tone crisp, Gus straightened his hat. "I'll have a word with Haze, get him headed out of my town." He nodded to Matt. "Thanks for the update. I'll see you next week." Then he directed another nod at Nate. "Rolfe."

"Anything new?" Matt asked, as they watched Gus personally speed the process of returning Randy's weapon then engage the man in conversation.

"Same as last time. Trying to provoke me." Nate gestured toward the corral some yards away, eager to get his horse and head out of town. "You ready to—"

Suddenly Haze stomped off, heading in the direction of the livery. Fresh impatience flooded Nate. Unwilling to suffer a second encounter with Randy, he became a statue, tracking the other man with a hooded glare until he entered the building.

"Hell."

"Best to avoid him," Matt cautioned.

"I do. The man does not like me."

"Because of Faith?"

"I guess." Nate stepped out into the street, restless. "But why? She chose him."

"Some men never warm to their wife's first love."

Nate kicked a rock. "Keen observation, Lawman."

"I aim to please."

Randy walked outside, leading his bay horse before Nate could reply. The shopkeeper looked at them and smirked before swinging up into the saddle. Without further incident, he rode away, heading out of town on the road leading to Fir Mountain.

"Let's get out of here." Nate didn't wait for agreement. On edge, he needed to move. His long strides ate the short distance to the corral.

"What's your rush? If we hurry we'll catch up to Haze."

"I need to get out of this town to where I can breathe."

Nate didn't pause, moving quickly past the split-rail fence and into the livery, not stopping until he reached the stall with his horse, Jack. With swift, sure movements, he readied the gelding for travel. Matt followed his lead, whistling, while he worked in the next stall. The men were back outside and mounted within minutes. They rode out of Silver Falls City at a brisk walk, an appropriate pace for moving through the outskirts of a heavily populated town, yet frustratingly slow, in his opinion.

"You told Evans you're suspicious of Haze."

"And you're wondering why?"

"Last time we talked, you weren't."

Several seconds passed. They continued forward, following a worn pathway through a stand of fir trees leading to a rougher, less-traveled road than the one Haze had chosen. Nate held to the slow pace, waiting for a response. After some time he almost prompted his friend but one look at Matt's solemn expression caused him to hold his tongue.

"I had a long talk with Mercy."

A sinking feeling settled in his gut after the sheriff finally spoke. His friend had seen Faith's little sister in the company of Miss Collier often but Nate couldn't believe she had any part in spreading the nasty rumors. She'd always been sweet to him.

"I don't think-"

"She said Miss Collier encouraged gossip about you. Mercy tried to rein it in but others sympathized with the woman."

"Why? I spoke to her *once*." Nate was succinct.

"I hear she has an artful way with the truth."

"What does this have to do with Haze?"

"I've reason to believe he learned about Ben and told her."

Nate's hand tightened on the reins. He resisted the urge to put his heels to his mount and let a long, hard ride bring calm. "New rumors?"

"No." Tension filled Matt's voice. "The original ones. The rustling started when he showed up in Fir Mountain. Speculation about his past. Stirring distrust without making an accusation."

"Allowing people to draw the *obvious* conclusion."

"Then repeat it as truth."

Nate shook his head, too frustrated to speak. There was no evidence his cousin had been an outlaw in Cedar Ridge but the fact that the Nash brothers had stalked Ben and his wife all the way to Oregon cast suspicion. The possibility haunted the man since he couldn't confirm or deny it. An injury caused him some permanent memory loss before they'd moved. Only family members, Matt, Sean, Matt's deputy, some Idaho lawmen, and a judge knew there was a chance he had a criminal past. Of that group, just those closest to him lived in Fir Mountain. It felt unbelievable one of them let the information slip.

Yet, one of them had, to Haze of all people.

Troubled, Nate squeezed his knees tighter, urging Jack to a faster pace. He'd met Ben for the first time last spring and believed his cousin had been honest, openly sharing concerns about his past with them from the start. He'd proven to be a hard, dependable worker on the Bar 7 and a good friend.

Matt had inquired about the Idaho crimes at Ben's request but there was no evidence of his involvement. Only one witness ever caught a good look at the robbers and he'd identified the Nash brothers. Since they were already set to hang, the sheriff from Cedar Ridge considered charging them with more offences a waste of time. A judge agreed. With the cases solved in the eyes of the law, and knowing he'd likely never recall the past, Ben accepted the ruling. He wanted to put it behind him now and not speak of it again.

Who, then, had provided fodder for gossip?

The slim possibilities flipped through Nate's mind for the thousandth time. Matt interviewed everyone with a connection, the Idaho lawmen, Judge Littleton, Claire and her family, Nate's brothers, even Evie, Ben's wife, hadn't been spared. His cousin had confided their relationship had gone through a rough patch but the marriage was rock solid and enviable now. The couple was expecting a baby soon and, in his opinion, deserved peace.

However, everyone Matt had spoken to denied speaking of Ben's past even as the rumors spread. His sheriff friend had a gut feeling that discovering who wanted to pin the rustling on his cousin would help solve the crimes plaguing his county. With no witnesses, tracks leading nowhere or promising trails washed away by rain, and no attempts to sell any of the branded cattle despite statewide alerts, there wasn't much else to go on.

The rattle of wooden wheels heralded an approaching wagon and wordlessly Matt dropped back, riding behind him. They rode on down the far right side of the road in single file, allowing the driver to travel past them. In the bed filled with people, Nate spotted Nancy's pouting face. He slouched in the saddle and bent his neck so the brim of his hat shadowed his face.

Nate straightened as soon as the wagon turned off the main road, rolling out of sight. He looked around while Matt moved forward, riding next to him once again. The road, visible for a good distance ahead and behind them, had no other travelers. He breathed a sigh of relief. The tension in his shoulders relaxed to some degree until his friend spoke.

"If Randy is guilty then I'm afraid—"

"It's not Faith." Nate jumped in. She was a good woman. It wasn't her fault she couldn't bear a life on River's Bend. Few women would be content to live so far from others. "She had no way of knowing about Ben's past before the rumors started."

"I know. This isn't about her."

His friend's almost hesitant tone had him slow his mount to a walk again. "Then who?"

"Claire caught Haze eavesdropping on some ranch hands in his store the other day."

"And you waited until now to mention it?"

"It was a bit crowded at the hanging."

"What about before?"

"I needed to think it over."

Matt was an excellent sheriff. His friend carefully considered all the facts in the crimes he investigated. However, in this case, Nate didn't understand what needed pondering. Haze, the man who always enjoyed amusing himself at other people's expense, seemed like a great suspect to him.

"If he's been lurking in shadows, spying, then one careless mention about Ben where he could've …" Matt winced, causing Nate to pause. His eyes narrowed, and certain he wouldn't like the answer, asked, "What haven't you said?"

"It may have been Claire."

"What?" The word exploded from him, both a question and a demand.

Although he and Claire were more distantly related, their mothers were cousins themselves rather than the closer blood tie he shared with Ben because their fathers were siblings, Nate had grown up with the woman. Her family lived down the road. Feisty and fiercely independent, she was as loyal as the day was long. He scowled. If his friend didn't understand her nature, he had no business marrying her.

Matt studied him for a minute before responding. "For a man who prides himself on his calm nature, you're testy today."

"For good reason," Nate bit out. A loner, even now, some miles away from the crowded city, he felt on edge. And this conversation didn't help. "You knew what to expect when you asked for my help."

"The skills of one of the best trackers in Oregon?"

"The best," Nate agreed, a quiet statement of fact without a hint of boast.

"The companionship of a good friend, who will have my back."

"Always."

"And a man grumpier than a bear roused from hibernation when forced to be among people."

"You're stalling. Stop," he demanded in a low, impatient rumble. "Explain what you meant about Claire."

Matt released a breath sounding just short of a sigh. "When we were apart, she and Evie talked a lot."

"So?"

"Sometimes they came into town for lunch and ... Look, she and Evie are close, like sisters. Claire would never deliberately do anything to hurt her or Ben."

"I know. Do you?" Nate's tone was unyielding.

"Yes. But if Haze had been lurking around the livery where they'd leave the buggy or ..."

A number of possibilities sprang to mind and some of his defensiveness eased. "I can see how it may have happened."

"Claire feels horrible."

"She shouldn't. If it's true, then the blame is Haze's and his alone."

"Remember, this is all speculation," Matt cautioned.

"You inferred he and Miss Collier are friends."

"He's been spending a lot of time at her bakery."

"A shop she opened right before the rustling started, and despite few customers or goods to sell, the woman lives well."

"The clever Miss Collier is notably seen in town during each rustling incident."

"And you suspect her of more than gossip, don't you?"

"If Haze is the brains behind the gang rustling, and has played me for a fool all these months." His friend's serious expression became grim. "I've no business being sheriff. The man is dumber than a mud fence."

"And Miss Collier?"

"Is guilty of more than being offended that you wouldn't walk her home. Of what exactly, I've no proof."

To his surprise, Nate found he missed his friend's earlier good humor and offered support. "You're making progress."

"Too damn little."

The truth of those harsh words weighed heavy on the two men. Over the next few miles conversation dwindled until they were barely exchanging a word. Each had been lost in their own thoughts for some time as they reached the anticipated fork in the road. When the friends moved a few feet off the road and pulled up, they focused on the reason for Nate's side trip.

"You think Alice is ready to come home now?"

The Rolfes' long-time housekeeper was like a second mother to Nate and his siblings. He gazed off to the south. She'd left several months ago to help her son following the death of his wife. "Hope so."

"Jed was … poorly when I stopped by."

Drunk, as he'd been at the funeral? The one brief letter Alice sent hadn't mentioned trouble but Nate sensed something was wrong. Concerned, he'd asked Matt to drop by Jed's place when the sheriff was in that part of the county last week. He looked back at his friend. The pity reflected in the other man's gaze seemed to confirm his notion. With a nod, he acknowledged the information.

"Come over when you get back."

"Will do."

The two men parted ways. Matt continued west, heading toward Fir Mountain, while Nate aimed for a small farm near Ashwood. As much as he longed to be heading home too, riding south granted something he treasured, time alone. Between working on the Bar 7 with his brothers while his parents were away and helping Matt, it was rare to have a moment to call his own.

With almost a day's ride ahead, he avoided towns and other travelers whenever possible. Nate had had his fill of people. By late afternoon, he felt more like himself than he had in a long while. He made camp in an empty meadow at dusk despite noting a few nearby farms.

Rain drizzled off and on. His tiny campfire provided more light than warmth. Jerky made a sorry dinner and his saddle a hard pillow. It wasn't the most comfortable night Nate had ever spent but he considered it far better than taking shelter with strangers.

Late the next morning Nate rode up the road toward Redwing Farm. Grey clouds covered the sky, lending an eerie light to the day. He pulled up then reached into his pocket for the crumpled bit of paper his brother, Sam, had jotted down crude directions for him.

Nate studied the scribbles. A glance around seemed to confirm he was in the right place. He turned onto a rutted path kindness could call a road, riding slowly around a stand of tall fir trees, letting Jack pick his way forward. Minutes later, he crested a hill and headed for the house set in the center of a few other scattered structures.

The recent rain dampened the earth, muffling Jack's hoof beats. He slowed his horse to a walk as he approached the wood-frame home. Dark and silent, with windows shuttered, the simple building looked deserted. No smoke drifted from the chimney.

Concerned, Nate scanned for other signs of life. Gently sloping fields stretched empty for a good distance around. The only signs of life came from a precious few chickens. This time of year, the lack of crops didn't disturb him but he'd expected to see more animals as well as a person or two.

Nate dismounted, looped his reins around a porch post then walked up to the door. No one responded to him knocking. At a loss, he returned to Jack and climbed back in the saddle.

The stillness pricked at his nerves even though silence didn't normally bother him. On his homestead only the sounds of nature filled most days. The quiet he found at River's Bend was peaceful. But here … what he felt was … disquieting.

Leather creaked as Nate shifted in the saddle, searching for someone, anyone. No one moved about tending chores. Not a flicker of movement caught his eye. The corral didn't confine one four-legged creature. Overall, the farm appeared neglected, almost deserted.

For a second, Nate flirted with the idea that his brother had given him wrong directions, then he dismissed the idea. Sam's handwriting might be horrid but the man was a stickler for details. It was far more likely he'd read them wrong.

A gust of wind pierced the outer layer of his coat. Nate hunched his shoulders, chilled, as he considered options. After last night's cold camp, he'd been looking forward to the warmth of a roaring fire, a hot meal, and a comfortable bed. Irritated, he was about to go in search of a neighbor for help when the sight of a board leaning against the barn stopped him cold.

Redwing Farm.

Although the cracked sign confirmed he was at the correct place, Nate felt frustrated rather than relieved. Worry weaved through his thoughts. Alice had known he'd arrive today. Well, she likely expected Sam, but still, she should be here, waiting.

Where is she?

His gaze scanned the area yet again. This time, from a new vantage point, Nate caught a flash of white on the side of the house. He urged Jack forward, riding past the building. On the far side, he discovered a woman with her back to him, battling to remove sheets from a clothesline in the rising wind. Silent, he pulled up and studied her for a moment although he knew she wasn't the one he sought.

While he'd never thought to ask her exact age, Nate knew Alice had to be in her fifties. Her hair, once as dark as the night, now had liberal streaks of silver. The woman in front of him was bundled against the chilly weather in a long, dark coat but nothing covered her head.

The long, tangled remains of her braid whipped in the wind, holding his attention. The color, a rich ginger shade of red, drew Nate to her, a moth to a flame. His gaze never left the woman as he dismounted. For the first time he felt empathy toward those women who'd pounced on him upon recognition. This woman's appearance compelled him. He left his mount ground-tied and strode straight to her, trying to make his approach as loud as possible so she wouldn't be startled.

Chapter 2

The wind ripped the sheet corner out of Hannah Brook's hand again. Frustrated, a huff of air passed her lips as she tried to wrestle the linen into submission, but even the aggravating task couldn't hold her full attention. Worry gnawed at her, causing distraction. Her gaze kept returning to where Alice and the kids had vanished into a clump of scrawny oak trees. Sam Rolfe should arrive by midday and she wanted to be elsewhere before then.

Although the older woman had repeatedly assured Hannah the Rolfes wouldn't harm her or her daughter, she couldn't quite believe it. The fiery tone Michael used when he'd spoken of his relations remained one of her most vivid memories of him. The easygoing man became downright grim at the mere mention of his family. He'd been emphatic, warning her to stay away from them, but never really explained why.

Maybe if we'd had more time...

Hannah swallowed a sigh. She should've pressed him for answers. On days like today, doubts plagued her. She kept second-guessing herself.

Do the Rolfes have a right to know?

Alice had earned her trust, becoming a valued friend over these past difficult months. She'd confided something few people had ever known to her, the identity of Jemma's father. The older woman promised never to reveal her secret but she wasn't shy about voicing her opinion. She dearly loved the family who'd employed her for over two decades and believed they deserved to know. And Hannah's daughter had the right to know them.

Hannah felt torn. As time ticked down to when Sam was due to come for Alice, she struggled to sort out her feelings on the matter and failed. Her decision, or rather lack of one, gave her a nagging sense of failure. Hiding never solved anything. Yet that was what she was about to do.

Alice pointing out the flaw in her plan hadn't helped. It wouldn't take long for the older woman to explain to Sam she wasn't ready to leave, but given the distance he'd traveled, the man would likely spend the night. With no relatives she could claim and no friends beyond those on Redwing Farm, there was no place she and Jemma could stay longer than a few hours. Running off for a short time when he'd probably still be here when she returned made no sense. She'd lain awake for hours last night, debating to stay or not.

Hannah blew out a breath. Maybe it was good Alice was late returning with the children. Her friend could be right. Sticking around, meeting Sam, and getting a measure of the man might be the wiser choice. Wind whipped her hair across her face. She started to raise a hand to brush it away then paused, a sound catching her attention.

Listening, she stilled. A long moment passed but all Hannah heard was moaning from the house behind her as wind battered old boards. She wiped at her face with an impatient motion, clearing some strands of hair from her eyes before returning to the chore at hand.

While Hannah battled to remove another sheet off the line, she inhaled the slight scent of lavender. Her lips curved as a pleasant memory tumbled through her mind. Michael had stumbled across her mother's place on another blustery day a little over five years ago. He'd caught her outside, charming her eighteen-year-old self with comments about her sweet-smelling clothing and his smile.

A soft sigh escaped her. Time had dulled the pain of losing him but sometimes a memory still brought the bittersweet echo of a dream lost upon awakening. With effort, Hannah pushed thoughts of Michael aside. She needed to focus on her present circumstances, not on what might have been. A decision had to be made and soon. Life didn't pause in times of struggle or sorrow. A harsh lesson she knew well.

In her life, Hannah had survived losing a number of people she'd loved: her parents, Michael, and recently Bessie. One day her best friend had been here, smiling, happy, talking about her plans for Redwing Farm, how it was going to be a famous breeding place, then the next day she was gone. How fragile life could be, even for a young, healthy woman, was no longer an abstract notion but an inescapable reality. A worry she had on occasion became a nagging concern after the tragedy. For comforting, Bessie's boys had their grandmother, Alice, and their father lived. Jemma only had Hannah.

If I die, who would care for my daughter?

The sheet twisted, wrapping around one of her arms. *Is it fair to keep Jemma from the Rolfes? Alice could be right.* Hannah tugged loose of the linen then threw it into the basket near her feet. *But what if Michael knew something she doesn't? Maybe I-*

The scrape of footsteps disrupted her musing. Hannah turned, expecting to see someone familiar and gasped at the sight of the stranger stepping up to her. He was an imposing man, standing some inches taller and being quite broad about the chest and shoulders. In the diffused light on this overcast day, with the wide brim of his hat throwing his face in shadow, his expression was unfathomable. Under the weight of his dark, steady gaze, she hardly dared to breathe. They stood, still and silent, for a moment. Then he reached up and removed his hat.

For an instant, the image of another man superimposed over the one before her. Confusion filled Hannah. She took a half step back, blinking hard. *Michael?* As soon as her thought formed, the illusion faded. She saw the stranger clearly again, noting any similarities between the two men were superficial at best.

Their physical builds and coloring were much the same but there were obvious differences. Jemma's father had green eyes that most often reflected inner amusement. This man's hazel eyes were somber and the left one had a faded scar around it. Michael would have hated a mark on his skin. He'd been almost vain about his appearance, keeping his straight hair neatly trimmed and well combed. The stranger, on the other hand, reminded her of a trapper who'd lived near Ashwood for a time. His dark-brown hair had a thick wave to it, tumbling around his face and over his collar to his shoulders, giving him an untamed, wild look.

Her gaze lowered, traveling over his full-length duster to the battered boots made for work. Michael had fancy footwear, shined for show. As she looked back up, Hannah noted well-worn blue jeans and a practical jacket visible between the open edges of oilskin. Both useful items of clothing Jemma's father would have never worn. His words, a memory, whispered in her mind.

No matter what, darling, a man has to look successful.

The stranger held out a hand. She stared at it for a moment still mired in noticing differences. Michael's hands had been soft, clean, and well kept, the hands of a gambler. This man's skin appeared calloused and travel-dirty, revealing he worked hard and outdoors often.

"Need help?"

Hannah shook her head, not in answer to his question but because she didn't know what to say.

"You sure?"

"I. uh." *What am I doing?* Michael was gone, had been for years. Comparing the men was silly and pointless. Hannah pushed away her memories and focused on the stranger. "Thank you, I'd appreciate it."

Her tone became a little squeaky as the likely identity of the man popped into her mind. Her heart beat faster. She'd met him once, years ago, and even though he didn't look like Hannah, remembered this must be Sam Rolfe, showing up early.

Should I tell him? Do I need to? Fear rushed through her veins. Hannah took a deep breath, gathering her composure. *Maybe it's enough that Alice knows.* She gave him a polite smile. "You must be Sam."

"Sorry, no, I'm Nate." His hand still extended to her, he moved closer. After a brief hesitation, she grasped it. The contact with his rough, cool skin sent an unexpected wave of warmth through her. "My brother couldn't make it."

"Oh." Which brother in particular didn't matter, the man was a Rolfe. His arrival decided the fate of her plan. If she dashed off now it might well create the very interest in her and her daughter she wanted to avoid. She pulled her hand free, then remembered her manners. "Pleased to meet you, I'm Hannah Brooks."

Nate smiled. The sweet, slow movement of his lips sent awareness dancing along her nerves. "Miss Brooks."

The wind gathered strength, buffeting her. Loosened hair stung her eyes and whipped her face. Despite the weather, Hannah stood, rooted to the ground, staring at Nate until he lifted an eyebrow in silent question. Her cheeks burned. With a gesture to the basket beside her, she turned away from him.

They wrestled the sheets into the large wicker container over the next several minutes. When they finished, Nate picked up the laundry, carrying it past his waiting horse and around the side of the house to set it on the porch. Hannah followed him slowly, taking some time to think over her behavior. She joined him near the steps almost a full minute later.

"I apologize for my bad manners, Mr. Rolfe. We don't get many visitors and you startled me."

28

"I'm sorry."

She shook her head, confused.

"That I startled you, Miss Brooks."

"It's all right, Mr. Rolfe."

His expression remained polite but something flickered in his dark eyes as he nodded. "Nate."

"Very well … Nate." Something about his name had tugged at her memory. She sifted through the information Alice shared with her about the Rolfes, thinking furiously. "Oh, you must be—"

"Don't."

His abrupt change of tone, now rough and bordering on rude, took Hannah by surprise. Confused, she ventured softly, "The oldest brother?"

"I am." The man rubbed a hand over his face. "Sorry." Dark smudges beneath his eyes painted a picture of exhaustion. "It's been a long few days."

"It's all right."

Nate acknowledged her words with a shake of his head and a brief smile. An awkward silence fell between them then. Hannah, a quiet, somewhat shy, woman often felt uncomfortable in social situations. Circumstances had led to her having few friends as she grew up and, following Jemma's birth, her world narrowed even further. Until Alice came, Bessie and her husband, Jed, had been her only friends for a long time.

Words flitted through her mind, considered then dismissed unspoken. Her gaze flickered from him to the yard beyond, then back again repeatedly, praying to see the older woman returning with the children each time. Unfortunately, aside from the man with her, the chickens were the only creatures in sight.

After another endless moment, Hannah stopped trying to come up with something smart and engaging to tell him. "I'm sorry. I don't know what to say."

"It's all right, Miss Brooks." Though his smile had faded, his tone, low, rich, and warm repeated the phrase she'd offered him with quiet sincerity.

"Please call me Hannah."

"Hannah."

His voice held a note she couldn't define but it sparked a response nonetheless. Fire spread over her cheeks again. Silence returned. Hannah shifted her weight from one foot to the other, uncertain of what to do next. With Jed in his current state she might as well be alone and was reluctant to invite anyone into the house.

After several seconds, he prompted, "Would you let Alice know I'm here?"

"I will, as soon as she returns."

"Where is she?"

"She took the kids fishing."

"Fishing?"

His obvious puzzlement was understandable. It wasn't a common activity this time of year but the children needed a break from the oppressive atmosphere at home. Jed had worsened. This week even the hours spent away at school didn't seem to ease his sons much. Even Jemma, once a sunny child, had been too quiet lately.

"Odd, I know, but the boys were restless. They're probably pitching rocks into the water instead of casting out line."

"Wasn't she expecting me?"

"We didn't think Sam, well, you, would be here before noon."

"Sorry."

"No need. *I'm* sorry she isn't here."

Nate studied her from the other side of the steps, not attempting to move closer. "Should I come back later?"

"No," Hannah answered, sounding almost breathless. She cleared her throat before continuing in a stronger voice. "You don't have to leave. It's just ..."

"I'm troubling you."

30

"No I … It's not you."

"Did Jed go?"

Do something fun with the boys? Hannah stuffed her chilled hands into the pockets of her coat. "No, he did not."

"He's home?"

"Yes, he is." *When is he not?*

"Would you tell him I'm here?"

"I'd rather not." With effort, Hannah kept her tone even, masking exasperation. They'd had an exceptionally bad morning with Jed.

"Why?"

"I don't think it'd be a good idea."

"He's … poorly?"

Hannah drew in a deep breath. Something about the way he responded told her Nate knew, or at least suspected, Jed's affliction. Still, she believed it was best not to say much.

"He's … having a bad day. When Alice gets back, I'm sure she'll explain."

Instead of pressing her further, Nate simply nodded. The only sign of his displeasure was in the slight downturn of his lips, a suggestion of a frown. She almost sagged in relief. Even with Alice, his mother, the changes in her friend's husband were difficult to discuss. The light-hearted man Jed had been before Bessie's death existed only in their memories now.

"Would you like to sit while we wait?" Hannah gestured to the pair of rockers on the sagging porch.

As soon as the words left her mouth, Hannah started feeling self-conscious. She looked down at the ground by her feet. Few people shared her enthusiasm to be outside when nature decided to be rowdy. Slowly, she brought her gaze up to meet his.

"Thank you." His tone reflected a sincere appreciation for her offer. "But I need to take care of my horse." He waved his hand in the direction of his mount. "Is there room for him?"

"Room?" *He thinks the farm is still functioning.* The words to explain stuck in her throat. Without talking about Jed, it'd be impossible. "Yes, there is."

"Would you mind showing us?"

"Us?" Startled, Hannah glanced around, looking for his companion.

Nate nodded toward his horse. "Jack and I."

"Jack?" In all the years Hannah had known Bessie, she'd heard several strange names given to horses but they usually bordered on fanciful. "You named your horse Jack?"

"Yes." Nate headed toward the young, reddish-brown horse. "It suits him."

"I'm sure it does," she affirmed, more to herself than him.

The wind carried the clean scent of recent rain to her as she waited, reminding Hannah a storm threatened. *Why hasn't she brought the kids home?* She turned, looking at the spot where they'd most likely emerge from the tree line along the south field. There was no sign of them. Despite having complete trust in the other woman, worry nagged at her.

"Hannah?"

His voice, soft and deep, drew her attention. "Yes?"

"You all right?"

For a second or two, she thought about sharing her concern, then dismissed the impulse. "I'm fine, but would you excuse me? I'd like to put the sheets inside first."

"Of course."

Hannah darted up onto the porch, where she picked up the basket before slipping into the house. She moved quietly inside, tiptoeing across the main room to put the laundry down near the table. Her mission complete, she turned, heading toward the door, then halted midway. This was still Jed's house. By rights, she should inform him of visitors. After taking in a deep breath to steady her nerves, she changed direction and headed to his room.

In front of the closed door, she stopped, hesitated a few seconds, then knocked. There was no response but Hannah hadn't really expected one. She turned the knob and opened the door some inches.

"Nate Rolfe is here," she announced softly, yet loud enough to carry to the occupant.

Hannah waited several seconds, then took Jed's silence as an answer itself. She bit her lip hard, preventing the release of a heavy sigh of disappointment. Wordlessly, she pulled the door shut, leaving the man alone in the shadow-filled room again.

Her strides were swift as she crossed the room, blinking back tears. By the time Hannah reached the front door, she'd recovered her composure. She exited the house, finding Nate waiting patiently, and hurried down the steps.

"Follow me." With a polite smile, she paused at his side briefly, then continued on, heading to the barn.

Nate's long stride brought him even with her in a matter of seconds. Their arms brushed. Startled, she stumbled on a tuft of grass. Her companion reached out, grabbing her arm to steady her.

Hannah pulled free almost immediately. "Thank you."

"You all right?"

"I'm fine, just fine, thank you."

Flustered by the unexpected contact, Hannah moved on at an even faster pace. They crossed the yard, scattering chickens as they came upon them. She was vividly aware of him every step of the way, feeling uncomfortable yet intrigued.

Like it'd been with Michael.

The memory of how swiftly she'd fallen for Jemma's father rose like a specter in her mind. Hannah had given him her heart in a matter of days. *But this isn't the same.*

Hannah reasoned away the disturbing thoughts. It had been a troubled day. Circumstances stirred up her emotions. Naturally, doubts and worries were haunting her. That's why Michael had been on her mind. That's all it was.

And although she'd just met Nate, Hannah could tell the two men were nothing alike. In fact, she remembered Alice saying the Rolfes had adopted their eldest son. He and Michael didn't even share blood. It was *impossible* she felt the same kind of instant attraction.

True, the man was handsome. Hannah glanced sideways. Nate was striking in a much *different* way than Jemma's father. His rugged good looks would have an effect on *any* woman. Besides, she was older and far wiser now. Nothing would happen. She knew better than to repeat history.

At the barn, Nate handed her his reins, then pulled open one of the heavy doors. A headache pulsed to life, pounding behind her eyes while Hannah watched him stare into the building. The sad shape of the interior appeared a hundred times worse to her now than it had this morning. The improvements Bessie dreamed of doing never became reality. She and Alice, with the children's help, had done the best they could, which wasn't much. Everything needed time, attention, and money and those were in short supply.

Hannah walked forward, leading the horse. After several steps, she paused to return the reins. The sight of Nate's grim expression gave her pause. As she stood with him in the shadowy structure, it suddenly occurred to her she had no proof the man was indeed who he claimed to be.

Unease slid through her veins. Why had she made it clear that, essentially, she was on her own? Why hadn't she insisted Jed come out to greet him? Hannah shifted, putting some space between them. At least if something happened, Jed could hear her scream then rouse himself to help.

No. A sick feeling gathered in her gut as certainty settled over her. *He wouldn't.* Jed would ignore her as he had earlier, as he did everyone. Hannah stiffened her spine. She would be okay. Her nerves were likely getting the best of her. The man with her had to be Nate Rolfe, a good person, according to Alice.

"Something wrong?"

Nate moved closer, and even in the low light, there was no mistaking the concern in his eyes. Hannah slowly released the breath she'd held and a calming bit of logic came to mind. He had asked after Jed and Alice. A drifter wouldn't have known about them. She needed to rein in her imagination. There were enough legitimate concerns to worry about without creating more out of thin air.

"No."

"You're pale."

"I'm fine." She gestured to his horse, wanting to get his attention off her. "You're welcome to put Jack in any stall but the one next to Meadowlark and her baby. She is very protective of Tanager and wouldn't enjoy close company."

"She isn't used to other horses?"

The note of surprise in Nate's observation caught her on the raw. Many people thought her friends were crazy when they'd invested every dime they could borrow into buying this run-down farm and two quality broodmares. They'd worked hard to prove the naysayers wrong, adding horses over time. Meadowlark had once been used to a barn filled with other animals.

Now, the mare and her foal were remnants of a dream. Months of neglect had unraveled those years of hard work. After Bessie died, everything changed.

"She's gotten used to being alone." Without giving him a chance to respond, Hannah moved away, heading deeper into the building.

Chapter 3

Enough light streamed through cracks on the far wall and the open door that she didn't bother with a lantern. She stopped by a stall that put almost the length of the barn between the gelding and the mare. After Nate nodded his approval, she showed him where to hang his tack and get clean straw for bedding. While he set to work making Jack comfortable, she fetched the horse a bucket of water, some grain, and hay.

Nate thanked her for the meager offerings. Still intensely aware of her companion, however, Hannah noted his first reaction was a critical tightening of his lips. Certain the poor animal deserved more, she felt bad but there was no help for it. They had limited feed.

Hannah worried for a moment he'd ask about having more and she'd have to explain, but Nate didn't say a word, carrying on with his task in silence. Relieved, she stepped over to stand near the open doorway while he finished. Her gaze wandered over the interior to the yard outside as she waited. Neglect was clear in every direction. She could only imagine how it might appear to fresh eyes. The man had to see how run-down the place was and that there was a shortage of many animals besides horses.

Tears welled up, threatening to spill. It wasn't all Jed's fault.

The farm had sat abandoned for years before he and Bessie bought it. Hannah couldn't honestly say she'd seen any potential in it. She glanced back at Nate, finding him still brushing his horse. According to Alice, the Rolfes' ranch covered over three hundred acres. The meager forty of Redwing Farm, a vast stretch of land to her friends, probably seemed insignificant to him.

A burst of cold air moved over Hannah. For a second, she could've sworn it carried the sweet scent of lilacs, even though it was the wrong season for Bessie's favorite flower. She turned her attention outside. Ramshackle buildings dotted the area, the chicken coop, sheds, house, a second small barn, and the lean-to against this barn where hired help would've slept, sadly looking much the same as the first time she'd seen them. The memory of her friend's excitement as she'd shown her around the farm then, pulling her from one falling-down structure to another, bursting with plans, filled her mind. She closed her eyes, trying to shut out reality.

"Done."

Did the man ever say more than a word or two at a time?

Hannah opened her eyes and turned to face Nate. "Are you hungry?"

"A little."

"Why don't you come up to the house?" She stepped out of the barn. "I'll fix you something."

"I can wait." Nate pushed the door shut.

"If you do, Alice will wonder at my manners."

"I don't want you to go to any trouble."

His full sentence tempted her to smile. "It's no trouble."

"But—"

"Alice and the children will be here soon." Hannah headed off toward the house without giving him the chance to respond.

Undecided, Nate remained near the barn a moment, then, with a shake of his head, he followed her. He would've preferred to wait for Alice outside. Although intrigued by Hannah, she made him uncomfortable. Besides, he wanted a look around. Jed had to be here somewhere and he wanted to see what exactly was causing the man's bad day. Unwilling to be rude, he disregarded those inclinations and kept walking.

His gaze swept the area while he crossed the yard. Boards were missing from the corral. The chicken coop showed a number of clumsy repairs. A closer look at the house as Nate approached it revealed a porch on the verge of collapse. Evidence of decay was everywhere.

How many bad days has Jed had?

Nate caught up with Hannah as she opened the door. While an answer to the question dominating his thoughts would be nice, he didn't ask her about Alice's son again. The young woman reminded him of a nervous horse, visibly wary, although he doubted she'd care for his comparison. Patience was in order. Thankfully, he developed that virtue working with wild mustangs.

Inside the small home, Hannah stopped a step from the door and removed her coat. She hung it on a peg on the wall. With a silent gesture, she invited Nate to do the same before unwinding an old, faded shawl from her shoulders.

Hannah's easy grace was a pleasure to behold. He couldn't help watching subtly as she removed bulky clothing, revealing the soft swell of her chest and generous curves of her hips. His gaze lingered on her form, clad in a plain, brown work dress, several seconds before moving up to focus on hair the rich red of autumn leaves. It'd been a while since he'd taken the time to enjoy the beauty of a woman and he found himself on the verge of being rude.

Nate shifted his gaze, staring at the wall while shrugging off his duster, but couldn't resist another glance at her after hanging it up. This time Hannah caught him, their gazes collided as she draped her shawl on top of her coat. She tilted her head to one side, puzzlement filling eyes the shade of the chocolate candy

Alice made at Christmas. A blush bloomed over her cheeks, charming him. He couldn't look away.

"Excuse me," she whispered, turning her back to him, then walking away.

His ill manners sank in. He knew how uncomfortable being gawked at felt. "Sorry."

"It's all right," Hannah called over her shoulder, her tone polite but a little cool as she crossed the room. "Please, have a seat at the table."

Believing further apologies would make matters worse, Nate moved to do what she'd asked without offering another. He looked around the space while heading for the decent-sized, rough-hewn table with six chairs sitting in the center. Along the wall to his right there were three doors and on the opposite one some shelves, hanging pots, a cupboard, and a small cook stove. Motion caught his eye. Hannah stood near the fireplace, in the middle of the wall directly across from the door. Within it, he noticed a pitiful pile of half-burnt sticks on top of dying coals, which explained why the air inside wasn't much warmer than outside.

Nate eased his frame onto one of the rickety wooden chairs, still watching his companion. From a small stack of fir rounds, Hannah added one onto the pile with careful precision. The sway of her skirt drew his attention as she bent over, blowing on the coals. The fire grew, showing off crackling flames after a few minutes of coaxing.

Hannah straightened and he brought his gaze up as she turned to face him. "Would stew be all right?"

Be charming. Put her at ease. Think of something Rowdy might say. "Yes." *Feeble, Nathaniel. Try again. Use more than one word.* "It would."

"Good." Although her tone remained polite, there was a hint of amusement in her short answer.

Not charming but, maybe, entertaining.

Never good with small talk, Nate chose to remain silent as she walked over to the cupboard. Hannah reached up, took a spoon and bowl out, then pulled a ladle off a nail on the wall. She turned and, from a pot left warming on the black metal stove, scooped him up a portion. Given the cozy size of the room, it took the woman only a couple of steps to reach his side, placing the meal before him a moment later.

"Thank you."

"You're welcome. Would you like some coffee?"

"Yes." Eagerness seeped through his voice. Nate hadn't bothered with a campfire in the morning and was craving the bitter brew. "Please."

Wordlessly, Hannah returned to the stove. She took two cups off a shelf and filled them both from a coffee pot beside the stew pan. As she walked back, Nate glanced down at the contents of the bowl. He dipped his spoon in and stirred, inhaling the fragrant scent of herbs. Thick with vegetables but no sign of meat, the sight was consistent with serious financial troubles.

After setting a cup down by his bowl, Hannah sat at the other side of the table, directly across from him. "Aren't you going to have some?"

"I'll wait for Alice and the children."

"Then I'll wait too."

"No need." Hannah shook her head. "You can have a second helping with them."

"But-"

"There's plenty. Please."

"But I—"

"I insist."

"Okay," Nate agreed, unwilling to offend her. "Thank you."

"You're welcome."

Hannah sipped her coffee while he ate. For the next several minutes there was no pressure to converse. The silence between them felt almost comfortable. By the time he finished, Nate had relaxed a little.

"It was very good."

"Thank you." Hannah rose to her feet then picked up his bowl, taking it over to the worktop of the cupboard. His eyes followed the gentle movement of her hips as she walked away. Near the stove, she waved toward the coffee pot. "Want more?"

Nate promptly lifted his gaze. "Please."

As she folded a cloth around the pot's handle Nate became conscious he was staring at her. He shifted in his seat and looked over at the fire. The flames barely licked the wood. It was still a bit chilly inside.

Should I offer to build it up? The soft falls of her boots on the worn wood floor announced Hannah approaching. Nate almost spoke, then hesitated. *If it's small to conserve wood, offering may embarrass her.* A second later, she stood beside him, filling his cup, the sleeve of her dress brushing against the skin of his wrist and the back of his hand.

Heat whispered through his veins. Hannah smelled sweetly of fresh air and flowers. He breathed in, leaning ever so slightly closer. Roses, she smelled like roses. The scent was a favorite of Nate's. He nurtured several blooming plants on the south side of his cabin, grown from cuts of his mother's garden.

Hannah moved away. Feeling the absence of her warmth, Nate wrapped his hand around the mug, welcoming the burning heat the fresh brew brought. The pretty woman intrigued him. Pursuing her was a tempting thought. Seconds later, he dismissed the idea.

It'd be pointless. Nate squeezed the mug tighter and raised it off the table, staring down at the steaming liquid. He had to keep this attraction under control. She wasn't a woman who'd welcome a casual flirtation and attempting anything more serious would be foolish. In his experience, women didn't care for the isolated way of life he loved.

Nate took a long drink of his coffee as Hannah reclaimed her seat. Her lips curved in a shy smile, causing his heart to beat a fraction faster. Despite knowing it wasn't wise, he found himself offering her a brief grin in return.

Although he sensed Hannah had a lot on her mind, she didn't break the silence. The quiet between them didn't seem to bother her. In Nate's opinion, it was a rare and attractive trait. Few people he knew resisted making casual conversation. Enjoying her company, he sipped his coffee over the next several minutes.

A noise from another room broke the pleasant mood. Nate put his cup down as he looked in the sound's direction. He'd thought they were alone. Silence followed. He turned his attention back to Hannah a moment later. A shadow flickered in her lovely eyes then her gaze skittered off, away from his.

"Who's here?" he asked gently.

Hannah shook her head, glancing at a door on the far wall.

A closer look revealed the one she was staring at was now slightly ajar. *Jed perhaps?*

Without thinking, Nate stood up and went to investigate. He heard her whispered plea to stop but didn't heed it. A step from the door, as he reached for the knob, a soft hand gripped his arm with surprising strength and stopped him. He turned to study Hannah for a second, then drawn by an unexplainable force he leaned forward, peering into the room through the opening.

At first, Nate only saw darkness, then his vision adjusted to the low light. His gaze swept the room, catching movement by a small covered window. There was a lone figure, slowly rocking in a chair. The sight disturbed him and heeding Hannah's tugs on his arm, he turned away.

Her displeasure was clear, full lips pressed thin together instead of curving in a smile. A part of him wanted to stomp into the room behind him and confront the man sitting in there. From her expression, however, he doubted she'd welcome that action.

"Jed?"

Hannah shook her head. She dropped her hold and moved away, returning to her chair. Nate waited a moment, watching her. She picked up her cup and stared down at the contents, turning it slowly around in her hands.

"That's not Jed?" He kept his tone even, not allowing even a hint of his disbelief.

Hannah's sigh floated across the room. "It is."

"But you don't want me talking to him?"

"As I said, it'd be better if you spoke to Alice first."

"Why?" He demanded with quiet intensity. Something was very wrong with the other man. The feeling, growing within him for some time, now settled in his gut with certainty. "I've known Jed most of my life."

"I know. Alice told me she started working for your folks when Jed was small, soon after losing her husband. But he's not the same anymore. He's …"

"Drunk?"

A sick feeling rose in her stomach. *Is it so obvious?*

The bleakness of the situation weighed heavy on her. While she struggled for words, Hannah looked over at the door Jed used to shut out the world. In less than a minute, she knew there was no nice way to present the truth.

"It's likely."

"Then I should definitely speak to him."

"It's not that simple," she muttered under her breath, resentment crashing over her.

Jed wasn't the only one who mourned Bessie, yet he behaved as though his pain was all that mattered. The rest of them had to grieve while continuing to handle the daily tasks necessary in life. They had an extra burden now, taking care of him. Her sympathy for the man was in short supply.

"Why isn't it?"

Her cheeks heated when Hannah realized she'd spoken loud enough for him to hear. She shifted her gaze to meet his. "I … just feel you should talk to Alice first."

"But won't explain why?"

"Please."

"I think—"

The sound of high-pitched voices pierced the thin walls, interrupting Nate. Hannah stood, smiling with relief. There was no need to debate further. She headed across the room.

"They're back."

As Nate watched Hannah walk away from him, the front door burst open. One minute the small home was almost dead quiet and the next energy flowed through it. A little girl, followed by two young boys carrying homemade fishing poles made of long sticks and string hurried through the door. Their presence soon filled the space as only children can, with eagerness, excitement, and the joy of simply being alive.

Nate felt a sudden and unexpected longing for his family. Normally he spent long stretches of time alone and knowing his loved ones were nearby, within a day's ride should the urge to visit overtake him, pleased him. Now it was different. His parents, sister, and Alice were all away from the Bar 7. Ben and his brothers remained on the family ranch but all had been busy with their own concerns. He worried his close-knit family was drifting apart.

"Mama, look." The little girl ran up to Hannah waving a large pinecone.

Disappointment shot through Nate while Hannah admired her daughter's prize. It wasn't logical but a part of him wanted to pursue her. He should've known she was married. The men around here would have to be blind not to notice her.

Hannah smoothed back the little girl's hair, drawing his gaze to her hand. She wasn't wearing a wedding ring. Although some couples couldn't afford rings, another option intrigued him. She could be a widow, young to be so, but possible. He shouldn't care. Even so, the thought lightened his mood.

Footsteps sounded on the porch. Nate looked over in time to

44

see Alice appear in the doorway. The older woman was a welcome sight. Pleased she was finally here, he smiled. As she stepped inside and shut the door, he closed the distance between them.

"Nathaniel." Alice smiled her delight, then enveloped him in a hug. "However did Sam convince you to come in his place?"

"I was helping Matt near here."

"More rustling?"

"Yes, but right now," Nate kept his voice low as he eased out of her embrace so it wouldn't carry to where the children had gathered near Hannah, "I'm more concerned about you."

"I'm fine."

Nate studied the woman a moment. Although Alice was years older than his mother, it had never been readily apparent until now. New wrinkles lined her face. Dark circles smudged her eyes, giving her a bruised look. Since he'd last seen her, she seemed to have aged years instead of months.

"I don't believe so. Things are rough here, aren't they?"

"I am fine." Her expression turned somber. "As much as I can be." She nodded toward the little ones. "We'll talk after they're in bed."

"That won't be for hours."

"Is there someplace you need to be?"

"Well, I came to bring you home," he stated in a matter-of- fact tone.

Alice raised an eyebrow. "Did you plan on leaving now?"

"I figured you'd be ready to go."

"I'm not, but if I was, you really want to leave this late in the day?"

"Yes, but an early start tomorrow would make better sense."

"Exactly, so make yourself comfortable."

"Couldn't we step outside?" He all but whispered, noticing the children were quiet, likely listening.

Alice shook her head. "Little pitchers have big ears."

"But-"

"It'll keep, Nathaniel, trust me."

Her words were gentle but Alice gave him a look Nate had become familiar with growing up. Nothing would change her mind. She gestured with one hand toward the table, calling to the boys. Long experience told him arguing with her was like talking to a fence post, pointless, so he gave up.

"Who are you?" The oldest boy, who couldn't be more than seven, stepped in front of him while his brother went straight to Alice.

The stubborn angle of his jaw, dark-blond hair and bright-blue eyes proclaimed him as Jed's son. The anxiety and bravado in his tone stirred empathy. This child felt threatened, regarding him with clear suspicion.

"I'm Nate." He sank down, crouching before the boy. "Do you remember me?"

"No."

Alice started to chide the boy for his rudeness but Nate glanced up at her, asking silently for her to let him handle the matter. To his surprise, she did. The woman resumed peeling off the other boy's jacket without another word.

"It's been a long time, Jason."

"How do you know my name?" The child's tone was only a shade more polite.

"Your grandmother became our housekeeper when I was about your age. I grew up with your father."

Jason's expression became mulish. "Grandma ain't never mentioned nobody named Nate."

"Jason." Alice spoke in a gentle tone as she moved beside them, placing her hand on the boy's shoulder. "Ain't never mentioned nobody?"

"You ain't—You haven't mentioned someone named Nate." The boy corrected himself.

Alice squeezed his shoulder in approval. "I use his proper name; Nate is short for Nathaniel."

Jason's mouth dropped open. His eyes rounded, becoming saucers. "He's Nathaniel?"

"In the flesh."

"Oh." The boy's gaze found his, staring at the man in wonder. "You're the—"

"Don't say it," Nate cautioned in a tone gentle but weary.

Chapter 4

Nate looked down at the floor, expecting an innocent remark echoing some part of the gossip. Instead, silence stretched over the next few seconds. He brought his gaze up and found the boy staring at him, puzzled. Shame heated his neck. He should have known better. No grandson of Alice would repeat rumors.

"You're not the one that works with horses?" Jason asked, sounding tentative.

"I am. Sorry. I thought you were going to say something else."

His expression made it plain Nate's explanation didn't make sense to Jason but he moved on. "Would you tell me, um, us, about your horses?"

"Sure, later, if your grandma says it's okay."

Jason beamed his eagerness then scooted around Nate to hang up his coat. The younger boy, John, darted away from Alice to join Hannah and her daughter at the same time. He and the older woman crossed the room at a more sedate pace. As they approached the others, the little girl drew his gaze. She looked about the same age as John, three if he remembered correctly, with ginger braids falling over her shoulders. When the child noticed him nearing, she sought the cover of her mother's skirt folds.

"Jemma, I'd like you to meet Mr. Rolfe." Eyes, green as the fir trees of his home, peered out at him, shyly. "Nate, this is my daughter."

Once more, he crouched down to a child's eye level. "It's a pleasure to meet you, little miss."

"Hi," She greeted him with a timid whisper.

Nate smiled, then trying not to overwhelm her, straightened back up. He reclaimed his seat and cup of coffee. Jason started peppering him with questions about horses and, over time, as he patiently answered them, his brother grew comfortable with him as well. To his surprise, he found himself enjoying their quiet but non-stop chatter while washing up then settling around the table.

The following hours, though pleasant, seemed to go on forever. They ate, tended chores, and had polite exchanges. Both women tried to be cheerful but, at times, Nate could tell their smiles were forced. Tension haunted them. The presence of a man unseen but felt, Jed. He never emerged.

During the day, no one ventured into Jed's room, knocked on his door or suggested including him. No one, not even his boys, spoke about the man. And, for all their chatter, the kids were subdued inside the house, far more than good indoor behavior warranted. Outside, however, the boys were boisterous. The stark contrast disturbed him. By evening, Nate was growing restless, eager to talk it all over with Alice.

Luckily, the children offered distraction. While not one of them complained about having warmed-over stew again, they each had a demand. John wanted more butter on his cornbread. Jemma asked for more carrots. At the same time, Jason started pleading for Nate to tell the promised story. The kids weren't trying to be noisy but each had raised their voice, trying to surpass the others.

The high-spirited chatter put Nate at ease, reminding him of his childhood. It sounded so familiar, in fact, he almost grinned. Even now, when his family gathered for a meal, the result was much the same.

Hannah took her daughter's bowl, carrying it to the stove to appease Jemma's request. Alice spread another thin layer of yellow on John's bread and, with Jason tugging on his sleeve, asking please yet again, Nate tried to think of an entertaining story. In the midst of all the activity, he somehow heard the low creak of a floorboard.

"Jed," Alice announced softly before he could look in the direction of the sound.

Silence fell, swift and sudden. The older woman's pale face filled Nate with concern. He glanced over at Hannah, wanting to see her reaction. She stood still, a statue by the stove, her expression a blank mask. His gaze next traveled to the children, each one silent, heads bowed with eyes cast down, then finally to the doorway behind him. The man standing there was an unsettling sight.

Jed and Nate were of equal height but he appeared shorter, standing stooped over like an old man. Clothing hung off limbs like the sticks of a scarecrow. Blond hair appeared a deep shade of brown, falling about his face in dirty, greasy locks. His face had the pale, grayish tinge of a person too ill to go outside for long. He barely recognized the man.

"Too." Jed's voice came out harsh and gravely as though it had been long unused. He waved one badly shaking hand at them. "Loud."

"Sorry, Pa." All his earlier eagerness gone, Jason's tone was low and flat.

Jed nodded in response then went back into his room without another word. He didn't bother to shut the door. Nate watched him shuffle across the bedroom to sit facing the window again, looking out into the dark, rocking. John made a wordless sound of distress. In silence, Alice got up and went over, shutting her son's door with a soft click that sounded almost explosive in the dead-quiet room.

As Alice walked back, Jason pushed away his half-eaten bowl of stew and stood. "I have chores."

John slid from his chair, joining his brother by the front door. Barely making a sound, the boys shrugged into their coats and mittens, then went outside. Nate stared after them, worried by their transparent excuse to escape the house. Their chores were already finished, done before supper.

His gaze shifted to Alice. She'd returned to her chair and sat staring in the direction of Jed's room, the sheen of tears in her eyes. Troubled, he looked away, seeking Hannah. The woman had also moved back to the table. He heard a flow of comforting words murmured to her daughter as she snuggled Jemma in her lap.

His appetite lost, Nate stood up and headed for his coat, feeling the need to check on the boys. Hannah joined him as he fastened his last button. She handed him a lantern.

"You'll find them in the barn with Meadowlark."

Though it was common for even young children to have chores involving animals, seeing how upset the boys had been, Nate was concerned. "If she feels protective of her foal, she may snap."

"They know better than to get into the stall with her."

"At a time like this, you trust they'll remember?"

"No, one of us follows them out." She didn't sound offended, just tired and matter of fact. "Tonight, it seems, you are."

"Oh." Nonplussed, he accepted the lit lantern, started to open the door, then halted. "Why go to the horse?"

"Meadowlark was their mama's favorite." A small, somber voice drifted up from where Jemma stood among the folds of her mother's skirt again.

Nate looked down at the red-headed child. Several strands had escaped her braids, giving her a messy halo of hair. As she peeked up at him, her sad, serious green eyes appeared familiar somehow.

"They miss her."

Three simple words relayed an understanding far wiser than her years. With a solemn expression, Jemma studied him. Nate got the impression she was measuring his worth, waiting for a response. He found himself not wanting to disappoint her.

"I understand."

"Good." The child turned around and scurried over to Alice, crawling up into the older woman's lap.

Without another word, Nate headed out into the night. Worry quickened his steps on the unfamiliar dark path but he reached the barn safely. Once there he blew out the lantern and eased open a door, slipping inside.

One swift glance down the length of the barn revealed the boys standing in front of Meadowlark's stall. Nate moved closer quietly, trying not to let them know he was there. He stepped up onto a hay bale for a better vantage point next. The foal lay in a nest of straw in a corner of the stall while the mare stood against the door. Only the murmur of voices and the soft nickers received in response were clear but he didn't need to know what they were saying. All that mattered was they were safe.

Finding comfort in the company of horses was something Nate identified with strongly. Loath to disturb them, he remained in the shadows, allowing the boys a measure of privacy. They stayed for some time but when they finally shuffled by him, their tears had dried.

Nate trailed them home. Once they'd slipped safely inside, he relit the lantern and returned to the barn. There he spent a few moments with Jack, giving him affection, then did one final check on all the animals before returning to the house. Alice answered his soft knock, opening the door for him. The room was still almost eerily quiet and not one child, or Hannah, was in sight.

Assuming the young woman was settling the children down for the night, Nate followed Alice to some chairs, taken from by the table, near the fire. He waited until she sat before taking a seat himself.

For a moment, Nate studied the woman, who was like a second mother to him, while he figured out the best way to start what promised to be a hard conversation. Her hands clasped together in her lap surprised him. She always had a project. Even at the end of a difficult day, he'd seen her sewing or knitting. Once he'd asked her why she didn't rest and she'd said it was her way of relaxing. At fifteen he'd found her answer odd, now an adult, he understood.

"Tell me." His words were simple, delivered in a kind tone.

Her sigh, almost soundless, washed over him with a wave of emotion. "I can't get through to him. He won't listen to me."

Nate kept his jaw from dropping with effort but couldn't help shaking his head. Although he'd witnessed the sorry state of the man himself, her statement was hard to accept. Jed had always been especially close to his mother. He treated her with the utmost respect. Even after he moved away, a grown man, he'd returned to the Bar 7 as often to visit as to get advice because he genuinely valued Alice's opinion.

"Hard to believe?"

"Yes."

"For me too."

"What changed?"

"What hasn't?" Heart-deep sorrow filled her eyes, then she shifted her gaze from his to look at the fire.

"I noticed he'd been drinking at Bessie's funeral. I thought … I figured he was grieving …"

"He was and is."

"Grieving or drinking?"

"Yes."

Nate reached out, covered her hands with his and gave a gentle, comforting squeeze. The creak of a door opening drifted to him. He looked over to see Hannah stepping into the room. Her expression took on a worried cast when the young woman noticed them. She started to turn around.

"Please stay." Alice's request made Hannah change course, cross the space to the older woman's side and she knelt beside her.

Concern filled Hannah's tone. "I didn't mean to intrude."

"You're not."

"Are you sure you want me here?"

"It'd be a blessing if you'd help explain what's happened to my son."

"All right."

Nate stood and waved Hannah toward his chair, stepping away when she attempted to decline his offer. He walked off, quickly grabbing another chair and carried it back over. In less than a minute, they sat flanking Alice, each being supportive.

"Jed isn't … coping well with losing his wife."

"She's been gone less than a year. Isn't that expected?"

Alice smiled sadly. "Grief doesn't have a time limit. My Harry has been gone twenty years and I miss him every day. It's fine for him to mourn still. But …"

"His drinking is out of control?" Nate guessed.

"There's that but …"

The older woman fell silent. After a time it became clear she wasn't going to continue immediately. Nate looked to Hannah, hoping for assistance. She drew in a deep breath then picked up where Alice had left off.

"It's beyond normal grieving. Losing Bessie the way he did devastated him."

"The way he did?"

"You don't know?"

"Alice was upset and we didn't want to pry."

"Evie had confided she was in the family way and Ben was nervous already. I thought it best to not share details," the house-keeper offered in a whisper.

"It probably was," Nate assured her. "And I don't need to know now if it's going to bother either of you."

Hannah shifted in her seat, painful memories filling her with restless energy. "It's still hard to talk about but … I think knowing what happened to Bessie makes it … easier to understand how he is now."

"You're sure?"

Over the last several months, a deep friendship had grown between her and Alice. The older woman had no relatives besides those in this house. There was no one who'd help her except, perhaps, the Rolfes, who Alice claimed considered her family. It was important Nate understood the situation. Once he did, Hannah would see if her friend's faith in those people was justified.

Or not.

"I am." After another deep, fortifying breath, Hannah began. "Bessie was expecting. She had trouble carrying a baby after John but that day she had made it past the months when she had problems before. She hadn't been sick in weeks. I thought ..."

Alice reached over, taking her hand. "You couldn't have known."

"I thought she'd be fine." Tears welled up and Hannah let them fall. "So Jemma and I went to see my mother. She had been feeling ill for some time. The doctor didn't know what was wrong with her and I was worried." She paused, steeling herself for the hardest part. "I should've been worried about Bessie too."

"Hannah," the older woman chided her softly.

With a shake of her head, Hannah went on. "Jason said after their noon meal Bessie felt tired. Jed took the boys out in the field with him so she could rest. They found her collapsed in the grass on their way home hours later. While Jed carried her home, Jason ran to the nearest neighbor, the Hendersons, for help. She'd miscarried and kept bleeding. Dr. Benton told me that when he arrived, Jed was cradling her, rocking in the chair he's likely sitting in now. She'd already passed on."

"I'm sorry."

Hannah wiped her cheeks with her free hand. "Thank you."

"You think Jed feels responsible for not saving her?"

"Yes, without a doubt, and the guilt is destroying him."

"Alice." Nate sounded shocked by the sound of her despair.

"I keep hoping with time he'll recover." The older woman

slowly shook her head. "But, the truth is, he's getting worse."

"He doesn't look well."

A moment passed before Alice responded to Nate's gently delivered statement. "He rarely comes out of his room, doesn't bathe, change his clothes, or eat. Mostly, he guzzles whiskey."

"Perhaps a doctor?"

"He threw Dr. Benson out of the house." Hannah grimaced, remembering. "The doctor refuses to come out again unless it's at Jed's request."

"So everyone just leaves him alone now?"

Her spine stiffened. The redhead's temper threatened. "What are you trying to say?"

"Easy." His tone lowered, pitched to be soothing. "I'm only trying to understand."

A silence fraught with tension ruled for a few seconds then Alice interjected, "I reach out to my son every day."

"I'm sorry. I didn't mean to imply you don't."

"She wanted to come here and help him from the start but he refused." Hannah wanted Nate to know Alice had tried. Memories from the weeks after Bessie's death ran through her mind. She'd had great sympathy for Jed at first. But, as time went on, she'd grown both worried about, and frustrated with, his behavior. "When I wrote to her about his difficulties, asking her to disregard his wishes and come anyway, she did, straight away."

"Alice is an amazing lady and mother."

His sincerity sounded genuine and Hannah's indignation on behalf of her friend eased. "Before, Jed spoke of his mother often and with great fondness. I'd hoped her presence would bring him out of it."

"But it didn't."

"No." Alice's single word hung in the air a long moment.

Fresh frustration welled up. Hannah wanted to give Jed a swift kick in the rear for the hurt he was causing. "You've been a Godsend for me and the children."

Alice patted her hand. "You're trying to make an old woman feel better."

"It's the truth."

The other woman smiled briefly. She shifted, bringing her hands back together in her lap. Her back straight, chin lifted, and expression proud, her gaze traveled from Hannah to Nate.

"The hour is late. We need to speak of practical matters."

"This place is falling apart." Nate kindly didn't point out why. "You need at least one farmhand."

"There's no money for one. Last week, I had to charge the supplies we needed to Jed's store account because there was no cash. I'm selling off anything of value bit by bit to keep the roof over our heads and food in our bellies."

"Jed isn't working at all?"

"No."

"Why didn't you tell us? You know we'll help."

"As I said, I kept thinking he'd get better." Alice reached up and patted Nate's cheek, as she did with the children. "And I know you all would help. For now, understanding I can't return any time soon is enough. I just can't leave Jed and the boys like this."

Hannah, knowing how much working for the Rolfes meant to Alice, couldn't help speaking up. "If you need to go, I won't leave."

"You're an angel but, as we've discussed, staying isn't best for Jemma. In fact, it may become necessary to take the boys away and I need to be here to make that decision."

"Perhaps a man-to-man talk would help?"

The older woman's sigh filled the room. "If I thought a talking-to would snap my son out of this I'd have herded you into his room straight away. We've tried." She paused, glancing over at Jed's door, then back at Nate. "Many times. But if you want to take a stab at it, please do. Just wait until the boys are at school tomorrow. I don't want them exposed to another ruckus so soon."

"His *bad day*?" Nate looked at Hannah as he referenced their earlier conversation.

"A bad morning for all." Alice grimaced. "Because I tried to change the bed linens."

His brow furrowed. "And?"

"Jed wants everything as it was the day Bessie died," Hannah added in. "Changing even something small upsets him."

Nate's expression went from surprised to thoughtful. "Ben saw this fancy doctor in Corvallis maybe-"

"I thought of that. Jed won't go."

"What about bringing the boys and Jed to the ranch?"

"I knew you'd make that offer. I appreciate it." With the stubborn tilt of her chin Alice indicated to all arguing with her would be futile. "But I want to give my son every chance here, in his own home, first."

"I understand but if things continue to go downhill?"

"I'll take you up on it. I may be a stubborn old woman but I'm no fool."

"I'd have words with anyone who said you were." Nate smiled at Alice, affection for her written on his face. "May I stay for a day or so? Fix a few things?"

"I'd be grateful."

"Make a list. I'll get started first thing in the morning."

Alice nodded. "There's one other matter I want to discuss this evening."

"Of course." His expression serious, Nate shifted, sitting on the edge of his seat.

The look in his eyes warmed Hannah's heart. The man seemed eager, hopeful of hearing other ways he could help. If so, Nate would soon be disappointed. She knew what the older woman wanted to address an issue they'd glossed over earlier. Her job.

"I don't know how long I'll need to stay."

"I understand."

"Jed could get worse, stay as he is or, given a miracle, my son could finally start to heal."

"Take as long as you need."

"I worry, wondering how all of you are getting by."

"Don't, we're fine."

"But I will. So I want you to—"

"Don't suggest we replace you." His voice suddenly became granite. "Not. Going. To. Happen."

The obvious effort behind Alice's threadbare smile was troubling. "I love you too. But the work still needs to be done."

"It'll keep. With Ma and Pa off visiting and Becca back east, the house is barely used. The boys and I usually eat with the hands. There's nothing to worry about."

The expression on Alice's face said she didn't believe him.

"We are fine."

"I have no doubt. But is the house clean?"

"We haven't been making it dirty. Only I sleep there."

"The laundry?"

"Evie is taking care of it."

"Evie?" Alice raised an eyebrow. "Isn't she getting close to her time?"

"Yes, but starting next week, we'll be hauling our stuff to town. It's a small matter. We're fine. Don't worry about us."

"But I do."

"Don't."

Alice studied Nate in silence, patiently waiting.

"I am not hiring a stranger to replace you."

"I don't want you to."

"Good."

"I want you to hire Hannah."

Chapter 5

"What?" Nate and Hannah spoke as one, sounding shocked.

"Alice." Hannah tried to control her reaction. "We've talked about this."

"Yes, we did."

"I've a serious concern."

"Your husband?" Nate put in.

Husband? Startled anew, Hannah's gaze shot from Alice to the man beside her. "I don't have a husband."

"Sorry." While his tone relayed sympathy, another emotion flickered briefly in his eyes.

Satisfaction? No, it couldn't be … Hannah pushed away the thought. "It's a natural assumption."

"I'm sorry you have to leave us."

Alice's gentle words brought tears up, stinging Hannah's eyes. "So am I but …"

"You *have* to leave?"

"I …" Hannah hesitated, feeling awkward about sharing more financial woes with Nate. She decided to keep it simple. "Yes."

"Jed can't pay her," the older woman stated bluntly.

"And you need to support your daughter."

"Yes, I do." The calm response she gave him was in direct contrast to the knotted anxiety within Hannah.

"You don't believe Jed will recover soon?"

"I pray he does, but even so he wouldn't be able to afford hired help, not for some time."

"You've made plans?"

"I discussed them with Alice soon after she arrived." *When she confronted me about not drawing my pay.* The older woman had been quite upset. Hannah didn't regret the decision, though, and given the same circumstances, she'd do it again. If she hadn't, there wouldn't have been enough for necessities now. "I don't *want* to go, not when …"

"Bessie would understand." Emotions – sorrow, love, and concern – flickered in the older woman's eyes like the flames warming the room, but her statement carried conviction.

Hannah knew Alice was right, logically. Bessie had loved Jemma. Without a doubt, her friend would've understood the needs of her daughter coming first. Reason, however, didn't dispel the wrenching feeling in her gut.

"I still don't like it."

The older woman nodded her understanding before returning to her original concern. "Taking on my job would solve your immediate problem."

"Your job." Hannah leveled a look at her new friend. A mule would be less stubborn. Alice probably met few challenges she couldn't overcome. *Failing to help Jed has to be one.* Sympathy snaked through irritation, softening her tone. "Hasn't been offered to me."

Alice waved her hand in a dismissive gesture. "Nathaniel will. It's the logical solution."

"I will?" The man referenced cut into the women's exchange.

"Of course."

"Alice." Nate and Hannah spoke in unison again, expressing mutual frustration.

Startled, their gazes met and held. Silence stole the next few seconds. Her heart beat faster. Hannah shifted in her chair, unaccountably nervous. Finally, she glanced away, looking back at the other woman.

"You know, it's more than a job I need for Jemma."

"You're worried it might be temporary?"

"Might be?" Nate interjected firmly, brooking no argument. "We're not replacing you. So *if* I considered your suggestion, it would only be until you returned."

"And if I can't come back?"

"You will."

"I appreciate your faith. I'm not so sure. For my piece of mind, Nathaniel, I want you to hire another housekeeper. Offer the job to Hannah. It's what she and Jemma need."

Shocked, Hannah's mouth dropped open. It took her several seconds before she regained composure. Exasperated, but trying to be patient, she stated softly. "You're not listening to me."

"Of course I—"

Jemma cried out from other room, cutting the older woman off. Hannah immediately got to her feet. In a distracted air, she excused herself before hurrying off to her daughter.

"Poor baby, she's probably having another nightmare."

"Another?"

"Almost every evening lately." Alice's expression morphed from troubled to one of determination as she looked away from the door Hannah had disappeared through to him. "Nothing some time in a happier home wouldn't fix."

"And you think that home should be on the Bar 7?"

"I do."

"I don't believe you've thought this through."

"Don't underestimate me, young man." The look in her tired eyes was sharp and direct.

Nate gentled his voice. "You're under a lot of strain."

"Yes, I am and if you hire Hannah it'd relieve some of it."

"How?" he prompted, hoping to finish the discussion before the young woman returned.

"It'd ease my mind about you boys."

Nate shook his head, dismissing the notion. "We're grown men. No need to worry about us."

"Oh?" Her eyes narrowed. "If there's no need, why do I have a job?"

"Alice."

"Nathaniel." She patiently stated his name.

"We need *you*."

A pleased smile was her immediate answer. "I miss you boys too." Alice reached over, patting his hand. "But my son needs me more."

"Yes, he does. That doesn't mean someone has to take your place at home."

"Sweet boy, no one can take my place."

"That's what I've been trying to tell you."

"Hannah wouldn't take my place. She'd just be doing my work for now." She tried to reassure him.

"That's different, how?"

"While your folks are gone, you're doing work they would've done on the Bar 7. But you're not taking their place."

Nate shook his head, although he understood her point. Alice was right. Her suggestion made sense. He just didn't like it.

"If I hired her, *temporarily*, what would happen to her and Jemma when you come back?"

"Offer Hannah a permanent job."

"Doing what?" Surprise colored his voice.

"The Bar 7's books? Helping with your breeding program?"

Nate ignored the reference to his plans. He was particular about who assisted with his horses. Up to now, he'd only allowed family to lend a hand. "She's a bookkeeper?"

"Yes, but Hannah did more than the books here. Because they

were still building up the place, she also worked with Bessie on the breeding charts and helped out in general."

"That's nice, but Pa handles the books."

"And he's hated doing them for as long as I've known him."

"He does?" As Nate thought about it, a few vague memories surfaced. There were times his father grumbled under his breath or made an occasional grimace before heading into his study but he remembered no complaints. "I didn't know."

"Wouldn't it be nice to have a bookkeeper in place before they return so your father would never have to do them again?"

Nate admired her persistence. Alice had a plan and wanted it done. "What then? I put Pa out to pasture?"

"No, lazing about for days on end would drive the man crazy but I'm certain he'd enjoy spending his time on other things."

Restless, Nate got up. He put another fir round on the fire and listened to a bit of pitch crackle in the heat. "Pa could've hired someone himself years ago."

"Jeremiah doesn't trust outsiders easily, especially with money."

"I know." He turned to face Alice again. "That's why your bookkeeping idea won't work."

"Hannah is a longtime friend of my son and his late wife and is now a close friend of mine. Your father won't consider her a stranger."

"I'm not so sure. And I—"

"Could do with some proper help."

Distracted, he shook his head. "I'm doing fine."

"Still keeping all the information in your head? What if you get sick or hurt?"

"Ben knows enough to help then." Nate reclaimed his seat, leaning forward and assuring Alice, "I appreciate your concerns, truly." He paused, taking a small breath then moved on, bringing up the point he'd wanted to make before. "You know I share Pa's aversion. Bringing a stranger to live on the Bar 7 doesn't sit well with me."

"Hannah's not a stranger."

"You just met her."

"Yes, but I've heard plenty about her over the years. She and Bessie were closer than most sisters." Calmly, Alice looked him square in the eye. "Hannah's a good person. If I had any doubts about her character, I wouldn't ask this of you."

"I know but … I'm not convinced hiring her is a good idea."

"Nor am I," Hannah announced from the open doorway.

But time's running out. In measured strides, she crossed the room and rejoined those by the fire, a mask of composure concealing the nature of her thoughts. The notion of turning down a job, even a temporary housekeeping one, knotted her stomach.

"I meant no offence."

"None taken." Hannah clasped her hands together in her lap to hide how they shook. She couldn't stop the effect of growing fear but refused to allow it to overcome her. So far, no other place had offered her work. Her choices were few. "But, should you be inclined, I'm willing to discuss Alice's idea."

Nate studied her a moment before offering a few polite words. "Another time, perhaps?"

"Of course," Hannah agreed graciously. *It's fine. I really don't want a job with the Rolfes anyway. Michael must have had a good reason to warn me away.* Tension tightened a band around her chest. *He must have.*

Alice cleared her throat, drawing Hannah's attention. "Will you both to give my suggestion some serious consideration?"

"I will," she promised, in a whisper.

Somber, Nate also assured her. "As will I."

"Good." Alice got up. "Now, I'm heading to bed. It's been a long day and this old lady needs to rest." Nate stood, offering her his arm. She refused it with a weary smile. "Good night."

The older woman walked away. After the dull thuds of her

boots faded, only the occasional hiss from the fire disturbed the silence for a long moment. Uncomfortable, Hannah murmured an excuse, got up, and went over to start clearing the table. Nate followed, helping, unasked. Working together provided a short-lived but surprisingly pleasant experience. However, as soon as they finished fresh tension filled her.

Either she or Alice routinely tried tempting Jed to eat something around this time. Hannah dished up a small portion of stew, took a deep breath, then looked over at Nate. "Excuse me, I'll be back shortly."

"Taking Jed supper?" At her nod, he continued. "Would you ask if he'd like to visit with me?"

Hannah held his gaze a moment. "I'll ask but ..."

"It's pointless."

The young woman didn't have the heart to respond. Without a word, she strode off, carrying the food into Jed's bedroom. She moved easily through the dimly lit area straight to him. Hannah placed the bowl in his hands, then waited several seconds until his fingers flexed, gripping it before she stepped back.

"Nate is still here." Jed didn't give any indication he heard her. His gaze remained focused beyond her, out into the darkness. "Would you come out and talk with your friend?"

After waiting for an answer for some minutes, Hannah headed toward the door. The soft chink of the bowl being set on the side table next to Jed sounded loud in the quiet space. A step from exiting, she stopped and looked back, saddened. He hadn't eaten all day again, to the best of her knowledge. She missed the man he'd been before: a good friend, playful father, and loving spouse. Bessie would be appalled to see her husband now.

Hannah blinked back the urge to cry and continued forward, closing the door behind her a moment later. Her gaze found Nate sitting near the fire again. He lifted an eyebrow and she gave a small shake of her head in answer to his silent inquiry. Without a word, she slowly walked over to join him, pausing on the way to grab the sewing basket.

"Would you like some more coffee?" She put the basket down on the floor next to a chair.

"No, thank you."

As soon as he declined, Hannah sat down, picking up Jemma's spare dress out of the pile of clothes needing mending. Pulling the needle out from where she'd left it, she settled back. There was comfort in tending to a familiar task, yet more than a sliver of guilt traveled through her.

Her little girl was growing fast. She'd outgrown all but the dress she'd worn today, filthy from running around with the boys, and the one Hannah held. The repair had to be finished by morning. She focused, keeping her stitches strong and small.

I need to provide better for my daughter.

It was past time to sew Jemma more clothes. *I should've taken care of it weeks ago.* It felt like there were never enough hours in a day. For a moment, the weight of her responsibilities threatened to overwhelm her. Hannah swallowed a sigh, unwilling to draw Nate's attention to her inner turmoil. After a short time, she dug up her determination. Tomorrow, she'd go through her trunk and pick out some of her mother's old dresses to cut down for her little girl.

If only all my problems were so easily solved.

Unexpectedly, Nate broke the silence. "Alice isn't replaceable."

"I agree. She's a special woman." Although Alice's blunt proposal had been a bit embarrassing, Hannah knew her friend had the best of intentions. She glanced up at Nate then back down to her stitching, trying to think of what to say next. "Your ranch must do well to have a housekeeper for so long."

As soon as the words left her mouth, she regretted them. It sounded like she was fishing for information. Her hand stilled mid-stitch while Hannah considered if an apology would make it better or worse.

"We do fair." Nate got up, gesturing to the wood stacked beside the fireplace. "May I?"

Relief coursed through her upon hearing his casual response. He wasn't offended. *Stop over-thinking every word.* She relaxed and resumed sewing. "Please."

He added another round on the low-burning flames. "My mother likes working outside. Time often gets away from her. A housekeeper was a wise investment."

Curiosity brought her gaze up from the little dress to the man standing nearby. "Your mother works as a ranch hand?"

"On our ranch, yes."

"Even when you were young? With Jemma underfoot, simple chores around the house often take twice as long."

"When it was just me, Ma claims it wasn't too hard." Nate returned to his chair. "Then she married Pa and, in short order, I had four siblings. According to my mother, Alice was a gift from Heaven."

There was a slight curve to his lips, a suggestion of a smile, which intrigued her. In a few simple words, the love he felt for his family was obvious. Hannah smiled at him and for a second a thread of connection seemed to weave between them. She looked away, jabbing the needle into cloth nervously.

"How long has she worked for your family?"

"Since I was eleven."

"Then you know Jed well?"

"He's closer to Sam but, yes, I do."

Hannah finished mending the tear, knotted the thread, then snipped the needle free. The hour was late. She folded the tiny dress and set it on top of the basket. *It's best to know.* She met his gaze and held it squarely. *Time is short.*

In a pleasant but forthright manner, she inquired. "Are you giving serious thought to Alice's idea?"

"I am." The look in his eyes was unreadable. "Would you take the job if it was offered?"

"I don't know."

"Perhaps we should sleep on it, talk more tomorrow?"

A wave of exhaustion crashed over her. Tomorrow promised to be another long day. Suddenly, sleep held great appeal. In the morning, rested and refreshed, perhaps the problems facing her wouldn't feel so overwhelming.

"That's a great idea." Hannah pushed herself out of the chair, up onto her feet. "In fact, I believe I'll turn in now."

As she turned, Nate caught her wrist in a firm but gentle grip. Her heart pounded. She looked down at him, wide-eyed.

"Hannah?"

Her mind stalled a moment on a single thought. His fingers were on her skin. With her next breath, she whispered, "Yes?"

"Where would you like me to sleep?"

An image of a fresh-stuffed mattress, tangled sheets, and damp skin flashed through her mind. Desire raced through her veins for a number of seconds before reality killed the flight of fantasy. She had no business entertaining such thoughts, ever again, especially now.

"I'm so sorry." Her cheeks on fire, Hannah stepped back, pulling free. "I forgot about you needing a bed. You must be exhausted."

"I am tired."

"Of course you are. Wait right here. There's an extra pallet in Jed's room. I'll go—"

"Will that disturb him?"

Her gaze went to the bedroom door. What should be a small matter unfortunately wasn't when Jed was involved. *How could I have forgotten, even for a moment?* She bit back a sigh and looked back at Nate.

"Probably."

"Worried about making him angry?"

Hannah answered in almost a whisper, "He's ... hard to handle."

"Maybe getting angry would be good."

"Snap him out of it?" She shook her head.

"You and Alice tried?"

"Getting Jed angry? It's easy enough without trying. But it doesn't change anything. At this late hour, what concerns me is disturbing Alice and the children."

"Don't chance it on my account."

"Thanks for being understanding." Hannah gestured toward her bedroom. "I'll gather some quilts and put you-"

"On the floor by the fire?"

"Oh no, I wouldn't make you sleep there."

"I won't take your bed."

"That's not," heat swept up her neck and spread over her cheeks at the thought of him in her bed, "what I was thinking."

"What do you have in mind?"

His tone seemed to hold a hint of suggestion. Certain her face was the same shade as her hair, Hannah resisted the urge to put her hands up to cool her cheeks. "There's a room attached to the barn, where they'd planned on hired hands staying. It has a bed and little stove, far more comfortable than the floor."

"Sounds fine."

"Good." Feeling flustered, she gestured toward a lantern hanging on a peg near the door. "Would you mind lighting that while I fetch you bedding?"

"Not at all."

Grateful for a moment alone to regain her composure, Hannah quickly headed to the small room she shared with her daughter and Alice. She dug a couple of quilts and other bedding out of the chest at the foot of the older woman's bed, being as quiet as possible. On her way out she paused, shifting the load in her arms, reached down, and pulled the covers up over Jemma. She ran a gentle hand over the little girl's hair, then returned to where Nate waited.

Unasked, the man had banked the fire. Hannah directed a soft, polite smile at him, pleased at his thoughtfulness. They met by the door. Wordlessly, they donned their coats and Nate his hat.

When she struggled to open the door with full arms, he gently took the bedding and handed her the lantern instead. She didn't protest, simply thanking him with another smile.

Together, they stepped out into the cold, crisp night. The wind had died, leaving the air still. Bright orbs dotted a clear black sky. Dull and distant, the half moon poured forth little light. Hannah shivered, despite her coat, while she moved across the yard, heading toward the left side of the barn. Her fingers tightened on the lantern's metal ring, comforted by its soft glow in the darkness.

Just past halfway along the building's wall, she stopped and pulled open a door. Hannah entered first. Inside, the room was big enough for two beds, a stove, a small table, and the two of them, barely. She set their light down on the table and glanced around.

Even this small space appeared neglected. Her sigh frosted the air. *Matches the rest of Redwing Farm.*

Eager to get him settled and return to the house, Hannah moved around the end of the first bed and accidentally brushed against Nate. His audible intake of breath startled her. She lost her footing, stumbled, and started to fall. He grabbed her by the waist, steadying her. She stiffened, uncertain how to react to the contact, easing away as soon as he loosed her.

"Thank you." Her tone was brisk.

"You're welcome."

Nate put the bedding down on the other bed, an arm's reach from the first one. "You brought sheets."

"And a pillow, it's old but …" Hannah shrugged.

"It'll be fine, thank you."

"You're welcome." After a brief but noticeable pause, she continued. "If you'll hand me a sheet, I'll make the bed."

"I can."

"You're the guest."

"How about," Nate twisted, grabbing a sheet before turning

back to face her. When his gaze met hers again, awareness flowed between them. Her breath quickened as he moved to the other side of the bed. Several inches separated them, but it felt like his presence filled the empty space. "We make it together?"

After a brief hesitation, Hannah agreed. She caught the edge of the sheet as he snapped it open over the mattress. Vividly aware of being alone with the man, her movements were jerky as she tucked it around and under. Nervous, she kept clearing her throat while they moved on, spreading a blanket out next.

"Something wrong?"

"Um, no. Um, Alice mentioned you breed horses?"

"Started to a while back."

Hannah waited for a time but when he didn't elaborate, she prompted. "So it's a new thing?"

"No. About five years now."

"I see. And, ah, before then your family ran cattle?" She smoothed the last quilt in place.

"Still runs cattle."

Hannah finished with the blanket and looked up at Nate. The man was between her and the door. She edged her way around the bed, halting about a foot from him. "So there are cattle and horses on the Bar 7."

"The Bar 7 is a cattle ranch." His brow furrowed. "There are enough horses to work the herd."

"You don't keep your horses on the family ranch?"

"No. They're on River's Bend."

Hannah tried to remember if Alice had mentioned anything about it, but her mind remained stubbornly blank. "Your place?"

"Yes."

"Too crowded at the family home?" She moved forward, trying to be careful, giving him as wide a berth as possible in the confined area.

"I just enjoy being alone."

"I understand." She nodded. "I should be going now."

72

"I didn't mean to be rude."

"You weren't. But it's late and this ... isn't exactly appropriate." Her hip bumped into the man, despite her efforts or perhaps because of them. Her gaze flew to his. Hannah couldn't look away. Awareness flowed through her veins now at a dizzying speed.

"You mean, being here alone?"

Nate moved, one small step, to stand directly in front of her. He leaned in, slowly. Her heart thundered. Entranced, she watched his face come closer. When he finally stopped, she could feel the warmth of his breath on her lips. His hand raised to rest his palm gently along her jaw line.

Hot and fierce, desire flooded her senses. Need threatened to overwhelm her. Hannah wanted to be held. It had been so long since she had been. His touch stirred temptation difficult to resist.

Chapter 6

Hannah allowed his hand to remain for a number of seconds, savoring the physical contact. After that, reluctantly, she did what was necessary. She reached up, pulling his hand down and away from her. Romance had cost her dearly before. She couldn't afford to pay the price again. Especially, not with a man named Rolfe.

"Hannah, I—"

Her fingertips covered his lips, stopping the words. She didn't want to hear he was sorry. When he quieted, she dropped her hand and stepped back, putting much-needed space between them. Her teeth chewed on the inside of her cheek, a nervous habit. Words seemed to stick in her throat. It took a moment before she could force them out.

"This isn't appropriate."

"I know. I'm—"

"Please. Don't."

Nate nodded, seeming to understand that she didn't want an apology. "What do you want me to do?"

Everything.

His sincere question fanned the flames of what Hannah was trying to douse. She couldn't help but wonder if a simple touch sparked such intensity, what a kiss would unleash. Their gazes, locked as silence, stretched between them. A cold bit of reality filtered through her emotions. Her wants didn't matter, Jemma's needs did. She must never lose sight of that.

Her spine stiffened. "Please forget this happened."

"But …" Something in her steady gaze must have conveyed there would be no discussion. "All right."

"It's best." Hannah started toward the door again. This time they both made certain to avoid accidental contact. "I forgot to bring an extra lantern. Would you like me to leave this one here?"

"You don't want me to walk back?"

Although the thought of going alone, in the dark, made her uneasy, Hannah asserted with perfect calm, "I know my way by heart. I'll be fine."

"I'd rather escort you."

"I don't want to trouble you."

"You're not."

"All right, if you're sure."

"I am." He reached up, settling his hat firmly on his head.

"Very well."

Hannah opened the door, took a step out, and shrieked. A small black shadow wove past her feet and disappeared through the doorway. Her hand on her chest, she struggled for composure.

Worried, Nate put his hand on her shoulder. "Are you okay?"

"No, Silas about scared the life out of me."

"Silas?"

"Yes. Sorry." Hannah shifted, pulling away. "I'm afraid the cat's in your room now. Would you like me to go find him?"

"He won't bother me." Lantern in hand, he closed the door and they started for the house.

"He probably won't," she agreed, paused for a moment, then added, "Silas was Bessie's pet."

"Was he?"

"It's strange."

Nate's gaze swept their surroundings, seeing only vague shapes and shadows past their tiny circle of light. "What is?"

"Jed hates anyone to touch Bessie's things. He's possessive of the littlest thing. But he won't allow her cat inside since she died. Poor Silas has taken to lurking around the barn."

"Usually a good place for a cat."

"Not for a pet used to sleeping on a cushion by the fire and having his cream in a saucer set out for him."

Hannah continued to speak in a hushed tone. He grinned, slightly amused. Something about being outside at night made most people whisper.

"Spoiled?"

"Very." Hannah blew out a breath. "I'm sorry I screamed. I should've expected him to appear near the barn."

"It's okay." They rounded the corner of the barn. "You were close?"

"Silas and I?"

"You and Bessie."

"Yes."

Such raw emotion filled her one-word answer Nate regretted asking. "Sorry."

"Nothing to be sorry about."

Her tone, even but almost empty of feeling, worried him. He wondered if he'd made things worse. For some reason, the young woman didn't seem to care for apologies.

"I shouldn't have asked about Bessie."

Hannah slowed her steps as if, suddenly, she wasn't eager to return to the house. "It's okay, honestly. Bessie was a big part of my life. Now, on most days, I can't even say her name aloud. And I'd like to."

"All right." Nate hoped he understood correctly. "How did you meet Bessie? Did you grow up together?"

"No, she moved here several years ago to teach school. We met at church. Bessie was so full of enthusiasm and energy. She made even impossible dreams seem achievable."

Nate moved his arm, swinging the lantern gently. "And this was her dream?"

"One of two. Having a large family was the other." Hannah's smile was fleeting. "She was an orphan, hated being alone and never wanted to be again."

"How'd she convinced you to help with this farm?" He leaned closer, interested in her answer. "You love horses too?"

"No. Sorry. I like horses fine on a one-on-one basis. I admire their beauty but being able to ride, if needed, is the extent of my skill set or interest."

"Are you trying to discourage me?"

"From offering me a job? No, simply being honest. Give me numbers and I'll make all the columns add up. With names, dates, and paper, I'll have your records organized in no time. If I've all the pertinent information, I'll track your breeding program to the smallest detail. But point to a group of horses and ask me who should be bought or be bred to who, then Jemma would likely give you a better answer."

"You like bookkeeping?"

"I love numbers the way Bessie loved horses."

"They give me a headache."

Hannah chuckled, a low husky sound. "I've heard that from many people. What can I say? I'm an odd duck."

"Nothing wrong with being different."

"That's what my ma used to tell me."

"Wise woman."

"I thought so." Hannah glanced up at the stars, falling silent for a moment before then looking back at him. "But most people believed the apple didn't fall far from the tree."

"Thought? You no longer think she's wise—"

"Ma passed away soon after Bessie."

"I'm sorry." Nate felt the urge to offer her a comforting touch, started to reach out, then thought better of it, his hand dropping to his side. "That must have been difficult."

"It was ... is. She was the only family Jemma and I could claim." Something about her odd phrasing nagged at him but Nate couldn't pin down exactly what. He filed her comment away in his memory. "Did your mother share your love of numbers?"

"No." Hannah chuckled. "Ma hated numbers. They were far too practical for her. People thought her odd for other reasons."

"So she didn't teach you how to keep records and such?"

"No, I learned from ... a man in town."

Again, something in way the young woman spoke caught his attention. Nate wondered why she'd be reluctant to share the name of a teacher or employer. His gaze studied her face in profile but the lantern didn't cast enough light to read her expression. It wasn't any of his business but it was curious.

"Bookkeeping is an unusual job choice for ... ah ...?"

Hannah stopped, turning to face him squarely. Even in the low light, Nate could see her raised chin. When she spoke, her voice was low, calm, and yet pure challenge.

"A woman?"

"Yes."

"No more unusual than choosing to be a ranch hand."

"Point taken."

A flash of white out of the shadows was her smile. Hannah resumed walking. *Interesting woman.* His gaze followed her. She'd made her point then let it go and didn't belabor it. *I like her.*

"But yes, you're right. It's unusual."

"Unusual isn't bad."

"You think so? Then you're a rare person."

"So I've been told."

"Is that good or bad?"

"Depends on your perspective."

Dark and mysterious as the night enveloping them, her gaze met his for a full moment before she responded. "Good answer."

When she looked away, Nate glanced ahead. An unexpected sting of disappointment pricked him. Despite their slow pace, they were nearing their destination. He didn't want the conversation to end. In fact, he wanted to know more about Hannah.

"Was this your first job?"

"Outside of helping Ma, yes. They didn't really need a bookkeeper yet but Bessie had a big heart."

"A big heart?" Nate echoed softly.

"Ma did the best she could but her health wasn't so good the last few years. Bessie knew I needed work."

"Like Alice wants to do for you now."

Pride stiffened her spine and sharp words raced to the tip of her tongue, eager to react to his soft-spoken statement. She wasn't a charity case. Hannah didn't need pity. Her lips parted to deliver a cutting defense then her flash of temper cooled as swiftly as it rose. The years she'd spent raising Jemma ground in the need for practicality. Pride wouldn't feed her daughter and the hard truth was he was right.

"Yes." Nate remained silent. After a few seconds, she felt compelled to add, "We're family." Memories of her friend and mother, both sweet and sorrowful, were so close to the surface they tugged at her composure. Tears threatened. Hannah took a breath. "Family isn't just people you're related to."

"I know."

His low-voiced sincerity ran through her like warm honey, soothing her jagged emotions. They shared a look of accord, understanding, and almost intimacy in the soft glow of lantern light. At first, it felt amazing and Hannah wanted to bask in it. Then it felt too comfortable, too much, too soon, and she didn't know how to respond. To her relief, they reached the porch steps in the next moment and she didn't have to do a thing. Their gazes met and held as they stood together.

Nate shifted, moving the slightest amount. "Would you mind if I took an armful of wood for the stove?"

"Of course not, the wood pile is on that side of the house." Hannah stretched out her arm, pointing.

"I noticed it earlier when we were bringing in the sheets."

"Oh, well, good." She put one foot on the first step. "Good night."

"Good night."

Quickly she climbed the steps then crossed the porch. As Hannah eased open the door, she looked back at Nate. His fingers tugged the brim of his hat, a soundless farewell. In reply, she gave a slight nod, even though it was unlikely he could see it, then stepped inside, shutting the door behind her.

Hannah stood by the entrance for a time. Her thoughts were spinning, driven by the emotions he'd stirred up. She listened to his footsteps, first loud along the side of the house then fading while he walked away. *Intriguing man.*

Exhaustion caught up with her as she removed her coat, hanging it up. When her gaze adjusted to the total darkness, she walked over to check on the fire. The gray mass of ash covering the coals exuded little heat. Satisfied all was well, she picked up a brick left to warm with a folded bit of cloth and entered her bedroom with it minutes later.

Alice snored softly in her narrow bed pressed against the right-hand wall. With care, Hannah avoided disturbing the older woman while she moved over to the far side of a slightly larger bed on the opposite wall. Her daughter was still, a small lump among barely disturbed covers. Many nights how quiet Jemma could sleep almost unnerved her. The child was dead to the world when she slept. Nothing disturbed her, until the recent nightmares.

In the cold air of the unheated room, Hannah shivered. She

placed the wrapped brick under the covers at the foot of the bed beside the one she'd put in when Jemma had gone to sleep. With quick movements, she changed into her nightgown. She tried not to think about how little warmth it provided. The garment was threadbare in places but replacing it wasn't an option now.

Weary, Hannah folded her clothes, setting them down on an old wooden chair. One tiny side step brought her in front of the dresser. Her image a shadow reflected in the old mirror. One by one, she worked the pins out of her hair and placed them on the wooden surface. Once the full length fell free to her waist, she took her time brushing her hair before weaving it into a loose braid. A brief private moment with time spent solely on her. She rarely got those.

A low wail sounded while a shaft of frigid air chilled her exposed skin. The wind had picked up again, sneaking in through the cracks between the planks. Hannah swallowed a sigh as she moved quickly to get under the covers. Bessie had fallen in love with this place, finding the plank-frame house charming. She'd overlooked all the flaws, including the gaps between boards.

Hannah shivered, then reached down and pulled up an extra quilt from the foot of the bed. Although it felt disloyal even to think about, she wondered if all this focus on the past was good for any of them. She scooted closer to Jemma. Some moments passed while she studied her daughter's sweet face half hidden by the feather pillow and long strands escaping her braids. The girl didn't stir once except for the gentle rise and fall of her chest.

Hannah turned on her back and stared up at the ceiling. As tired as she was, sleep remained elusive. Nate was drawing her attention in ways it hadn't been since before her daughter was born. She raised a hand and shifted her pillow, trying to get comfortable. At a time when she needed to focus on getting a job and providing for Jemma, he was a tempting distraction.

And a Rolfe, don't lose sight of that. Restless, she rolled onto her side. *What's so bad about them, Michael? Why does Alice sing their praises but you … ?* Hannah shifted onto her back again, frustrated. *Why didn't you explain?* She blew out a soft breath, closing her eyes.

Right now, it felt as if it took all she had to get through each day. A sudden longing for her mother filled Hannah. Her parent had always been a source of comfort. Guilt mingled with sorrow. With all the drama surrounding Jed swallowing up huge bites of energy, had she mourned properly? Losing Bessie was painful. She missed her friend a lot. It was just…

I miss you, Ma. She sighed softly, trying not to disturb the room's other occupants.

Although she hadn't always heeded her mother's advice, Hannah missed having the option to seek it out. She rolled back on her side, opening her eyes to look at her daughter. With one hand, she reached out, gently smoothing some hair off the little girl's cheek. She knew Ma would've told her to do what was best for Jemma. *I just wish you could tell me what exactly that is.*

With effort, Hannah quieted her thoughts. Her eyes drifted shut again. The need to rest trumped worries and sleep slowly claimed her.

Out in the small room off the barn, the stove had finally heated the place up enough to be comfortable. Nate blew out the lantern, settling back in the dark. A slight musty smell drifted from the feather pillow, but it was far softer than his saddle so he couldn't complain. The thin pallet beneath him, on the other hand, felt little better than stretching out on the ground. Not yet ready to sleep, he stared straight up, with his hands behind his head. His day had gone far different than he'd anticipated.

Alice wouldn't be returning to the Bar 7 for who knew how long. Jed's grief and drinking were out of control. He wished he hadn't come here in place of his brother, a close friend of the other man. If anyone had a good shot at getting through to Jed, it'd be Sam. Even so, tomorrow he'd try talking to the man. It couldn't hurt to try.

Nate tried turning his thoughts to planning repairs around the farm, but a certain redhead kept sneaking into them. After a few minutes, he'd forgotten about work and instead tried to find a logical reason for his attraction to Hannah. There was no denying she was pretty. *Those chocolate eyes.* Mostly she'd been pleasant company. *Didn't fill every second with words.*

His lips curved, recalling some of the quiet moments they'd shared. *I like her.* Tension followed. Nate didn't warm up to new people easily. *What's different about Hannah?*

Part of her appeal *had* to be how good it felt running into a woman who hadn't heard the rumors and wasn't set on trying to heal him. He most certainly did not need *healing*. His heart had mended long ago. Women did make him wary, but it didn't make him some tragic figure. *Being careful isn't bad.* People landed in a heap of trouble by tossing caution to the wind.

So it's completely understandable I—

Unexpectedly, the cat jumped up beside his head, startling Nate. Silas stood, calmly looking at him. Though it seemed odd, during that time he sensed the animal's loneliness and didn't have the heart to push him off the bed. He stretched out a hand, petting soft black fur. The cat remained in place, accepting the attention for several seconds before strolling away to curl up near his feet.

Nate closed his eyes, trying to relax. The image of a woman whose hair brought to mind a glorious sunset flashed through his mind again, keeping him awake. *What if she came to live on the ranch?* Heat swam through his veins. The strength of his reaction to the mere thought troubled him.

Restless, Nate rolled onto his side and faced the wall. A brief low growl reminded the man he wasn't alone. He looked down at his companion. Large yellow orbs stared at him, conveying annoyance.

"Sorry." He felt silly apologizing to a cat, yet was pleased when Silas closed his eyes and purred.

By the time silence fell, Nate had corralled his wandering thoughts. He slowed his breath and closed his eyes. After a few moments, he was asleep.

The next morning Hannah overslept. She didn't wake until Jemma started climbing over the top of her. A glance across the room revealed Alice gone. She scrambled out of bed and hurried through their morning routine. First, she helped her daughter dress before changing into her own day clothes. She then plaited the little girl's hair into two neat braids. Once done, she sent Jemma out into the main room, where the boys waited, judging from the sound of muffled voices.

Hannah twisted her hair up in a quick knot at the back of her head, pondering what to say to Alice. Her fingers fumbled as she tried to hurry, hoping to catch her alone before Nate woke up. The older woman knew she'd sent letters of inquiry to nearby ranches and farms and that all but one had replied using similar words with the same ending, no job for her. The Triple C Ranch hadn't answered yet and she was holding onto the slim hope it meant they were considering her for a position. However, if they also said no, there were other places to consider besides the Bar 7.

Did Alice push her idea because I'm running out of time?

Worry gnawed at her. Not many people were likely to take a chance on a female bookkeeper, especially a young, unmarried one with a child. Hannah opened the door and stood, observing the people in the room a moment. *Everyone might turn me away.* She bit the inside of her lip hard. *How long can I wait?*

As if she sensed Hannah's presence, Alice turned around and looked directly at her. The deep-seated worry clear in the older woman's expression almost shocked her with its intensity. A knot tightened in her gut. She'd known for some time their stay at

Redwing Farm was nearing the end. Her inability so far to secure a new home for Jemma was a heavy burden. Seeing how troubled her friend appeared underscored her concerns.

For her daughter's sake, Hannah maintained her outer poise while entering the room. Fierce determination soon steadied her nerves. Her gaze settled on the little girl. She'd do what was best for Jemma, whatever sacrifice it meant.

Any honest work. Laundry. Housekeeping. Hannah stepped up beside Alice, who was busy stirring a pot of oatmeal on the cook stove. *Sorry, Michael, but even a temporary job with the Rolfes if one is offered.* "I—"

A quiet rapping on wood distracted her. The boys left the table and hurried across the room. Seconds passed in a quiet but intense argument between them regarding who should be the one to open the door.

"Alice," Hannah whispered, trying to take advantage of the children's distraction, but before she could speak another word Jason opened the door. Nate, tall, dark, and exuding confidence, strode into the room, stealing her attention. His gaze met hers as he took off his hat and every coherent thought she had fled.

"Yes? Hannah … Hannah?"

With a shake of her head, she belatedly responded to the older woman. Hannah turned slightly and looked at Alice. The older woman studied her, frowning, her expression still one of worry. Before her friend could say a word, the sound of a man's low laughter floated through the room and she couldn't resist a glance at Nate. When she looked back, Alice's expression now had speculation mingled with concern.

Conscious of Nate and the children gathering around the table behind her, Hannah averted her gaze. She wanted to explain her glance meant nothing, but couldn't with them so close. *It's just been a long time since I've heard a man laugh.* As Alice started filling bowls, she picked up two at a time, carrying them over to those waiting. *That's it.* She set the man's food in front of him then moved in a perfectly reasonable pace to her daughter.

Breakfast was a subdued event. After distributing oatmeal, Hannah and Alice then joined the others, bringing a pitcher of fresh milk and a jar of honey with them. Few sounds disturbed the quiet room once they sat down. Children and adults alike concentrated on eating and volunteered little conversation.

As soon as he finished his meal, Nate excused himself and went outside. The boys followed him soon after with the stated intent of completing their chores. Minutes later, everyone else finished and Hannah started clearing the table while Jemma and Alice settled near the fire.

The older woman soon had her daughter helping unwind yarn from an old sweater. The task wouldn't hold Jemma's attention long. Hannah pitched her voice to carry over the clinking of the dishes as she started washing them.

"Alice." She paused, choosing her next words carefully so nothing the little girl overheard would trouble her. "Why did you bring it up with Nate?"

A few moments passed before Alice offered a measured response. "I wanted you to have another option. Although you've presented them in the best light, we both know what the numbers say."

"I didn't sugar-coat things."

"You didn't point out you hadn't been paying yourself."

Hannah scrubbed harder on the sticky pot. "I wasn't trying to mislead you."

"I'm certain you were trying to be kind."

"I was."

"I appreciated it then, but now … I believe we need to be brutally honest with each other."

"All right, last night I felt pushed into a situation I wasn't ready to be in."

"I felt I had to say something. Nate won't be here long and there isn't much time left to make arrangements."

"I have concerns." Hannah turned the pot upside down, placing it on the towel-covered surface to dry before looking over at the older woman. "You knew that."

Alice glanced down at the girl kneeling by her feet. "Yes, I do. I also know you'd do anything for this one."

"Of course I would, but there are other options."

"None with the same benefits."

Towel in hand, Hannah started drying a freshly washed bowl with vigor. "I'm not convinced what you speak of would be in my best interests."

"But they are in hers."

Hannah stilled. The calm words were a simple statement of fact. Alice's certainty was difficult to ignore, especially when all she had against the Rolfes was a warning from a man long dead. *But what if Michael was right?*

"I know you believe that. And I … value your opinion but—"

"You continue to doubt it." Alice's tone, while direct, held notes of sympathy. "Out of real concern or because you're afraid of making the wrong choice?"

Hannah stared down at the bowl in her hands. She continued rubbing the towel over it another minute although it was already dry. Finally, she put it away and reached for the next one.

"I'm afraid," she whispered, remaining focused on her task.

"I understand. I often struggled with the same fear after losing Harry. It's hard being the only parent. But sometimes not making a decision ends up making one you don't intend."

"I know you're worried about us." Hannah spoke slowly while she finished drying the last few dishes. "But you shouldn't have brought it up with Nate without my agreement."

Alice sighed, soft and weary. The sound caused Hannah to look back at her. "My patience isn't what it used to be. I'm sorry I made you uncomfortable."

"It's all right." Now Hannah felt bad for even mentioning it. It paled in contrast to what the older woman endured daily.

A quiet moment passed before Alice spoke again. "Perhaps …
if you spent some time with Nate today and got to know him a
little, it might help you with … certain decisions."

"He hasn't offered me a … anything."

"He will," Alice stated with absolute confidence.

Hannah wiped her damp hands on her apron. "I'll visit with
him if an opportunity comes up, if it will ease your mind."

"It will."

"All right."

"Mama." Jemma bounced up, scampering over to her side.
One small hand tugged on Hannah's skirt. "The chickens are
waiting."

"Are they? Well, go get the basket." She smiled down at her
daughter's eager expression.

While the little girl dashed away to do her bidding, Hannah
slipped her apron off and moved over to the door. Mother and
child bundled up and were ready to go out in minutes. As they
were exiting the house, Hannah glanced back at Alice and noted
how she sat, staring at Jed's closed bedroom door. Her somber
expression held a tinge of resignation. Sadness filled her, knowing
of nothing she could do to help.

Hannah gently pulled the door shut and walked out into
another depressingly gray day. She swallowed a sigh as her gaze
lifted to the heavens. The clouds seemed heavier, darker than
yesterday. She hadn't seen the sun in days. Winter had barely
started and already she felt it had lasted forever.

With Jemma holding onto her mitten-covered hand, skipping
along beside her, they crossed the yard and went down the path
to the chicken coop. It was a short walk to their destination on
the far side of the barn. To their surprise, the chickens had
company. Their visitor, with the boys' help, was repairing holes
in the building's walls.

The sight of John hammering with a lot of enthusiasm but
little efficiency brought a smile to Hannah's face. Her gaze moved

to Jason, working as he most often did, with painfully slow precision. She blinked back tears. It was hard to imagine not being part of their daily lives. She was going to miss them both so much.

For another moment, Hannah continued watching, pleased to see how patient Nate was with them, then her daughter drew her attention. The little girl became impatient. She darted forth, basket swinging, in search of eggs. Hannah followed her and together they quickly filled Jemma's bit of wicker.

Hannah called out to the boys, telling them it was time to leave for school. She acknowledged Nate with a polite smile, then herded the children back to the house. Jemma headed straight to Alice, presenting her with the eggs while the boys grabbed their things. As prearranged, a short time later she left her daughter happily chatting about chickens in the older woman's company, to head out with John and Jason.

As they walked near the barn, Nate stepped out from the shadows and directly into Hannah's path.

Chapter 7

Startled, Hannah stopped abruptly, staring at the man.

"May I join you?"

"Excuse me?" For a moment, his words didn't make sense.

Nate lifted one eyebrow as he repeated, "May I join you?"

"You want to walk to town with us?"

"If you don't mind?"

"Wouldn't you rather ride?"

"I'd prefer company."

"You would?"

"Yes."

At a loss for words, Hannah just stared at him again.

"So, is it all right?"

"Is what all right?"

"Is it all right if I join you?"

Fire swept up her neck and over her face. "Yes, of course it is. Please do."

"Thank you."

"You're welcome." She averted her gaze.

Seconds later, Nate moved out of her way and, with a sweep of his hand, indicated his desire for Hannah to go in front of him. An awkward silence fell but the quiet didn't last long. The boys were excited to have his company. They scampered about the man like eager puppies for the full mile walk from Redwing Farm to the small town of Ashwood. It was both sad and endearing to witness. She shivered as the wind picked up, chilling her even through her coat. Once upon a time, Jed would've inspired such high spirits in his sons.

The boys took off, lunch pails swinging, as they ran toward their friends soon after they entered town. After continuing at a leisurely pace for a few minutes, they passed near the school and Hannah paused. While the teacher greeted other students, the boys were playing in the yard with other children. It gave her a sliver of peace to know John and Jason had somewhere to go where they could still play with abandon.

"They're very different here."

"Than at home? Sadly, yes."

"I'm going to talk to Jed today."

Startled, Hannah's gaze swung to the man next to her. She'd almost forgotten his presence. A knot formed in her stomach when at last his words sunk in.

"You are?"

"Yes, I am," he stated with strong conviction. "Someone needs to get through to him."

Hannah read a familiar mix of emotions in his eyes. She'd seen the same reflected in the mirror: caring, compassion, the need to do something, anything, to help. "I see."

"You don't think I should?"

"It's not my place to say one way or another."

"But you don't believe it'll make a difference."

"I …" Her voice trailed off, words failed her and she shook her head in frustration.

"Don't you think he can get better?"

Hannah drew in a deep breath. Once, she'd thought so and even now she wanted to say yes, badly. For the boys' sake as well as Alice's, she wished for the faith that, in the end, he'd be well.

However, doubt far outweighed hope now and it wasn't in her to lie.

"I don't know. I hope so."

A bell rang out, the wind carrying its notes to them. She turned to watch the children swarm into the building that also served as the community's church. Restless, Hannah then started walking. Her goal, the mercantile, was at the other end of town.

Despite the cold, a good number of people were up and about their business. The few outside, besides her and Nate, occupied the other side of the street, which suited Hannah fine. Eager to get her errand done, she quickened her pace. The man stayed at her side without any obvious effort.

"May I ask you something?"

Hannah slowed, casting him a wary glance. "Of course. What do you want to know?"

"Is it just Bessie's death that's affecting Jed?"

"Yes," she answered, without hesitation. "Would you prefer more causes?"

"Yes."

Hannah studied him a moment. "Because then there might be something you might be able to fix for him?"

"I liked Jed, thought he was a good man." Her companion looked straight ahead, his expression somber.

"He was." She couldn't stop a tinge of anger from creeping into her voice. "And I want to believe he still is."

"But?"

"The boys miss Bessie. They need their father so much right now. This isn't fair to them."

"Out of sympathy?"

"For Jed? No, but …" Hannah paused, searching for the right words. "He's not the only one who loved Bessie. We all miss her, a lot. She was my best friend. But I can't stop taking care of Jemma because I'm grieving. My daughter needs me, regardless. Just as the boys need him. As heartless as it may sound, life goes on."

"Not heartless. Just realistic. Practical."

"Thank you. I hope so. Sometimes I feel guilty I'm not mourning her enough because ... I miss my mother too. Because ... I play with the children. Because Jed is ... grieving so much."

"What would Bessie say about that?"

"Bessie?" The young woman took a moment, considering the possibility. "She'd understand me, always did. But Jed." Hannah shook her head. "She'd be mad he's ignoring their boys."

"A sensible reaction."

"Thank you." Her smile offered him a flash of appreciation rather than expressing happiness.

"Don't feel guilty."

"I'll try."

They walked in silence for few minutes before Nate spoke again. "May I ask you something personal?"

"Yes," Hannah consented even as she tensed.

"May I be blunt?"

The young woman stopped, turning to face him. "Please."

"Does Alice want you to have her job because you can't find one?"

Even though she'd given him leave, his plain speaking made her bristle slightly. "I've applied to every farm and ranch within a half day's ride."

"Any offers?"

Not a genuine one. "No." Hannah took a breath, calming her pride. "Not yet."

"No responses?"

I need his good will. "I've heard back from all but one."

"And if it's a dead end?"

"Then I'll broaden my search. Send out more letters. And I may ..." Hannah drew up all the confidence she could muster. "Ask you to consider me for a temporary job."

His gaze held hers for a long moment. Nerves dampened her palms, threatening to crack her mask of poise. Hannah barely breathed as she waited for him to speak.

"I'm already thinking about it. Thank you for being so honest."

Her tension lessened in response to the warmth in his voice. The weight pressing on her chest eased. She started to relax, then a familiar giggle carried on the breeze. Careful to appear composed, allowing no hint of emotion, Hannah turned to look in the direction from which it came. Emily Harris and her sister, May, were approaching, exchanging excited whispers.

They were close to her in age; Emily a year older and May a few years younger, but they'd never been friends. With beady eyes and sharp features, Hannah likened them to a pair of weasels as they rudely stared at her. She looked each one dead in the eye for some seconds. To show any hint of fear or weakness would be an invitation to attack and these women didn't need much of one.

The women walked by so close Emily's skirt brushed against hers. Hannah noticed their gazes dart from her to Nate then back to her again. The speculative gleam in their eyes made her want to cringe. They continued their not-so-hushed conversation with hands shielding their mouths but she knew the subject under discussion without hearing one clear word.

Coming to town with him was a bad idea.

Thankfully, the sisters didn't pause, walking on down the street. Hannah wasn't sure what to do next. Nate had to have noticed the women's rude behavior. She looked blindly ahead, trying to think of the simplest explanation to offer him.

"Sorry about that."

Nate's gruff tone as much as his words startled her. Hannah turned her gaze to the man beside her. His hat brim pulled low obscured his expression but she noticed his clenched jaw. It revealed irritation. She understood the reaction. His apology, however, made no sense.

"Sorry about what?"

"Those women."

"You're apologizing to me for them?"

"You didn't deserve their rudeness."

Still puzzled, her brow furrowed. "Few people do."

"True, but I'm responsible. It wouldn't have happened if you hadn't been with me."

How does he know that? Alice wouldn't have told him. Could the boys have let it slip somehow? Hannah chose her next words with care. "What are you trying to say?"

"There are some rumors being spread about me. I didn't think it'd be an issue here." Nate reached up, resettling his hat. "But I should've known better. A friend told me the gossip is widespread."

"You are the victim of gossip?" Incredulous, she couldn't stop herself from asking.

"Anyone can be."

Instantly, Hannah felt bad. He was right. Just because Nate was handsome and came from a successful family didn't prevent a person from targeting him.

"I didn't mean you couldn't be but—"

"I should ignore it, be the better person."

"That's not what I was going to say." Upset, her tone had an edge to it. Hannah knew how cutting words could be, hurting a person down to the marrow of their being. She paused, regaining control, before offering him some soft sincerity. "I know it's not always possible to brush off what people say."

Nate grimaced. "Sorry, this is like a burr in my blanket but that's no excuse. I shouldn't have snapped at you."

"It's all right."

"No, it's not, but thank you."

"You're welcome." Hannah continued with careful politeness. "Perhaps you're mistaken about this?"

"I don't believe so."

"I haven't heard of those women spreading tales about you but … there are others they whisper about."

"You've heard about Ben?"

Michael's brother? Her stomach clenched but Hannah didn't react beyond shaking her head. *Is this why he wanted nothing to do with them?* She tried not to show too much curiosity. "Ben?"

"A cousin of mine who … never mind. This isn't about him."

"I didn't suggest it was," she assured him, then eager to know more gently prompted, "Why would you think this concerned your cousin?"

Nate shook his head, frowning. "It's not. Forget I said anything about him. They were definitely talking about me."

"How do you know for certain?" Mystified, she stared at her companion. "Did you hear something they said?"

"Not a word, but they were laughing."

"Laughing?" Hannah echoed.

"Didn't you hear them?"

"Uh, yes, I did. I'm confused about the connection. Why do you think it means they must have been talking about you?"

"Well, I admit it's usually men who laugh," Nate continued in an irritated growl, delivering the longest statement she'd heard from him. "The women mostly set their sights on figuring how they can heal the poor Recluse of River's Bend."

"The Recluse of—?"

"Me." Embarrassment entered his voice.

"You're a recluse?"

"No, that's the gossips' conclusion. I just spend a great deal of time alone."

And that's different from being a recluse how? Hannah tried to make sense of what he was telling her. "You think the Harris sisters consider you a recluse and somehow that's amusing?"

Nate shifted. "I'm not explaining well. I … They … Sometimes when women are speculating about healing my broken heart they …" His expression reflecting frustration, he shrugged. "Giggle."

"Your heart is broken?"

"No." His swift, emphatic denial made Hannah wonder if the opposite were true.

A wagon rattled through the frozen ruts running the length of Main Street, passing too close for comfort. As they shifted, moving nearer to the blacksmith's shop, Hannah noticed two men engaged in an animated discussion directly across from them. She squirmed inwardly, recognizing the one nearest to the saloon's closed door. The last thing she wanted today, especially in the company of Nate, was to run into Raymond Stone.

With a wave of her hand in the direction of the store still yards away, she started walking. "I'm sorry. I'm confused."

"I was engaged." Nate strode at her side. His words succinct, he sounded impatient. "She broke it off and married another man. Rumors say that's why I live in the wild."

"But it's not?"

"River's Bend is my home. Originally my father's homestead, I planned to live there since I was knee high to a grasshopper."

Hearing a phrase her mother had often used, Hannah almost smiled. "So living there has nothing to do with heartbreak?"

"No."

"And you believe those women were gossiping about you?"

"Yes."

Hannah didn't want to be rude to the man but his reasoning wasn't logical. "I—"

"It sounds crazy, I know. But that's how it is."

"Gossip can be crazy." They stopped in front of the mercantile and Hannah turned to face her companion. The information he'd shared with her was interesting but, on a gut level, she knew Nate was wrong. "But I'm certain the Harris sisters were talking about, and laughing at, someone else."

"Oh? Who?" He expressed doubt.

She sighed. "Me."

"You? Why?"

Hannah caught movement out of the corner of her eye. Her

gaze shifted, seeking the source and found Ray. The man stood on the plank sidewalk a few steps from the Long Branch Saloon, watching them. He smirked and she looked away, feeling distinctly uncomfortable. Without a word to Nate, she hurried into the store. A short distance from the door by the large front window she stopped and picked up a length of blue ribbon, pretending to study it while peeking out the glass.

"Something wrong?"

Even though Hannah had felt Nate following her, she started when he spoke. "No, not really, why?"

"You took off suddenly, without answering my question."

"Sorry." She turned in order to meet his gaze and held it steady while putting the ribbon back. "Could we talk about it later, somewhere more private?"

"If you'd like."

"I would. Thank you." Hannah didn't give him the chance to respond, heading off toward the counter running along the back wall, through the neatly stacked but crowded space.

"Wait." Nate touched her shoulder. She stopped, twisting to look back at him. "You okay? You seem," he paused, as though considering his next word, "unsettled."

Because I am. She didn't want to explain why seeing Ray, a fine upstanding citizen, disturbed her. "I'm fine."

Hannah moved on without waiting to see if Nate believed her assurance. When she neared the counter, Dennis Myers, a slightly older man she'd known since childhood, stepped out from the back room. They weren't friends but he'd always been kind to her. His wife, on the other hand, was a different story.

Mrs. Myers had never said anything spiteful to her face but the other woman's disapproval was always clear. It showed in the sour way her lips pursed whenever she had to look at Hannah and how Ruth always waited on her last, no matter who had entered the mercantile first. To her relief, Dennis appeared to be the only person, aside from them, in the building.

"Good morning." The man greeted her with a broad, welcoming smile. Unabashed interest gleamed in his blue eyes just before his gaze shifted to Nate, who'd stepped up beside her.

"Good morning." She gestured toward her companion. "Dennis, this is Nate Rolfe, he's visiting Alice. Nate, this is Dennis Myers, owner of the Ashwood Mercantile."

The two men exchanged pleasantries, then Dennis looked back at her. "What brings you into town today?"

Before she could respond, Nate excused himself, then walked off toward a display of canned goods. Her gaze followed him as the man picked up an empty box off the floor and wandered down an aisle. *He's giving me a little privacy.* It was a simple

act, a small gesture, but his thoughtfulness warmed her heart.

Dennis gently cleared his throat. Flustered, she turned her attention back to him.

"I, uh, was wondering if I have any mail?"

"You know, I believe you do." The shopkeeper stepped down to the end of the counter, turning his back to her in the process. He studied the tiny wooden squares on the wall a moment, then plucked out an envelope. In the act of handing it over to her, his expression became serious.

"Ruth said she talked to Alice."

Her cheeks flushed. She was grateful Dennis had kept his voice low and waited until after Nate went over to the other side of the store to say something. "Yes, she did."

"I wanted to say I'm sorry. I wish things were different."

Hannah shook her head. "Don't apologize. You've been too kind to us."

"I like Jed. I feel for him, I do, especially now that Ruth is finally expecting."

It was common knowledge the Myers desperately wanted a baby after being married for seven childless years. Though Hannah was happy for him, it was hard to show it at first. Any reference to a pregnancy triggered memories of Bessie. She swallowed hard, then plastered a smile on her face.

"Congratulations."

"Thank you." His grin reflected the depth of his joy for a full moment before his expression grew troubled again. "I wanted to explain why I can't keep him on my books any longer."

"We understand. You need to take care of your family. It's amazing you carried his account this long."

"It's a real shame about Jed."

"Yes. It is."

"If you or Alice need …"

"I'll let you know." Hannah assured him, even though she wouldn't, being polite.

"Good."

Tears stung her eyes. The shopkeeper was one of the few truly kind persons Hannah knew. Her lips parted, but before she could say a word, the bell over the door rang out. The man who worked with the blacksmith soon joined them at the counter. With a farewell nod to Dennis, she shoved the envelope into her coat pocket and went in search of Nate. She found him gazing out of the front window.

"I'm done. Did you need anything or are you ready to go?"

Nate turned to face her, his expression grave as his gaze locked on hers. "I couldn't help overhearing."

"That's understandable." Although they'd kept their voices low, in the small area it would've been difficult to avoid.

His breath caressed her ear when he leaned in close and whispered, "Do you need anything?"

"Excuse me?" Hannah stiffened even as her nerves sang with awareness.

"Is there anything needed at the house?"

Oh. Images of dwindling supplies flickered through her mind. Pride whispered for her to brush aside his question but she couldn't. Alice and the children needed help.

"Many things but I didn't make a list."

"Because of what Alice was told?"

Her gaze didn't waver. "Jed's account is closed."

"That won't do."

"Alice did her best. There's nothing I can do about it."

"No, but I can."

His boots hit the old wood floor hard as Nate strode up the aisle, collecting a variety of canned foods on the way. Hannah trailed him, watching in silence while he filled the box. Once the task was finished, he headed for the counter, reaching it as the other customer turned to leave. Before the door shut behind the man, he'd settled Jed's debt. She thought he might put some money down for future use, but what he actually did surprised her. He opened an account in Alice's name, making it clear only she could use it, then put quite a sum on it.

His action was stunning, further evidence the older woman was indeed like a family member to the Rolfes rather than just an employee. Hannah remained quiet, uncertain what to say, while her companion purchased the foodstuff he'd gathered. She didn't find her voice until after the men finished their business, when she and Nate, him carrying the loaded box, stepped back out onto the street.

"I … Thank you."

"This is nothing."

"It's kind and generous." Hannah glanced around and relaxed when she didn't see Ray. "This will feed them for a month."

"I wish she'd told us how bad things were … are."

"She kept hoping he'd get better."

"There's no shame in asking for help."

"I know."

"We could've helped like this." Nate paused, drawing her attention to the box he carried with a pointed look. "Before."

"We still have food." The sound of heavy footsteps from behind them distracted her. Even though Hannah hoped what she heard was only another person out for a walk, her stride lengthened.

His long legs easily matched her new pace. "Vegetable stew and oatmeal?"

"Not fancy, but filling."

"She should've let us know."

"If Jed wasn't better, Alice planned to ask for help when Sam came for her."

"All she's asked for is a job for you."

"Yes but—"

A man somewhere behind them called out her name. Unable to ignore Ray without drawing unwanted attention to the fact, Hannah stopped. She addressed Nate, who'd halted just ahead of her, first. "Would you please excuse me for a moment?"

He glanced beyond her. "Is there a problem?"

When Nate met her gaze again, he appeared braced and ready for confrontation. Hannah could read subtle challenge in his stance. For a split second, she was tempted to spill out her troubles and lay them at his feet. It'd be such a comfort to allow someone else to handle a problem for her. Pride rose up then, killing the thought.

"No problem, I just need to speak with him for a moment."

Nate flicked another glance behind her. The corners of his mouth turned down. "All right."

"You could wait by the livery." She nodded to the building a few steps further down the street.

"I'll wait here."

"But I'm sure the box is heavy. You could lean against-"

Without a word, he set the box down in the middle of the plank sidewalk then straightened.

"I'm fine, Nate."

He nodded, his gaze still focused beyond her.

"You don't have to—"

"I'm waiting here."

Stubborn man. "Fine."

Hannah turned around. In denims, an old wool coat, and a white hat, stood Ray. The courteous expression he wore gave no hint of his intention but his eyes, as dark as the night sky, seemed to hold her in place, a butterfly on a hatpin. He took a step nearer, deliberately standing too close for comfort.

Chapter 8

"Who is he?"

His interest puzzled Hannah but after their last exchange, Ray's intimidating manner didn't surprise her. She allowed a few seconds to pass before responding with a neutral greeting, "Good morning."

"I asked—"

"I heard you."

Ray frowned. Unruffled, Hannah slowly stepped around him and moved further down the sidewalk, hoping to gain a semblance of privacy. But the maneuver failed. When she faced the farmer again, Nate stood at the edge of his shadow. Their new positions only changed one thing. The men were now within arm's reach of each other.

"Are you ignoring me, *Miss* Brooks?"

The emphasis on her unmarried status put her back up. "No, Mr. Stone, I am not."

"Then answer my question, Hannah."

Why haven't you asked the man himself?

Her eyes narrowed. She'd never cared for Ray, though he was well liked in Ashwood. He'd always made her feel uncomfortable, more so after she had Jemma. A reason for how she felt eluded her for years. He'd never been less than polite to her ... that is until he made his one, and only, visit to Redwing Farm. "My companion isn't your concern."

"Careful," he warned with a smile. "A woman, especially one in your position, shouldn't alienate her neighbors."

What are you trying to do? Anxiety wove a band around her chest. Ray had support in the community. Hannah did not. Still, while it would've been prudent to give the man what he wanted, she didn't appreciate his not-so-subtle bullying.

"Is this about my refusal?"

Ray moved closer, invading her space again. "It was a good offer ..."

"For a woman like me," Hannah finished for him, repeating what he'd said to her alone. She planted her feet and lifted her chin. Not for anything would she retreat. About to deliver a carefully worded, thoroughly composed, protest she noticed Nate move and instead blurted out, "Stop."

Both her would-be defender and Ray heeded the demand, but neither man looked pleased about it.

"You really should reconsider." False concern molding his expression, Ray eased back slightly.

In the less-than-ideal weather, few people were outside, so Hannah easily heard both the sound of others walking closer and their animated murmurs. Then the footsteps stopped. Her lips pressed flat together. *They're listening.*

Somehow, the news that Hannah had declined a *respectable* job had gotten out. A sour taste filled her mouth. It was one thing to know she was the topic of gossip and another to have people she knew hovering behind her, waiting for a juicy tidbit to chew over later.

Hannah tried to ignore them, focusing on Ray. "I'm not going to change my mind."

"I thought you'd be grateful for the opportunity to earn a decent living."

Fire scorched up Hannah's neck. Her regrettably visible response triggered a fleeting glint of satisfaction in Ray's eyes. She was certain then he'd fed the current speculation about her out of spite.

"I already do."

Eyebrows raised, he offered disbelief. "As a bookkeeper?"

A quickly suppressed giggle from behind Hannah stung but she tried not to let it show. The fine citizens of her community had made their disapproval of her living alone with a man in the weeks before Alice's arrival quite clear. The fact that Jed was the recent widower of her dear friend hadn't mattered. Rumors had spread like wildfire. Public opinion seemed to be if she'd made a child with one man, then of course she'd crawl into bed with another at the first opportunity.

"Yes," she bit out.

"Oh? What records are you keeping? The horses are gone."

"Not all."

"Oh yes, my mistake, when I picked up Sun Dancer, there was one mare and her foal. They must keep you very busy."

Her fingers curled, making tight fists. The reference to their last encounter tested Hannah's self-control for more than one reason. First, the meager amount he'd paid for the stallion had been the nail in the farm's coffin. "You took advantage of Jed."

Then tried to prey on me. In front of his farmhands, Ray had maintained the guise of being a *good* neighbor. He'd offered her a housekeeper position, starting after him and Ester Harris married … to be proper. Between the dubious horse deal and her personal unease with the man, Hannah couldn't bring herself to accept it. Still, she'd been hesitant to turn him down. Jemma's needs were more important than some discomfort and for a short time, just until a better job came along, she could put up with almost anything. She'd asked for time to consider it, and he'd graciously agreed.

Later, while the others were busy, Ray had cornered Hannah

in the barn. They weren't alone long, moments at best, but it was all the time needed for him to explain the *duties* he'd expect from her, then for her to tell him no.

"I didn't *take advantage* of anyone. I make sound business transactions, benefiting both parties."

Hannah sensed Ray was speaking about both his deal with Jed and the arrangement he'd wanted with her, but kept her response strictly about the horse. "It may have been legal, but buying Sun Dancer for a pittance wasn't morally right, not by any stretch of the imagination."

"Hannah," he chided, as though she were a wayward child. "I hardly think you should be offering others guidance on … morals."

Stiff as a board, Hannah fought to hold the tattered edges of her composure together. Her fingernails digging into skin now, despite her gloves, she glanced at Nate. His dark expression signaled he wouldn't restrain himself much longer. She swallowed a sigh. The last thing she needed was to be the cause of a brawl in the middle of town. Such an event would have tongues wagging long after Nathaniel Rolfe returned to his homestead.

"You will have to excuse me. It's time I headed home."

"Of course, Jed probably needs your care."

He's amusing himself at your expense. Don't give him that satisfaction. Keep calm. "I'm finished speaking with you."

Hannah rounded the farmer and walked up to Nate. The man in front of her now made no effort to hide his glower. He didn't budge an inch, his gaze remaining focused beyond her. She looked back and discovered Ray coolly studying her companion. Suddenly, she felt caught in some sort of silent stand-off.

"You never did say who he is." Ray continued to address Hannah instead of the man next to her.

"No," she was blunt, bordering on rude. "I didn't."

"You won't get a better offer."

"Perhaps, but it's my choice."

"That choice," Ray treated her to a long, pitying look, "is one that will have you and your outlaw's little bastard out on the street."

Clever. Delivering all that information with your slur ... just in case the stranger with me doesn't know.

Although the term applied to her daughter never failed to tear at Hannah's heart, she struggled not to react. Expressing outrage wouldn't win any compassion from most of the people in this town. They believed she had no right to complain about someone stating Jemma was born out of wedlock, even if that person used crude language. It was the truth, after all.

Nevertheless, with Nate's solid presence giving her the feeling she had support, Hannah couldn't resist a few choice words. "I'd rather be out on the street than work for you."

"A sensible woman would accept any honest job."

"True." Hannah said nothing further, allowing those listening to draw their own conclusions.

Ray shook his head, turned, and walked away without another word. Hannah watched him go until he joined the Harris sisters standing some yards away. To her relief, the small group headed in the direction of the mercantile. The senseless confrontation was over.

"You all right?"

Hannah looked at Nate and nodded.

"Want to talk about it?"

"Not really, especially not here."

"Ready to go then?"

"Definitely."

Together, they moved down the street, pausing briefly for Nate to retrieve the box. They walked in silence at first, with Hannah focused exclusively on getting out of Ashwood. As each step brought them closer to the edge of town, she started to relax and enjoy his pleasant, undemanding company.

When they approached the second-to-the-last house on the street a gray-haired woman emerged from it. She reached the sidewalk as they closed the distance between them, shutting the gate of the pristine white fence surrounding the yard. With only a couple of feet separating them from her, she looked over and noticed Hannah. The old woman sniffed, loudly. With a sweep of her skirts, she strode across the street, away from them, then headed off into town.

"That was odd."

His quiet observation killed Hannah's tiny hope Nate hadn't noticed. *What must he think of me?*

Hannah kept her gaze averted from his, feeling her cheeks heat yet again. Her face had likely been an ugly shade of red a good portion of the time he'd spent with her. Blushing so easily was a curse. For a moment, she wished the earth would open up and swallow her whole.

Then who would take care of Jemma? Hannah glanced at Nate when her self-pitying thought brought up a real concern. *Is it enough that Alice knows? Or is it not?* The worry nagged her at all hours.

Hannah looked straight ahead. *Trust Michael? Alice?* She glanced over at the man beside her again. *Or find a way to judge him myself?* Her gaze wandered but she didn't pay attention to the familiar surroundings. *Maybe if I tell him … some. See his reaction.*

"Not so odd, given what she knows."

As soon as the words left her mouth, Hannah felt the weight of his gaze on her. She tensed, waiting for Nate to utter the obvious question. Minutes passed. They left Ashwood with him still silent. Finally, she realized he wasn't going to ask.

Hannah felt relieved at first. She rarely shared certain personal details. Too many people, including the older woman they'd just encountered, had judged her harshly for them.

The longer they walked, however, the more Hannah leaned back toward sharing a thing or two with Nate. How he reacted might tell her all she needed to know. *Or nothing but…*

Hannah mulled over possibilities until they were about half way to the farm before deciding to act. "I'd like to explain something Ray said."

"You don't have to," Nate answered softly.

"I'd rather share the truth before you hear more gossip."

"I doubt I'll be in Ashwood again."

"Still, rumors spread and once heard, burrow in."

"Personal experience?"

Hannah shoved her hands into her coat pockets. "Yes."

"I'm sorry."

"Not your fault."

"I sympathize. I despise and ignore gossip. If I want to know something about you, I'll ask directly."

"Thank you. I appreciate that." She gave him a brief, but sincere, smile.

"No need to thank me for doing what's right."

"I'm glad you feel that way but I'd still like to explain."

"Because you might ask for a job?" He inquired, polite yet serious.

"Partly." Hannah aimed to be as honest as possible while still protecting a few sensitive facts. "And because I prefer the truth, straight up, even when it isn't pretty. Besides, it has a way of coming out no matter how you try to bury it."

"And some people will always try twisting information until it pleases their way of thinking."

"Turning the beautiful ugly."

"You don't like gossip, do you?"

"No." Her one word made an emphatic statement. "And I try not to listen to it." She smiled again, this time sadly. "But it can be hard to avoid when you're the topic."

"I understand."

His words carried such certainty, Hannah believed him. "Good."

"But you still want to explain?"

"A little, yes."

"All right." His calmness went a long way toward steadying her nerves.

"Raymond Stone was a neighbor for a time when Jemma and I lived with my mother." She paused, still deciding what to say and what to hold back.

"Friends?"

Hannah shook her head. "I don't know him well. The place next to Ma's had been deserted for years. I was in my last year at school when Ray bought it."

"Just him?"

"Yes. When he came to introduce himself—" She hesitated, considering her next words with care. "Ma didn't ... like him."

"Why?" Nate prompted.

"Well ... she'd just get a sense about a person."

"A quick judge of someone's character?"

Hannah stepped around a mud puddle, lifting her hem to keep it from being soaked. "In a way." She glanced at her companion and noted his wrinkled brow. Attempting to explain her mother's quirks was challenging. "As I've said, Ma was ... different."

"People are, generally."

His casual acceptance eased her. "Yes, but her differences were ... noticeable. And she didn't try to hide them."

"Sounds interesting."

"Interesting?" She considered his word a moment. "Yes. Ma was kind, generous, loving, and *interesting*. She'd do things like take Jemma out to the barn and play with kittens while dinner burned on the stove, forgotten."

"Anyone can get distracted."

Hannah smiled, even as she shook her head. "When Ray showed up, Ma was inside cooking while I was sweeping the porch. I'd barely greeted the man when she stepped outside. After one long, hard look at him, she marched over, grabbed me by the arm and shoved me in the house. Standing in the open doorway, she told him to never to come back, then slammed the door in his face."

"Did strangers make her ... nervous?" Caution shaded his question.

"No. She loved Jed straight away. Hugged him before Bessie finished the introduction."

"Because she knew Bessie?"

"No." Hannah shook her head, then continued, offering him another example. "When your brother visited years ago, Jemma and I had gone to stay with my mother for a few days. John decided he wanted to be born during that time. Sam about scared the life out of us, pounding on the door at dawn. But as soon as Ma laid eyes on him, she smiled and put down her shotgun. Fed him peach cobbler while I dressed. She either liked a person or not, right from the first. Always."

"Was she ever wrong?"

"I never thought so."

"Even now, with Jed?"

Hannah hesitated, startled to realize the troubled widower hadn't entered her thoughts for some time. "Underneath it all, I still believe he's a good man."

"So do I."

A wagon rolled up headed toward Ashwood, interrupting their conversation. The older couple nodded in greeting but didn't speak a word, stop, or even slow down. After the strangers drove by Hannah decided to be blunt. There wasn't time to be otherwise before they reached the farm.

"I need to finish telling you about Ray."

"Sorry, I sidetracked you."

"It's all right. It was nice talking about my mother. But ..."

"You had something else in mind."

"Yes."

"Please, tell me."

"I've never felt at ease with Ray, especially after I had Jemma, but he's never been rude or improper to me until recently."

112

"What happened?"

"He offered me a job."

"The refusal you spoke of in town?"

"Yes." Hannah released a long, almost silent, breath. "There aren't many ways for a woman to support her child, so I tried to be practical and consider it. Then he informed me in private of certain expectations and I ... declined."

"I should've punched him."

"I appreciate the inclination but I'm glad you didn't."

"Would've caused you more trouble?"

"Likely."

"Wouldn't want to do that." Nate shook his head. "But ..."

"I understand, believe me."

"It was cowardly, trying to bully you, then insulting your daughter when you rightly walked away."

"Made me madder than a bald-faced hornet, but some people wouldn't think he insulted her."

Nate appeared confused by her statement. "Decent people don't call children names."

"Most of the *decent* people around here don't consider it name-calling because it's true." Hannah squared her shoulders, bracing for his reaction. "That's what I wanted to explain. Ray was rude but correct. I wasn't married to Jemma's father."

"Oh." Nate paused for a long moment, looking at her. She held his gaze steady, outwardly cool and composed. Others had judged her, so one more shouldn't matter, especially not a man she'd just met. Still, her chest felt heavy and tight while she waited for him to continue. "I thought you were a widow."

"I'm not," Hannah stated.

"Oh."

"I've shocked you?"

"It'd take more than that."

His sincerity touched Hannah. Her tension started to bleed

away. They left the road then, walking up to within sight of the house, where Nate stopped.

Am I about to hear his real reaction? Nervous, Hannah halted and turned to face him.

"Does Jemma know her father?"

The unexpected question took her by surprise. Hannah shook her head. "He died before I knew I was expecting." The wind picked up, its icy blast chilling her. "I've told her stories about him but ..." She wrapped her arms around her midsection, both to ward off the increasingly hostile weather and as a nervous self-protective gesture. "Why?"

"Sorry, that was rude."

"It's all right. Ask me whatever you'd like."

Nate was quiet for several seconds. When he spoke at last, his words came out slow, almost hesitant. "It's odd no one else seemed to be *troubled* to witness that man being unkind to you."

"After I had Jemma, most of the people around here expressed the opinion that a woman like me should expect unkindness as her due."

"You don't agree?"

"No, and, to be clear." Hannah lifted her chin, holding his gaze steady and direct. "I'm not proud of the choice I made, but I'm not ashamed of Jemma. I loved her father. I'm grateful to have his daughter. I wouldn't trade being her mother for the world."

His expression unfathomable, Nate responded to her declaration quietly and without apparent censure. "Understood."

Chapter 9

Silence gripped them for the next few minutes. Neither of them moved. Hannah felt she should say something, but words seemed to stick in her throat, unable to escape. Her cheeks grew numb and her fingers started to ache, yet she didn't make a move toward shelter, waiting, for what she knew not. At last, she broke eye contact, looking down at the ground.

"Hannah?"

The note of concern in his voice drew her gaze up. "Yes?"

"Is that Ray?" Nate indicated the direction of the road, still visible from where they stood.

Startled, Hannah turned to look. A man on horseback had pulled up at the turnoff to Redwing Farm. For a moment, she felt him staring at her, then he rode on, heading away from town.

"I believe it is."

"Does he follow you often?"

Hannah shook her head. "He's probably on his way home. His place is about a mile down the road."

"You're not concerned?" Nate remained, watching the other man until he faded from sight.

"I'm not anxious to have another run-in with him, but I don't think he followed me here hoping to make trouble."

"All right." After one final glance back at where Ray had disappeared, Nate shifted the box in his arms then started walking again. "May I ask another question?"

"Of course."

"What happened to your land?"

"My land?" Hannah echoed, confused.

"Your mother's place?"

"Ma rented from the Cowells." She waved her hand in the general direction of the neighbor's farm. "The lease ended with her death. I didn't try for a new one."

"You regret it?"

"No, it's… it doesn't seem right she's not there anymore."

"I understand. My parents left months ago to visit family in Ireland but whenever I'm on the Bar 7, it still feels strange to find neither of them at home."

They shared a look of accord. Once more, Hannah felt a few threads of connection weaving between them. She was hesitant to break them this time. After the rough morning, his understanding soothed.

"Did your mother farm?"

Memories fluttered through her mind. "Nothing so ambitious: a garden, a cow, some chickens, and a couple of pigs. We got by, nothing more."

"And your father?"

Taken by surprise, she didn't watch her step and stumbled over a good-sized rock, almost falling.

"You okay?"

"I'm fine," Hannah rushed to tell Nate, when he reached out with one hand, attempting to steady her. "Just clumsy." She waited until he withdrew his touch, then resumed walking. After a few steps, she cleared her throat. "My father heard of gold in Whiskey Fork when I was little. He left. Never returned."

"Sorry."

"Thank you, but he's been gone a long time."

"It must be difficult having lost both your parents."

"It is." Unexpected tears welled up. *Jemma's growing up without a father. Just like me.* She blinked rapidly, unwilling to let them fall.

"Do you have other family?"

Hannah bit the inside of her cheek while she thought of how to answer him. Her mother's relatives refused to acknowledge her and, as long as that was their choice, she wouldn't claim them either. On her father's side, there was no way of knowing if she had living family connections or not.

Hiram Brooks had been a traveling man who'd drifted into Ashwood one day and swept her mother off her feet. He was gone before Hannah was old enough to remember him. Her mother never met his family and said her father never spoke of them or his past. And since talking about her missing husband always upset her surviving parent, despite her curiosity about the man, she hadn't pressed for more information.

To her surprise, Hannah had found a ragged family bible among her mother's things soon after she passed away. The names scribbled on the first faded pages indicated the possibility of relatives somewhere in the world. However, without any clue of where to search for them, it was an unsolvable mystery. She was on her own.

"It's just Jemma and me now."

"I'm sorry."

For a moment, Hannah thought he was going to say something more, but Nate remained quiet. "Some days it's hard but," she shrugged, "I can't change what is by wishing it was different."

"True."

Thunder rolled through the heavens, loud enough to deafen, ending the conversation. They dashed forward, making it into the house seconds before the heavens opened and rain came pouring down. Nate crossed the room to put the box he carried down on the table while Hannah remained by the door.

Her gaze swept the room. Alice stood by the stove, stirring something in a pot. Jemma sat on the floor near the older woman, playing with her rag doll. Jed was nowhere in sight, which didn't surprise her.

"Mama," the little girl cried out, with happy excitement, and dashed over to give her a hug.

Jemma looked up, gave her mother a wide grin, then skipped back to where she'd left her doll as Hannah started unbuttoning her coat. The sound of Alice scolding Nate, affectionately, for buying the supplies drew her attention away from the child. She looked over at the pair and saw the older woman giving him a fierce hug. Even from across the room she could see the sheen of tears in her friend's eyes.

Hannah averted her gaze and took her time removing her coat to give her companions a moment. The crinkle of paper when she hung up the garment reminded her of the letter. Her hand shook as she pulled it out, at once eager to read the contents yet dreading to do the same. She stared down at the creased envelope while seconds passed, undecided until heavy footsteps behind her at last spurred action. Blindly, she shoved it into her skirt pocket.

"I'm going out to check on the animals." The deep timbre of Nate's voice caused her to turn around, leaning slightly in his direction as though pulled toward him.

"I … thank you."

The man walked by, leaving the house before Hannah could find something better to say. She remained where she stood for a few seconds, tempted to follow him and talk to him a little longer. *To determine his character? Or because I'm liking him too much?* Her heart pounded at the idea. She couldn't lose her head over another man. And yet…

Hannah moved away from the entrance, slowly going over to help Alice. She tried to concentrate on chores but the steady downpour made her feel both restless and trapped. Her gaze kept returning to the door, anticipating Nate's return. After a time, it became clear he wasn't returning to the house soon and she tried to put him from her mind. There were plenty of tasks to keep her busy. Unfortunately, none of them killed the whispering urge for his company.

Hours later, with Jemma settled down for a nap, Hannah gave up trying to be productive. She seized on a comment Alice made about Nate getting hungry, using it as an excuse to slip out of the house. She hurried to the barn, holding a shawl over her head for some protection. The door gave a mighty creak when she pulled it open, as if announcing her presence. Inside, she found the man she sought, mucking out a stall.

"Alice send you?"

"She made you lunch." Hannah put the dripping shawl on a nail on the wall beside where the lantern she'd left with him the night before was hanging, adding light to the dim interior.

"Almost finished." Nate glanced up at her but didn't pause from his task. "But don't wait on me."

"I fed Jemma but Alice and I would rather you join us."

Hannah looked around, seeing signs of hard work. The double doors on the opposite side of the building were open, letting in a little rain but also additional light and much-needed fresh air. He'd fed the animals and given them clean bedding. The old leather harness, freshly oiled, hung along with an assortment of tack. It wasn't perfect, but it now appeared as though someone cared.

"You've been busy."

"Wanted to help." Nate straightened, leaning against the upright handle of the pitchfork. "Lost track of time."

His sleeves rolled up to his elbows revealed a good portion of muscled arms. Hannah stepped closer. Her gaze wandered down, idly noting the way the faded red flannel of his shirt clung to his chest. Nate shifted and she realized what she was doing, quickly glancing away.

"Are you hungry?"

"I am." His casual statement sounded rich with meaning, bringing her gaze back to meet his.

The man wore a polite expression, with no hint of anything more, yet she had trouble finding words. "Ah … Alice made soup."

"Sounds good."

"Chicken with …"

"Vegetables?" Nate moved, carrying the pitchfork over to lean against the stall door.

His hair drew her attention next. He'd tied it back at his neck. The desire to free it, then tangle her fingers through it, whispered softly through Hannah. Nate turned to face her, his eyes reflecting curiosity.

Heaven above, what's wrong with me? "Um, yes, vegetables."

"Something wrong?"

"Wrong? No. Nothing is wrong. Not a thing." *Stop rambling.*

As Nate studied her, his eyes became dark and unreadable. He pulled leather work gloves off his hands. "Good."

"Yes." Nervous, she shoved her hands into her pockets.

"All right." He gestured toward the double door. "I need to shut those. Do you mind waiting?"

"Of course not."

The man gave her a brisk nod then strode off. Alone, Hannah closed her eyes and shook her head. *Stop acting like a silly school-girl, you're a grown woman.* Attraction like this had lured her into trouble before. She couldn't allow those kinds of feelings to control her.

"Sure you're okay?"

The rumble of Nate's voice by her ear startled her. She gasped. Her eyes popped open and she spun to face him.

"I'm …" She started to snap at him, belatedly realizing he was expressing concern. Her face heated. *He's going to think red is the normal color of my skin if I keep this up.* She took a breath, then offered him as much honesty as she felt comfortable giving. "Feeling … awkward after our conversation."

"I'm sorry." He blew out the lantern with a soft puff of breath.

Shadows enveloped them. Nate stood so close she felt the heat coming from his body. Her heart rate increased, beating in a fierce rhythm. Logic fled. She leaned closer to him without conscious thought.

For the second time in less than twenty-four hours, Hannah believed Nate was going to kiss her. The possibility sent liquid fire rushing through her veins. Her breath quickened. Her lips started to part.

Suddenly, Meadowlark whinnied to her foal. The gentle sound hit her with the force of a slap. Eyes wide, wary, she stepped back. *What is it about this man that makes me take leave of my senses?*

Hannah cleared her throat, averting her gaze. She should be polite, nothing more. "No need to be sorry. I'm being a goose."

"No, I understand."

His kindness cracked her new resolve. *Maybe we could be friends.* Hannah turned abruptly, tramping down a vague longing for more. She grabbed her shawl, then headed toward the door at a brisk pace. *Maybe.*

"I'm glad you do." She spoke softly, more to herself than to her companion.

"I feel awkward too."

It took a good portion of her self-control not to jump when he whispered. She'd expected him to follow but hadn't known Nate was already beside her. For a large man, he moved quietly.

Skeptical, Hannah demanded. "You do?"

"The gossip I told you about?"

"Yes?"

"Even friends have laughed."

Being mocked, whatever the reason, hurt. "I won't."

"I appreciate that."

They reached out for the door handle at the same time and his hand ended up covering hers. Hannah stilled then, sucking in a breath, snatched her hand back. She felt his gaze on her but kept hers focused forward. Her expression composed, she waited patiently. After a small, silent pause, Nate opened the door.

The rain had stopped. Bits of blue were now visible above as the cloud cover broke apart but the day remained damp, dark and dreary. Hannah twisted the shawl in her hands as they walked toward the house.

"Will the boys be home soon?"

"Not for a couple of hours."

"Hmm."

"Something on your mind?"

"Thinking about talking to Jed."

"Oh." A hint of disappointment crept through her. *What were you expecting? Him to say he was thinking about you?* "You wanted them to be gone?"

"Might be best if everyone was."

"If the weather holds, Alice and I can take Jemma and meet the boys after school. It should give you about an hour alone."

"I'd appreciate that."

Hannah responded with a nod. After the exchange, words seemed to dry up as if she'd spent them all. The soft squelch of boots walking through muddy grass was the only sound until they reached the house.

The afternoon passed swiftly. All too soon, the women, with a well-bundled Jemma, headed to Ashwood. The walk to town seemed to take forever. They met the boys at the edge of the schoolyard, then turned around, going straight back to the farm. Their trip was peaceful. The kids chattered as they moved down the road but the women were quiet, worried about what was happening at home.

"Jed," Nate called out, pushing open the bedroom door. He'd knocked several times without getting a response. "It's Nate."

The creak of the rocker on the bare wood floor was his only answer. Although he was a man who valued silence, here it felt unnatural. He hesitated, looking at the space. Shadows filled the curtain-drawn room. Dark shapes rendered some clues to the placement of furniture and the room's occupant.

Nate stepped into the room, crossing directly to the man in the chair. "Jed." After standing at his side a moment without getting a response, he moved in front of the other man. "I hear you've been having a rough time."

There wasn't a flicker of movement in response. Jed's gaze appeared unfocused, staring blankly forward. Hoping he wasn't seeing clearly in the dark room, Nate glanced around and spotted an oil lamp on a dresser nearby. A few minutes later, he had it lit and placed on the small table beside the rocking chair.

The soft glow of light wasn't kind to the other man. With his sallow skin and distant expression, Jed didn't look far from the grave himself. Nate crouched down as he would for a child or frightened animal. "I'm real sorry about Bessie."

Jed's gaze shifted, glancing at Nate. Desolation filled his stare for a few seconds, then his eyes blanked. And the silent man looked away.

"I understand it hurts." Nate paused, hoping for a response, then continued when it was clear he wouldn't get one. "But the boys need you." He allowed another moment to pass. "They're hurting too." Jed was so still it was hard to notice him even taking a breath. "Your mother is worried about you. We're all worried."

Jed never responded again. Nate continued speaking to him for the better part of an hour. *So much for being the hero.* His voice was hoarse and his knees ached when he finally gave up, straightening. *Didn't make a damn bit of difference.*

Weary, Nate leaned over and blew out the lamp. He studied Jed one last long moment. "I remember how you talked about her that day when you brought the boys up to see the horses." He put one hand on the man's shoulder. "You gushed about Bessie like a boy courting his first girl." He withdrew his touch.

"Everything I've heard about her tells me she wouldn't want you to grieve her like this."

Jed didn't stir. Nate shook his head, then slowly crossed the room. In the doorway, he paused and looked back. The other man remained unchanged. *I was a fool to think a few words would set him to rights.* He stepped out into the main room, easing the door shut behind him. *I hope Alice isn't too disappointed.*

As she neared the farm, Hannah's pace picked up. There was no reason to expect Nate could work a miracle, yet she couldn't help hoping for one. She glanced at Alice as they walked up the rutted path from the main road. The tension in the older woman's expression worried her. She hoped whatever happened while they were gone wouldn't be too hard on her friend.

Unexpectedly, the sound of a hammer rang through the cold air. The boys took off, running. Jemma trailed after them as fast as she could with her short legs. The women also moved faster, but in a restrained manner, following them to the smaller barn.

Hope died the moment Hannah saw Nate's face. He didn't have to say a word. She gently touched Alice on the arm, knowing her friend would make the same, quick deduction.

"I'm okay." Her tone hollow, the older woman gave her a wobbly smile. "I didn't think he could change anything."

"But you hoped?"

"Every day."

"I'm sorry." Hannah wrapped an arm around her and squeezed, letting go before the children noticed.

Alice called the boys to her then herded them over to the house, despite their protests. As they were walking away, Jemma spotted Silas and ran over to pick him up. The girl plopped down on an old board with the black cat snug in her arms. Knowing her daughter would be safely distracted for a few minutes, Hannah moved closer to Nate.

"It went badly?"

"It didn't go well."

"No reaction?"

"He just sat in the damn rocker." Frustrated, Nate focused on the wall in front of him. "Sorry." He blew out a breath. "Pardon my language."

"It's all right. I understand."

Wordlessly, Nate shook his head, then drove home a nail.

"It's good that you tried."

"I failed." He reached down, picking up a small board from the pile by his feet.

"Doesn't mean it wasn't good of you to try."

Nate turned his head and met her gaze. "Thanks."

That feeling of connection returned, at once comfortable and a little unnerving. Hannah decided it'd be prudent to take her leave. "I should head up to the house. The boys are likely pestering Alice. And she might need …"

"Send them out."

"You wouldn't mind?"

"No." The man resumed working.

Hannah recalled how patient he'd been with them that morning. "You're used to children?"

"I've been around a few."

"Oh?" Despite her urge to leave, curiosity got the better of her. "Neighbors?"

"My brothers. Sister … Jed."

"You're the eldest so they seemed like little kids to you."

"A lot of years between us."

"Did they pester you?"

"Still do." His simple answer held obvious warmth. Nate glanced at her and to her surprise continued. "Jason and John remind me of when they were small and eager to help."

Charmed, her lips curved in the slightest measure. *There's a lot to like about this man.* Her gaze slid from his, needing to check on her daughter. Jemma was still happily playing with the cat. *Still, for her sake, I need to be cautious.*

"I'll go pry Jemma away from Silas then let the boys know they can join you." Focused on her daughter, Hannah started to move toward the little girl.

"She's welcome too."

Startled, she stopped mid-step, her gaze swinging back to Nate. "She is?"

"Unless it makes you uncomfortable."

"You don't care about ..." Hannah glanced at her child, then back at the man.

"Her birth?" Nate lowered his voice. "Not her fault." His expression grave, he studied her a moment, then continued. "And not my place to judge you."

The tension knotting in her gut unraveled. Warmth filled her heart. Few people offered easy acceptance of her daughter.

She smiled. "Thank you, I'm glad you feel that way. But actually I was surprised you'd want her out here, since she's a girl."

"Why would that matter?" His brow furrowed as puzzlement filled dark eyes.

"Jed has fixed ideas on what men and women, boys and girls, should do when it comes to physical labor."

"He does?" Nate looked over her shoulder in the direction of the house. "But he supported Bessie's idea of a horse farm and hired you, a female bookkeeper."

"He's never doubted a woman's ability to use her mind, but the notion that they should be protected is deeply rooted in him. It was one of the only things he and Bessie argued about."

"Wanting to protect your wife." Nate looked over at Jemma, who could be heard carrying on a one-sided conversation with the cat. "Or daughter." His gaze returned to meet hers. "Or sons. I understand."

"So you wouldn't allow my daughter to hammer a nail?"

"One doesn't exclude the other."

126

"You don't have a problem with girls doing boys' work?"

"A woman or a girl can do about anything she sets her mind to doing. My mother taught me that."

"Because she worked as a ranch hand?"

"Because she took pride in doing it well."

Before Hannah could say another word, Jemma dashed up and tugged on her skirts. "I'm cold."

"Okay, honey." She glanced up from her daughter to Nate. "It appears this little one has had enough time outside, but I'll see if the boys would like to come out to help you."

"I'll be here." The man returned to his task, his hammer descending, filling the air with sound as mother and child left.

The boys were eating some warmed-up soup when Hannah and her daughter entered the house. Upon hearing Nate's offer, they slurped down the last of their snack, rushed over and snatched their jackets off their pegs, but didn't stop to put them on before running outside. They spent the rest of the day outside, helping Nate. By dusk, they'd finished a number of repairs on the outbuildings and the corral, as well as the evening chores, all before trudging in for dinner.

Hannah helped Alice dish up a simple but filling meal of beans and stewed tomatoes. While the older woman took a seat, she piled slices of sourdough bread on a plate, then carried it, along with a jar of butter, to the table. The unopened letter weighed on her as she moved, feeling like a stone in her pocket.

After dinner, Jason brought out a book the teacher had lent to him. Hannah gathered the children around her by the fire and started to read. For a full chapter the charming tale held their rapt attention, then they started fading. One by one, each child displayed drooping eyelids while small hands tried covering huge yawns.

When she reached the end of the page, Hannah placed a bookmark she'd fashioned from a scrap of cloth in to mark the spot and closed the book. Together the women quickly got the children settled for the night. The little ones donned their night-clothes with few protests, then crawled into their beds, warm beneath layers of quilts. All three were sound asleep in minutes.

To her surprise, when Hannah returned to the main room she found it empty. While she didn't know where Nate had gone, the muffled sound of Alice's voice told her the older woman was in with her son. *There won't be a better time.* She walked over to the chair near the fire, sat down, then slowly pulled the letter out of her pocket.

Miss Brooks,

Thank you for your letter but we have no need for a book-keeper.

Hannah didn't bother to read further. She crumpled the single sheet of paper, along with the envelope, into a ball and tossed them into the flames. As she watched them burn, she considered her options, which were few.

Find another kind of job nearby doing anything that will include providing shelter. A dull ache started at the back of her skull. She'd already inquired after every form of honest employment in the community. No one had work … except Ray.

And he can go jump in a lake.

Her lips pressed together. Bitterness left a sour taste in her mouth. *Correction, no one is willing to give me decent work.*

Hannah had wanted to secure a job nearby so she and Jemma could visit Alice and the boys often. She hadn't wanted to face reality. Whispers, giggles, and snide remarks hurt but, in the end, were a trivial matter. It was clear the majority of Ashwood wanted nothing to do with her. Their steadfast refusals, in most cases politely but firmly turning her aside, meant she had to leave her community.

I hope you're pleased, Grandmother. Hannah stiffened her spine. *We'll be gone soon. Somewhere we won't embarrass you.*

She clasped her hands tightly together in her lap. *Moving is best anyway.* Jemma would soon be old enough to understand the unkind words and suffer from them. Hannah released a soft breath just short of a sigh. *I should've left long before now.*

Could've, would've, should've, does you no good.

Her mother's voice rang so clear in Hannah's mind she half expected to see the woman step out of the shadows lurking in the corners of the room. Her lips curved with fondness. Grace Brooks gave excellent advice even from beyond the grave. Looking back never solved a thing.

I need time to figure out where to go. Hannah rubbed damp palms over her wool skirt. A temporary housekeeping job with the Rolfes would give her that luxury plus a place for her and Jemma to live until she found a permanent position. She squared her shoulders. *Now I need to convince Nate to hire me.*

Nate entered the house, carrying an armload of wood. With a bump of his hip, he closed the door. A lamp set in the middle of the table cast a small circle of light. He started crossing the room, then paused after only a couple of steps, catching sight of Hannah sitting alone by the fire. Her expression unreadable, she stared at the flames in front of her.

She's worried. Nate couldn't fix Ben's memory, Jed's all-consuming grief, or Alice's concern for her son. He hadn't been able to kill the rumors about his cousin or himself. Despite his best efforts, neither had he been able to track down the elusive rustlers. But, he could ease Hannah's mind.

What's holding me back? Alice wouldn't feel replaced. It'd be temporary so the *slight* attraction he felt wouldn't have time to get messy. Besides, he'd be out helping Matt and wouldn't be at the ranch much.

We'd be sleeping under the same roof. "Um." *Just me and her ... and Jemma, of course.* He cleared his throat and resumed walking toward the hearth. "Hannah."

"Yes."

"I ..." *I can bunk out with my brothers.* Although the thought of sleeping in a small space with a number of men wasn't a happy prospect, he could bear it for a short time. "I'd like to …" He emptied his arms, stacking the rounds on the floor next to the fireplace. "Offer you a job."

Chapter 10

Thank Heavens. Hannah got to her feet and held out her hand. "Thank you, I accept."

They shook hands, sealing the deal. "I'd like to leave for the ranch the day after tomorrow. Can you be ready?"

"It won't take long to pack. We don't have much."

"Good, then it's settled." His hand continued to clasp hers, as though he'd forgotten how to let go.

"What's settled?"

Alice emerged from Jed's bedroom and walked over to join them. Hannah pulled free, turning to face the older woman. "Nate offered me the job."

"And you accepted?"

"Yes."

"Good." Alice put her hands together, smiling with obvious relief. "It's what's best for everyone."

"I know." Hannah enfolded the other woman in a tight hug.

"We'll miss you and Jemma."

"Hopefully, we'll see you again soon."

"I hope so." Alice stepped back. "Now I assume Nathaniel wants to leave soon, so let's make plans."

The rest of the evening and the next day passed in a blur of activity. Nate wanted to leave Alice in the best way possible, so he worked hard to fix up the farm while Hannah readied her and Jemma to leave. Hours flew by. It felt like she'd blinked once then it was time to go.

In the early morning hours, she stood on the porch watching Nate lug her trunks out of the house and load them up onto the farm's wagon. Hannah couldn't stop a few tears from falling as she gave Alice and each boy one last hug. On her way down the steps, she hesitated, looking back through the open door into the home. She held some hope that Jed would stir himself enough to make an appearance. He did not.

Hannah turned around and continued to the wagon. Nate assisted her up, then lifted Jemma up to her. She settled her daughter on the seat beside her as he climbed up on the other side. With a snap of the reins, they drove away a moment later.

Rays of sunlight filtered through the clouds above as Nate turned left onto the main road. A number of skinny trees lined their way for a long, straight stretch. Naked of leaves, the bare branches swayed in the breeze, as though waving farewell. Hannah kept glancing back toward the farm until they rounded a corner, entering an expansive forest. A dense grouping of fir trees soon all but surrounded them, blocking her line of sight.

Hannah looked down the road. Miles of road cut a narrow path through the woods ahead. Jemma, tired in the early morning hour, dozed, leaning against her. After a while, she shifted, trying to get comfortable without disturbing her daughter.

"Hard leaving them?" His low husky tone distracted her from the dilemma.

"Very." She kept her voice low as well. "I heard you trying to convince Alice to come home again this morning. Regretting offering me a job already?"

"I had to try."

Hannah ran a gentle hand over Jemma's hat-covered head. "She's not going to leave her son."

"She could bring Jed. She's being stubborn."

"She says the same about you."

"She's right." Nate flashed a boyish grin at her.

Charming. The fingers of her free hand smoothed out a wrinkle in the wool blanket draped over her lap. *Those rumors he spoke of had him all wrong.* True, the man was quiet a lot and, even in the few days she'd been around Nate, he'd spent noticeable time off by himself. *When the boys weren't able to tag along.* She'd lived with a person who'd withdrawn from the world and there was a marked difference between Jed and this man.

"I see."

"Sorry if I upset you."

"It's okay." *A recluse?* Hannah doubted it. "It's endearing how much you care for her."

"I love her," Nate asserted with the easy assurance of a confident man.

Warmth spread through her chest. "Me too."

A moment passed. On either side of them, light and shadows danced through the evergreen trees. The steady muffled clops made by the borrowed mules' hooves filled the air. Jemma sighed and one small hand fisted the quilt covering their laps.

"It'll be all right."

His sincerity eased some of her tension but she didn't look over, remaining focused on her daughter. Hannah made a low, wordless, comforting sound. Soon the little girl relaxed, sleeping peacefully again. Only then did Hannah shift her gaze to Nate, giving him a brief smile.

"Thank you. I hope it'll be. But if it's not, I'll adapt."

"Don't believe good things happen to good people?"

"Good things can happen to anyone." Hannah glanced down at the sweet face of her beloved child. After a moment, she looked up, staring down the road stretching out ahead of them. "And so do horrid things. I believe how a person responds to what comes their way determines whether they'll be all right or not."

"Don't believe in luck?"

"A person makes their own."

Hannah felt his gaze on her for a number of seconds before he responded. "I agree."

A comfortable quiet settled over them. For the next several miles, they rattled down the road, with few exchanges until they exited the forest, entering a wide, flat plain. A ball of gold hovered above the distant hills in a patch of blue sky. Hannah sighed with pure pleasure at the vision.

"You okay?"

"Better than okay, I just saw the sun."

"A pretty sight, isn't it?"

"Yes, I've missed it." She smiled. "I was starting to think it'd forgotten us mere mortals."

A small hand tugged on her. "Mama."

"Yes, Jemma."

"I need to go."

"Okay, honey." Hannah glanced over at Nate as she helped her daughter sit up. "I need you to stop."

"I'd like to keep moving."

"I understand but—" Jemma pulled on her dress, distracting her. She shifted her gaze to the little girl. "Just a minute."

"We need to keep up a good pace to reach the Bar 7 before nightfall."

Impatient, Hannah looked back at him. "When a little girl says she needs to go, she needs to go now."

"You mean she needs to … go?"

"I do."

"Oh, sorry. I didn't … I'll stop."

Nate pulled off on the side of the road, setting the brake soon after he finished speaking. He hopped down and stretched up his arms for Jemma. Once he set the little girl down, he reached back up. The strength of his hands on her waist caused Hannah's breath to catch. When her boots hit the ground, she turned and faced him. Their gazes met and held for a heartbeat or two then he loosed her, stepping back.

Hannah averted her gaze, breaking the contact. She glanced around for Jemma and her heart stilled. The girl was gone. Her daughter had scampered away while she'd been distracted. Seconds felt like hours as she scanned the area, looking for her child.

Panic threatened to engulf Hannah by the time she spotted Jemma. Only yards away, the little girl was skipping around a scrub oak tree. She hurried over to her daughter.

"Jemma Lynn Brooks."

"Yes, Mama."

"What did I say about running off?"

"To not to." The little girl peered up at her with an earnest expression. "But I had to go."

"No running off without telling me, understand?"

"Okay." Jemma agreed readily, with a wide grin, then ran back to the wagon without waiting.

Hannah shook her head, knowing they'd be having the same conversation again soon. She waited, watching until Nate had her daughter and was lifting her back up onto the wagon seat before seizing a bit of privacy for herself. The steady beat of hooves hastened her pace when she headed back moments later. A group of people approached as she settled in next to Jemma once more. The men rode past them without pause, a couple of them lifting their hats in silent acknowledgment.

"Ready?"

At her nod, Nate set them in motion again. "You think we'll reach Fir Mountain tonight?"

"If all goes well."

"Are we taking a short cut?"

"A short cut?" Nate echoed, clearly puzzled.

"You told Alice it'd taken you a week to reach Ashwood."

"I didn't come straight from the ranch."

I wonder where he went. "Oh."

Jemma, now wide awake, hobbled further discussion. She'd never traveled beyond Ashwood. Excited, the little girl had a hard time sitting still. Every animal her daughter spotted, even ones she'd seen before, like deer, were amazing sights. Pressed against her mother's side, she pointed out pretty shapes in the clouds and released soft squeals of delight whenever they hit a bump in the road.

Hannah answered Jemma's numerous questions patiently, doing her best to keep her daughter entertained. However, soon after the noon meal, she felt her energy flagging. She had made up a pallet in the wagon bed hoping the little girl would settle down enough for a nap at some point. To her surprise, she did.

One second Jemma was chattering about the red-winged black bird she'd seen and the next moment she was dead quiet, slumping against her mother. Hannah released a sigh of relief, welcoming the respite. As much as she loved her girl with all her heart, she needed a quiet moment now and again.

"If you can handle the team?" Nate held up the reins, offering them to her. "I'll move her to the bed you made."

Hannah nodded, accepting control of the team. Although it was an awkward undertaking, he shifted Jemma from the seat onto her makeshift bed without disturbing the child. His thoughtful act gave her a warm, cared-for feeling.

"Thank you."

Nate nodded, reclaiming control of the team. "Glad I didn't wake her."

"Once she's asleep." A hint of a grin played on her lips as fond memories meandered through her mind. "A stampede wouldn't wake her. Usually."

"You're lucky. My brothers hated napping."

"Yes, I am." Reflective, Hannah considered some of the ways she'd been fortunate. *Jemma's health. Alice's friendship. The temporary job.* She glanced at Nate. *His kindness.*

"Has Jemma camped?"

His question scattered her thoughts. "We won't make it to the ranch tonight?"

"Afraid not."

"Because of Jemma and I?" Suddenly nervous, she tucked some loose strands of hair behind her ear.

Nate lifted one shoulder in a half-shrug. "To make this a day trip we needed to move faster."

"I'm sorry."

"It's all right."

"But if it wasn't for Jemma …" She shook her head.

"I enjoy her company."

"You do?"

"I get excited to see animals too."

Hannah stared at him. "You were excited earlier?" Clear skepticism rang in her words. "From watching wildlife?"

"Yes."

"Really?"

"It's one of my favorite ways to spend time." Nate turned to look at her, his expression serious yet earnest. "Nature is amazing. Too many people don't pause to notice."

"You're an interesting man."

"Is that good or bad?" His voice, low in deference to the sleeping child, sounded a little amused.

Hannah had to smile. "Good."

Nate held her gaze for a long moment. He didn't turn his attention back to driving until they hit a deep rut. She waited until the road smoothed out before speaking again.

"We won't make it to a town before nightfall?"

"Fir Mountain is the next town, sorry."

"Oh."

"Nervous?"

"Will we be okay?" She avoided a direct answer, glancing up at a gray sky.

137

"Alice packed plenty of blankets."

"That's good."

"We might get a little cold, but we'll be fine."

Fine? Hannah was alone with her daughter in unfamiliar territory with a man she barely knew. 'Fine' wasn't the word she'd use. "I trust you'll keep us safe?"

Nate glanced at her, one eyebrow raised. "Hard having faith in a stranger?"

Yes. "No, of course not, I've complete faith in Alice. She wouldn't have encouraged all this if she hadn't considered you trustworthy." *Whatever troubled Michael, please don't let it have to do with this man.*

"You two became close quickly."

"We did."

"Someday, I hope you'll trust me because you know me."

What's he implying? Her eyes narrowed as Hannah studied him. *That, in the future, we might be close? Not possible.* Real life was a far stretch from the fairytales her mother told her as a child. She shifted uneasily on the seat. *I'm likely reading too much into a few words.*

"That will depend on you."

"That's honest."

From his tone, she knew her words had hurt. "Sorry."

"Don't be. I prefer honesty even when it stings."

Hannah stiffened. "Sometimes absolute honesty is difficult, especially with someone you've just met."

"I agree. Trust takes time to build."

"Sounds like you speak from experience."

"Working with wild horses takes a lot of patience and understanding while building trust."

"So you're a patient, understanding man?"

"I think so."

I hope you are. "Good to know."

The sense of accord Hannah had felt before in his company

returned, settling over her again. The urge to confide in Nate became strong. Words filled her mind and almost flowed straight out of her mouth. She bit down on the inside of her cheek until the temptation passed.

"It was good of the Cowells to lend us their mules." Hannah abruptly changed the subject.

"It was."

"I was curious about why you didn't ..."

"Put Jack in a single harness?"

"Well, yes. It's a small wagon and I didn't bring much."

"The mules are better suited for the task."

"But you'll have to return them."

"Someone will, yes."

Hannah mulled over his responses a moment, then suddenly his motivation was clear. "You wanted an excuse to check on Alice."

"And the boys. And Jed."

"You're going right back? I thought there was a reason you had to go home."

"There is. I'm not going."

"Sending one of your ranch hands?"

"One of my brothers."

"Sam," she guessed.

"He and Jed were close. I thought it'd be worth a shot."

"Oh, Nate."

The man kept endearing himself to her. Thoughtful and kind, he hit on all the same traits of Michael's that hooked her. Yet his caring gestures were not dramatic or impulsive, like those of her first love. Nate handled himself with the confidence of a mature man. She liked him far too much already and if she didn't watch it, he'd steal her heart.

"Yes?"

"Nothing I ... I just think that's sweet."

"He'll probably have no better luck than I did."

139

"But, it's worth trying."

"Yes."

A moment passed. Her gaze wandered, looking over their surroundings as she wondered what to say next. Selfishly, she didn't want to talk about Jed anymore.

"Ever cooked over a fire?"

"Testing me?" She turned her attention back to the man next to her. "Trying to find out if my cooking is up to your standards?"

"My standards are not burnt beyond recognition."

"I can manage that."

"I'm sure."

"Thank you."

"Cooking over an open fire can be a challenge."

"You hired me to do a job."

"We're not on the Bar 7 yet."

"I considered myself hired when I shook your hand."

"Well, yes."

"Rest easy, Mr. Rolfe, although it wasn't outside, I cooked over a fire at Ma's house. I'll serve you something edible."

"Great. I'd offer to help but I can't make the same claim."

"You can't cook over a fire?"

"I can. Make it edible?" Nate shook his head. "That's a whole other kettle of fish."

"You usually live alone but can't cook?"

"I eat a lot of burnt beans and jerky at home."

"Oh my."

"It's not too bad."

"I'll take your word for it."

"Think you can do better?"

"You seemed to like the meals at the farm."

"You only helped Alice."

"I only …" Hannah started out indignant, trailed off, then continued in a measured manner. "You're right. While you were there I didn't cook a full meal. You took a risk in hiring me."

"I've complete faith in Alice." He echoed her earlier statement.

"Well said."

His only response was a grin as he maneuvered them around a large mud puddle.

"How long before we stop for the day?"

"We'll reach Bear Creek in a couple of hours. It's the best place to stay the night. There's water for us and the animals."

"Okay."

"Do you need to stop now?"

"No."

"Mama." A soft, sleepy voice drifted over the seat.

"Change that to yes."

The rest of the afternoon passed pleasantly. Hannah enjoyed visiting with him, much to her surprise. She didn't realize the day had flown by until Nate pulled off the road. They drove into a clearing and he parked the wagon in a well-worn spot obviously favored by travelers.

After helping her and Jemma down, Nate started setting up a simple campsite. He lowered the tailgate and pulled a large box onto it, putting the supplies within easy reach. Next, he asked the little girl to 'help' him build a cooking fire by gathering pine-cones. The child hadn't warmed to him at the farm, neither avoiding the man nor seeking out his attention. Until this point in their trip, she'd directed her chatter solely at her mother, so Hannah was surprised when her daughter did as he asked.

She kept an eye on Jemma while she prepared the evening meal. She heated up some canned beans, flavoring them with bits of salt pork, and made some fry bread as her daughter stayed in Nate's company. Though quieter than normal, the little girl shad-owed the tall man, 'helping' him tend all the animals then move bedding beneath the wagon.

By the time Hannah called them to eat, Jemma's feet were drag-ging. Dinner was an almost silent affair. Afterward, Nate's few but sincere words of appreciation filled her with warmth. A smile still tugged at her lips while she led her daughter over to the wagon, intending to settle her down for the night. As she knelt down the lantern light revealed a sight Hannah hadn't expected to see.

One bed?

Tension cast out the warmth she'd felt. Outwardly composed for her daughter's sake, Hannah carried on with the task. She tucked the child under the layers of blankets fully clothed in deference to the cold. Exhausted by her long day, Jemma's eyes closed immediately.

Hannah waited several minutes, wanting to be certain the little girl was sound asleep, then went in search of Nate. He'd vanished from the campsite along with their dinner plates but she could hear movement nearby. Spine stiff, she stomped down a trail in the direction of the sounds, clutching both the lantern handle and her anger tight. A few yards away, she found him by the creek washing the dinner dishes.

"Why is there only one bed?" She demanded softly but with clear displeasure.

Nate looked up at her. "It's best we share the blankets."

"Excuse me." In disbelief, Hannah stared at the man in front of her a full moment before she could continue. "We most certainly will not." Her back now so rigid it felt as though her spine might snap. "Do not assume because I … That I … Because with Jemma I … It doesn't mean I'd … I won't. I'm—"

"Whoa. Hold on. I didn't assume anything and I meant no offense." Nate stood up, stepping closer.

A fraction calmer but with outrage still pumping through her, Hannah lifted her chin. "What exactly did you mean by it?"

"It's cold."

"Oh." His simple statement of fact took the wind from her sails.

"Your breath is frosting the air now and it'll get colder before morning. I wanted to be sure the little one stays warm."

Jemma. She glanced back. Although the distance was short,

142

Hannah didn't like being too far from her child. "I need to go back." She turned, walking toward the wagon. Nate fell in step with her without a word. When they entered the campsite, she took a breath, then apologized. "Sorry, I misunderstood."

"I should've explained." Nate continued on, moving to the tailgate. He slid the dishes into the box then shoved it further into the wagon bed.

"Still, I'm sorry."

"No harm done." Nate studied her for a minute. "Would you like to sit with me a spell?"

Her heart beat faster. "Sit with you?"

"Yes."

"Ah … On the ground?"

"No." He took a seat on the tailgate then offered her a hand. "Up here."

"All right."

Cheeks hot despite the chill in the air, Hannah accepted his help and climbed up beside him. Nate leaned over, blowing out the lantern as soon as she settled. She sucked in an audible breath when the night abruptly enveloped them.

"I'm right here."

"It's so dark."

"Look at the fire, see the coals?"

Hannah followed his suggestion. "Yes." The tiny orange glow somehow steadied her nerves. "Thank you."

For the next several minutes, the couple was silent. Wind moved through the trees. A couple of frogs croaked down by the creek. Hannah shifted, smoothing her coat over her skirt.

"Have others made assumptions about you?"

"Aside from Ray's job offer, no one else has expected me to share their blankets. I'm sorry I leapt to the conclusion you meant to be disrespectful." Hannah set the lantern down on her right. "It's just that …"

"That?"

"Gossip is rarely kind, yet people mostly believe it."

"Sorry."

"You didn't do it."

"I'm still sorry."

"Okay." She shifted again, restless. "Did you ask me to sit with you so you could ask me about that?"

"No." Nate leaned back on his elbows. "Look up. Stars are peeking out around the clouds."

"You wanted me to look at the stars with you?"

"Yes."

Nate's simple answer swayed her. Hannah copied his position, then glanced up, trying to ignore how their shoulders were brushing. "Beautiful."

"They are."

"I'm glad it hasn't rained."

"Me too."

"The day started out beautiful."

"It did." His voice, warm and relaxed now, soothed away the last of her edginess.

Hannah released a soft sigh. "This is nice."

"Yes, it is."

"Hmm." She sighed again.

"You okay?"

"Just tired."

"You want to go to bed?"

"Not quite yet."

"Jemma's a quiet child."

"She's being a bit shy around you." She continued gazing up at the heavens. "Usually she's full of spirit, often more than me. Sometimes I wonder where she gets all that energy."

A minute went by in comfortable silence. Hannah relaxed, despite the dropping temperature, lulled by the sound of water running over rocks in the nearby creek. Her eyelids started to droop.

144

"Maybe from her father?"

Her eyes snapped wide open. *Does he know?* She turned her head to stare at the man beside her, going from at ease to tense in seconds. *Or is that just a casual suggestion?* In the dark, she couldn't read his expression. Her heart beat against her chest wall, sounding as loud as thunder to her.

"It's possible," Hannah stated honestly, then paused, taking a breath, calming herself. "But most likely it's just something about being a child. My experience with the boys and Jemma has been, unless something's wrong, children have almost boundless energy."

"My brothers and sister ran around like startled deer when they were little."

His reaction eased her mind but, a little paranoid, she seized the opportunity to shift the conversation. "You've one sister. How many brothers?"

"Three."

"I'm an only child," Hannah stated, envious.

"I was too for a time."

"I wanted a brother or sister. Which did you like better, being an only or having company?"

"Some of both." Nate moved, sitting up. "I liked having all of my parents' attention. After my siblings were born, it was nice having someone else to blame for stuff like when Ma's roses were trampled."

"You blamed things you did on your brothers?"

"And sister."

"And your mother believed you?"

"Which time?"

Hannah laughed softly, then an icy gust of wind almost stole her breath. "It's getting colder. I should go and lay down with Jemma now."

"Do you need the lantern lit?"

"Just to walk around the side?" Her hand brushed his thigh as she sat up. Nervous, Hannah withdrew it swiftly, sliding off the tailgate to stand by the wagon. "No, I'll be fine." She'd been intimate with a man, was raising the child born from that union, but she'd never stood next to a man knowing he'd soon be joining her in bed. Although she believed Nate to be honorable and the situation was innocent, it was awkward. She cleared her throat. "Thank you."

"I'll be there shortly."

Not knowing what to say, she nodded then felt silly. *He can't see me nod in the dark.* "Okay."

With one hand touching the side of the wagon for guidance, Hannah walked around to the side. She took off her coat, spread it over Jemma, who was in the center of the bed, then slid under the covers on her daughter's left side. It took a few minutes to check on her child then find a semi-comfortable position. Once satisfied the little girl was fine, she stared up at the underbelly of the wagon, unable to sleep.

I'll be there shortly. Nate shook his head. *She's already nervous and that made it worse.* It was already bad enough they had to spend a winter's night outside. If anyone found out him and Hannah, an unmarried couple, had camped overnight, let alone shared blankets, no matter how innocently, the gossiping he hated so much would again spread like wildfire. *I should've just said goodnight.*

Nate reclined back on his elbows again. *Should I wait until she's probably asleep?* It was late. It'd been a long day and he was weary. *Or go now?* On his own, he would've already hit the hay. Torn, he decided to give her a few minutes, then follow.

His thoughts continued to center on Hannah. The young woman seemed straightforward, but he was certain there was more to her past than she'd shared. Her subtle but notable reactions when he commented on her daughter, or the little one's father, made that obvious. *Understandable, though, and none of my business.*

146

Still one of the comments Ray made in Ashwood nagged at the man. *Your outlaw's bastard.* Maybe it was because only days prior Nate had attended the Nash brothers' hanging. Or perhaps it was because the gossip about his cousin troubled him. In any case, the phrase caught his attention and wouldn't let go.

Had the man been a nasty piece of work like the Nash brothers? Or someone like Ben, who'd made bad choices but deserved a second chance? Or neither? Maybe gossip is twisting the truth.

Maybe Hannah doesn't deserve yet another person speculating about her. Nate sat up. He eased off the tailgate, leaving it down for access in the morning. *Then again, if I'd speculated a little about Faith I'd have saved myself a world of hurt.*

Every beat of her heart felt labored. Each shallow breath sounded louder than the crickets singing in the brush. Because Hannah was straining to hear, she heard Nate walking down the other side of the wagon from his first step. It took her a few seconds to become aware she'd started holding her breath. She forced herself to relax, releasing the breath in an audible huff, right as he crouched down.

"Are you all right?"

Her face heated, realizing he'd heard her. "I'm fine."

"Good."

Nate tossed his hat down then removed his jacket before crawling into the bed. With her vision adjusted to the darkness, Hannah watched him turn onto his side, facing her. Although the shadows made his features impossible to read, she could feel him looking at her over the sleeping form of her daughter. There was a curious intimacy to being with him like this in the dark, so close yet separate.

"She looks peaceful."

At his whisper, Hannah's gaze shifted to her daughter. Her voice matched his in volume, trying to avoid waking Jemma. "After a hard day, I sometimes watch her sleep for awhile. It reminds me that no matter what has happened, she's worth it."

"It must be difficult, raising her on your own."

"At times."

"What about her father?"

"He's dead." Hannah's tone softened the harsh statement of fact. She'd known Michael for only a short time and he'd been gone so long. Her memories of him were now more like half-remembered dreams. "What about him?"

"Sorry, it's none of my business."

Oh, but it is. "What about him?" she repeated cautiously.

"I wondered … Did he have family that could help you?"

Yes, he does. Guilt gnawed at her. All she had to do was open her mouth and let the words flow out. Her lips parted but fear still kept her from being completely honest. "He was estranged from his family."

"Because he was an outlaw?"

Chapter 11

"How did you know about that?" Her whispered words shot out swift, just short of being accusatory.

"Overhearing Ray."

That will have you and your outlaw's—The other man's words returned to haunt her. "Oh, yes, I remember."

"I didn't mean to upset you."

"You didn't."

Nate had been kind and caring. Though she'd known him only a short time, Hannah had no doubt how much family meant to this man. Nothing in his behavior justified Michael's warning … so far. Part of her wanted to spill the whole truth. But, caution won out. She'd known him a matter of days.

For Jemma's sake, I can't trust too easily. "He wasn't a bad man."

"Who?"

"Jemma's father." Hannah rolled onto her side, facing him squarely.

"Oh?"

Nate said nothing further, waiting patiently. She took a minute to organize her thoughts before continuing. "He wasn't a completely good man either."

"You're describing every man I've known, including myself."

"But you're not a wanted man, are you?"

"No." His voice held no inflection.

Hannah cleared her throat gently. "He was."

"I'm sorry."

"So was I."

The little girl between them made a soft, sleepy sound then rolled onto her stomach. Hannah reached out, pulling one of the blankets back up over her child. Silence reigned until they were certain she still slept.

"Would you mind telling me what he did?"

"His crimes?"

"If you don't mind."

Hannah did mind, a little. Michael was more than the crimes he'd committed. "He was a cardsharp and a robber."

"You knew from the start?"

"No, but I should have."

"Oh?" Once again, Nate fell silent, letting her continue as she would without further prompting.

"He stumbled across our farm late one evening looking for help. Someone had shot him. The wound was only a graze along his side but there was a lot of blood. Any rational person would've found it odd."

"You didn't?"

"Honestly, at that moment, I didn't care."

"Love at first sight?"

"I'd say instant attraction now, but then … I was young and naïve and soon lost my heart."

"In spite of him lying?"

"He didn't exactly lie, though he wasn't in any hurry to tell me the truth. He kept … redirecting conversations with a great deal of charm."

"What about your mother? Did she slam the door or hug him?"

"Neither." Hannah paused, thinking how best to explain. "I

found him in the barn. Despite being charmed, I had enough sense to holler for Ma. She came running then stood there, staring at him for the longest time. Finally, she said I could bring him up to the house to get patched up but he was trouble."

"And he was."

"He was."

"Had he been shot by the law?"

"No, by someone who took exception to him dealing from the bottom of the deck."

"I see. So you patched him up?"

"We did. Afterwards Ma let him sleep in the barn loft while he recovered. One day led to another. It wasn't long before I couldn't bear the thought of him leaving."

"Did you know what he was by then?"

"Looking back … I probably did." She took a breath. "Making his way through life like that was all he knew. It's what his father taught him."

"That made it acceptable?"

The question stung, although he didn't sound judgmental. "Of course not. He was responsible for his choices whatever his upbringing." She paused for a long moment, considering her next words. "But he could've chosen another path. I hear his brother did, eventually. But Jemma's father … liked the excitement."

"Some always do."

"He promised to stop."

"And you believed him."

"I did."

"Then he seduced you."

"No," Hannah stated firmly, brooking no argument. "I allowed myself to be seduced."

"I'm not sure I understand the difference," Nate offered cautiously.

"Seduction is luring an unsuspecting woman into a snare to be caught. I made a conscious choice to be with him that night."

"Hmm."

"I know in most people's eyes—"

"I'm not most people."

"I hope that's a good thing." Her attempt at a lighthearted comment fell short. She paused briefly then posed a serious question. "Does this lower your opinion of me?"

"No." His swift, firm answer left no doubt in her mind he spoke the truth.

"It wasn't a wise choice."

"It happens to everyone."

"To you?"

"Yes." Nate paused and for a moment, Hannah thought he was going to share an experience he'd had but the man wasn't that forthcoming. "Makes a person … cautious."

"Yes, it does."

Silence fell. She waited for Nate to speak again, listening to the sounds of nature and her daughter's soft breathing. Just when Hannah started wondering if he'd fallen asleep, his husky whisper reached her.

"What happened to him?"

"You mean when he-" Her throat tightened unexpectedly and for a moment she couldn't continue.

"You don't have to tell me."

"I want to."

"All right."

"I refused to marry an outlaw." Hannah turned to lie on her back, staring upwards.

"He proposed?"

"Yes." Her lips curved. The memory was sweet. "He did. And when I told him why I couldn't, he promised if I said yes he'd change." Her voice became flat with a hint of sadness. "He'd be a better man."

"Was he sincere?"

"Yes." She pulled in a deep breath before continuing. "The next

152

day, he left before dawn. When I woke, I found a note saying he needed to make some things right. Weeks passed without a word, then I received a letter sent from Idaho."

"He ran out on you?"

"No." Her tone was heavy with remembered loss. "He killed a man."

"What?"

"He said he messed up, shot someone, and was sorry."

"Did you see him again?"

"He'd written me from jail. He'd already been hung by the time I received his letter."

"Are you sure—"

"It wasn't some tall tale he spun as he ran out on me?"

"Ah, yes."

"I took the train to Elk Bend. Spoke with the Marshal. Put flowers on his grave. I'm sure."

"I'm sorry."

"So am I." Her words were barely audible. Time had dulled the pain but an echo of heartache remained.

A couple of minutes passed without another word. *Is she tired of talking?* It had been a long day and the deeply personal subject had to be difficult for Hannah. Nate shifted onto his back. *It's very late. Maybe she's fallen asleep.*

"Do you have any lost loves?"

Startled, Nate's first thought was to avoid answering her directly. *But she didn't.* It had taken a lot of heart to share all she had. Hannah had endured a lot more than some annoying gossip and heartbreak. People tended to be cruel to women who had children out of wedlock. Giving her an honest response was the least he could do.

"Yes. I mentioned her the other day."

"The one you were engaged to but she married someone else?"

"That would be Faith."

"What happened?"

"River's Bend."

"I don't understand."

At first, neither did I. The entire time I courted her, I didn't ask half the questions I've already asked you. I assumed…

"Rebuilding my father's old homestead, and living there, is a lifelong dream. The land borders the Bar 7 but it's almost a full day's ride from Fir Mountain. Although she would've put up with living on my family's ranch, Faith really wanted to live in town. She thought if I loved her enough, I'd change."

"And you didn't love her that much?"

"Loving someone shouldn't mean giving up your dreams," he challenged.

"Loving someone, in my opinion, involves a willingness to sacrifice almost anything."

"I could give up almost anything but not River's Bend. It's a part of me. When I'm there … I can't explain."

"Then perhaps she didn't love *you* enough?"

"Apparently not. She broke up with me and married the man who owned the general store the next month."

"I'm sorry."

"So am I." He echoed her earlier statement.

"Is it hard seeing her around town?"

"No, it's been years and I'm rarely in town anyway." Nate turned his head, looking in her direction. "I was petty enough for a short time to find it satisfying she married a thoroughly unpleasant man. Does that lower your opinion of me?"

"Do you still feel that way?"

"No. Now, I feel sorry for her."

"Then ah … I, ah …" Hannah tried stifling a yawn. "I think that's good."

"Feeling sorry for her?"

"No, not holding onto bitterness. That takes a good man."

"Not as good as some."

"I'm certain better than others."

"I'd like to think so."

Nate heard her yawn yet again.

"I'm sorry, I've enjoyed talking with you but I don't think I can stay awake any longer."

"Don't be sorry." Nestled close to her daughter, Hannah was with an arm's reach of him. Nate watched a stream of moonlight caress the curve of her cheek. "It's all right, I'm tired too."

"Okay, then good night."

Her soft, sleepy voice stirred images in his mind, sending an unexpected burst of desire rushing through him. Nate closed his eyes, taking a deep breath. After a few seconds, he turned so he faced away from her.

"Good night, Hannah."

The morning dawned frosty. When she woke, Nate had already left their makeshift bed. Hannah could hear him walking around, though, his footsteps crunching the crusty earth. Careful not to rouse Jemma and resisting the warmth of the blankets tempting her to stay, she crawled out of bed. Shivering, she snatched up her coat and hurriedly slipped it on as she stood up next to the wagon.

Her gaze found Nate busy tending his horse. Before he could notice her, she rushed off to where the trees would afford her privacy. After taking care of her needs, she washed up at the creek then finger-combed her hair, securing it into a knot with a couple of pins from her pocket.

Anticipation flowed through her veins as Hannah headed back to the wagon. The time she'd spent with Nate, just talking, left her wanting more. He looked at her and smiled as she approached. Her step quickened. Several words danced through her mind, yet upon reaching his side she couldn't think of a single thing to say.

"Good morning."

Of course. "Good morning."

"The weather is taking a turn for the worse." Nate finished tying Jack to the back of the wagon.

Hannah looked up. There wasn't even a hint of blue in the sky. "It's going to rain?"

"It's cold enough for snow."

"Oh." Concern chased away lighthearted feelings.

"I don't think a storm is imminent but I'd like to get moving soon."

"Breakfast?"

"Best we eat on the go."

"Mama." A small head poked out from under the wagon. "Where are you?"

"I'm right here," she called out to her daughter before addressing Nate again. "I'll fix up something as soon as I take care of Jemma."

"Good. I'll hitch up the mules."

Hannah headed straight to her daughter. She helped Jemma into her coat, quickly braided her hair, then took the girl down by the creek to finish her morning routine. When they returned, Nate had finished with the team. He helped them up into the bed of the wagon. While he moved on to packing up the blankets, she spread strawberry jam on thick slices of the bread for a quick meal. Only minutes later, they were heading down the road.

Jemma made short work of the simple fare. Hannah used a little water from the canteen on a handkerchief to wash her child's sticky hands and face before giving her a drink. She next tugged mittens over the girl's hands then placed a blanket over both of their laps, tucking it snugly around her daughter.

"What's wrong with your eye?"

"Jemma," Hannah exclaimed. Her child had obviously grown more comfortable with Nate after yesterday.

"Yes, Mama?"

"That's not polite."

"Why?"

"Because it's … personal."

The little girl tilted her head to one side as she stared up at Hannah, her forehead crinkled. "Personal?"

"We don't ask people about their faces."

"We don't?"

"No, we don't."

"But—"

"Jemma." Hannah was gentle but firm. "We don't."

"Okay." Her daughter agreed but her disappointment was obvious.

"I don't mind answering."

"She shouldn't have asked."

"But she already has." Nate looked over at her, his expression amused.

Curious herself, Hannah gave in. "If you don't mind."

"We had an issue with a neighbor several years ago. His sheep kept helping themselves to our grass. My parents decided to put up a fence. While my brothers and I were stringing some barbed wire, a strand came loose. It caught me across the face."

"You're lucky you didn't lose the eye." The picture painted by his words horrified Hannah.

"Yes, I am."

"Did it hurt?" The little girl's concern was as obvious as her curiosity.

"It did."

Jemma reached out, patting him on the arm. "I'm sorry."

"It was a long time ago, little one."

"Okay. Did the sheep stay out?"

Nate smiled down at the girl. "They do now."

"Good."

Satisfied with his explanation, Jemma returned to directing most of her conversation to her mother. However, her occasional question for Nate was a noticeable difference in behavior. It pleased Hannah to see her daughter warming up to the man. The change eased one of her worries.

Despite her efforts at reassurance, Jemma had become withdrawn, almost fearful, around Jed and men in general. The man had been a good friend to both Hannah and her child before Bessie died. He'd treated Jemma as if she were one of his own. Already dealing with the loss of her grandmother as well as Bessie, his sudden transformation bewildered the little girl. Voluntarily speaking to Nate, even this tiny amount, was a sign of healing.

As the day progressed, their conversations revolved around Jemma's chatter most of the time. The clouds covering the sky broke apart and allowed the sun to peek through occasionally after a while but the air never warmed. Concern for her little girl grew. Hannah put another blanket over them, cuddling the child close. Thankfully, they rolled into Nate's hometown before noon.

Fir Mountain, though clearly a small town, appeared larger than Ashwood. She looked around, noticing a post office, church, restaurant, schoolhouse, sheriff's office with jail, and bakery, in addition to the mercantile, while they rolled down the main street. An uneasy sensation crept over Hannah within minutes. It felt as though people were watching them with more than average curiosity.

Gossip couldn't have traveled this fast. Could it?

"Nate—" Hannah started, intending to ask him about it, then stopped abruptly, feeling foolish. *I'm imagining it.*

"Yes?"

"Um … how far out is the ranch?"

"About an hour. Why? Do you and Jemma need a break?"

"Well … Um …" *Get a hold of yourself. There's nothing going on here.* "Actually yes, it'd be nice to stretch our legs if you don't mind?"

"I think we'll be fine. The weather is looking better. How about getting some lunch?"

Hannah nodded. "I'll make it right after I tend Jemma."

"I must be rusty." Wearing a wry grin, Nate looked over at her. "What I meant was, may I escort you and your daughter to Judith's, our finest, and as it happens only, restaurant?"

"Would that be proper?" She didn't want to spark whispers her first day in town. Envisioning old gossip following her was troubling enough. "I work for you."

"We're also friends."

Startled, Hannah stared at him. "We are?"

"I'd like to be." His grin had faded, leaving a somber expression.

Friends with a Rolfe? "I ..." She studied the man who'd talked to her until the wee hours of the night and had shown nothing but kindness to her daughter. "I'd like that as well."

"Good."

"And have you taken other women friends to lunch?"

"Yes." He was quick to assure her. "Alice most recently."

"I'm sorry. I'm nervous. This is a new start for Jemma and I and I don't want to mess it up."

"You won't."

His two words conveyed conviction. A hint of tears stung her eyes. Warmth bloomed in her heart, spreading with each beat.

"What do you think, Jemma? Would you like to go to lunch with Nate?"

"I'm hungry." Her daughter nodded emphatically.

Hannah chuckled. "I guess that settles it. We'd love to have lunch with you."

"Great, I'm starving."

Nate pulled up in front of the livery a moment later. He helped Hannah and Jemma down, then went inside the old building to arrange for the animals' care. After he was done, they walked down the sidewalk with the little girl in between them. Jemma clung tightly to her mother's hand, peering around with wide eyes at her new surroundings. At the restaurant, he held the door open for them.

Charmed, Hannah smiled, herding Jemma in front of her. They stopped a few steps inside. A woman's voice rang out just then.

"Nate."

A petite, dark-haired young woman jumped up from a nearby table, hurrying up to them. She launched herself at Nate and he caught her to him in a tight hug. Hannah stiffened, watching the pair as several sharp pricks of jealousy stabbed her without warning. After what seemed a *very* long time, he loosed her.

"Where's Alice?" the stranger demanded. "And who do you have with you?"

"It's good to see you too, Claire."

Claire punched him playfully in the arm. "I hugged you. Now tell me what's going on."

"It's a long story."

"Those are my favorite kind."

"Alice had to stay." Nate nodded at his companions. "And this is our new temporary housekeeper, Hannah Brooks and Jemma, her daughter. Ladies, please meet my cousin, Claire McConkey."

Hannah almost sagged with relief. The stunning beauty with a heart-shaped face was a relative. It shouldn't have mattered, since she and Nate were only friends. But, it did.

"Pleased to meet you."

"Lovely to meet you." Claire shook Hannah's hand. She next crouched down to Jemma's eye level, offering the child her hand just as she had to her mother. "And you as well." She stood back up. "Come and join me."

Hannah glanced at Nate. He nodded and she looked back at the other woman. "We'd love to."

They settled around the table quickly. Hannah removed Jemma's coat, then her own. Claire asked a waitress, Ginny, to bring over a small wooden box. She swiftly returned with one, placing it on Jemma's seat. As Nate lifted her daughter up onto it, Ginny shared the day's special. Within minutes, the waitress had taken all their orders and headed off to the kitchen.

"Did Evie finally give in to Ben's pleas?"

Claire grinned, nodding. Hannah's confusion must have been obvious because the other woman tried to explain. "Ben's a cousin of ours. He's from a different branch of the family than mine, though."

Yes, Michael's.

"Evie is his wife."

Hannah smiled, liking Claire's warm enthusiasm. "Alice told me about Ben and Evie moving onto the Bar 7 last year. However, I'm not clear on all the family connections."

"Ben and Nate's? Their fathers were brothers."

"Oh." Hannah paused, catching movement out of the corner of her eye. She glanced over to see Nate pulling a bit of string and some coins out of his pocket to entertain Jemma. After a few seconds, she turned her attention back to Claire, feeling it was important to understand the Rolfe family dynamics better. "How are you related, then?"

"Nate's mother and mine are cousins. If you want to be specific, we're second cousins."

"Oh, and do you live on the ranch too?"

"My folks have a farm down the road from the Bar 7."

"It must be nice to have so much family around."

"It's great. Evie and I are good friends now. You'll like her. She's sweet. She'd be here but she's expecting. The baby should come this month and Ben's worried, even though the doctor says she and the baby are fine. All he's doing by not wanting her to do anything is driving her crazy. She used to come to town with me to get the potato soup here because she craves it something fierce but Ben-"

"Claire, pause, take a breath," Nate interrupted, obviously amused.

"Sorry, I get carried away sometimes."

"Sometimes?"

"Yes." Claire speared him with a look. "Sometimes."

"Would Matt agree?"

"Of course he would." Her smile was wide and confident.

Nate shifted his gaze from Claire to Hannah. "Matt Marston is the sheriff of Silver Creek County and—"

"My fiancée."

"I was going to say, a good friend of mine."

"He's that and so much more."

"Spare me the gushing, little cousin."

"What's wrong with being loving? And I am not little."

"Yes, you are. And there's nothing wrong with loving but the two of you have been spouting so much sugar, you'd give a child a bellyache."

"I like sugar." Jemma piped up, causing the adults to laugh softly.

Smiling, Nate reached over and tapped her on the nose. "So do I, little one, but too much will make you sick."

"Okay." The girl agreed but her expression reflected such clear disbelief everyone chuckled again.

The waitress returned just then and the delivery of their meals consumed the next few minutes. Ginny set down a glass of milk for Jemma and cups of coffee for the adults, apologizing for not bringing their drinks earlier. She rushed off without waiting for a response, returning almost immediately with bowls of potato soup, plates of sliced ham and buttermilk biscuits on her next trip. Lastly, she brought them honey and butter, then left them to enjoy their lunch.

Hannah cut Jemma's ham into bite-size pieces then helped her drizzle honey on half of a biscuit. After taking care of her little girl, she turned her attention to her own meal. She let a minute go by then posed another question to Claire.

"Did I understand correctly? You're engaged to Sheriff Marston?"

"I am." Claire's slow, broad smile lit her whole face. The woman positively glowed. "Have you met him?"

"I haven't had the pleasure. He was going to stop by the farm about a month ago but something came up."

Pink spread over Claire's cheeks. "He was busy here."

"Oh, well." Hannah had the distinct impression there was a lot more to the simple explanation. "The sheriff came by the farm again a week or so ago but I was in town."

"Tracking down the rustlers?"

"Rustlers? No, I don't think so. Alice thought he was there to check on Jed."

"Why?"

Hannah glanced at her daughter. "It's a long story."

"As I told Nate, those are the kind I love to hear."

"Little pitchers have big ears, Claire. I think it's a tale best told at home. Ride over for a visit and I'd be happy to share everything with you." Nate turned to Hannah. "That is, if you don't mind?"

"It's your ranch," she protested, although pleased he was being so considerate.

"Actually, it's my parents' ranch, but for now it's your home. Please tell me if you'd rather not have visitors and do invite anyone over you'd like, even if it's my little cousin."

"Hey." The woman in question swatted his shoulder.

Hannah watched their interaction, fascinated by how relaxed and talkative he was around his cousin. Distracted, she almost forgot to speak up. "It'd be nice if Claire visited."

"I'd love to. I'll ride over tomorrow afternoon and, if the weather holds, take you and Jemma on a tour of the ranch."

Nate cleared his throat. "That's a bit soon. Give her some time. Let her settle in. And I'll show them around."

"You want to do that?"

"I do." The tips of his ears turned red.

"All right." Claire drew the two words out, studying her cousin intensely for a second before continuing. "How about I come out in a couple of days?"

"I'd like that." Hannah smiled.

Nate wiped his soup bowl clean with the last of his biscuit. "So where is our good sheriff?"

Chapter 12

"He was called out to Myrtle Point." For the first time Claire's expression became somber.

"More missing cattle?"

"That's what the telegram said."

"He went alone?"

"No, he took Sam with him."

A tense silence followed. His jaw clenched, Nate picked up his coffee cup and stared down into it. A moment passed before he spoke again.

"Sorry, I didn't mean to be rude." He looked at Hannah then glanced around the crowded restaurant. "I don't feel comfortable explaining here. I'll tell you about it later."

"You don't owe me an explanation."

"I'd like to give you one anyway."

"All right."

Jemma started to fuss a little. She was finished with her meal and getting tired. Hannah got up and knelt by her side, speaking to the child in a hushed, comforting tone.

"Time for us to go?" Nate asked.

"Sorry, but yes."

"Don't apologize." He stood. "I'll go settle the check."

Both women got to their feet when he walked away. As she helped Jemma into her coat, Hannah got the feeling someone was watching her. Subtly, she glanced around. No one appeared to be looking at her.

"Is something wrong?"

"This may sound odd." Hannah shifted her gaze to the young woman beside her. "But I feel like someone is staring at me."

Claire's friendly expression became a polite mask. Her gaze slid away, scanning the room. Seconds later, barely moving her lips, she offered Hannah a possible answer.

"Don't look but there are some chattering magpies seated by the window. Lizzie Jane and her cacklers likely wonder who you are and why you're with Nate."

Hannah straightened, holding Jemma's hand. "Why?"

"I suspect she's still stirring up old gossip and spreading a little new as well."

"Nate told me about that." She matched Claire's whisper, shrugging into her coat.

"He did?" The other woman seemed surprised.

"Only about himself." Hannah smoothed her daughter's hat back on. "Though he mentioned rumors about Ben once."

"I'm impressed."

"You are?"

"Nate doesn't share personal things often."

"He doesn't?"

"I only know the gossip bothers him because Matt told me."

Then why did he tell me? Mute, Hannah stared at the other woman. Nate returned a few seconds later and the opportunity to respond was lost. Together, they left the restaurant.

Nate went to fetch the wagon while she and Claire waited on the sidewalk with Jemma, firming up their plans for a visit. Two women walked by them, offering subdued greetings as they passed without pause. It reminded Hannah too much of what had happened in Ashwood.

To keep Jemma from hearing, she kept her voice low. "Are they gossipers?"

"The younger one is Mercy Ellis." Claire leaned close. "She has some friends who spread words faster than telegraph wire but I don't think she joins in. In fact, I get the impression their behavior embarrasses her. The other woman is her sister, Faith."

"Nate's Faith?"

"He told you about her?"

"Yes."

"Interesting." Curiosity gleamed in Claire's chocolate-colored eyes as Nate pulled up in the wagon. "I look forward to us having a nice long visit."

"Do you want a ride home?" Nate addressed Claire, climbing down.

"No thanks. I rode Storm in."

"Go ahead and saddle up. We'll wait."

Claire shook her head. "I need to check out something before I head out."

"You have a lead?"

"Maybe."

"Want to share, little cousin?"

"Not yet."

"We can wait until you're finished."

"No need."

"It's no bother." Nate helped Hannah climb onto the seat then lifted Jemma up to her.

"My pistol is in my saddle bag, Nathaniel. I'll be fine."

"I'm surprised it isn't on your hip."

"A compromise, my dear cousin." Claire reached up, giving him a peck on the cheek. "Just a little compromise." She called out a quick cheery goodbye to Hannah and Jemma then strode off.

Nate climbed back up onto the seat and set the mules in motion. Not long after leaving the outskirts of Fir Mountain, the wind picked up, nipping at them. Dark clouds billowed across the sky and soon filled it. The temperature dropped, chilling any exposed skin. Hannah pulled yet another blanket out of the bed and wrapped it around her daughter.

Although Nate urged the team up to a faster pace, it still took almost an hour for them to reach the turn off for the Bar 7. They traveled down the private drive for a number of minutes, winding around a vast stand of pines until finally arriving at their destination. Eyes wide, Hannah tried to take it all in.

Several buildings were spread over a large clearing with dense forest ringing it on three sides and the fourth a seemingly endless field of winter grass dotted with shaggy cattle. In the distance, she could see a huge snow-covered mountain. They drove past some sheds, a cabin, a huge barn, and a long, low structure she assumed was their bunkhouse. In front of a sprawling log home, easily four times the size of the house at Redwing Farm, Nate brought the wagon to a halt.

A few ranch hands emerged from the low building, which seemed to confirm Hannah's guess. Given the increasingly hostile weather, Nate didn't waste time with introductions. He hustled her and Jemma into the house, leaving the care of the animals and wagon to the other men.

The air inside the house wasn't much warmer than it was outside. Nate herded them through a mudroom, then the kitchen and into the living room. With a broad gesture in the direction of the couch, he headed for the fireplace. Hannah and her daughter sat down and watched him go to work. In minutes, he had a nice blaze going.

"I'll go light yours. Stay here and warm up."

"Mine?" She stood, bringing Jemma to stand near the fire. "You've more than one fireplace?"

"There's three: this one, one in my parents' room, and one in Alice's room, where you'll be staying." His answer floated over his shoulder as he strode away, intent on his purpose.

The flames soon started warming the large room, as well as Hannah and her daughter. She and Jemma remained close to the heat but were comfortable enough to have removed their coats by the time Nate returned. Before he could say a word, the sound of a door opening echoed through the house.

"Nate, where are you?" a man called out.

"In here."

The sound of heavy footsteps sent her daughter into the folds of Hannah's skirt. She laid a gentle hand on the little girl's shoulder. A band tightened around her chest. *What if it's Ben?* Knowing the man worked on the ranch was one thing, but it was quite different from the prospect of meeting Michael's brother face to face. If he walked in now, she honestly didn't know what she'd do.

Seconds later, two men entered the room, each carrying one of her trunks. Both were dressed for the weather in worn denim pants, heavy coats, and hats covering their hair and shadowing their faces. Although Hannah had never seen a likeness of Ben, Michael had once said people knew from one glance the two were brothers. Rigid with tension, she waited for the introductions.

"Hannah, Jemma, I'd like you to meet," Nate gestured to the man on the left, "two of my brothers." The young woman released the breath she'd held. "Jacob." He indicated the other man. "And Isaac."

The man on the right put down his burden, then took off his hat. Hannah couldn't suppress a small gasp. With dark hair, like every Rolfe she'd met and green eyes the same shade as Michael's and her daughter's, stood a man so handsome, looking at him had to be a sin. The cocky grin Isaac wore as he walked over to shake her hand said he was well aware of his devastating appearance.

"Pleasure to meet you, ma'am. Call me Rowdy, everyone does."

"Pleased to meet you... Rowdy." Hannah greeted him with a polite smile, clasping his hand briefly.

In the face of his overwhelming self-assurance, bordering on arrogance, the young woman felt a measure of reserve. Her opinion of him improved when, like Claire had earlier in the day, Rowdy knelt down to Jemma's level and offered her his hand as well. A man who was kind to children must have some redeeming qualities.

"Jemma. What a pretty name for a pretty girl."

The little girl stared at him, eyes wide. She pressed against her mother, one hand clutching Hannah's skirt. Her whispered response surprised them all. "You're pretty too."

Rowdy gave a full-throated laugh. "Why thank you, little miss."

The man then stood, moving aside for his brother. Hannah's attention shifted to Jacob. He was an inch or two taller than Rowdy, with similar green eyes. His brown hair had a shaggy look, hanging over the tips of his ears, as if he'd forgotten to get it trimmed. His features didn't boast the near perfection of Rowdy or the rugged good looks of Nate, but were simply nice, almost boyish. Hannah felt instantly at ease with him.

"Pleased to meet you too."

"And you, ma'am. Please call me Jacob, everyone does." His voice was rich with amusement, taking an obvious but gentle jab at his brother while shaking her hand.

"Hi." Jemma took one small step forward but didn't loose her mother's skirt.

"Hi." Jacob knelt down in front of her and offered the child his hand. "I'm glad to meet you."

"Thank you."

To Hannah's surprise, her daughter actually shook his hand briefly. "Jemma, say 'glad to meet you too.'"

"Oh, okay. Glad meeting you. Did you bring Daisy?"

"Who's Daisy?"

"My dolly."

"Did your ma put her in a trunk?"

Solemn, the little girl nodded.

"Well, then probably."

His answer brought a smile to Jemma's face. Jacob grinned in response straight off but a few seconds later his expression started changing. Hannah noticed a little puzzlement enter his gaze. Her stomach clenched. She reached down for her daughter's hand, hoping to disrupt the man's focus.

"Daisy is in the trunk next to Nate."

"You know." Jacob chuckled. He straightened beside her as Jemma carefully scooted around him, heading for Nate. He shook his head when Hannah looked at him, one brow raised in silent inquiry. "For a moment, she reminded me of our sister."

Hannah managed to keep her calm facade in place. "She did?"

"Strange, huh?"

"Becca's our baby," Rowdy interjected. "Makes sense, you'd think about her when meeting a little girl."

"Yeah, that must be it." Jacob agreed, but doubt lingered in his expression.

Hannah smiled, although it felt stiff, because she didn't know what to say. It was a relief to hear Jemma asking Nate to open the trunk. Her daughter's high-pitched voice was edging toward a whine. With a nod in the direction of her child, she excused herself.

Quickly, Hannah crossed the room and addressed Jemma's concern. "I'll find Daisy for you in a minute." She glanced at Nate. "Someone is tired. Is there somewhere I could lay her down?"

"Of course, let me show you where you'll be staying." He turned, speaking now to his brothers. "I'm giving her Alice's room. Follow us."

Nate then took them down a short hall. He stopped at the first door and pulled it open, gesturing for her and Jemma to enter. Inside, Hannah found a room that was twice the size of the one she'd shared at Redwing Farm.

A small fire crackled in the fireplace on the wall directly opposite the door, warming the space. To her left, a good-sized bed sat, made up with a quilt in varying shades of red, and two plump pillows. An oil lamp burned, casting out a soft circle of light from where it stood on the nightstand. On the other side of the room was a tall, oak wardrobe and a short but wide, four-drawer dresser, both pieces appearing old but sturdy.

Nate's brothers walked in a moment later, carrying her trunks. They set them down on the floor near the dresser. "Thank you."

"Our pleasure, ma'am," they chorused, then took their leave.

"Will this work? I planned to give Jemma the room next door, but it doesn't have a bed now. I'll have one of my brothers help me bring a cot down from the attic shortly."

"She isn't going to share with me?"

"She can if you wish." Nate spoke slow and soft. "The room I had in mind hasn't been used in years because it's so small but I thought it'd be perfect for a little girl."

"You're probably right."

"If she misses her mama, you'd only be a shout away."

"You're very thoughtful." She smiled at him. "Thank you."

"You're welcome. I'll go catch up with my brothers while you settle Jemma down and unpack. Please, let me know if you need anything."

"I'm an employee, not a guest."

"Employees are better. Often they're like family."

Family. His words, clearly offered with the intent to make her comfortable, had the opposite effect. As he walked away, she twisted her hands together in front of her. Her conscience nagged at her to tell him about Michael now.

"Nate." The man paused in the doorway, looking back at her with an expectant expression. "I—"

"Mama," Jemma whined, tugging on her skirt. "Daisy?"

One glance down at a small unhappy face and Hannah lost her nerve. *Now isn't a good time.* Her daughter was exhausted and on the verge of a tantrum. *Maybe after Jemma's had time to adjust.*

"I'll find her, honey." She knelt down next to the trunks, opening one at random.

"Did you need something?"

Heat rushed up her neck and over her face. Her gaze shifted over to the man in the doorway. "No. Sorry. I just… wanted to thank you again."

"You're welcome." Nate offered her a smile then exited the room, leaving the door open.

Hannah turned back to her task, listening to his footsteps echo down the length of the hallway while she dug through their belongings in search of the doll. It didn't take long before she found it, still wrapped in the quilt her mother made for Jemma when she was a baby. Her hand tightened over fabric, soft and faded from countless washing. She bit her lip to hold back a sigh, wishing her mother could advise her now.

"Mama."

Her daughter's petulant tone focused her attention. Hannah handed over Daisy, then gathered Jemma in her arms. She stood up and in three long steps crossed over to the bed. With one sweep of her hand, she pulled the covers down and laid the child on the sheet. The little girl clutched the doll tight but closed her eyes without one whispered protest while she tucked her in, smoothing the old baby quilt over her last.

Hannah sat on the bed beside her daughter for the next few minutes. Once certain Jemma slept, she got up and silently went about unpacking. A quick check of the opened trunk confirmed everything within should remain undisturbed. There was no need to take out her mother's china set, bedding, towels, dishes, or cast-iron pans until she had a home of her own. However, she couldn't resist one item. She pulled out the crazy quilt she'd pieced together with her mother when she was not much older than Jemma, placing it over the foot of the bed.

After carefully securing the lid of the first trunk, Hannah moved onto the other one. She removed all of Jemma's belongings, stacking them on top of the dresser. If she allowed her to be in a room of her own, they'd be easy to move. Hairpins, ribbons, and her brush went beside her daughter's things. She then tucked her clothing and shoes into the wardrobe and dresser drawers. After that, only a few keepsakes remained in the container.

Hannah took out a little wooden box and looked inside. It held the pitiful amount of coin she had, some paper, a couple of envelopes, her mother's wedding ring, and a silver necklace Grace had always worn. With it still in one hand, she reached back in with the other and picked up two books. One was an old book of children's fables her mother had read to her as a child and she now read to Jemma. She got to her feet and walked over to the nightstand, placing both the box and book of fables beside the lamp. The other book remained in her grasp.

Her teeth worrying her bottom lip, Hannah gently opened the old bible. Pressed between the ragged pages she kept two pieces of treasure. One was the only photograph she had of her parents, taken in Salem on their wedding day. She studied their smiling faces a long moment before putting it back, wishing for more than memories. From a separate location, she removed a yellowed bit of paper and unfolded it. The only likeness she possessed of Michael, a printed image cut from a wanted poster she'd grabbed in Elk Bend, stared up at her.

Her gaze moved to her daughter. The way the lamplight and shadows fell, her bright hair looked dark and, in that moment, the resemblance to her father was striking. Jemma deserved to see a picture of Michael someday but Hannah wished she had a better option. Although she trimmed off the damning parts, most adults would realize what she'd cut the picture from. She sighed softly and folded the image up again, putting it back. Maybe, she could ask Ben if he had a picture of his brother.

I'd have to tell him about Jemma first. Hannah glanced over at the doorway. If she concentrated, she could hear the Rolfe brothers' voices, rising and falling in the rhythm of conversation, but couldn't make out a word. *What if it was Ben Michael was truly worried about?* She swallowed another sigh and walked over to the dresser, sliding the bible into the drawer with her stockings. *Best meet the man before leaping to rash conclusions.*

Hannah remembered leaving their coats on the couch as she closed up the second trunk. Embarrassed, she went off at once to fetch them. She moved swiftly down the hall, then paused in the opening to the living room. It appeared unoccupied. Uncertain where the Rolfe brothers were, she moved slowly into the space.

Curious, Hannah studied the contents. All the furniture had a rugged but comfortable appearance, giving the room an almost masculine feel. Yet, upon a closer look, there were soft touches visible throughout the space. Some multi-colored rag rugs were scattered over the plank floor, an afghan crocheted in shades of green hung over the couch back, and a bright painting of a cabin in the mountains took up a large part of one wall. Drawn to the image, she stepped nearer, admiring the cheerful colors depicting spring.

"My sister painted that."

Hannah turned around and found Nate standing in the doorway leading to the kitchen. "It's beautiful."

"It's River's Bend." Nate smiled with obvious pride while he walked up to her. "Becca's very talented."

"That's your home?"

"It is." Strong emotion permeated his words. His gaze focused on the painting, he stopped at her side.

"You miss it."

"I do. Can't wait to go home."

"You're leaving?" Sudden anxiety filled her.

"No, not soon anyway."

The resignation in his voice brought her guilt along with relief. "You're not staying because of me and Jemma, are you?"

"No." Nate turned, facing her. "I've made commitments."

"Do you mind me asking what they are?"

"Helping out here while my parents are gone is one."

"Must be hard to do that and tend to your own place."

"They hired a couple of extra ranch hands." Nate moved to the fireplace, shifted some coals with a metal poker before adding another round of pine. "I was supposed to ride in twice a week, lend a hand if one was needed."

"Something changed?"

"Sam caught one of the new hires smoking in the barn and fired him on the spot. We don't tolerate carelessness."

"Understandable."

"Then Matt asked for my help."

"The sheriff? Was it about the missing cattle you mentioned at the restaurant?"

"Yes. Ranches all over the county have suffered losses."

"Why does the sheriff need your help?

"I'm the best tracker in the state."

"His matter-of-fact statement affected Hannah as much as his claim. She had no doubt what he said was true. "I'm impressed."

"Thank you."

"Why didn't you and your brothers hire another ranch hand or two, especially after you agreed to help the sheriff?"

"Wanted to. No one is willing to work for us now."

"Because Sam fired that man?"

"Because of the gossip." From Nate's sour expression, it looked like the subject left an ugly taste in his mouth.

Confusion filled her. "Men don't want to work here because some women speculate on your broken heart?"

"No, rumors about my cousin."

"Claire?"

"Ben."

Ben? "Oh?" She stiffened slightly but otherwise kept her reaction in check. *Maybe if he'll tell me what these rumors are this*

176

time, I'll learn why Michael warned me away. "I assume they aren't about heartbreak."

"No." Nate paused, studying her for a long moment. "Ben's a good man. But … he has a troubled past. The law suspected him of being an outlaw in Cedar Ridge. He and Evie moved here, wanting a fresh start. The rumors … people say he's behind the rustling."

Michael wouldn't have cared if his brother had trouble with the law. "What do you believe?"

"I'd trust him at my back."

"Sometimes, when you love someone." She chose her words with care. "You trust beyond reason."

"Thinking of Jemma's father?"

Silently, Hannah held his gaze some seconds, then nodded.

"Ben told Matt all he could remember, and what he suspected about himself, when he and Evie first rolled into town."

"Alice mentioned he'd been hurt and had trouble remembering some things."

"Several years of his life."

Or is that just what he's telling everyone? "It must be hard on him."

"It is."

Hannah drifted a few steps away, moving near the couch. She waited several seconds before speaking again, trying to keep the pace of her questions reflective of casual interest. "And the sheriff's reaction?"

"Matt asked Ben to help investigate the rustling."

To keep an eye on him? She reached down, picking up Jemma's coat. "Is he a good tracker too?"

"He's okay. Not as good as me." Nate came to stand beside her. "There's a place by the door for your coats."

"Oh?"

"I should've put them up while you were settling Jemma."

"You don't have to pick up after us." Hannah offered him a

177

brief smile then scooped up the rest of her and her daughter's things. "I appreciate the thought but I'm the housekeeper."

Nate held out his hands, indicating with a look he wanted to relieve her of the bulky clothing. "Which is no reason for me not to be helpful."

"You don't …" Feeling ungracious, she hesitated a moment then handed him everything. "Thank you."

"You're welcome."

Hannah followed him across the room to a door on the far wall. Nate went straight to a series of pegs beside it, hanging their coats next to a couple of other ones. *Two entrances. Three fireplaces.* It was a little overwhelming. She'd never been in a house so large.

"Thank you again."

Nate turned, facing her. "You're welcome again."

Her mind blanked. For a moment, she held his gaze, feeling heat creep up her neck as the silence stretched on. *Ben. Finish asking about Ben.*

Nervous, Hannah cleared her throat. "So why did the sheriff want your cousin's help?"

"Well." Nate gestured toward the fireplace. He waited until she took a step then fell in beside her. "Did Alice tell you Ben's father and brother were wanted men?"

She didn't have to. "She may have mentioned something."

"Ben was told he might have useful insight into criminal behavior because of his experiences with them."

Something in his phrasing struck her as odd. "He remembers them?"

"His memory loss is only for the last few years."

"Oh." *Convenient.* "Was that the sheriff's real reason?"

Nate took a few seconds to respond. "No. It was to keep an eye on him. Matt wanted to either get the evidence to convict him or rule him out."

"And?" Hannah gently prompted.

"He ruled Ben out."

"But that didn't stop the gossip?"

"No, it's only worsened. Rumor has it our good sheriff has gone soft where the Rolfes are concerned."

"Because of Claire?"

"Because he and Ben are friends now. Because Matt and I are close friends, have been since childhood. And, yes, they say love is clouding his good sense."

"But you don't think so?"

"No."

They stopped in front of the fire once more. Hannah held her hands out to the warmth. "In essence, then, the rustlers are keeping you from River's Bend."

"In essence, yes." His gaze returned to the painting. "I can't go home with this hanging over my family."

"Family is important to you, isn't it?" she asked softly.

He looked at her, dark eyes reflecting strong emotion. "Family is everything to me."

Guilt twisted inside of her. He had family right down the hall and didn't know it. Hannah wished she could tell him. But Michael's warning haunted her and what she'd learned about Ben so far didn't ease her mind. She had to be sure, first.

"Something wrong?"

"No," Hannah croaked out, then cleared her throat. "Speaking of family, are your brothers going to join us?"

"A section of fence needed to be checked. They'll be back later to help with Jemma's bed."

"Oh." She thought they were in the kitchen. Tension of a different kind rose up as Hannah realized she and Nate were alone again except for one sleeping child. With the curtains closed, the only light in the room came from the fire and a few oil lamps. Suddenly, the atmosphere seemed intimate. "That's nice of them but it doesn't have to be done tonight."

"One small bed is no trouble."

"Um …" Hannah glanced around the room, trying to think

of something clever to say. The painting caught her eye again. For the life of her, she couldn't remember Alice saying anything about his sister except there was one. "Is your sister home?"

Nate shook his head. "She's back east, studying art with a friend of our family."

"How wonderful for her. Will she be gone long?" Hannah looked back at him.

"Becca left almost two years ago." He grimaced. "But she should be home this spring."

"She's very talented. I hope I'm still here then, it'd be nice to meet her."

For a long moment, Nate studied Hannah. "You'd like her, everyone does." He paused, glancing at the painting then back at her. "She's a lot like you, sunshine on a cold winter day."

Chapter 13

Shocked by the poetic words, Hannah could only blink in response, unable to speak or move. Her palms dampened when Nate moved closer. His body brushed against hers, causing her heart to race. She swallowed hard but still couldn't say a word. His hand lifted slowly and his fingers traced down the side of her face, leaving a trail of nerves on fire.

"Mama."

Trance shattered, Hannah stepped back, putting much-needed space between her and Nate. She turned to face Jemma. "Yes."

Her face heated upon hearing the breathless quality of her voice. Her daughter looked up at her, wearing a grave expression. "My tummy is growly."

"Well, now, we can't have that." Nate stepped around her, reaching down to sweep up the little girl. With Jemma in his arms, he strode away, calling over his shoulder, "Follow us."

Now he's … playful? Startled anew by his shift in behavior, she stared after him. *How's Jemma taking this?* She hurried to catch up to them. To Hannah's surprise, her daughter appeared all right with the tall man carrying her. Although the little girl wasn't smiling, neither did she look in the least upset.

Reassured, Hannah trailed the pair into the kitchen. She'd

barely noticed the room earlier when they'd entered the house and now slowly looked around. There was a large stove, a table, two cupboards, and a sink with an inside pump. The welcome sight brought a smile to her face. *I don't have to haul water.*

Off a shelf in the walk-in pantry, Nate snagged a jar of canned pears. The sight of her favorite fruit caused Jemma to make a sound of pure pleasure, drawing Hannah's attention. She moved over and took her daughter from the man, settling her at the table.

Nate filled a bowl for the child, then poured her a glass of water. While Jemma ate her snack, he gave Hannah a tour, showing her where to find everything. After showing her how to work the sink, the man made a casual statement that took her by surprise.

"By the way, our hands have their own cook and they eat where they sleep, in the bunkhouse."

"Oh, so it'll just be you and your brothers at the house?"

"We bunk with the crew."

"And your meals?"

"We've being eating with them too."

Worried the housekeeping job was really just an act of charity, Hannah studied him closely. "What exactly did you hire me to do, then?"

"The house needs more than a lick and a promise. It's been looking as though no one lives here any more."

"Cleaning the house with only me and Jemma living in it won't take much."

"I'll be here too." Hannah stiffened, even as he went on to add, "I didn't mean … I'll be sleeping in the bunkhouse."

"You weren't staying there before?"

"Ah … No. I prefer to be on my own."

"I don't want to kick you out."

"You're not. I knew I couldn't stay here when I hired you."

"Because people would talk." Grim, she looked out the small window over the sink at the dusky landscape.

"No doubt. Regardless, it wouldn't be proper."

"No more than sharing blankets with a man."

"It was necessary and no one ever has to know. But sleeping arrangements here, however innocent, would become known."

"You're trying to protect my reputation?"

"Of course."

"Can't be done. It was destroyed years ago."

"In Ashwood not here."

Hannah looked back at him. She lifted her chin and asked in a soft, slightly sad tone, "You think it'll be different here?"

"You deserve a chance for it to be."

"I don't know it's possible but I appreciate the thought."

The slurping sound of Jemma finishing her pears broke into the serious moment. They both glanced at the little girl then back at each other, sharing amusement. Hannah stepped over to the sink and pumped some water over a cloth. The convenience of it made her smile again as she washed her daughter's face.

"All you expect of me is cleaning this house?"

"I'd like to take my meals with you. My brothers may wish to also, at least occasionally."

"You don't like the fare at the bunkhouse?" Hannah moved on to cleaning sticky little fingers.

"I'd enjoy eating where it's a bit … quieter."

"I see."

"If that's no trouble."

"No trouble at all, but even if it was, you're the boss."

"You'll do anything." Something in his tone made her look at Nate. A crooked grin had spread across his face. "I ask?"

For a few seconds Hannah stared into his twinkling brown eyes. *He's teasing me.* With a shake of her head, she lifted Jemma down from the chair and sent the child off to find her doll.

"Within reason."

"And who determines what's reasonable?"

Maintain boundaries. "I do." She leveled a look at Nate then

183

went back to clarifying her duties. "Cleaning the house and cooking for you and maybe your brothers, is all?"

Nate cleared his throat. "Well, Rowdy has been feeding the chickens and pigs since Alice left. I'm sure he'd appreciate it if you'd take that on."

The man asking instead of telling her what to do, as if she were a guest or visiting relative, increased the guilt already gnawing holes in her stomach. "Not a problem. I'll need to know where they're housed and where to find their feed."

"I'll show you in the morning."

"Okay, is that all?"

"Isn't that enough?"

"I want to be certain I earn my keep."

"You will. Any other questions?"

"Why …?"

"What?"

"Never mind." Hannah shook her head. "Nothing."

One eyebrow lifted, Nate crossed his arms over his chest and waited in silence.

"Well, I didn't want to be rude but … Rowdy?"

Nate laughed. "My handsome, and he knows it, brother likes to play hard. He was always up to something as a child and now has quite the reputation with the—" Jemma skipped back into the room, Daisy in hand. "I'll tell you his story another time."

"I get the gist."

"I'm sure you do." He stepped closer. "Why don't I show you how to work the stove?"

"Hinting I should start supper?"

"My tummy *is* a little growly."

Hannah couldn't help but smile at his silly comment. The next few hours passed pleasantly. With Nate's help and a well-stocked pantry, she pulled together a meal of fried salt pork, boiled potatoes, biscuits, and the last of the pears, in a short time. After they finished eating, he left to attend chores. The kitchen seemed too quiet then, even with her daughter's chatter.

Once she tossed the scraps into the slop bucket, washed the dishes, and tidied up the room in general, Hannah spent some time with Jemma. She retrieved her daughter's other doll, then settled in front of the living-room fireplace to play. Some time later, Nate and Jacob entered the house. They hauled her trunks up to the attic and brought back down a small bed frame, carrying it directly to what would be the little girl's bedroom.

With her daughter's help, Hannah made up the bed with fresh bedding, then brought Jemma's things into her new room. Although the girl seemed excited at the prospect of sleeping in her own bed, when her bedtime neared she became clingy.

While Hannah helped Jemma into her nightgown, tears started to flow. The little girl missed the boys, Alice, and even Silas. Notably she didn't cry for Jed, a man the child had called uncle. She held Jemma, soothing her until, worn out, she fell asleep.

Hannah tucked her daughter into bed beside her. In time, the little girl would adjust to changes. It didn't have to start on her first night in a new home. She lay next to Jemma for some time, listening to the soft sound of her sleeping. Tired but unable to relax, she couldn't fall asleep herself.

Restless and uneasy, Hannah finally gave up trying to sleep and crawled out of bed. She pulled on her robe and walked across the room, checking on the banked coals in the fireplace. They were still giving off some heat but her thin robe offered little protection against the cooling air. She shivered while walking back to the bed, wrapped a quilt around her, then wandered out of the room.

Down the hall, in the archway leading to the living room, Hannah paused. No lamps burned. The only light came from the fire but she sensed Nate was in the room. Flickering light cast from the low-burning flames danced over a pair of boots resting on the hearth. Her gaze searched the shadows, looking for the man. She found him sitting on the far edge of the couch, quiet and alone.

"Not tired?" Nate called out as she turned, intending to return to her room.

Hannah abandoned the idea of a quick retreat, turning back to look at him. "Exhausted, but I can't sleep."

"Me too."

"Is that why you're here instead of the bunkhouse?"

"All the snoring was disturbing my peace."

"I'm sorry." She entered the room but stopped a few feet from him.

"Not your fault."

"If I wasn't here, you'd be sleeping in the house."

"I've ignored worse. Tonight, I've a lot on my mind." Nate indicated the empty area next to him. "Care to join me?"

Hannah hesitated, then sat down, deliberately keeping a good amount of space between them. For a few moments, the only sounds came from the pinesap crackling in the fire. She shifted, moving the quilt until it draped easily around her.

His hand reached out and touched her blanket. "Cold?"

"A little."

"Looks pretty comfortable."

Memories of learning to sew and choosing the now-faded colors flickered through her mind. Her fingers trailed over the fabric. "It's the first quilt I made with my mother."

"Missing her?"

"Always."

"I'm sorry."

"I know nothing can bring her or Bessie back but..." She released a barely audible sigh. "Sometimes, it's hard... because I need a friend or just... want my mother."

"For comfort or advice?"

"Both. Ma always knew when I couldn't sleep. She'd come up to the loft and hold me, even when I was a grown woman."

186

"Sounds nice."

"It was." She stared into the flames, lost in memory. "We'd go back to her place for a night every so often after Jemma and I moved in with Bessie and Jed, just to be together."

"She sounds like a good mother."

"She was. Her *differences* made most people uneasy but they never bothered me."

"Most people think I'm ... different too."

"Oh? You seem fine to me."

To her surprise, Nate chuckled. She turned her head to look at him, puzzled by his response. In the fire-cast light, his expression was impossible to read.

Hannah decided to be direct. "What's funny?"

"Not funny exactly. Just ... you're a rare person."

"I am?"

"Few people are so accepting."

"More should be."

"Wouldn't that be nice?" Nate paused. "I think your mother and I would've been birds of a feather, so to speak."

"You're nothing like my mother."

"You don't find the Recluse of River's Bend odd? People are whispering about me all over Oregon."

"I had a child out of wedlock fathered by an outlaw, who was hung for murder. People whisper about me daily. Being gossiped about doesn't make you different, it just means you've been singled out."

"Even if part of the rumor is true?"

"Gossip starts with some truth which people distort for entertainment," Hannah stated, then curious, asked, "What part is true?"

"I do like being alone a lot. Perhaps I am a recluse."

"Are you politely trying to tell me I'm disturbing you?"

"No. To be honest, you are, but not in an unpleasant way."

Hannah stared at him, shocked speechless. It was a moment before she could speak again. "Are you flirting with me?"

"A little." A rich amount of self-amusement flavored his words.

"I don't know what to say."

"No need to say anything." He fell silent, holding her gaze some seconds before continuing. "The reason I couldn't sleep ..."

Nervous, she blurted out some possibilities. "The gossip? Rustling? Family?"

"You."

"I—"

"I wanted to talk to you again though we'd just parted."

His words touched Hannah but she shook her head. "Nate, I—"

"We've only known each other a matter of days but—"

"Nate." Her voice was low, a warning in itself.

"I like you." He continued as if she hadn't spoken. "And I'd like to get to know you better."

I can't be impulsive. I can't repeat past mistakes. "I like you too but ..."

"But?"

"But ..." *I can't encourage him, not without telling him about Michael. And I can't tell him that yet.* "It's complicated."

Silence fell. Hannah felt his tension rise. Seconds passed like hours. The desire to explain better filled her. Her lips parted but she lost her nerve, remaining quiet.

Nate finally offered a soft, bitter statement. "No woman wants to consider a man who is determined to live on the edge of a wilderness."

"This isn't about your home. To be clear." Her gaze sought out the spot where the painting hung, even though she couldn't see it well in the mostly dark room. "From what I've seen, I think River's Bend would be an amazing place to live."

"A place of near isolation, with no quick way to reach help in an emergency?" Nate challenged.

Hannah looked back at him. "Redwing Farm is a twenty-minute walk from Ashwood, less by horse, and Bessie still died. Life doesn't come with guarantees."

"Some people want them."

"I'm not some people," She asserted.

"That's what I hoped."

A number of responses swirled in her thoughts but only two words escaped her lips. "You were?"

"Yes."

"Nate, I … I can't talk about this now." Hannah clutched her blanket tighter as she got to her feet. "I need to go to bed."

"I'll be back in the morning." His casual statement sounded like a promise.

Hannah stared down at the shadowed man. "Excuse me?"

"For breakfast?"

"Oh. Yes. Of course. Good night."

"Sweet dreams."

Would getting to know him better be so bad? Hannah walked swiftly down the hall and into her bedroom. She closed the door, standing a moment with one hand resting on the knob. *As long as if I didn't allow attraction to overrule good sense, everything would be fine.* She moved across the room and put the quilt back over the foot of the bed. *But how would he react later on when, if, I tell him Michael fathered Jemma?* With a sigh, she removed her robe, slipped under the covers and closed her eyes. Sleep was a long time coming.

When Hannah woke up the next morning, sunlight streamed in through curtains not fully closed. She got up, careful not to disturb the mounded blankets on the other side of the bed, and peered out the window. A pretty winter day greeted her with a pristine blue sky above and frost dusting every surface below fuzzy white. The sight charmed her. It seemed to be a good omen for her first morning on the Bar 7.

Into the perfect scene rode a man on a black horse with four white-stocking legs. A shiver shot down her spine. Hannah shifted her weight from one foot to the other, uneasy without knowing why. The stranger pulled up and dismounted by the barn, in clear view of her window. After tying his horse to one of the corral posts, he started walking toward the house. He took off his hat a few feet from the porch, raking fingers through his hair.

The blood drained from her face and, for a second, Hannah couldn't breathe. Alarm flooded her mind, screaming at her to back away from the window, but her feet rooted to the floor. She couldn't move. Eyes wide, she continued to stare at the man.

The sound of laughter startled her as it traveled through the house. Within it were two voices, one deep and amused, Nate, and the other high-pitched and excited. Her gaze swung to the bed. The lump Hannah had assumed to be her daughter was, in fact, a pillow. Panic flooded her.

Jemma is in the kitchen.

The need to protect her child overwhelmed all else. Sweat broke out on her brow the moment she heard the front door open and shut. In a rush, Hannah dressed and pinned up her hair. She stomped her feet into her boots as another male voice joined the first two. It took great control to stride quickly instead of race down the hall. She paused in the doorway, taking a calming breath before greeting everyone.

"Good morning. I'm sorry I overslept on my first day."

"Don't worry about it." Nate smiled at her, his expression relaxed, with no hint of last night's tension. "Jemma and I had fun getting to know each other."

Hannah noted the flour covering most of the kitchen table and her daughter. "That's what you call this?"

"We made you pancakes, Mama." Jemma looked up then, a messy angel with a bright smile.

The little girl was still in her nightgown but had a large apron wrapped over it. Most of her hair had fallen out of her braids, a tangled mane of flour-dusted red flowing over her shoulders. Big splotches of white powder covered her face and hands. Hannah smiled back. The child was adorable.

"Did you now?" She leaned over and kissed the top of her daughter's head. "Thank you so much."

"Hannah." Nate touched her shoulder. She stiffened, knowing what was about to happen. Polite mask in place, she turned to face the man who rode in minutes before. "I'd like you to meet my cousin, Ben."

"Pleased to meet you."

Michael was right. Ben looked so much like Jemma's father it felt surreal. Hannah shook his hand. "Hi. It's good to meet you in person. I've heard so much about you." *Stop, you're rambling.* She pressed her lips together, stopping the nervous flow of words.

"Good things, I hope."

"Yes." She paused, then couldn't resist adding. "Alice is very fond of you."

"She wasn't sure of me at first but I grew on her."

What should I say? "I, um ..." *I know we just met but please tell me why you and your brother were estranged.* "It looks like you've met Jemma."

"Yes, ma'am. She offered me one of your pancakes. I'm afraid I couldn't resist."

"That's all right. And, please, call me Hannah."

"Hannah." Ben nodded in agreement, then looked over at her daughter, who was perched on a chair by the stove helping Nate scrape batter out of a bowl onto the griddle. "She's charming."

"Thank you. She gets that from her father."

"Nate mentioned he'd passed on. Must be rough."

"It can be." *Especially when I don't know if I should trust his family or not.*

"I'm sorry for your loss."

As am I, for yours. "Thank you."

More words caught in her throat when she noticed his gaze lingering on her daughter. Her heart started beating faster. *Can he see the resemblance?* Hannah cleared her throat. Ben looked back at her, his expression sheepish.

191

"Sorry, I can't help staring at her."

"You can't?" To Hannah's dismay, her voice shook.

"Bad choice of words, cousin."

The confusion on Ben's face was almost laughable. "What?"

"Think about it. A strange man telling a mother he can't help staring at her daughter," Nate said pointedly.

"I didn't. I mean I did, but ..." Ben shook his head, his ears turning brick-red. "I meant no offense. I'm going to be a father soon and I can't help staring at every child I see, wondering what our baby will look like."

Probably a lot like Jemma. "That's sweet."

"Did he upset you?" Nate's concern stirred up guilt.

"No, of course not." She assured him, then to Ben. "It's all right. I understand."

"I'm glad my cousin didn't offend you. His baby is certain to be beautiful as long as the little one takes after Evie."

"Thanks." Ben shot a mock glare at Nate, then looked back at Hannah. "I'll be thankful as long as he or she is healthy." He smiled, but she noticed a hint of sadness in the man's familiar-looking green eyes. "Evie would love to meet you. May I bring her over tomorrow?"

"That would be lovely." *Maybe during the visit I can learn something significant.*

"Great, we'll see you then." Ben shifted his gaze to the little girl Nate was helping up to the table. "Good bye, Jemma." He started for the door, calling over his shoulder, "I'll be in the barn."

Nate pushed a plate of scrambled eggs and a pancake closer to her daughter. "He meant no harm. Ben's good man."

"So I've heard."

"From Alice?"

"And others."

"Oh? Who?" He walked toward her, his expression curious at first, then smoothed. "Claire spoke of him yesterday, didn't she?"

"Yes."

"What about me?"

"Yes, you talked about him."

"No. I meant did Alice talk about me?"

"Some."

Without a single point of contact, she felt his presence physically. Wisps of desire traveled along her nerves. Nate bent his head, leaning in so close she felt his breath on her lips when he spoke.

"Like what?"

Hannah licked her lips. "I can't remember exactly now."

"Why?" He asked softly, a whisper meant only for her, as his gaze held hers prisoner.

"Because you're … you are …"

Nate straightened. He studied her a moment then, blinking rapidly, took a step back. "I need to head out soon. Ben and I have a lead to track down." In silence, she watched him stride back to Jemma. "I'll be back after noon to take you on a tour of the ranch." He tousled her daughter's hair, then moved toward the door. "Please pack us a basket lunch."

A minute later, Hannah heard the front door open then slam shut. He was gone before she could respond. She stared at the empty doorway for a number of seconds, gathering her scattered wits. Needing an outlet for all the energy humming through her veins now, she got busy.

Nate entered the barn and followed a low soothing voice until he walked up behind his cousin. Jack, his horse, and Ben's mount, Sugar, flanked the man. "Ready?"

"Yes." Ben rubbed a gloved hand down his mare's neck as he handed Nate Jack's reins.

The men walked their horses outside, mounted and headed toward town. Nate flipped the collar of his wool-lined jacket up, protecting his neck against the icy wind. Hooves crunched against frozen earth. When they reached the curve in the Bar 7's drive, he glanced back at the ranch house. *I wonder what she's doing now.*

"She's a pretty one."

Nate turned his attention to the road ahead. "Jemma?"

"Her mother."

"Don't think Evie would appreciate you noticing."

"Evie knows she's the only woman for me," Ben asserted calmly. "But she'll find it interesting how much you're *noticing* ..."

"Hannah."

"Hannah," he echoed, amused.

"I'm just being friendly."

"Exactly."

"I'm friendly to people."

"Family and those few you know well."

Nate tried changing the subject. "How's Evie?"

"She's fine, as I told you before. Claire is with her." Ben kept pace right beside him. "Are you sweet on Hannah?"

"I'm not a schoolboy."

"You didn't answer my question."

"I'm the only person she knows here. I'm trying to make her feel welcome."

"By entertaining her daughter? Making her breakfast?"

"I didn't plan to ... It just happened."

"Interesting. You usually avoid women."

"Believing gossip now?"

"No, believing Claire. And my own eyes."

"There's just ..." Nate shook his head then glanced over at his cousin. "Something about her."

Ben studied him for a long moment. "I understand."

Silence fell. Several minutes passed. The outskirts of Fir Mountain appeared in the distance before Nate spoke again.

"Did our dear little cousin tell you anything more than what you told me earlier?"

"About your lunch with—"

Nate speared him with a hard look. "About Miss Collier."

"Oh …" Ben didn't appear in the least cowed. Nate braced for further inquisition, then relaxed when his cousin moved on. "No, pretty much all she said was the woman has been receiving too many deliveries. In Claire's opinion, far more supplies than could possibly be used."

"So Miss Collier is either bad at managing her business or there's something more than flour in her store room."

"Exactly."

"And you think this connects to the rustling because?"

"My criminal—" His cousin broke off when Nate delivered another glare, looking back at the man calmly for a couple of seconds before going on. "I appreciate you don't want to think of me as such, but my past is what it is."

"Whatever you may have done before, you're a good man now."

"Yes, and I strive hard every single day to remain so."

"Then why bring up your past? All you've recalled of that time are a few flashes."

"Because Claire's right. My gut tells me there's something off about that woman." A look of pure frustration flashed in Ben's eyes. "But I can't tell you what."

"Ever think it's just instinct or smarts giving you that impression? She's made it a point to share the *observation* that you arrived in Fir Mountain about when the rustling started."

"Which is true."

"As is the fact that she moved here shortly before you and Evie did."

"I know, but—"

"And Claire, the friendliest person I know, took an instant dislike to her."

"I know."

"Now add in these odd deliveries. In a town this small, how likely is it all explained by coincidence?"

"Not very."

"Leave your past where it belongs, behind you."

"Working on it."

The men entered Fir Mountain, riding by the first few buildings. "Sean meeting up with us?"

"Our good deputy isn't back yet."

"Thought he was only escorting the marshal and his prisoners to Bend."

"Stagecoach ran late."

"So we're on our own."

"Yes, and I promised Evie we wouldn't do anything crazy."

"Well, then, let's find a spot to lay low, watch and learn."

"Exciting." Ben grimaced. "Think I'd rather be home helping crochet booties."

"I'd rather be home too." To Nate's surprise, an image of Hannah, not his homestead, drifted through his mind.

His cousin turned off the main street, riding at a walk into an alley. Nate followed. Already, he found the constant noises of town annoying. *It's going to be a long morning.*

Hours flew by for Hannah. First, she sat down with Jemma and ate, with appropriate gusto, the breakfast her daughter had made for her. A beaming smile was her reward. Next, the young woman tackled the kitchen, setting it to rights. Once the surfaces were clean, she heated water on the stove, pulled a tub out of the pantry, then bathed the little girl.

When Hannah carried a towel-wrapped Jemma into her bedroom, she noticed little light streamed in through the curtains. She took a moment to open them fully before grabbing fresh clothing for the child. Gray clouds filled the sky. Disappointment dampened her spirits as she helped her daughter dress. A ride around the ranch seemed unlikely now.

Nevertheless, Hannah swiftly completed the familiar task of braiding Jemma's hair, then did what Nate had asked of her. She returned to the kitchen, making lunch, while her daughter played on the floor near her feet. She baked a pan of biscuits, boiled eggs, and put those items, along with some jam and butter, into a hamper she found in the pantry. As she finished washing the last dish dirtied by her efforts, the eldest Rolfe brother returned.

"A storm is rolling in. I'm sorry but the tour will have to wait." Nate seemed a bit distracted.

"That's all right." Hannah started unpacking their lunch, setting the food out on the table. As she finished, rain began to fall, hitting gently on the roof. "We'll find another time."

"I'll make sure," he promised.

When she turned, offering him a smile of thanks, the look in his eyes captured her attention. After a moment, her cheeks heated as Hannah realized he'd been speaking but she hadn't heard a word. "I'm sorry, what did you say?"

"Can you both ride?" His tone held some amusement, signaling he knew why she'd been distracted. She noted with interest that her daughter went to Nate for assistance getting onto a chair instead of asking her.

Regardless if it was because they'd left Jed's household or Nate's kind interactions, her little girl was behaving more like the fearless, happy child she'd once been every day. Last night, despite all the tears shed before falling asleep, her daughter hadn't suffered a nightmare. A warm feeling washed over Hannah.

I made the right decision.

"I do." She set plates down for each of them while Nate settled the girl. "But Jemma doesn't, she's only four."

"That's a little old to start, but there's still time to teach her."

He must be joking. "Excuse me?"

"It's best she learns soon."

"Don't you think she's a bit young?" Hannah filled her child's plate then nodded permission for her to start eating without waiting for them.

"I was in the saddle before I could walk."

Eyebrows raised, she held his gaze. "You remember that?"

"No." Nate chuckled. "Ma told me. Said my father started riding around with me sitting in the saddle in front of him when I was still a babe. I don't remember not being able to ride."

Imagination painted a picture in her mind of the boy he once was with his father. She almost smiled but then the image shifted. The tall cowboy became Nate and the little boy in his arms, Jemma. Then the child transformed again, becoming a small boy with his father's hazel eyes and her bright hair. She shook her head, mentally pushing the imagery aside.

"You don't believe me?"

"I've no reason to doubt you."

"Then, may I teach her?"

"Will you keep her safe?"

His gaze caught and held hers. Something in his expression made her breath quicken. Lost in the moment, she leaned closer.

"Mama," Jemma piped up, startling her mother.

Hannah closed her eyes for a couple of seconds, pushing down disappointment for what exactly she couldn't say. "Yes."

"I'm done. Can I play?"

"May I," She gently corrected.

In a sunny mood, her daughter's smile was wide, making dimples on her cheeks that were endearing. "May I, Mama?"

"Yes, you may." She smiled back at the little girl.

Jemma didn't wait for help. She wiggled off the chair, then skipped straight out of the kitchen. After a moment, her voice drifted through the walls, talking to her toys. Nervous, Hannah got up from the table, put fresh grounds in the coffee pot, then set it on the stove to heat.

"She doesn't mind playing alone?"

"Jemma is used to it." Hannah walked back, taking a seat at the table. "Jason and John were often busy with chores or at school."

"Does she miss them?" Nate pulled out the chair next to her and sat as well.

Hannah picked up a biscuit, broke it in two halves, then spread blackberry jam over them both. "We both do. I hope Alice can bring the boys for a visit soon."

"But not Jed?"

"No." She sighed, looking down at her food without touching it. "Not until he's better. Jemma is …"

"Happier?"

"She is but I feel badly for Alice and the boys … and Jed. I wish something could be done."

Nate reached out, covering her hand with his. "As soon as Sam gets back, I'll send him down."

"You really think he can help?"

"As I said before, I hope so. They were close once."

"I feel guilty for leaving." Their physical connection drew her gaze. His touch was both comforting and distracting.

"As do I. If I didn't have prior obligations …"

Hannah glanced over at him. Nate was staring at their hands as she'd been doing. She moved so their palms touched and squeezed.

"What could you have done?"

"I don't know."

"That's the root of the guilt, isn't it?"

"Not knowing what to do?"

"Yes."

"Yes," he agreed, lifting his gaze to meet hers.

The sound of her heartbeat filled her ears. Her breath hitched. Uneasy, Hannah pulled her hand free and stood up.

"Would you like some coffee?"

"Sure."

Hannah poured them each a mug, then set the pot back on the stove to keep warm. On the way back to the table, she paused in the doorway and checked on Jemma. Her daughter was playing some sort of game with her dolls and crocheted animals. She watched the little girl for a moment, then walked on, handing Nate his steaming cup before reclaiming her seat.

For the rest of the meal their conversation focused on less personal matters. They chatted about the weather, the need for more firewood and how the borrowed mules, Nell and Molly, were faring. After several minutes, Hannah relaxed. It was amazing how easy it was to be around Nate at times. Finished with her meal, she stood up and started clearing the table.

We could be friends. Hannah placed the dirty dishes by the sink. *As long as I ignore the attraction.* She turned, intending to go back for more and gasped.

Chapter 14

"Are you all right?"

One hand came up, resting over her pounding heart. "Heavens no, you startled me."

"Sorry." Instead of moving out of her way, Nate reached around her and placed the dishes he'd carried over beside those she'd stacked.

"How on earth do you move so quietly?"

Nate shrugged, giving her a crooked grin. "Ma threatened to put a cow bell on my belt a time or two while I was growing up."

"I could see the benefit."

"Do you now?" His smile broadened and there was a twinkle in his eye. "I need to go. Thanks for lunch."

"You're welcome. Will we see you for supper?"

Nate nodded, then strode away. Her gaze followed him as he headed toward the mudroom. At the doorway, he paused and looked back at her, his expression now somber. "I enjoy your company."

With those four words, Nathaniel Rolfe stole a piece of her heart. She chided herself for allowing the man to stir up her affections inwardly. But that didn't stop the flood of warmth from flowing through her veins or wipe the smile from her face much of the rest of her day. Her pleasant mood carried on for hours while she tidied the kitchen, made a routine for the chores, then settled Jemma down in her own tiny room for a nap.

The storm started gently, the first snowflake falling at almost suppertime. Jemma danced with excitement when she woke up and heard the news. The little girl kept running to the large living-room window, pressing her nose against the glass every few minutes to see how much snow had piled up, until it was too dark to see. The three Rolfe brothers walked into the house as Hannah was promising yet again that she'd take her outside to play in it soon.

"Do you mind if they join us tonight?" Nate indicated his companions with a wave of his hand.

"Of course not."

"I didn't give you any warning, though. Will there be enough to go around?"

"I made a roast. There's plenty," Hannah assured him, with a smile, hiding her disappointment it wouldn't be just the three of them and the slight panic she felt, trying to figure out how to stretch a meal meant for three to accommodate five. "Should we move to the dining room?"

"We'll be fine in the kitchen, a little cramped but cozy."

His warm smile eased her anxiety. "All right, if you all will wait with Jemma, I'll have supper ready shortly."

The men settled in the living room while she quickly moved to the pantry. Hannah grabbed an armful of supplies, items she'd gathered earlier, intending to use tomorrow. She added onions and dried mushrooms to the fried potatoes. After doubling her normal recipe, she poured cornbread batter into a pan. She pulled the roast out of the oven, slid the bread in to bake and moved on to opening several cans of beans, dumping them into another pan to heat. Lastly, she added more roast drippings to the gravy, thickening it with starch.

Hands on her hips, Hannah looked everything over. *It's the best I can do.* She set out extra plates, then called everyone in for dinner. Although she anticipated an awkward evening, it ended up being fun.

Nate's brothers shared good-natured ribbing as well as interesting bits of news. She learned Jacob would be returning to Corvallis College soon and Rowdy never dated a girl longer than a month. Sam thought his feelings for a daughter of another rancher were a well-kept secret but all his brothers knew. And the latest gossip in town wasn't about any of the Rolfe men, but Claire. Some townswomen were shocked her wedding dress would be red, her favorite color, not an 'appropriate' blue or brown.

When the meal was over, Hannah was sad to see them go. The kitchen felt too quiet after the younger brothers left. After giving Jemma her doll to play with, she started clearing the table. Nate pitched in despite her protests and the clean-up went fast. With the last dish washed, she turned from the sink and noticed her daughter's droopy eyelids.

"Excuse me. I need to put Jemma to bed." She took off her apron and hung it on a hook on the wall.

"Are you going to bed too?"

"Did you need something else?"

"Um … no."

"If you're still hungry I can make you something as soon as she's asleep."

"No, I'm fine. Thank you, though."

Hannah studied him closely, worried that she'd misunderstood something. Nate looked uncomfortable. "Did I do something wrong? Would you rather Jemma and I take our meals separately?"

"No. No. That's not it."

Her daughter came over and leaned against her skirt. Hannah reached down, smoothing the little girl's hair. "What is it, then?"

"Would you like to … sit by the fire … with me for a while?"

Relieved, she smiled. "I'd like that."

Nate nodded, then immediately walked away, heading into the

living room. She scooped up her daughter and followed him. As he moved in the direction of the fireplace, Hannah crossed to the hallway and strode quickly to her room. Once there, she focused on settling Jemma down for the night.

Almost an hour later Hannah walked back toward the living room, feeling a little nervous. Tonight there was an oil lamp burning on a side table near the end of the hallway. When she entered the room, Nate was again sitting on the couch.

"Hello."

Her gaze met his, then skittered away, looking at the flames dancing high. "Hi."

The sound of wind howling pierced the walls, capturing her attention as it battered the window. Hannah moved over to look through the glass. In the dark, she saw little beyond shadows.

"The storm is picking up. We have a good foot of snow now and I expect double by morning."

Hannah turned, moving across the room toward him. "Is this normal?"

"Yes."

"I've never seen it snow so much."

"We'll have storms like this, or worse, until spring."

"Really?" She sat down on the opposite end of the couch from Nate. "Jemma will love that."

"She seemed excited."

"Very."

A long moment passed in silence, then Nate cleared his throat. "I doubt you'll have company tomorrow."

"I assumed the snowfall would keep them home, especially Evie." Hannah shifted, adjusting her skirt with nervous sweeps of her hands.

"Ben is very protective of her."

"Because of her condition?"

"Because he loves her."

"That's good." She shifted again. "Um … speaking of Ben, did you find out anything new this morning?"

Nate lifted his arm onto the top of the couch back. His fingertips barely brushed her shoulder yet her nerves hummed with awareness. His weary sigh brought her focus back to the conversation.

"Maybe."

"You don't seem pleased about it."

"Had to spend the whole morning in town."

"Oh, did you track someone there?"

"No. Claire discovered something and with both Matt and his deputy gone, Ben promised we'd check it out."

"I'm guessing it didn't involve tracking."

"No, just hours of lurking about, surrounded by people."

Her eyebrows shot up. "Surrounded?"

"Well." He grinned. "Surrounded might be a strong word."

"You don't like being around many people do you?"

"No, a few at a time is enough."

"Do you mind if I ask why?"

"No grand explanation, just how I've always been."

"Even as a child?"

Nate nodded. "Used to worry Ma half to death disappearing for hours by myself."

"I can understand. If Jemma ran off I'd be beside myself."

"You're a good mother."

"Thank you."

Silence fell between them. After a moment, Hannah turned the conversation back to his activity in town. "Can you tell me what you were in Fir Mountain checking on?"

"Matt suspects a particular business person is involved in the rustling somehow. He's all but certain she's the one who's feeding the gossip about me and Ben, which also ties in somehow."

"This business person, is her name Lizzie Jane?"

"You've heard of her?"

"Claire pointed her out at the restaurant."

"Interesting. Now I know why my little cousin was in town for lunch alone in questionable weather."

"You think she was spying on her?"

"Yes."

"Does Claire help the sheriff too?"

Nate laughed. "No, but she writes for a few newspapers and loves nailing down a good story. Recently, her curiosity landed her in trouble."

"With the law?"

"No. With Matt and our family."

"What happened?"

"She followed a dangerous man alone. He tried to ride off with her. Lucky for her, Matt and I were riding toward town then. If we hadn't been ... well, Billy Nash had killed before."

Her eyes open wide, Hannah stared at him. "One of the Nash brothers kidnapped her? The ones hung in Silver Falls City?"

"Yes." Nate stood up, went over and put another round on the fire. He stared into the flames for a few seconds before turning to look at her. "Claire is a lot more careful now."

"Heavens, I hope so."

Nate sat back down on the couch. "Anyway, she noticed Miss Collier receiving *a lot* of deliveries at her bakery."

"How does that connect to rustling?"

"I don't know, but my gut tells me it is ... somehow."

"I'm guessing you didn't find any stolen cattle today."

"No, she just received another wagonload of full flour sacks though her store room appears quite full."

"Did you sneak down and rip one open?"

"Wanted to. Didn't. Best to wait for Matt."

"You're quite a patient man."

"I am." His tone held the solemn ring of a promise given.

Instinctively, she knew those words weren't in reference to the rustling investigation. Hannah felt a soft touch on the back of her hand and for five heartbeats she hesitated, feeling him waiting. *Friendship or ...?* Her gaze met his as the lamp sputtered out, leaving them with only the firelight. She turned over her hand slowly and held his. *What if I—?*

Hannah didn't finish her thought. She didn't want to be logical. She just wanted to enjoy the moment. They sat like this, without exchanging a word, until the clock on the mantel chimed. Alerted to the late hour, she pulled free. *Is it wrong to like his company so much?*

"Good night," she quietly wished Nate, taking her leave.

Over the next two weeks, while the bitter cold and deep snow kept visitors away, sitting with Nate by the fire each evening became routine. Every day Hannah felt they grew closer, building a friendship and her desire for a deeper relationship. But she continued to hold onto her secret. Trust was difficult. Trusting him. Trusting herself.

Getting to know Nate and two of his brothers to some extent hadn't eased her mind. Hannah liked them. Jemma liked them. And they seemed to like her and her little girl. With her daughter happily settling in, revealing her father's identity troubled Hannah even more. *What am I missing, Michael?*

One afternoon the sky finally cleared, allowing the sun to cast down warmth. The snow started melting. Hannah knew their time virtually alone wouldn't last much longer. Visitors would come. Somehow, she needed to talk to Ben about his brother. She had to make a decision at some point. Then things would change.

Her thoughts wandered while Nate told her about his plans that evening. She barely heard him mention welcoming this break in the weather so he could check in with the sheriff. Rustling was the farthest thing from Hannah's mind. Matters of the heart held her attention.

It can't be love. I loved Michael. She glanced at the man sitting beside her, then back at the dancing flames. *And this is different.*

With Jemma's father, her emotions had always been in a tense or excited state. *That intensity is part of falling in love.* A twinge of sadness touched her heart. *Isn't it?* Hannah suppressed a sigh. She'd never know if that riding at full speed into the wind while standing in the stirrups feeling would've remained or faded over time.

I can't be falling for Nate. With him, she'd felt the same immediate draw, but the emotions he stirred were not. *Well, not exactly.* Hannah glanced at him again, letting the richness of his deep voice wash over her before looking away. She enjoyed listening to him but loved spending time with the man, even when he barely spoke a word. Warmth filled her when he walked into her sight and when he wasn't she missed him. *It can't be love.*

Maybe affection? Hannah considered the idea a moment, then set it aside. She was fond of Nate's brothers but her feelings for the man himself differed.

Friendship perhaps? She and Bessie had a close bond, like sisters. The emotion was similar but not the same. *Because he's a man? No.* She rejected the thought almost immediately. Before Jed fell apart, they'd been good friends for years. However, her feelings for the man paled in comparison to those Nate inspired.

It can't be love, though. Her feelings for him were strong and growing stronger each day but they weren't intense. *Except … Whenever Nate touched her, or was about to, suddenly she became aware of him in a deep, primal way.*

"I need to go home soon." His statement drew her attention.

"You miss it?"

"Need to check on my horses."

"You have horses there?"

"Yes. A trapper friend is wintering at River's Bend, caring for them while I'm gone. I trust him but …"

"You need to see them in person." She glanced over at his sister's painting. "Why did you name it River's Bend?"

"I didn't. My father did so because he built the cabin on a bend of the North Santiam River."

"Is that the one he built?" She waved toward the painting.

"Yes, but I've added on to it since then."

The undercurrent of deep emotion in his tone made her look back at Nate. Their gazes met and held. Hannah felt … safe, like she could lean forward into his arms and be sheltered. But, at the same time, temptation beckoned. His voice flowed over her but the words went unheard as desire crept in, a slow-building yet powerful heat. Her gaze dropped to his mouth.

"Hannah." The intense way he said her name got through to her. She looked up, into his eyes. "We're friends?"

Sort of. Maybe. Yes. "I think so."

"Good, I—"

"Do you ever kiss friends?" As soon as the question popped out of her mouth, Hannah wanted to run away and hide. Yet she couldn't move or even look away, needing his answer.

"Sometimes." His eyes seemed to darken. Nate shifted to face her, sitting sideways. "On the cheek."

"But not a proper kiss?"

"No."

"Would you now?"

"Would I what?" He leaned closer.

Hannah felt his breath warming her lips. "Kiss me."

His gaze became more intense. His hand rose, touching her cheek briefly before moving to cup the nape of her neck. "I can, but I can't promise anything more."

"All I want is a kiss."

Chapter 15

Nate studied her for so long she worried he was going to make a polite excuse and leave. Instead, so slowly her heart almost exploded in her chest, he lowered his mouth to touch hers. The kiss was soft, sweet, and lingered on. He pulled away, leaving her senses flooded. In that moment, nothing existed for her but him. She shifted closer, wanting another taste of him.

His hands came up and gently gripped her arms, holding her apart. "I think you best go to bed now."

Hannah stared at him for several seconds before coming to her senses. With a shake of her head, she pulled back, then stood up in a clumsy fashion. She mumbled good night, and without waiting for a reply, scurried off.

Inside her room, Hannah sagged against the closed door. Her limbs laden, she shuffled over to the bed, plopping down. She put her heated face in her hands. *What was I thinking?*

I am a mother. I have responsibilities. Acting on impulse, allowing romantic notions to sweep away her good sense couldn't happen. *Not again.*

Hannah stood up, wearily changing into her nightgown. She then crawled into bed and curled up on her side. Without concern for her future or the possible impact on her daughter, she'd let herself be caught up in the moment. *In him.* She pulled up the blankets, leaving only her face uncovered. *I know better.*

She reached out a hand, touching her sleeping daughter's shoulder. Although Jemma now consistently napped in her own room, at night she still wanted to be in her mother's bed. She'd allowed feelings for Nate, whatever they were, to distract her from what was important. Redwing Farm would belong to the bank sooner than later, Alice would then bring the boys to the Bar 7, and Hannah would be out of a job. She had to secure a permanent position to support her little girl. Tomorrow she'd write new letters of inquiry and ask Nate and his brothers for suggestions on where to send them. She drew in a deep breath and closed her eyes, praying sleep would come soon.

Out in the bunkhouse Nate remained wide awake. Usually the loud snoring and ripe odor of numerous unwashed males in a small space disturbed his peace. Tonight, he barely noticed. A certain woman occupied all his thoughts.

It was just one kiss. Nate rolled on his side and pulled part of his pillow over his ear, muffling the obnoxious sounds around him out of habit. Eyes closed, an image of Hannah flowed through his mind. The curve of her cheek bathed in firelight was so clear he could count the dusting of freckles on her skin. And he wanted to kiss each one. He flopped onto his back with a growl of frustration, staring at the ceiling.

How did she become so important to me? He'd found a number of women attractive in his lifetime but only with one other had Nate felt such a strong emotional response. *But this isn't the same.* His relationship with Faith had grown out of a childhood friendship and the way he'd loved her had been … gentler.

However, his physical draw to Hannah often threatened to, and occasionally did, overcome his good sense. *I shouldn't have kissed her.* Control had never been an issue before. But, with this woman … He couldn't stop thinking about her, how sweet her slightest touch felt, the scent of roses on her skin and how much he wanted to be in her company again only moments after leaving her side.

It's pointless. She was leaving as soon as Alice came back and given the state of Jed's farm that wouldn't be long. *What if I hire her to do the books?* The housekeeper's suggestion tempted him. If she accepted and Pa approved it'd keep her and Jemma on the Bar 7. *But what then?*

Despite her comments to the contrary, Nate wasn't convinced Hannah would actually like living at River's Bend. Faith grew up with him. She'd known his plans for years, long before agreeing to marry him. Yet, she'd thought he'd change his mind and give up his dream. The memory of her crestfallen expression when he shared his plans to improve the cabin for her, his soon-to-be bride, remained vivid. She'd broken their engagement by the end of that conversation.

For quite some time, he'd been angry at Faith, especially after learning she'd married Randy Haze. Nate hadn't been fit to be around anyone for weeks following the news. Slowly, the hurt lessened, his outrage faded, and he'd come to realize the break-up was mostly his fault. Every woman interested in him since his ex-fiancée expressed a desire to *heal his heart so he'd move out of the wilderness.* They believed the gossip because it made more sense to them than the truth. Obviously, few people wanted the mostly isolated life he preferred. And he refused to compromise.

Daily, his feelings for Hannah deepened. The logical thing to do would be to put up boundaries and stick to friendship. *But what if she's one of those rare women who might enjoy living on River's Bend?* If Nate backed away from starting a relationship with her, he'd never know. *What if I discover she hates it after losing my heart? What if I've already lost it?* Troubled, sleep remained elusive long into the night, questions haunting him.

Hannah felt awkward the next morning as Nate entered the house with his brothers. He greeted her with a smile, treating her no different from the day before. Her tension started to ease. Listening to the men's familiar bantering while she served them biscuits and gravy further melted her reserve. By the end of the meal, she felt almost normal.

It didn't take long to set the kitchen to rights after the men left. Once the morning chores were finished, Hannah brought out some wooden blocks Jed had cut and sanded for her daughter last Christmas. She started writing letters with Jemma happily playing on the floor. While she worked, sunlight streamed in through the large living-room window. She'd just finished her third letter when a noise outside drew her attention.

A buggy drove into the yard, pulling up right in front of the house. Claire stepped out, bundled up for the weather but easily recognizable, as a lone rider came up next to her. Ben dismounted, tying his horse to a post, then going over to help a second woman out of the horse-drawn vehicle. Although she too wore bulky outer clothing, Hannah guessed her to be Evie, his wife. He pulled out a huge bag from the buggy, then escorted the women to the front door.

Hannah glanced down, checking to see if her daughter was still entertained. Jemma had built two block towers and her rag dolls were in the process of knocking them down. She stood up and took off her apron, quickly crossing the room to hang it on the back of the kitchen door. A knock echoed through the house as she wiped damp palms on her skirt. After taking a deep, calming breath, she went over and answered the door.

"Hi, I'm finally here to visit." Claire greeted her with a broad smile, waving at the other woman. "I brought Evie to meet you. She was going crazy stuck in the cabin with Ben hovering over her."

"Hello, please come in."

The women stepped inside but Ben didn't. "I'm going to go settle the horses then tend chores while you visit, if that's okay?"

Evie reached up and flipped back her hood, smiling at her husband. "Go on now, I'll be fine."

"You'll send Claire out for me if—"

"I feel the slightest twinge. Promise. Now go." Although her words were firm, loving amusement infused her statement.

Ben leaned in, giving his wife a lingering kiss through the open doorway. Their interaction had a smile tugging at Hannah's lips. They seemed to be a lovely, loving couple. When he finally walked away, she closed the door and helped her guests out of their things, hanging them on pegs by the doorway.

"It's so nice to meet you." Evie grinned at her.

"And you as well, please take a seat by the fire."

"Thank you."

As Hannah led through the living room, she called to her daughter. "Jemma."

"Yes, Mama."

"Come say hello to our visitors."

The little girl ran over, stopping by Hannah to smile shyly up at the women. "Hello."

Claire held up the big bag she carried so Hannah could see something though the opening. "May I?"

"Of course. That's so nice of you, thank you."

"Hi, Jemma." Claire knelt down in front of the child and pulled out a doll made of rolled yarn, offering it to her. "I made this for you."

Her eyes wide, Jemma clutched the doll to her chest. "Thank you."

"You are most welcome."

"Hello, Jemma." Evie sat down on the couch while Claire got to her feet. "My name is Evie."

"Hi. Why do you have a big tummy?"

"Jemma." Appalled, Hannah choked out her daughter's name.

"It's okay." Evie smiled. "It is big."

Hannah shook her head. "Jemma, you need to tell Mrs. Rolfe you're sorry. It isn't polite to ask a question like that."

Jemma looked at her mother a moment before turning back to Evie. "I'm sorry, Mrs. Rolfe."

"It's okay, sweetie."

The little girl leaned closer to her mother, then whispered in a tone that carried across the room. "Why can't I ask about her really big tummy, Mama?"

Hannah's face heated. She could hear the laughter the other women were trying to stifle. She tried not to think of how worse the situation might have been if Evie had been merely a large woman instead of one who was expecting.

"Because it isn't nice to ask people about their body."

"Even when their tummy is really, really big."

"Yes."

"Oh." For a moment, Jemma's face scrunched up as if she was thinking it over hard. "Sorry, Mama."

"It's okay."

Her daughter stretched up on the tips of her toes, trying to whisper in Hannah's ear. "But why is her tummy big?"

"Jemma." Hannah gasped, wishing the floor would open up and swallow her. "Mrs. Rolfe is going to have a baby."

"Oh, like Meadowlark." Satisfied with the explanation, she immediately scampered away to play with her new toy.

"Meadowlark?"

"A mare that foaled this year."

"I see." Claire sounded as though she was still suppressing laughter.

"I'm so sorry."

"There's nothing to be sorry for." Gracious, Evie smiled. "She's adorable." She patted her stomach. "If this one is a girl, I hope she's like Jemma."

The chances of that are greater than you know. "That's nice of you to say."

"I mean it."

"Thank you." She liked this woman already. A needle-sharp feeling of guilt pricked her. Every day her secret felt heavier to carry. Hannah prayed that soon, maybe even today, she'd learn something to put her worries to rest. "Would either of you like a cup of coffee?"

"I'd love a glass of water if you don't mind?"

"Not at all. Claire?"

"Water would be great."

"I'll be right back."

Hannah hurried into the kitchen. She pulled a large glass pitcher from the cupboard near the door. Thankful, once more, for the convenience of having water piped into the house, she filled it, then set it and four cups onto a tray, carrying it all into the living room.

When she returned, Hannah noticed Jemma was showing Evie her favorite rag doll, Daisy. She put the tray down on the table by the couch then poured each of them a cup. The girl took a few swallows from hers and set it back down on the tray, skipping off to play again.

"Thank you." Evie sipped from her glass. "Your daughter really is quite charming."

"Thank you."

"All right." Claire moved around, almost pacing. "Before we start asking the important questions, do you knit or crochet?"

The other woman's energy was a little overwhelming, but in a nice way. "I crochet."

"Great, we do too. I brought a few of the projects we're making, for Evie's baby and my wedding. Would you like to help work on one while we visit?"

Pleased to be included, she nodded with enthusiasm. "I'd love to. Excuse me a moment and I'll fetch my things."

Once more, Hannah rushed out of the room. She returned in minutes with a bag of her own in hand. Before sitting back down on the couch next to Evie, she added a couple of rounds to the fire. On the cushions between the women were several projects, a couple of blankets, numerous white yarn roses and many booties.

"Are the roses for your wedding?" Hannah glanced at Claire.

The other woman nodded. "Not many flowers bloom this time of year and I wanted a bouquet that would last forever."

"They're pretty." Hannah pointed to one half-finished baby blanket, recognizing the stitch. "May I work on this one?"

Claire reached down and picked it up, handing her the item in response. "Some people think crocheting flowers is crazy."

"I don't," Hannah assured her with a smile. "A relative of mine made all sorts of things by crochet, including flowers."

"How nice."

"I thought so."

"So … what do you think of the Bar 7?" Claire moved a chair, positioning it so she could sit facing the other women.

Hannah put her hook to pale-green yarn. "It's peaceful."

"Does it bother you being so far from town?" Evie picked up a sunshine-yellow blanket.

"No. I grew up on a tiny farm with only my mother and our few animals for company most of the time."

"You don't mind the quiet?"

Claire's question seemed pointed and almost too casual. Hannah felt as if she were missing something. "No … though I guess it depends on the reason for it."

"Oh?"

The other woman said nothing more as she started working on a pair of brick-red booties. Hannah considered offering a polite non-answer but hesitated. She didn't want to chance wrecking the potential for friendship. Although Alice was a wonderful person and a good friend, she missed talking to a woman her own age.

"Quiet because we're snowed in or night has fallen is …" she paused, searching for the right word. "Comfortable. But when it's because no one knows what to say or is worried how someone else will react then it's … not good."

"Is that how things are at Jed's place?"

Startled, she struggled to respond. "I …"

"We know about Jed," Evie said gently.

Hannah looked at each woman in turn. "You do?"

"Nate told Ben. Ben told me. I shared with Claire."

"Oh." She'd been trying to think of a simple way to explain how it had been at Redwing Farm since Bessie's death. Now, she felt both relieved and at a loss.

"I'm told Jed is a good man. Maybe all he needs is more time." Evie spoke softly and with obvious sympathy.

"I hope so."

"Sorry about Bessie." Her dark eyes pools of compassion, Claire interjected. "She was a lot of fun when they visited. I understand you were close."

A lump formed in her throat. It took Hannah a moment to respond. "Like sisters."

Evie reached out, putting a hand on her arm. "I'm sorry."

"Thank you."

Hannah looked down at the work in her hands, needing to shore up her composure. As if sensing that, the other women crocheted in silence until Claire finished her booties. When she started another pair, in forest green this time, Nate's cousin moved the conversation along.

"What will you do when Alice comes home?"

"Claire." Evie sounded aghast.

"I meant no offense."

Hannah smiled briefly. "None taken."

"Do you have another job lined up?"

Evie shook her head but remained silent.

"Not yet. And that worries me."

"Would it help if I ask around and find out if anyone is looking for a housekeeper?"

"If it's not an imposition, I'd be very grateful."

"It would be my pleasure."

"Thank you. By the way, though I don't mind working as a

housekeeper and will again if that's all the work I can find, I'm trained as a bookkeeper."

"Bookkeeping." Claire looked thoughtful. "Interesting. Most businesses and ranches around here handle their own books. Few hire outsiders."

"I've run into that, a lot." A grim note entered Hannah's voice, all too aware of the challenges she faced.

"Don't worry. I'm sure Nate won't turn you out in the cold before you find something."

"He's been very kind but I don't want charity."

"Something will turn up. Have faith," Evie put in.

"Thank you." Out of the corner of her eye, she saw Claire's lips part. To forestall another question Hannah asked one of her own. "If you don't mind, when do you expect your baby?"

"Any time now."

"Really? That's exciting."

Evie smiled, glowing with happiness. "Honestly, I'm a bit scared but I can't wait to hold this baby. I feel like I've been waiting forever for him or her."

"I felt like that with Jemma. Maybe all women feel that way with their first child."

"Actually, this is my second." Evie glanced over at the little girl playing on the rug to the left of the rough circle they'd formed. "Our first was born too soon and passed away."

"I'm so sorry."

"Thank you. Mostly I'm at peace with it, but sometimes as we wait for this baby it's hard not to think of him and wish there was a little James Michael Rolfe with us."

Michael. The name couldn't be a coincidence. They'd named their firstborn son after Ben's brother. *Why would they do that if something went seriously wrong between the men? Did that mean the issue was with the other Rolfes? With Nate?*

Evie had to know the answer. All Hannah had to do was ask and the mystery would be over. But how?

By the way, even though we just met, may I ask you a deeply personal question about your husband? Yeah, no. Even if that didn't offend her, how would I explain knowing there's a problem in his family in the first place? Maybe if I can get her talking about Ben...

"Evie, I—"

Without warning, the sound of heavy footsteps echoed through the house. Hannah forgot what she was going to say and looked over at the kitchen doorway. Nate and Ben walked into the room, both carrying an armful of pine rounds. Confused, she glanced over at the stack of wood on the wall near the fireplace then back at the men. There was no need for what they were doing.

"You didn't need to rope Nate into unnecessary work so you can check on me, my dear husband. Just come and ask."

"But you said you were tired of me doing that." Unabashed, Ben grinned while crossing the room to unload his burden.

"I am," Evie replied with exaggerated patience. "But it's better than you trying to be sneaky."

"Okay, doll, so how are you doing?"

"Fine, I am fine."

"Good." Ben stood by the fire and took off his mittens, holding his hands out to the warmth.

"Pretend he isn't there, hovering," Claire told Evie, then addressed Hannah. "Would you and Jemma like to attend church with us tomorrow?"

"Evie can't travel all the way into town now."

"I was speaking to Hannah, but if Evie wants to go then—"

"Excuse me, I'm sitting right here, you two, and with child or not, am quite capable of speaking for myself."

"Sorry." The two contrite voices speaking as one brought a slight curve to Hannah's lips.

"Good, you both should be. Now, darling, does the fact that you're in here bothering me mean you've finished playing poker?"

Ben turned to look at his wife. "I was working."

"Really? Doing what exactly?"

"Repairing harnesses and tending animals."

"And you didn't play one hand of cards?"

"Well …" He winked. "Perhaps one or two."

"And what did you win?"

"What makes you think I won?"

"Because, love, you always win."

Ben walked over and leaned down, kissing his wife full on the lips with a loud smack. "Rowdy and Jacob will be helping me build another room on our cabin this spring."

"Lovely."

"Are you getting tired? Ready to go home?"

"Almost." Evie patted his hand.

"I can go hitch up Bella."

"Not quite yet."

"You look a little pale."

"I'm fine, love."

"Are you sure?"

While Evie worked at convincing her husband she was really, truly, completely all right, Hannah's mind wandered. She hadn't been welcome at church since before Jemma was born. *I could make a polite excuse.* However, sharing some of her story now, as she had with Nate, might make it easier if, or when, the time came to tell the rest. Her gaze went to her daughter, still engrossed with her toys, not paying the slightest bit of attention to the adults. As long as she chose her words carefully, the little girl wouldn't hear anything upsetting.

Hannah took a deep breath, looking back at Claire. "Thank you, but I don't think it would be a good idea-"

"Matt." The other woman cried out, jumped to her feet and raced out of the room.

Both men quickly excused themselves and trailed after their cousin. Hannah turned, looking out the large window. Two riders were dismounting in front of the house. One might be Sam; he had the look of a Rolfe brother but she couldn't be sure. The other man had to be the sheriff, since Claire had jumped into his arms.

A sharp intake of breath brought her attention back inside to the woman seated beside her. Evie's face had paled. She bore an expression of intense concentration. *Oh no.*

"It's time, isn't it?"

She nodded. "Could you go get Ben?"

"Yes. Of course. Stay right here."

"Wasn't planning on going anywhere," Evie said wryly.

With a sheepish smile, Hannah got up and darted out of the room. As soon as she yanked open the front door, Ben turned to look in her direction. She could see the blood drain from his face even from yards away. Before she could say a word, the man sprinted by her into the house. The others streamed after him, leaving her to bring up the rear.

Hannah returned in time to hear Nate ask Evie, "Did you want to go home or stay here?"

"Go home? She can't go home. Didn't you hear her? She's going to have the baby," Ben burst out, glaring up at his cousin from where he was kneeling in front of his wife.

"She should be wherever she feels most comfortable."

"Once again I'm right here and can speak for myself." Evie interjected firmly, with a hint of exasperated amusement. "And I'd rather stay here, if you don't mind?"

"Of course not," Nate assured her.

Everyone gathered around Evie, wanting to comfort the soon-to-be mother. In the midst of the excitement, her daughter came over and grabbed Hannah's hand in a tight grip. She looked down at the little girl's tired, confused expression and swept Jemma up into her arms.

"I'm hungry, Mama."

As her daughter whispered in her ear, Hannah's gaze swung to the mantel clock. Guilt stung her. The hour was past when she normally fed Jemma lunch.

"Sorry, sweetie, I'll fix you something to eat in a minute."

Evie loudly cleared her throat. "I appreciate everyone's attention but could someone fetch the doctor and Maggie?"

The room erupted in sound as everyone starting talking at once. Jemma clutched her tighter. Hannah reached out, touching Claire on the shoulder.

"I need to grab something for Jemma to eat then put her down for a nap. As soon as I can, I'll ready a room for Evie. If she needs one sooner or anything else in the meantime, please let me know."

Claire nodded, then turned away, rejoining the debate on who should ride where. Minutes later her daughter ate a quick meal of a boiled egg, piece of cheese, and bread with butter in the kitchen. Nate, Sam, and Matt soon entered and filed past them with only nods of acknowledgment, exiting the house. Worried, she hurried Jemma though the living room as soon as she finished eating, noting both Ben and Claire remained with Evie, talking quietly. To her relief, the little girl settled down to sleep without a problem, allowing Hannah to get on with setting up a spare bedroom.

The rest of the afternoon flew by with everyone doing his or her best to stay busy. When Maggie, Claire's mother, arrived, the women retired into the room Hannah had prepared. They helped Evie change into a borrowed nightgown, then slowly walk back and forth between the walls. Outside, Ben paced the wide wrap-around porch, waiting restlessly. The ranch hands came up occasionally, checking on him before retreating to the barn again. It wasn't until after dinner that Nate returned with the doctor.

Leaving her daughter with him, Hannah showed Dr. Wright down the hall to where Evie labored. Ben followed, trailing in behind them. When she opened the door, a moan floated out and he insisted on seeing his wife. Afterward, to everyone's surprise, the man remained, refusing to leave her side again.

As the setting sun colored the clouds purple, pink, and red, the Rolfe family grew by one. A beautiful, healthy girl was born to Evie and Ben and named Lillian. Once everyone had admired the newborn, the doctor left, taking Maggie and Claire with him to drop home on his way back to town. Nate's brothers retired to the bunkhouse. Ben and Evie closed the door, resting with their new daughter. In a short time, the house went from bursting with noise to being mostly quiet.

After all the excitement, her own daughter was ready for bed early, sleeping after listening to only a few pages of her bedtime story. Tired but not ready for bed, Hannah headed to the living room as she had on previous nights. Logic whispered she should avoid being alone with Nate, that she was tempting fate, but her feet kept moving forward.

Hannah paused, standing in the doorway. Neglected, the fire wasn't much more than glowing coals. One lamp, turned low, sat on the mantel next to the clock. It cast little light beyond the hearth but she could see well enough. The couch was empty. Her heart sank as she realized how much spending time together at the end of the day meant to her.

"Ben says she's the best Christmas present ever."

Chapter 16

Relief cascaded through Hannah. She turned and found Nate by the window. "Children are little miracles."

"Never thought much about having my own until I spent time with Jemma. Then today, well, holding Lily was pure pleasure."

"Yes, it was."

"Do you want more children?"

"I once wanted a houseful."

"Not now?"

"Now I know not every dream is possible."

"Some are."

"Perhaps." Hannah crossed the room, joining him by the window, then deliberately changed the subject. "Is something on the porch?"

"Rowdy cut us a Christmas tree. We can set it up tomorrow."

"It's hard to believe it's that time of year already."

"Will you and Jemma help decorate?"

"I'm sure she'd love to."

"And you?"

"Me too."

"Good." Shadows played over his face. She sensed more than saw his smile. "Are you done with her gift?"

"I finished her new mittens but I'm only partly done with crocheting the bunny."

"She'll be a happy girl on Christmas morning."

"Jemma always is."

Nate lightly touched her shoulder. "Is something wrong?"

"Why do you ask?"

"Something in your voice."

"It's been a long day. And I'm worried about a few things."

"Like last night?" His hand moved up, cupping her jaw. *I should tell him to stop.* "I didn't sleep well."

"Neither did I."

"I shouldn't have been so forward. I'm—"

His fingers gently covered her lips. "Don't be sorry."

Hannah reached up, gently pulling his hand down. "Could we pretend it never happened?"

"No. I'll never forget our first kiss."

First. That implied there would be another. She shook her head, not knowing what to say.

"Can't we take each day as it comes? See what happens?"

"I can't be casual about relationships, not with Jemma. I have to be careful for her sake as well as my own."

"I'd never take advantage of you."

"I believe you. But … sometimes when I'm with you it feels like I've lost all good sense."

"Me too."

The look in his eyes almost hypnotized her. It took effort to avert her gaze. "I need to focus on taking care of Jemma."

"Of course you do."

"I need to find another job."

"You're not happy here?"

"I am, but we both know that it won't be long before Alice comes home." She shifted, staring out the window, where moonlight had turned evergreen trees silver.

"Sam is returning the mules in the morning."

A measure of her tension eased. "That's good."

"You're worried about her and the boys?"

"I'm worried about a lot of things."

"Everything will work out." He reached out, clasping her hand. "Sam will help with Jed and the farm, so there's no need to worry about Alice or the boys. We'll help you find a job when she does come home. And we'll be careful with each other." His thumb moved over her skin. "Have I eased your mind?"

"Somewhat." Hannah felt conflicted. His desire to relieve her worries was endearing. At the same time, it was irritating that he imagined them so easily solved.

"You don't like what I suggested or is something else troubling you?"

Hannah avoided answering the first part of his question by responding to the second half. "Before she left, Claire invited me and Jemma to her wedding."

"That's nice." He sounded slightly puzzled. He clearly didn't understand why it troubled her.

"Christmas Day is only a couple of weeks from now."

"Yes, we were just talking about that."

"They're getting married, then."

"I know." Nate took hold of her other hand, turning her to face him. "You object to them getting married on Christmas?"

"No. I assume the ceremony will be held at the church."

"Of course."

"She wanted me to join them at church tomorrow. I turned her down."

"You don't like going to church?"

"It's not that. I was going to tell her why but Matt showed up, then Evie … Later, when Claire spoke of her wedding the doctor was standing right there and …" Hannah paused, frustrated with herself. *Just tell him.* "I haven't been welcome at church since it was obvious I was expecting Jemma."

Hannah shivered, memories sending a chill through her. She

pulled her hands free then, feeling restless, walked over to stand by the fire. Nate quietly followed. His arms came around her from behind, pulling her gently against him and she allowed the embrace. For a long moment, he simply held her.

"Only those without sin should cast stones." His breath feathered her skin as he spoke softly, close to her ear.

"Not everyone takes that to heart."

"They should."

"I agree." She stared at the flames. "But they don't."

"I rarely attend church, preferring to be outside in God's creation instead of trapped in a building. But on the occasions I've gone." Nate eased his hold, turning her to face him. "The minister welcomed me." He gave her an encouraging smile. "Give this church and community a chance."

"If someone finds out about Jemma they might make a fuss and I don't want to spoil their day."

"Nothing could spoil the day for those two."

"But—"

Nate placed a finger on her lips for a second, then lowered his hand. "If anyone has the bad manners to pitch a fit at the wedding, it'll be their fault, not yours."

"You really think it'll be all right to go?"

"Yes, in fact." He hesitated. A look of caution entered his eyes. Without inflection, Nate continued. "I'd be honored if you'd allow me to escort you."

"Are you asking me on a date?" she blurted out in surprise.

"I am."

"But you said we'd be careful and take one day at a time."

"The wedding is one day."

She shook her head, trying not to laugh at his silliness.

"Is that your answer?"

"No." *But it should be.* "I mean, no isn't my answer. Yes is." *Heaven help me.* "It'd be very nice. Thank you."

His arms rested loosely around her waist. *I should go. I need to*

walk away now. It's bad enough I'm going to the wedding with him.
Hannah lifted her arms, but instead of breaking his embrace, she placed her hands on his chest. *Maybe-*

"Hannah." He pulled her closer, one hand coming up to cup her jaw.

"Yes?"

"When I finally slept last night, do you want to know what I dreamed of?"

"What?"

"Kissing you again." His hand slid over her skin, moving ever so slowly until he was caressing the nape of her neck.

Her mind fogged. She stared at him for several seconds before being able to respond. "You did?"

"Yes, I did." His tone roughened as his fingers wove into her hair, loosening pins that fell unheeded to the floor. "May I?"

Nate didn't make another move, waiting. Her gaze flicked from his eyes to his lips, then back again. *I shouldn't. I really shouldn't.* "Yes, please," Hannah breathed, leaning into his warmth, unable to resist.

His kiss wasn't sweet and soft as before. This time his mouth claimed hers with barely leashed passion. Lips crushed together with almost bruising need. His fingers tightened in her hair while his free hand roamed, first over her back in sweeping motions, then moved over the side of her ribs and up to cup the swell of her breast.

Shocked, Hannah gasped. Nate seized the opportunity to delve his tongue inside, tasting her. Heat burned through her veins. Passion chased away all rational thought. She wrapped her arms around his neck, arching against him. Suddenly, the high, shrill cry of a baby split the night, shattering the mood.

They froze. Their mutual rapid breathing seemed impossibly loud, a small roar to Hannah's ears. When a comforting female voice drifted through the walls, likely Evie answering her infant's distress, they slowly pulled apart.

Her gaze locked on his, Hannah took a step back, putting more space between them. "I need to go."

"So do I," Nate replied, but neither of them moved.

Finally, she headed for the doorway. "Good night."

"Sweet dreams."

The simple phrase sent suggestive images through her mind, promising a restless night. She hurried from the room, down the hall, and into her room. After closing the door behind her, she crossed to the window. *He's offered no promises.* In the moonlight, she could see Nate's shadowy form walking toward the bunkhouse. *Is he worth the risk?* Her fingers touched her lips, swollen and throbbing from his kiss, then closed the curtains.

And what about Michael's warning?

Some worry remained, a persistent whisper of caution, but it was fading. Each day spent with the Rolfes had lessened her concern. They'd all been kind, generous, and welcoming. Hannah had witnessed nothing troubling. There were moments when she forgot about it. *Like when I'm in Nate's arms.*

Slowly Hannah walked over to the dresser and pulled out a nightgown. Her heart still beat fast. Even now, she could feel Nate's touch. Before the sensation would likely have caused her no little distress, but tonight it was different. *Or maybe I'm different.*

A range of emotions dwelled within her: excitement, worry, desire, and concern. Yet, she felt almost calm. *What's changed?*

Hannah undressed and slipped her nightgown on. *I still need to be cautious and take care of Jemma first. I still don't know what happened between Michael and his family.* She crawled into bed. *Do I trust Nate more now?* She turned on her side, looking into the darkness. *Not anymore than yesterday.*

Then what is it?

Tired, her eyes closed. After a few more minutes of silent pondering, realization seeped through her. *I trust myself ... more, at least.* She tugged the blankets up over her shoulder, relaxing in her warm cocoon. *I'm not a girl anymore. I can indulge in a little flirtation without losing my head.*

My heart, though? Hannah didn't allow herself to speculate further, shifting her focus. The hour was late. Jemma would be up early. Guests meant extra work. And … her heart might already be lost.

Nate found it difficult to have a moment alone and almost impossible to steal a moment with Hannah over the next several days. He agreed with his cousin about not taking the new mother and baby out in the freezing weather, even the short distance to their home, for at least a week. However, that meant he couldn't predict privacy. He never knew when someone might come up to the house to see Lillian or be awake caring for the newborn.

Throughout each day, Ben would go in to check on his wife and Lily. Maggie and the doctor individually traveled out to check on the new mother. Claire showed up every day, visiting Evie and helping with the baby for hours. Either Rowdy or Jacob tagged along every time Nate went up to the house, neither man making the slightest attempt to hide their fascination with the little one. Even Matt, when he rode out to the Bar 7 to discuss their suspicions regarding Miss Collier, had to hold the baby before leaving. As frustrating as it was to have so many people around, he understood the draw. Lillian was a joy.

Hannah's daughter seemed a little overwhelmed by the sudden influx of people. Nate identified with the feeling. He made it a point to spend time with Jemma, taking her out to the barn for short periods. Quiet in the house, the little girl jabbered away when it was just the two of them.

"Can I feed the chickens?"

"Didn't you and your ma already?"

"Uh huh." Jemma skipped through the few remaining inches of snow, her little boots kicking up bits of white.

"Then no."

"'kay. Can I pet the kitty?"

"Sure, if she's around."

"Can I brush Jack?"

"With me there."

"Can I sit on him?"

"Maybe."

Each time they went outside, her words never slowed but the constant stream of speech didn't bother him. In fact, Nate found it charming. He thought the newest Rolfe was darling and Jemma no less precious. He'd quickly grown attached to Hannah's little girl.

As the week progressed, Nate could see friendships forming between the Rolfe women and Hannah. His gaze returned to their temporary housekeeper repeatedly the evening they decorated the Christmas tree with a roomful of his relatives. *It was different with Faith.* His family had liked the other woman, but throughout their engagement remained more polite than friendly. Hannah, on the other hand, already appeared to be fitting in well.

His doubt about a long-term relationship lingered. However, Nate found the positive interactions between the people he loved and the woman who'd captured his interest encouraging. *Maybe, we can have more than one outing. Maybe…*

Nate felt somewhat guilty when his cousin announced during dinner the next day that he, Evie, and baby Lily would be heading home in the morning. Anticipation pumped through him and he had a hard time paying attention to the conversation afterwards. He relished the thought of tomorrow. A few smiles, occasionally touching her arm as he walked by, and one quick, daring kiss in the pantry had only made him miss their quiet times more.

As soon as he'd finished eating, Nate went outside to tend some chores and check on their firewood supply. When he entered the kitchen about an hour later, Hannah was giving her daughter a bath in a copper tub. "Sorry, little lady, I didn't realize you were indisposed."

Jemma giggled. Nate started to walk away, grinning at her delight, then stilled. His gaze lingered on the little girl's face. Something about how she looked now, with her hair darkly wet and slicked back, nagged at him.

"What's wrong?"

"Ah … Jemma looks … different but familiar."

"Of course she's familiar."

Hannah sounded a little odd. *Can't blame her, I'm not making sense.* "I meant she reminds me of someone."

"Is that so?" Hannah motioned for her daughter to stand up, then wrapped a towel around the child before plucking her out of the water. With the little girl in her arms, she faced Nate. "I think she looks like her father."

And who is he exactly? You've never mentioned his name. "I thought she looked like you."

Hannah shook her head. "Just the hair."

The sound of a rider entering the yard interrupted their exchange. Curious to see who was visiting so late, Nate strode over to the window. The full moon cast enough light for him to recognize the sheriff.

"It's Matt." He turned, facing Hannah.

"I need to get Jemma dried off and ready for bed."

Elements of strain were in her expression, although her tone was pleasant. *What's bothering her? That Jemma looks like her father or that I noticed?* "I'll go meet him at the barn."

"I'll make some coffee after I'm done with Jemma."

"Thank you."

"You're welcome." Hannah gave him a brief smile then, carrying her sleepy-eyed daughter, left the room.

Nate grabbed a lantern from a shelf by the door then made his way to the barn, striding to where his friend stood tending his horse. "What brings you out so late?"

"Just wanted to see your handsome face." Nate arched one eyebrow and waited. Matt removed his gloves, stiffly flexing his fingers. "Remember those men Sam and I told you about?"

"The ones seen by a couple of farmers the day before the cattle went missing from the Circle K Ranch?"

The sheriff nodded. "Sean has been keeping a close eye on Miss Collier, waiting for her next delivery."

"All right." Nate was confident his friend would connect the two seemingly unrelated statements.

"She had one today." The sheriff patted his horse before looking directly at Nate. Exhaustion had etched deep lines in his expression. "Her delivery men match to the description the farmers gave me."

"You arrest them?"

"For what? Possibly riding near Myrtle Creek or driving a wagonload of heavy flour sacks?"

"Ah no proof, just suspicion."

"They're suspicious as hell, but I need evidence." Matt took a few steps forward, sat down heavily on a hay bale, then leaned his back against the wall close behind him.

"Come up to the house. Have some coffee while you tell me how that brought you here."

"Coffee sounds good. Give me a minute … maybe two." Matt closed his eyes. "As for how I ended up here." His friend opened his eyes to slits, staring up at him. "Trailed those men since they left town late this morning." He stretched out long legs, crossing one wet, mud-splattered boot over the other. "You're not the only one with tracking skills."

"I know. I'm just better."

Matt closed his eyes again. "Yep. The best."

"Those men are near the Bar 7?"

"No." With a sigh, the sheriff opened his eyes and took his time getting to his feet. "They're holed up in the line cabin a mile west of Bear Creek Meadow."

Nate's jaw clenched. "They're on the Bar 7?"

"Yes, and I want you to leave them alone."

"Because?"

234

"The sheriff, your good friend, asked you to."

"I don't like it."

"I didn't expect you would."

"Waiting for them to act, using our cattle as bait?"

"Yep."

"I really don't like it."

"I understand, but if you or your brothers run them off this investigation will likely drag on several more months at least."

Then I'd see Hannah more but ... I'd miss spring on River's Bend. It was Nate's turn to sigh. "Setting a trap?"

"Yes."

"Think it'll work?"

"Hope so." Sounding weary, Matt shrugged. "No guarantees."

"And I suppose you want us to keep an eye on them?"

"I'd be obliged."

"I'll set it up." Nate grimaced. It would be cold, boring work. *And long hours far from the house.*

Matt's eyes narrowed. "Something besides stalking rustlers in December troubling you?"

"Why do you ask?"

"Why did you avoid answering the question?"

For a long moment, Nate studied his friend. "I'm escorting Hannah to your wedding."

"That so?" Matt grinned, sitting back down. "Tell me how this happened."

"I asked her."

The sheriff held his gaze but didn't say a word. When Matt wanted to, he could outwait just about anyone and they both knew it. Nate shook his head, plopping down beside the other man, then slowly started explaining what had been going on between him and the temporary housekeeper.

Hannah pulled her bedroom door shut then hurried off to the kitchen. It'd taken her longer than she'd anticipated for Jemma to fall asleep. Her daughter managed to keep her eyes open until almost the end of a second bedtime story. Worried that Nate and the sheriff were waiting, she was relieved to discover the room empty. She swiftly made up the promised pot of coffee, set it on the stove, then took a seat at the table.

Minutes passed. Water soon boiled through fresh grounds. A tantalizing aroma started drifting from the pot. Alone, waiting for the men to come up from the barn, Hannah's thoughts centered not on them but on Michael. The choices she'd made regarding him and his vague warning had created a difficult situation.

Fingers intertwined, her hands rested on the tabletop. She gazed through the open doorway into the darkened living room without seeing a thing. Ben had been in the house for days but there hadn't been an opportunity to ask him about his brother. *Or maybe I didn't try very hard to find one.* Now with him and Evie heading home she'd have even less chances to speak to the man. Hannah sighed softly. *That's just another excuse. Next time I see-*

"Do I smell coffee?" Ben walked in, startling her.

"Ah … yes." Her mind blanked, thoughts scattering. Hannah stared at him for a few seconds, then cleared her throat as she got to her feet. "Would you like some?"

The man offered her a weary smile. "I'd love some."

"Please." She gestured to the other chairs. "Sit."

"You don't have to wait on me."

"It's a small thing and you look tired."

Ben nodded, taking a seat at the table. "I am. Thank you."

"You're welcome." Hannah moved over to the cupboard. She pulled out a mug, filled it, then brought it over to him. "Sugar?"

He shook his head, sipping the bitter brew unaltered.

"Lily asleep?"

"Her and Evie both."

"That's good. She should rest when the baby does."

His gaze met hers. "Voice of experience?"

"Some good advice I was given." Hannah reclaimed her seat.

Ben acknowledged her words with a nod. Silence stretched on for a full moment. "Sorry. I'm poor company."

"You're fine." *This is my chance. I just need to bring up Michael somehow.*

"You're a kind woman."

And you seem like a nice man but ... "I was wondering—"

"Mama."

Her gaze shifted to the doorway. Blood rushed through her veins as she watched her daughter walking toward her, carrying a book. *Oh no.* "Jemma." Calmly, she pushed back from the table and stood up. "What are you doing out of bed?"

"Want another story." Her words slurred as she reached up with one small hand, rubbing her eyes. From her other hand dangled the old bible.

The book fell, landing on the hard wood floor with a loud thump before Hannah could take a single step. Startled, Jemma's eyes rounded. The little girl dashed across the room and pressed against her. Gently, she gathered her daughter up in her arms, murmuring comforting words.

"Here you go."

Ben's statement drew her attention from Jemma. Hannah looked up. Her heart thundered. The man stood in front of them, holding out the bible to her. Without a word, she stretched out a hand to take it. As he handed her the old, battered book Michael's picture fell out, drifting softly down onto the floor.

"Oops, I'll get it."

A sense of inevitability settled over her while Ben bent over, picking up the yellowed paper. Hannah sat down, cradling her daughter. The trimmed bit of old wanted poster unfolded as he picked it up by an edge. He froze, staring at it. His face lost all color. After a moment, he stumbled over to his chair.

"Are you okay?" Hannah asked softly, one hand rubbing over her daughter's back.

Ben glanced up at her then down at the picture in his hands before back up again. "This is my brother."

Chapter 17

"I know."

"Why do you have this?"

"Well …" Hannah shifted the bible up from her lap onto the tabletop. She glanced at her little girl. Snuggled close and eyes half shut, Jemma appeared to be falling back asleep. "I—"

"You knew Michael? Why didn't you say so before?"

"He was in Ashwood for a short time." Hannah ignored his second question.

"When?" Ben's tone was low and rough with emotion.

"About five years ago."

"Five years … I always wondered where he went then."

"He wasn't there long."

"Just a few months, I'd assume." Ben paused. His face, a sickly shade of white, grayed. "Then he … died in Elk Bend."

His raw grief brought tears to her eyes. In a gentle whisper, she confirmed his guess. "Yes."

His gaze lowered to the image he held. A long moment passed in silence. Another glance down revealed Jemma had closed her eyes. Hannah shifted her daughter into a position slightly more comfortable, praying she'd sleep through the conversation. The little girl muttered a wordless protest then resumed her even breathing.

"Did he mention me?"

"Yes but …"

"It wasn't nice."

"Um …" Hannah paused, studying the man across from her. *Is it necessary to tell him?* Her daughter released a soft sigh. She looked back at the child's sweet face for some seconds. *I must know what was behind Michael's warning. For Jemma's sake.* "He warned me to stay away from all Rolfes."

"We didn't part on good terms." His expression unreadable, Ben looked up at her.

"A nasty argument?"

He snorted, staring down yet again at the picture of his brother. "You could say that."

"May I ask what you argued about?"

"Family. Loyalty. Honor." He took a breath. "And the law."

"Sounds complicated."

"Seemed so then. Not so much now."

"Oh?" Hannah gently prodded him.

"Did he talk about our family?"

Her arm ached from supporting her daughter, but she didn't dare move. Any interruption threatened her chance for an answer tonight. If Hannah drew attention to her discomfort, he might suggest she go put the child to bed. By the time she did, Nate and the sheriff would be here. In fact, she was surprised they hadn't walked in before now.

"I know your parents have passed away and Michael was your only sibling."

"We were close once."

"You and Michael?"

Ben nodded. "Our father was a small-time outlaw, like his father before him, and that's the trade he taught his sons."

"Hard to know right from wrong then."

"Perhaps. When we were young."

"Your ma didn't …?"

"She loved my father. Never said a word against him." He blew out a breath. "But there was no way to hide the times Pa spent in jail."

"I'm sorry."

"Don't be. It was his choice. He could've come out here with Uncle Miah."

"You wish he would have?" she offered gently. The man looked like an invalid. *Because seeing the image of his dead brother shocked him or ...?*

"Yeah." Ben looked up, his eyes dark with emotion. "If he had, Michael would be alive today."

"Because he wouldn't have been an outlaw?"

"Neither of us would've been."

"Didn't you walk away from that life?"

"I tried to, several times before now. It's why we fought."

"Because you wanted him to quit too?"

"Yeah." He shifted the picture, staring down at his brother once more. "I'd gone through a rough patch but was dead certain I had everything figured out. Evie was expecting. We were moving again, making another fresh start. I was full of self-righteous enthusiasm. *I know what's best, little brother.*" Scorn laced his voice. He shook his head. "Michael didn't buy it. Said something would happen and I'd fall back into old habits. And that he was better off staying an outlaw than becoming a hypocrite like me."

"That must have hurt."

"Like a knife to the chest." Ben grimaced. "The worst part is he was right. Soon after we parted, I had some bad dealings with the locals in Cedar Ridge. Then our baby died. As Michael predicted, I fell all right, hard."

"But you're doing well now."

"Yeah, that only took some hard blows to the head and almost dying."

Although the history was interesting, each minute ticking by increased her tension. "Are you saying Michael warned me away

241

from your family because you didn't want him to be an outlaw?"

Ben closed his eyes, shaking his head. His expression grew more pained. "I told Michael if he wouldn't do as I asked, I'd turn him in. For his own good. I lied, said I'd been in touch with Uncle Miah and the whole family agreed with me. They were just angry words. I'd never …" He opened his eyes, showing her deep green pools of pain and shadows. "I got a letter from him weeks later. He'd seen a wanted poster and believed I'd done as I'd threatened. He wanted nothing to do with our family or me. I hoped with time …"

Anger over an argument? That's it? Dismay chased relief through her. *That's what I've been so worried about?*

"You remember that?"

Startled, Hannah glanced over and discovered Evie standing in the doorway.

"Yes."

"Do you remember everything?" The other woman asked with clear but cautious hope as she walked slowly into the room, focusing on her husband.

Ben shook his head, his face still ashen. "Some. Enough."

"Us?"

"I don't recall courting you."

"It's okay." Evie hastened to reassure him, placing a hand on his pale cheek when she reached his side.

"But I remember a bit of our wedding. It was spring, a pretty day. I stood with the minister in the shade of a grand old tree, watching the most beautiful woman I'd ever seen walk toward me."

"Oh Ben."

"And you still are." He took her hand in his. "Beautiful."

A pleased flush spread over Evie's cheeks. "I'm a mess."

"Gorgeous."

"Ben."

"Love you."

"I love you too." Evie bent down, gently kissing him. "I'm happy you've remembered more."

"See this." He indicated the picture.

"Is that Michael?"

Ben nodded. "Hannah had it."

"She did?" Confusion evident in her expression, Evie looked at Hannah. "How? Why?"

Uncertain if the woman was addressing her or her husband, Hannah held her silence, waiting to be sure before attempting to respond. She didn't want to speak out of turn. And, she needed a moment to figure out how best to answer.

I should tell them everything, get the whole story out, be done with it. But … it's late. Ben looks … ill. Evie is clearly tired. Nate isn't here. Maybe that should wait. Give a short answer now. He's Jemma's father. Period. End of story. Or …?

"Doll?"

"Yes." Evie's attention swung back to the man next to her.

"My head hurts something fierce. Would you walk with me to our room? I need to lie down."

"Of course." The other woman helped Ben stand, putting an arm around his waist.

The couple faced her. Evie's gaze seemed to focus on Jemma for some seconds before meeting Hannah's again. *She knows.* Her heart beat faster, though the other woman's expression appeared thoughtful not critical. *How could she not? Why else would a woman keep a picture of an unrelated dead man?*

Ben held up the image of Michael, drawing her gaze. "May I keep this a while?"

"Please do."

"We need to talk more." Each word emerged slowly, delivered in a pained tone as if he was forcing each one out. "Later."

"When you feel up to it."

Ben nodded. The couple then moved away, heading toward the living-room doorway. Hannah got up from her chair, suppressing a sigh at the effort it took. It always felt as if Jemma doubled her weight when she slept.

While shifting her daughter to rest more on one arm than the other, Hannah heard the outside door opening. She noticed Ben and Evie stop in response. They turned slightly, looking back as Nate, with the sheriff close behind him, entered the kitchen.

"Good, you're up. Matt wants us to …" Nate's voice trailed off. "What's wrong?"

"Long story." His cousin shook his head. "Can it wait?"

"Ah … sure."

After a nod of acknowledgement, the man and his wife walked out of the room. Nate turned to Hannah. "What happened?"

"Ben remembered a few things."

"And that made him sick?" His brow furrowed.

"He said his head was hurting."

Her soft, almost hesitant, response troubled him. "Do you know what triggered it?"

"The picture I had of his brother."

"You had a picture of Michael?" he echoed. "Why?"

"I …" Hannah stared at him for a moment, then released a long breath. "Could I tell you in the morning? I really need to get Jemma back in bed."

And you can't come out afterwards and explain? Nate almost pressed her, then noted her strained expression. "All right."

"The coffee is on the stove." Her gaze shifted from his to Matt, addressing them both. "Good night."

Before he could respond in kind, Hannah hurried out of the kitchen carrying her daughter. Nate turned to his friend. "That strike you as odd?"

"Ben remembering things?" Matt shrugged. "He's had flashes occasionally since I've known him. Can't say I've ever seen him looking like that afterwards, though." The sheriff pulled a mug from the cupboard and filled it with the casual ease of a person

244

long familiar with the Bar 7's kitchen. "Or were you referring to Hannah having a picture of your outlaw cousin?"

"Both." Nate got himself some coffee, then led the way over to the table.

Matt waited until after they sat down and he'd taken a long drink before answering. "Odd? Yes."

"Keeping a picture? It means something."

"Probably."

"Like he meant something to her."

"That'd be my guess." The sheriff took another long sip.

"Jemma's father?"

"Could be." Wearing a serious expression, Matt offered calmly. "Or not. Don't leap to conclusions. Ask her."

"If he is, why would she hide it?"

"I don't know."

Nate stared down at his untouched coffee. "I thought she was honest."

"*If* he fathered Jemma, how would that make her dishonest?"

"If Michael's her father, then Jemma's a Rolfe. And Hannah's been welcomed into our home, offered friendship and I …" He shook his head.

"It's just speculation right now."

"Yup."

"Not saying something isn't the same as lying."

Nate didn't look up, moving his mug around in his hands. "Faith never came straight out and said that she didn't want to live on River's Bend. There were hints I should've caught but—"

"Faith knew what you expected when you proposed. Accepting without telling you she wanted something else was dishonest."

"And Hannah working for us, living here and … not telling us her daughter is family isn't?"

"First, you don't know for certain yet who Jemma's father is. Second, the situations and women involved are different."

"Seem similar enough to me," Nate muttered.

245

Matt shook his head. "Before rushing to judgment, why don't you listen to what she has to say?"

"Nate." His gaze sought Hannah and found her standing just inside the doorway. "Can we—"

Suddenly the rattle of wagon wheels disturbed the quiet of the evening. A shout brought both men to their feet. Nate looked toward the window. Thin muslin curtains blocked clear vision but the glow of a lantern in the yard was clear. He strode over and pulled them aside.

"It's Sam. He brought Alice home."

"The boys?" Sadness flowed through Hannah. She already knew the answer. *They're here because Jed's worse.* Still, she had to ask. The miracle Alice had been praying for could've happened.

Nate glanced at her, his expression unreadable. "Them too."

A two-word sentence when speaking to me. Guilt rose within her. *It's my fault.* She'd overheard enough of Matt's cautionary words to be certain of that. *I should've told him.*

Could've, would've, should've Hannah. Her mother's voice whispered through her mind. *Yes Ma, I remember. I can't change what I've done.* She stiffened her spine. *I can only explain and apologize.* Her gaze followed Nate as he walked away, heading outside. *I just hope he'll understand.*

The next hour passed swiftly. She moved over to the window, peering out in time to see several men walk up, coming from the direction of the bunkhouse. In minutes, they helped Alice and the boys down off the wagon and unloaded a few items. When Matt started walking the older woman toward the front door, Hannah headed for the cupboard. She had a steaming cup of coffee ready for her friend by the time they entered the house.

With quick strides, Hannah left the kitchen to join the sheriff and Alice in the living room. She set the cup down on the small table by the couch then gave the older woman a short hug. While she whispered words of welcome, Matt lit the lamp on the mantel then added a few rounds to the low-burning fire. Nate walked in as her friend sat down on the couch, carrying both of the sleepy boys. Before she could do more than offer Jason and John a smile, Rowdy entered the room. He headed straight to her, then promptly deposited a box containing one very unhappy cat in her arms.

Startled, for a moment Hannah couldn't think of what to do with Silas. She didn't want to banish him to the barn. His low, repetitive yowls stirred sympathy. However, it wasn't her place to decide if the pet could stay in the house. Her gaze turned to Nate.

"My old room."

"Thank you."

Nate nodded. "The boys too."

"I'll settle Silas there then make up the bed."

"Wait." He stepped over to a side table and picked up a small lamp, lighting it. "Follow me."

Nate led the way down the dark hall and into the chosen room. He set the lamp on a tall dresser by the door as Hannah walked in behind him. She set the distressed animal in a corner, still in the box.

"I'm going to fetch him something to eat."

"Take the lamp."

"Are you coming?"

"I'll stay."

Hannah hesitated, looking at him. For a moment, she felt the urge to blurt everything out now. Another, louder, yowl from the box snapped her back to reality. This wasn't the time. Right now, she needed to calm Silas down before he woke up Lily or her daughter.

"I'll be right back."

Moving quickly, Hannah gathered fresh bedding in addition to some scraps and a saucer of milk for the cat. Surprise held her fast just inside the door when she returned a few minutes later. The murmur of Nate's voice was the only sound in the room now. The man sat on the floor beside the opened box with

Silas curled on a blanket by his thigh, one hand soothing black fur.

"Amazing."

"He is."

"I meant you."

Nate shook his head as he slowly got to his feet. "He just needed attention."

Her mind went stubbornly blank. Nate moved closer, stopping right next to her. Silently, he took the lamp from her, putting it on the dresser again. He then removed the treats for Silas from their precarious perch on top of the bedding and placed them near him. Lastly, he slid the blankets and sheets out of her arms, setting them on the bed.

When Nate turned back, facing her again, several thoughts suddenly flooded her. Her lips parted. He waited, holding her gaze a full moment, but Hannah couldn't speak.

"I need to check on Alice."

Of course you do. Hannah nodded, feeling foolish while she watched him walk away. As the sound of Nate's footsteps moving down the hall faded, she released a heavy sigh. *I thought I was done being awkward and tongue-tied around him.*

Hannah put aside her feelings and focused on getting the bed ready. The door eased open while she smoothed the last quilt in place. Sam entered, carrying Jason, followed by Jacob with John, then Rowdy holding two pillows. Both children were sound asleep and didn't wake during the process of tucking them in. The men then filed out as quietly as they came in. She lingered to drop a kiss on each boy's head before heading off. With one foot in the hall, she glanced back and saw Silas leap up onto the bed, settling down in between the boys. The sight made her smile as she shut the door.

In the living room, Hannah discovered the sheriff about to take his leave. She slipped into the kitchen and set up a tray with coffee-filled mugs and a plate of sugar cookies. When she returned to the other room, only the Rolfe brothers and Alice remained. She placed the refreshments on a side table. While everyone took a cup, only Rowdy seized a handful of sweet treats.

"Have you forgotten your manners, Isaac?" Alice calmly inquired, with an expectant look.

"Rowdy, everyone calls me Rowdy."

"I do not."

"Yes, ma'am." The man grinned at her, then picked up the plate, passing it to Jacob. "Better?"

"It'll do."

Each brother took a cookie or two, then handed the plate to the next man. In silence, they completed the task before setting the almost-empty plate back on the tray. With the exception of Rowdy, no one took a bite, but Hannah didn't take offense. She sensed the other men were more interested in talking to the older woman.

"If there's nothing else I can get anyone I'll go-"

"Please stay," Alice interrupted softly.

"I don't want to intrude."

"I'd rather say this once."

The notes of strain in her friend's otherwise calm statement changed her mind. "I'll stay, then."

Nate stood, offering her his chair. With a grateful smile, Hannah accepted. Alice started speaking as soon as she sat.

"I assume you all know what's been happening." The older woman paused, waiting for each brother to nod. "The bank manager visited on December first. The next morning Jed was gone."

With a shaking hand, Alice pulled a torn piece of paper from her skirt pocket and handed it to Nate. Silence ruled the room while the note passed from person to person. Hannah was the last person to read it.

> *Sorry Ma, but I'm no good for anyone now.*
> *Tell the boys, I do love them.*
> *Jed*

"My son's gone and not coming back, not anytime soon."

"Why didn't you come home, then?" Jacob spoke gently.

"I hoped he'd come to his senses. I sent Sam looking but …"

"You couldn't find him?" Nate addressed his brother.

His tone grim, Sam answered. "Oh, I found him."

"And he refused to come back." Alice took control of the conversation. "So I packed us up. We brought Meadowlark and her foal because …" She cleared her throat. "I wanted the boys to keep the mare Bessie treasured, to have something of value."

"They have you," Hannah put in.

"That doesn't feel like much." The older woman gave her a sad smile then looked to Nate. "You said the boys were welcome."

"Yes."

"Thank you. May I ask another favor?"

"Anything."

"You don't know what I want."

"Anything," he reaffirmed.

Alice shook her head, her lips curving with a hint of a smile. "Before I left to help Jed, you were planning to fix the roof on the foreman's cabin. Are you hiring one?"

"No, Pa plans to offer Sam the job when they return."

"He is?" Sam's surprise was clear to all.

"I wasn't supposed to tell you, he wanted to himself."

His brother stepped closer. "Why did Pa ask you to help *watch over* the ranch if he had such faith in me?"

"He knew you were offered a job on the Circle K. And since you've been making cow's eyes at Hazel Kline he-"

"That's over," Sam bit out.

"Sorry."

The younger man nodded once, his expression stone. Sam didn't say another word. After a moment, Alice directed her next question to him.

"Will you want the cabin?"

"And have a whole house to take care of? No, ma'am. I'm happy in the bunkhouse."

"Would you mind me and the boys living in it? It'd be good for them to have a home instead of staying in someone else's."

"It's yours if you want it, as far as I'm concerned."

"The roof's repaired but it's been vacant for some time."

"I'm aware of that, Nathaniel."

"It'll take a few days for us to make it livable."

"You don't have to—"

"Yes, we do," everyone surrounding Alice chorused.

"I … thank you."

Jacob reached out, tapping the older woman's arm to gain her attention. "How are the boys doing?"

"They're quiet. Shed a few tears when we left the farm but I think this year has left them about cried out."

"We'll start working first thing in the morning," Rowdy promised, sounding uncharacteristically somber.

"You're a good boy, Isaac." The older woman's voice shook, reminding them all of her obvious fatigue. "Thank you."

Everyone but Alice got up, joining Nate, who was already standing. Hannah gathered up the mugs back onto the tray. She then carried it into the kitchen, washing the few dishes while the brothers said good night to Alice. Jacob, Sam, and Rowdy passed through the room, heading toward the back door as she finished with her task. She returned to the living room to hear Alice inquiring about a bed.

Hannah quickly crossed to her friend's side. "You'll stay in with me, of course. After all, I'm in your room."

A further sign of her exhaustion, Alice merely nodded. She accepted Nate's arm, slowly rising from the couch. The man picked up her carpetbag with his free hand, then escorted the older woman down the hall. Hannah followed. He stopped at the bedroom doorway and gently hugged Alice.

Nate straightened. "Sweet dreams."

"You too." Alice shuffled into the room.

Hannah waited patiently while Nate stepped back into the hall before turning to face her. Without a word, he handed her the bag. A moment passed as they stood there, gazes locked.

"Good night," she finally offered softly.

"Good night."

Reluctantly Hannah walked into the bedroom and shut the door. The two women readied themselves for bed, exchanging little conversation. A short time later, the lamp extinguished, fire banked, and both of them settled beneath multiple blankets, she felt sleep begin to claim her. Then Alice spoke.

"In the morning, we need to talk."

Chapter 18

Hannah stiffened. "About?"

"You know." The older woman yawned audibly. "Good night."

Nate. Had someone mentioned him spending time alone with her after dinner? Or Ben. He and Evie had remained in their room when Alice arrived. *Maybe someone told her how sick he looked earlier, after talking to me.* "Um …" As much as Hannah wanted an answer, she couldn't press her exhausted friend. "Good night."

After a long night spent tossing and turning, sleeping in short spurts, the sound of cheerful humming woke Hannah the next morning. She opened her eyes and discovered Alice was already out of bed. Her friend stood across the room. She was dressed and in the process of winding her hair up in its customary bun.

"Good morning." Alice looked into the mirror above the dresser, meeting her gaze in the reflection without turning around. With barely a pause, she went on. "You and Nathaniel seem to have grown close."

Hannah, stilled in the act of getting out of bed, was surprised although she shouldn't have been. One of the things she liked about the older woman was how she cut to the heart of whatever was on her mind. Alice told her the habit came with age. She was too old now to waste time beating around the bush.

"I think so."

"Either you have or you have not."

"I believe ..." Hannah paused, doubt niggling at her as she slid her feet down onto the cold wood floor. She pulled off her nightgown then picked up the faded, but serviceable, blue calico work dress from the foot of the bed. "We have."

The older woman pushed one last hairpin in place, then stood up, walking over, while Hannah slipped the dress on. She sat down on the side of the bed, patting the covers beside her. "What are your intentions?"

"I don't know." She focused on fastening buttons.

"Have you told him about Jemma?"

Hannah glanced toward the door. "Are the boys up?"

"I haven't heard them stir."

"I'm surprised Jemma didn't crawl in bed with us. This is the first night she's stayed in her own room."

"She's growing up and you're avoiding the question."

"Nate knows I wasn't married to her father."

"And?"

"He didn't judge me."

"Because he's been judged enough himself. It's made him more tolerant than most." Alice studied her a moment before continuing. "He's a good man."

"I agree." She walked over to the dresser.

"Have you told him who Jemma's father is?"

Hannah picked up her hairbrush. "Not yet."

"How can you believe you're close without trust?"

Her friend's gentle words hit her hard. "I trust Nate ... I just ... I'm going to tell him soon. Today if possible."

"What would get in the way?"

"Lack of privacy. Interruptions. Cowardice."

A loud series of knocks sounded on the door. "Grandma, are you in there?"

"Yes, just a minute, Jason," Alice called out. She got to her feet, then addressed Hannah again. "You need to tell them all. Ben especially."

"I talked to him yesterday." She paused, took in a deep breath, then quickly relayed what happened.

"Sweetie … you need to talk to Nate; the sooner the better."

"I know." Hannah finished fixing her hair and turned to face the older woman. "Any advice?"

"Open your mouth and spit it out."

Another knock hit the door. Alice gave her a long look, then walked over, stopping in front of it. Instead of opening it, the older woman bent down and picked up a sheet of paper from the floor. A moment later, she held it out to Hannah.

Worried, she hurried across the room and took it from her. Evie's note was short.

Hannah,

We're heading out at first light. Ben isn't well and needs to be at home. We'll be back to visit, and have a talk, as soon as he's better. Please tell everyone, especially Alice, we're sorry to leave without saying goodbye.

Evie

"It'll be all right."

"I hope so."

"Grandma." John's impatience was clear. "We're hungry."

Alice reached out, squeezed her hand, then pulled open the door. Jemma skipped in, followed by Jason and John. The older woman herded the boys right back out, stating the need to find them clean clothing, leaving Hannah alone with her daughter.

Excited by the boys' arrival, it took twice as long as it usually did to get Jemma ready for the day. The little girl was bursting with energy by the time Hannah finished braiding her hair and helping her dress. When they finally headed to the kitchen, she almost raced down the hall.

In the large, stove-warmed room, all the Rolfe brothers were already present. They'd brought in extra chairs from the dining room and sat crowded around the table with Jason and John among them, carrying on multiple discussions. Jemma rushed over to join them, running straight to a certain man's side. She then waited in silent expectation. Without being asked or missing a beat in the conversation, Nate reached down, picked the little girl up, and settled her on his lap.

"You're not the only one getting close to him." Alice spoke softly, close to her ear.

Her gaze shifted to the older woman as her daughter's chatter joined the chorus of male voices. "I think she's coming out of her shell."

"I think it's more than that."

So do I. Hannah glanced back at her child as she slipped an apron over her dress. Jemma had relaxed around all the brothers but she had a marked preference for Nate. *She's already attached to him.* The thought gave her a warm feeling, but concern shadowed it closely. *What if something goes wrong like it did with Jed?*

"You can't keep her apart from others."

Hannah gave a slight shake of her head. Sometimes it felt like Alice could read minds. She started cracking eggs into a large frying pan while the older woman stacked fresh biscuits onto a large platter.

"I know but …"

"Wanting to protect her is natural." A pained look briefly appeared in Alice's eyes. "No mother wants her child to hurt."

Before Hannah could say anything, her friend walked away, carrying the platter over to the table. There was no chance for any more personal exchanges as they finished cooking and serving breakfast. After the meal, the children begged to go with the men when they headed out to work on the cabin for Alice. While they bundled up the kids, she convinced the older woman to leave the clean-up to her and join them. A welcome silence descended when everyone else was out the door.

Hannah took her time tidying the room and preparing meals for the rest of the day, relieved to have some minutes alone. *By the way, Michael is …* A fresh pot of coffee went on the back of the stove to keep warm. *No, too casual.* She moved on, making ham sandwiches for a cold lunch at the cabin. *Remember when I told you about meeting Jemma's father? Well …* In a basket, she put in a jug of water and the sandwiches. *No, it's best to start with Ben seeing the picture.*

Her approach decided, Hannah put a large roast into a pan and slid it into the oven. She heard the outside door open as she straightened. When Nate stepped inside seconds later, she stared at him, mute.

"Alice wanted me to fetch the broom."

More likely, she wanted us to talk. "It's in the pantry."

"I know," he stated, but didn't move.

"Nate, I …" Hannah bit her bottom lip. *Just tell him.* "I'd like to tell you what happened yesterday with Ben and-"

"Is Michael Jemma's father?"

So much for easing into it. "Yes."

"Why didn't you tell us … tell me?"

"Michael warned me to stay away from all Rolfes."

"Why?"

"He never said, but yesterday Ben explained they'd argued."

A muscle jerked over his jaw. "You took this job."

"Because Alice vouched for you all and … I needed to support my daughter." Hannah wanted to be honest.

"You spent time with me. Kissed me. Agreed to attend the wedding with me. But you don't trust me? In fact, you lied to me." He delivered the uncharacteristic barrage of words with tightly held anger.

"I didn't lie."

"You withheld the truth."

"Before I got to know you, I was worried. I didn't know who to trust, the man who fathered my child or the kind woman who'd just befriended me."

"What about Bessie? Jed grew up here. She knew us."

"It was hard for me with Michael dying, finding out I was expecting and … I refused to talk about your family."

"Refusing to talk seems to be a habit with you."

"Nate—" She tried to protest.

"And after you knew me?"

"I was scared."

"Of me?"

Hannah shook her head. "Of making the wrong decision for Jemma. Of everything changing. Of you being so angry you'd toss us out."

"Oh, I'm angry all right." A sick feeling gathered in the pit of her stomach as Nate stalked up. "Even more so because you thought I might kick you out."

Past and present flowed together. "I worried you would."

"I was a fool for thinking we knew each other well."

"I—"

"We don't know each other at all, do we?"

"It's not that simple."

"Oh? Have you lied about something else?"

"I didn't lie," she insisted, as he stared at her hard.

After a moment, Nate walked over to the window. "You know how important family is to me."

"I do."

"I'd never throw out my flesh and blood." He turned to face her again. "I can't imagine what made you think I'm the sort of lowlife who'd do that."

Nate held her gaze for several seconds before heading for the pantry. He retrieved the broom and, in a few long strides, reached the back door. His hand was on the knob when Hannah found the courage to explain.

"Remember that older woman in Ashwood?"

Nate stilled, hearing the thickness of her voice. Empathy welled up in him. He needed to cool his temper and talk this over with her calmly. As he turned around, her words echoed in his mind. *An older woman in Ashwood.* He sifted through his memories of that day. "The one who—?"

"Acted as though it was distasteful to be on the street with me."

His fingers tightened on the broom handle. *Patience.* Nate took a breath and consciously relaxed them. "What does she have to do with this?"

"You wanted to know how I could think such a thing of you."

"Yes."

For a long moment, Hannah simply held his gaze. As a blank but composed mask became her expression, a sour feeling settled in his gut. *I'm not going to like this.*

"I played in her yard as a child. When I was a young woman, knowing my love of numbers, she persuaded her husband to teach me his trade." Hannah moved closer to him, stopping about a foot away, near the wall. Silently, she removed her apron and hung it on a peg. Her hand went to the old shawl hanging beside it. For a few seconds her fingers trailed over the faded blue yarn. "She crocheted me a shawl in my favorite color every Christmas." Her gaze shifted, meeting his as her hand dropped, falling to her side. "She loved me once. I knew that as surely as I knew the sun would rise."

The stark pain reflected in her eyes made him want to stop her next words. "Hannah—"

"When I told her I was expecting, I knew what I'd done was wrong. I figured she'd be … upset." Tears shimmered in her eyes but didn't fall. "I begged for forgiveness." Her chin lifted a fraction. "And received none." She paused briefly, then continued in a tone emptied of emotion. "That woman is my grandmother."

"Hannah …" His thoughts and feelings a tangled mess, Nate fumbled for words. "I don't know what to say."

"How about you understand and it's okay?"

That would be kind. It'd be appropriate. But it wouldn't be honest. "I need some time to think about it."

Hurt flashed in her eyes. Guilt swept into his internal emotional storm. He took a step toward Hannah. *I should-*

Someone pounding on the door interrupted the moment. Nate turned, going to answer the summons. The ranch hand he'd sent to watch the deliverymen stood on the porch. Hank informed him the suspected rustlers were on the move and he'd lost their trail.

After instructing the man to ready his horse, Nate closed the door and walked back to Hannah. "I have to go."

"All right."

"I think your grandmother is wrong. Dead wrong."

"Thank you."

"And this isn't about you having Jemma out of wedlock."

"I know." Her gaze never wavered from his. "It's about me messing up and someone being unable to forgive me for it."

A long moment passed, tense silence filling the room. Her words hung in the air between them. Then Sam walked in.

"I saw Hank ride in and…" His brother stopped, looking from him to Hannah, then back to him. "Am I interrupting something?"

"No." She replied before Nate could.

Hannah grabbed the basket off the table, took the broom from his lax grip, then headed into the mudroom, where they heard her putting on a coat. She left the house a few minutes later, shutting the door with a firm thud. Only then did Nate meet his brother's gaze.

"Want to share what's going on?"

"I'm heading out to find the deliverymen's trail."

"I know. I talked to Hank. I meant with you and Hannah."

"Nothing I want to talk about now."

"I'm surprised." Sam's tone was dry.

"Later, little brother, I need to think it through first."

"I'll hold you to that."

"I'm sure you will." Nate headed for the door. "For now, though, let's get back to work."

Sam followed on his heels. "You need my help?"

"Don't think so. Stay and get the cabin ready. I'll send Hank back if we run into trouble."

The men walked to the barn together, then parted ways. Nate watched his brother amble off as the ranch hand led their horses out. He mounted, cast a glance in the direction of the old cabin where Hannah was, then rode off deep in thought.

Feeling hurt, worried, and guilty, Hannah was mostly quiet as she spent the rest of the cold, foggy day with the children, Alice, and the three younger Rolfe brothers. They all worked hard to get the cabin livable. Jacob and Sam cleared a squirrel nest out of the chimney and built a nice fire. They next stacked a generous supply of firewood along the south wall. Rowdy fixed the cooking stove, repaired some holes in the floor then, with the children's help, filled gaps in the outer walls with mud and moss. The two women cleaned away cobwebs, put fresh linens on the beds, swept the plank floor and scattered several rag rugs around. By the end of the short winter day, the place was move-in ready.

Tired, they decided to wait until morning to unload Alice and the boys' possessions. Dinner back at the main house was a quiet affair. The children were sleepy, Nate hadn't returned, and his brothers didn't stay long, tucking into their food then leaving to tend chores. While her friend settled the kids into bed, Hannah cleaned up, then both women retired for the night.

Early the next morning Jacob, Sam, and Rowdy drove the wagon from Redwing Farm from the barn where it had been stored over to the cabin and unloaded it. The men returned to their normal workday as soon as they finished. After helping Alice unpack and arrange things, Hannah brought Silas down to his new home, setting him down in the boys' room, where he hid under John's bed. The women then took a few moments to enjoy a cup of coffee, watching the children play.

"Did you tell him?" Alice pitched her voice low.

Hannah nodded, her gaze focused on her daughter.

"He didn't like you not telling him sooner."

"No. He calls it lying. Said he needed to think."

"And you didn't like that."

"No." She stirred more honey into her hot brew, then looked over at her friend. "I didn't."

"Want to talk about it?"

Movement caught Hannah's eye. She looked past Alice to the window behind her. "Ben and Evie are headed up to the house."

The older woman nodded. "Anytime you need to talk, I'm right here." She held her gaze for a moment, then got to her feet. "Let's meet them there. I'm not ready to entertain yet."

The sound of hoof beats carried on the icy breeze as they headed out some minutes later. Nervous yet hopeful, it was Nate coming back, anticipation rushed through Hannah. A full moment passed before she could identify the rider.

Claire pulled up, dismounting beside them. Hannah pushed aside disappointment and welcomed her with a smile. *It's nice to see her. I just …* While the petite woman hugged Alice, her gaze swept the surroundings but found no other rider. *I miss Nate.*

The day, though sunny, was bitterly cold. Hannah hustled the group onward, eager to get everyone to the main house. The new mother and baby were already inside warming by the freshly stoked living-room fire when they reached it. Alice took a seat on the couch by Evie, brushing aside her apology for entering without them. Claire plopped down next to them while the kids crowded close, peeking at Lily. Ben stood by the front door and

Hannah felt the weight of his gaze as soon as she walked in.

Nervous, Hannah turned to face him. She was pleased to see Ben appeared a little tired but healthy. "Hi."

"I need to tend the horses," he stated, sounding almost cautious, as though he didn't want to worry her.

"We'll talk when you get back."

Ben nodded as Claire got to her feet, stating her intention to accompany him. He waved her back. "I'll take care of Blue."

Claire smiled her thanks and sat back down.

Hannah excused herself, ducking into the kitchen as soon as Ben slipped out the door. She made coffee and peppermint tea to calm her stomach. For a snack, she made up a tray with a large plate of buttermilk biscuits along with jars of strawberry jam and apple butter. Her daughter drew her gaze as she carried it into the other room.

I should tell Jemma first. Hannah set the food tray down on a side table and hurried back for the drinks. Her hands had just closed on the second tray when the door to the outside creaked open. She glanced over her shoulder, expecting to see Ben. The sight of the younger three Rolfe brothers startled her.

"Hello."

"Ben said he brought Lily over." Rowdy grinned at her as he and Jacob ambled by, going directly into the other room.

Sam paused by her. "Are you all right?"

"Too much coffee." *And having to tell all of you, all at once.* Hannah conjured up a smile. "My stomach is a touch upset."

"Oh? Try some peppermint tea." He plucked the tray out of her hands, then followed his brothers.

"Thanks for the advice," she muttered to herself, shaking her head.

Hannah walked over to the window, picking up her mug of cooling tea off the table along the way. The sound of happy voices drifted through the wall. *Maybe it's good they're all here.* She sipped the soothing brew, gazing outside without paying attention. *Maybe Alice had the right of it the other night. Say it once and be done.* She took a deep breath. *First Jemma then-* Two riders entered the yard, disrupting her thoughts.

As soon as the sheriff dismounted, the other man rode off toward the barn, taking Matt's horse with him. *I'm starting to understand why Nate likes solitude so much.* Hannah put her mug back on the table, then went to welcome the lawman.

"Afternoon, Sheriff, please come in."

"Good afternoon, Hannah." Matt stepped inside and she closed the door. "Has Nate made it back yet?"

Fresh worry welled up. "No, is there cause for concern?"

"I don't believe so. Sean crossed paths with him earlier today. Said Nate reckoned he'd be home soon."

"Good." She felt some of her tension ease.

"Would it be all right if we wait here for him?"

"Yes, of course." She waved to where he could hang his coat and hat. "Would you like some coffee?"

"Please."

Hannah went into the kitchen and filled a mug, handing it to Matt when he joined her. "Did you know Claire is here?"

A slow smile spread across his face. "She is?"

Hannah nodded. "Care to join her in the living room?"

"I'd love to." Matt headed for the other room, pausing at the door. "When Sean comes up, would you send him in too?"

"I will."

"Thanks."

Knowing Ben would be returning soon, Hannah followed the sheriff though the doorway. She softly called her daughter over to her, then led Jemma out of the room. In the kitchen, she took a seat at the table, lifting the little girl up onto her lap.

"I've something important to tell you."

Jemma's eyes rounded. "Yes, Ma."

Her daughter was so solemn it was endearing. Hannah gave her a gentle squeeze. "This is about your daddy."

"Oh." Jemma nestled up against her.

"Well … he's part of a special family."

"Uh-huh."

"His family name is Rolfe."

"Like Nate?"

"Exactly like Nate."

The little girl shifted in her arms, looking up at her with her head tilted slightly to one side and brow furrowed. As Jemma was considering her words, Hannah heard the outside door creak open. Whispers of movement came from the mudroom. She glanced over as Nate stepped into the open doorway, looking cold, wet, and tired.

"Does that mean Nate could be my daddy?"

Hannah sucked in a breath as she returned her gaze to her daughter, fire racing over her cheeks. "Sweetie, you know your daddy's in Heaven."

"Like Bessie and Grandma."

"Yes." She hugged Jemma gently. "Nate is your cousin."

"Rather have a daddy," the little girl whispered.

Hannah rubbed her daughter's back. "I'm sorry."

"Is Rowdy …" Jemma sighed, snuggling closer. Her eyelids drooped. "A cousin too?"

"Yes." Guilt rose up as she realized it was way past the little girl's naptime. *Some mother I am.*

"Jacob?"

"Him too."

Cradling her daughter, Hannah got to her feet. She glanced over at the man watching them. Words escaped her. Silently she looked at him for a long moment, then walked away, carrying Jemma to her bedroom.

"Sam?" the little girl asked softly in sleep-slurred speech when Hannah laid her on her bed.

"Yes."

"Ben? Claire?" Jemma yawned. "And Evie?"

"Claire is, but Ben is your uncle. Evie is your aunt."

"Oh. Okay." With that underwhelming response, her daughter closed her eyes.

Hannah remained, sitting on the side of the bed a few more minutes, watching Jemma drift off to sleep. It was clearly more dramatic for an adult to learn about her daughter being a Rolfe relation. She smoothed another blanket over her child, then stood up. *It's time to tell them.*

Nerves tightened a band around her chest but Hannah steeled her spine and went forth. Nate was standing by the fire, staring into the flames, when she stepped into the living room. Claire, Alice, and Evie remained on the couch. Ben stood behind his wife, one hand on her shoulder. Jacob and Sam leaned against the wall on either side of the window while Matt, Rowdy who was holding Lily, and a blond man she assumed to be Sean occupied chairs near the other women. She hesitated, intimidated by the gathering.

Hannah shifted. A board squeaked under her foot. Everyone fell silent, turning to look at her. Her heart thundered at the sudden, undivided attention. *They were waiting for me.*

Chapter 19

Much like Nate days before, Ben didn't wait for her to speak. "Jemma is my niece, isn't she?"

"Yes," she affirmed, focusing on him instead of the group.

"Did Michael know he had a daughter?"

"No." Hannah took a breath, then explained. "He died before I knew I was expecting."

"How did you meet him?" Evie interjected gently.

"He stumbled onto our farm, wounded and looking for help."

"Wounded?" Claire observed. "So not injured by accident?"

Hannah shook her head. "Another gambler shot him, thinking he cheated."

"He probably did." Ben stated, matter-of-fact. "Still an outlaw, wasn't he?"

"Michael said he was a wanted man."

"And you didn't care?"

Although his tone remained even, the shadows in his eyes spoke volumes. *How can I tell him Michael was going to give it up for me when he refused to for him?* "I …"

"She gave Michael an ultimatum, remain an outlaw or marry her." Alice came to her rescue. Hannah looked over, giving the older woman a grateful smile. At that moment, she noticed

Jason and John weren't present. As if she'd read the unspoken question in her expression, her friend volunteered, "Hank took the boys out to visit Meadowlark."

"And he chose to remain an outlaw." Ben drew her attention back.

"No. Michael said he wanted to marry me."

"Then why did he end up in Elk Bend?"

"I don't really know." Hannah held his gaze steady, hoping he'd read the truth in her eyes. "Michael said he needed to make something right and left. A couple of weeks later he was dead."

"He was hung." Pain accented each word.

"I know. I went there, looking for answers. All the marshal would say was Michael murdered a man. I couldn't believe it."

"My memory is still …" Strain was evident in Ben's expression. "Spotty." Evie reached up, clasping his hand. "But after what you said … I believe my brother went to Elk's Bend looking for me. It's where we met up last."

"How then—"

"Did it end in murder? I don't know exactly. My little brother could charm birds out of trees. Violence …" Ben shook his head. "Wasn't how Michael handled situations. I couldn't believe he was guilty either. Then I learned he killed an ex-partner of mine who ran off with all my money. And I knew …" He cleared his throat. "Our father taught us a skewed sense of family honor."

"You think he was trying to avenge you?"

"I think he ran into Dan. Confronted him. And …"

Ben didn't spell out the rest, but Hannah accepted what he inferred. His words rang true. A measure of peace settled over her. Although she'd hoped Michael had been innocent, it was good to have a better understanding of what happened to him.

"Thank you for sharing that with me."

"You're welcome."

"I am sorry I didn't tell all of you about Jemma sooner."

Ben came around the couch, walking up to her. "I wish you

had but it's water under the bridge now." To her surprise, he reached out and hugged her briefly. "Welcome to the family."

"But I'm not—"

"Don't argue with a Rolfe. We always win in the end."

Hannah shook her head while Evie moved up beside him, hugging her as well. "I'm happy we're family."

"But I …" Seeing the same determination in the other woman's expression as her husband's, she gave up arguing. "So am I."

Minutes later, Hank brought the boys back and the impromptu gathering started winding down. The deputy left, returning to town. Rowdy grudgingly handed Lily back to her mother next and the younger Rolfe brothers headed back to work. Evie made one mention about feeling tired and Ben promptly bundled up his wife and baby, taking them home. With the dinner hour approaching, Alice went to the kitchen. Hannah was trailing after her when Jemma woke up and wandered in.

While the other adults decided to follow the housekeeper into the other room, Hannah stayed. She took her time, settling her daughter with Jason and John in the living room. The moments spent fixing her little girl's braids, pulling out the basket of toys again and adding another round of pine to the fire allowed her to regain composure. She then joined the others in the kitchen, leaving the children playing happily together.

Everyone but Alice sat around the table. The only sounds in the kitchen were the older woman's footsteps as she moved and the sheriff's voice. Hannah overheard the name Lizzie Jane Collier while crossing the room to get her apron. In the process of tying it on, she watched the Bar 7's regular housekeeper set a bowl of potatoes on the table between Nate and Matt, handing each of them a knife. *My time here is ending.*

Melancholy welled up. *Soon, I'll be leaving. What will happen to us then?* Her gaze shifted to Nate. *What's happening now?*

"You want to use your wedding to catch the rustlers?"

Alice's incredulous tone cut through her thoughts, drawing

Hannah's attention. Eyebrows raised, the housekeeper was staring at Matt. Hannah moved over and began helping with preparations for dinner, paying closer attention to the conversation.

"Sort of." The sheriff patiently explained. "Everyone knows when I'm getting married and the whole community is invited to the reception. I believe Miss Collier is aware I've had her and her deliverymen watched but she hasn't pulled up stakes. I've a gut feeling she's planning something for when I'm not here."

"You're responsible for the whole county and often called out of town."

"In those cases no one knows when I'll be gone. The wedding date, on the other hand, has been public knowledge for months."

"Your deputy and," Alice glanced pointedly at Nate, "those you press into service will still be around. You don't think their presence concerns her?"

"She knows they're all friends and family who will be in attendance at our reception long after my bride and I leave."

The older woman shook her head, looking at Matt as if he'd lost his mind, then addressed Claire. "Creeping around in the dark trying to catch vermin doesn't sound like a very romantic wedding night. What do you think of this?"

Matt grinned, answering for his fiancée. "It was her idea."

"There will be other nights for romance." Claire leaned over, kissing the sheriff on the cheek. "We have a lifetime."

Alice shook her head and moved into the pantry, calling out from inside it. "Why do you want to move the reception here?"

"I'm hoping to make the opportunity irresistible by giving her the impression everyone is here, miles from town."

"What do you need from me?" Nate asked in a low tone.

Hannah looked over at him as Alice emerged from the pantry with an armload of supplies. It was the first time she'd heard the man speak since he returned. She walked over to the table and gathered up the potatoes and peelings.

"Your presence will be the most important thing."

Why? Matt's answer worried her. *What's Nate going to do?*

"Especially when Randy kicks up a fuss," Claire added.

"How do you know he will?" Hannah wanted to know.

"Randy always does. He's moody and malicious. Easily angered. Jealous and possessive of his wife. Enjoys creating drama and needling others, in particular Nate." Claire rolled her eyes. "Something always sets that man off."

"The perfect wedding guest." Alice's sarcasm floated across the room.

"In this case, yes," Matt responded calmly. "Randy's weak, and once he's worked up, Nate will tell him we're rounding up the rustlers. That should rattle him into doing something stupid."

"But hopefully not dangerous," Hannah said softly, then headed to the sink.

While the sheriff laid out details for Nate, Hannah sliced onions and potatoes into a frying pan. Alice soon joined her at the stove. The two women made quick work of cooking a meal of salt pork, potatoes, green beans, and gravy, letting the others hash out the particulars of the plan undisturbed.

Afterwards, Claire and Matt declined to stay, riding off together as Hannah went to get the children for dinner. Her gaze kept wandering to Nate during the meal. He was quiet, even for him. Only she and Jemma would be in the house tonight. *I hope he'll come up, ready to talk.*

Long after dark, Nate walked alone from the bunkhouse. The moon provided ample light, allowing him to set forth without a lantern. He moved along at a quick pace, unwilling to linger in the bitter cold. The house was dark, giving him pause. Still he entered, maneuvering through the darkness of his childhood home easily, in search of Hannah.

Nate found her by the living-room window. With the fire banked and no lamps lit, she stood mostly in shadow. A single moonbeam illuminated a section of her face, suggesting a pensive

271

expression. His mind leapt back in time, recalling how Faith had looked right before she'd broken their engagement. An icy needle of fear entered his heart. He already cared for this woman more than he'd ever intended.

Without announcing his presence, Nate studied her. Hannah had dominated his thoughts the entire time he'd spent tracking the deliverymen to a cattle yard in Eugene. He should've been excited by the apparent confirmation they were after the right suspects. Instead, all he cared about was seeing her again.

His temper had cooled out on the trail, but home again, his heart and mind battled. No one else seemed overly troubled by what Hannah had done. *But no one else spent as much time with her.*

I'm probably overreacting. But what if I'm not.

How many clues to Faith's real outlook did I dismiss? Maybe the past is clouding my judgment. But remembering the past keeps a person from repeating it.

Really, it's a matter of trust. Can I trust her?

Then there was the issue of intent. *What is mine?*

Jemma's soft words about wanting Nate to be her daddy left him reeling. Part of him had wanted to sweep the little girl up into his arms and make her promises. He already loved her. *But.* Doubt riddled his feelings for her mother. *And.* On River's Bend, she'd have no playmates. Visits from friends and family would be rare. *Would that be fair to her or …?*

He took a breath and stepped forward. "Hannah."

"Hi." She turned to face him.

"I've been thinking about you."

"Is that good?"

"I … don't know." Nate aimed for honesty but didn't know how to express to her what didn't make sense to him. "I can't seem to sort out my feelings."

Hannah didn't respond for a moment, then cautiously asked, "Would you rather not escort me to the wedding?"

"No. Yes." He shook his head. "I mean, I would like to if you're still so inclined."

"I am, if that's what you want."

"It is."

"All right then."

"Good."

Silence stretched between them. A minute passed. Hannah cleared her throat. "Um … Did you learn anything new while you were gone?"

"I tracked them to a cattle yard. Sean's checking it out."

"That's good."

"Yes." Nate thrust his hands into his coat pockets. "It'll be Christmas in a couple of days."

"Yes. Hard to believe."

"Did you…?"

"I finished Jemma's present."

"Good."

"Yes."

"Well … I should go." He turned and started walking away.

The hesitant way she wished him *good night* made Nate long for the ease they'd shared only days ago. *I probably just need some time. By Christmas, I'll have it figured out.* "Good night."

Christmas dawned with clear skies, breathtaking cold and Nate no less troubled. However, as the day progressed, his mood lightened. He, along with his brothers, Alice, and the boys joined Hannah and Jemma at the main house, gathering around the tree to exchange small gifts. Each child's delight in receiving a present was a pleasure of its own. His favorite moment of the morning was seeing a delicate flush spread over Hannah's cheeks as she opened his gift to her: several skeins of yarn spun from a neighbor's goats dyed in various colors. Her smile when she looked up to thank him was a vision he'd never forget.

After a family breakfast of sausages and pancakes, they all

separated to get ready for the wedding. When it was time to go, he took Hannah and Jemma to the church in his parents' buggy while his brothers brought Alice, Jason, and John in the larger wagon. During the ceremony, the little girl sat between him and her mother in the pew. Nate couldn't stop glancing over at his companions, warmth spreading though him. *We look like a family*.

Afterward, everyone took turns hugging the bride, radiant in her deep-red dress and long lace veil. People embraced the groom, fair to bursting with pride, next. It took some time for each of them to complete the process but Nate didn't mind. Even the crowded confines of the filled-past-brimming church failed to bother him. The happiness of the newly married couple seemed to flow into him. He buried his doubts, allowing himself to enjoy every moment.

Finally, the guests made their way outside, heading to the Bar 7 for the reception. Nate had hired some local girls to set up, serve food, and clean up so Hannah and Alice could simply attend the party. Therefore, everything was ready when they arrived home. The regular living-room furniture was gone. The space now held numerous chairs and a table, loaded with food dishes and a large cake sitting on one end, pushed up against the wall.

Lizzie Jane Collier had insisted on providing the wedding cake, her present to the bride and groom. Although it looked beautiful, his cousin had been suspicious. She'd read about a woman in Texas who killed an entire wedding party by poisoning a cake. Claire told him she'd tasked her youngest brothers, George and Daniel, with taking care of the problem. She wouldn't tell Nate what the boys were going to do but he had a feeling it'd be at very least entertaining.

Nate took his companions' coats, hung them in the mudroom then stood in the kitchen doorway, trying to locate either of them in the packed living room. After a few minutes, he spied Jemma in the corner farthest from the table. She was with John and

Jason, playing with their Christmas presents, wooden horses from him and various crocheted animals from Hannah. He watched them, feeling sad for a moment. *Jed should be here.*

Donald, Faith's son, joined the children, shifting Nate's attention. Curiosity took hold of him. He glanced around again and found his ex-fiancée near her son, standing with her sister, Mercy. Her face was pale with dark circles under her eyes and she was painfully thin. Although he avoided listening to gossip, Claire mentioned once the woman's marriage to Randy Haze seemed to have little joy.

Her expression a blank, polite mask, Faith looked over at him as though she'd sensed his gaze. Empathy for the woman he once loved welled up and Nate walked over to her. He had no romantic interest but it was time to stop avoiding her. When he stopped in front of her, some not-so-hushed whispers sprang up among the guests surrounding them.

Ignoring the hum of gossip, he focused on Faith. "Hi."

"Hello," she greeted him politely.

"Enjoying the party?"

"Yes, we are. Thank you."

The stilted exchange held more words than they'd shared in years. He shifted his weight, trying to think of something to say. "Um … your son is a handsome boy."

"Thank you." Faith gave him a brief, pleased smile.

The din of countless people talking started eating away at his peace. His head began to throb. *Why did I think this was a good idea?* Nate felt the urge to walk out the door and join Jack in the barn, but he smiled back at her instead. For a second, the conversations around them paused. He felt the weight of others' increased interest, then the chatter around them resumed.

"Your date is pretty."

His smile broadened, becoming natural rather than simply polite. Just the thought of Hannah eased some of his tension. He glanced around, searching for her bright hair. "She's special."

"I'm happy for you."

Her words barely registered. Nate had at last spotted his date. Hannah was in the opposite corner from her daughter, with Randy standing way too close to her. A bright flush suddenly spread over her cheeks. *What nastiness is Randy sharing now?*

"Excuse me." Without waiting for a response, he headed straight for Hannah.

"Do you enjoy working here? Must be hard out here all alone with so many men." Hannah noted the unpleasant glee in the man's gaze. Despite the considerate facade, she understood Randy intended his words to bite.

"Excuse me. I need to go check on something."

Without another word, she walked away from the loathsome man. Hannah took three steps before a hand clamped on her arm, halting her mid-stride. She looked back at Randy and gave him a cold smile.

"Remove your hand, now."

"Certainly," Randy agreed easily, his tone implying she was overreacting as he released her. "I just wanted to introduce you to Miss Lizzie Jane Collier."

The rustler. Gossip-monger. Hannah shifted her attention to the dark-haired woman beside him, keeping a polite expression firmly in place. "A pleasure to meet you."

All of a sudden, Randy muttered something rude, his mouth puckering as if he tasted something sour. He stalked away seconds later. Relieved, Hannah didn't give him a second thought.

"So you're the woman who's finally lassoed the Recluse."

Now if I can just get rid of her. "I'm afraid I don't know what you mean."

"Don't be afraid, love," she mocked, setting Hannah's teeth on edge. "Nate's a fine stallion. He'll serve you well as long as you like being stuck out in the wilderness."

"That won't be an issue."

Lizzie Jane threw back her head, giving a deep-throated laugh. "Broke his spirit already? Congratulations."

She walked away without another word. Hannah stared after her. *I don't know who's creepier, that woman or Randy Haze.*

"Having a good chat?"

Hannah turned to face Nate, troubled by the odd note in his voice. "Not really." Aware of all the people around them, she added in a whisper, "She's different."

"That's one word."

"Is something wrong?"

"I heard what you said."

Puzzled, she thought back but couldn't figure out what could've disturbed him. "I don't understand."

"I should've known."

"What are you talking about?"

"You wouldn't want to live at River's Bend."

Chapter 20

For some seconds Hannah was too stunned to speak. They'd discussed this. She'd thought Nate believed her and had set aside his notion about all women not wanting to live on his homestead instead of just some. However, the bitterness he expressed now had her rethinking that conclusion.

"What are you talking about?"

"Never mind." He nodded to the door. She looked over to see Claire's brothers entering the room. Daniel had something under his shirt. "We'll talk later."

"Indeed, we will." Steel threaded her promise.

Screams and shouts rang out before she could say anything else. With wide eyes, Hannah watched the two McConkey boys chase a large black cat across the room. Before they, or anyone else, could catch the cat, it ran into the wedding cake, knocking it to the floor.

Suddenly, Maggie's voice cut through the din and commanded silence. Everyone froze as the boys' mother strode across the room. She plucked the cat out from under the table, then, with it firmly held in her arms, marched her sons out of the room.

Hannah and Nate went over to help clean up the mess. They shoved the cake remains onto a couple of empty platters, then, while Alice and the hired girls washed off the table and mopped the floor, carried them into the kitchen. Inside, Claire had her arms around her brothers, quietly praising them. Maggie cleaned up Fluffy then handed Mrs. Bishop her pet. The old woman, seated at the table enjoying a cup of tea and cookies, settled the cat on her lap. Quickly they scraped the cake into the belly of the stove, then one by one each of them returned to the party, the boys attempting to look chastised instead of triumphant.

As Hannah entered the living room, she noticed Lizzie Jane, clearly furious, marching toward Claire. She heard Alice call out for single women to gather so the bride could throw her bouquet and smiled. The older woman had impeccable timing.

The group of women snared Hannah when they gathered. She was surprised, moments later, to catch the bouquet. A rush of emotion filled her as she held the soft, fake flowers. Heat crawled up her neck when she looked up and realized everyone had focused on her. Thankfully, Alice then announced that the newlywed couple was about to depart and the crowd's attention shifted from her to them.

Most of the guests followed Claire and Matt outside to a waiting buggy and waved them off despite the cold. Right after they drove away, before everyone went back inside, one of the Rolfe's ranch hands rode up. The man made a show of delivering a message to Nate as planned. A number of people paused, obviously curious, and then the sound of a loud, obnoxious voice came from the house.

Their attention diverted, the guests streamed through the open door. Hannah entered the house last, following Nate. Hushed silence fell over the gathering when she walked into the living room again. Although told to expect such a public display, the sight of Randy standing in the middle of the space, red-faced and glaring at everyone, still astonished her.

"I told you not to speak to him." The man scooped up his son and grabbed Faith by her arm, in what looked like a painful grip. "We're going home."

A grim-faced Nate stepped in front of Randy. "You shouldn't leave without hearing the good news."

"Not interested in anything you have to say, Rolfe," the other man snapped as he stepped around him.

"You should be." Nate turned, raising his voice so that it carried throughout the room. "I just learned the rustlers have been connected to a local business." Randy stopped and glanced back, his face now pale. "Our deputy is already rounding up the guilty and is confident he'll have the whole gang behind bars by tomorrow."

"Good for him." Randy scowled then exited the building with his family in tow.

Concerned, Nate followed them outside. When he was within arm's reach, Faith looked over her shoulder and gave him a tiny shake of her head. He stilled, sensing any further interference might make matters worse, and held his tongue with effort. From the edge of the yard, he watched them go over to the barn, then drive away several minutes later.

When Nate headed back to the house, he discovered another witness to the Haze family's departure. Faith's sister stood in the doorway. Mercy ducked inside soon after he noticed her but returned, bundled for the weather, when he reached the porch steps. In silence, she moved past him and started walking off into the twilight.

"Wait," Nate called out. "I'll get someone to take you home."

"No. Thank you."

"It's cold and it'll be full dark before you reach town."

"I'll be fine."

"I insist."

The young woman stopped, turning to look at him. "I under-stand you're trying to be kind but I *will be fine*."

Nate shook his head as Mercy resumed walking. Even if it had been a spring day, with Matt's plan unfolding, he believed she needed an escort. He hurried into the house, seeking one of his brothers. To his surprise, he found Rowdy just inside the door, shrugging into his coat and already intent on seeing her safely home.

Well if that doesn't beat all. Nate stared at the empty doorway, where his brother had stood seconds before. Rowdy had wasted no time on his typical banter, immediately going after Mercy. *He's sweet on her.*

Another Rolfe/Ellis romance will be complicated. With a shake of his head, Nate walked into the living room. He scanned the thinning crowd until he found Hannah. *But matters of the heart usually are.*

Hannah noticed Nate heading in her direction as she watched Lizzie Jane, coat in hand, moving toward the doorway. The other woman stopped and turned around when he passed by her. *If looks could kill...*

"What's wrong?" Nate stepped in front of Hannah.

"Miss Collier appeared." She paused, moving to unblock her view, and frowned. Lizzie Jane was gone. "Livid with you."

"Good."

Hannah shivered. "I'm not sure I agree."

"We hoped my little announcement would disturb her. Angry people make poor decisions."

"I know but—" A small hand tugged on her skirt, distracting Hannah.

"I want to see the kitties."

"Can you ask nicely?" She knelt down beside her daughter.

"May I please see the kitties now?"

There was more than a trace of ill humor in her tone but Hannah decided to ignore it. She gathered the little girl in her arms and stood up. "Okay, pumpkin."

"I'm not a pumpkin, Mama," Jemma protested.

"You're not?" Hannah pretended to consider that. "Are you a watermelon, then?"

One small giggle was her reward. "No."

"Perhaps you're a turnip." A deep voice joined in the game.

"Nate." A series of giggles erupted from the bundle in her arms. "No, not a turnip."

"A potato?"

"I'm a little girl."

"You are?" Nate affected amazement.

"I are."

Hannah smiled before correcting her daughter. "I am."

Jemma's expression became serious. "No, you're a woman."

After giving her a gentle squeeze, she bent over and put her daughter on her feet. "You are quite right, little miss. Now, if you'd like to go see those kitties, go get your coat."

Jemma clapped her hands in delight and raced off, slowing her pace slightly when Hannah called out for her to walk.

"She's tired of the grown-ups' party?"

"I'm afraid so."

"Don't be. I'm tired of it too. May I accompany you?"

"Please do." Hannah shot him a serious look. "It'll give us a chance to talk."

"All right, I'll go fetch our coats and let Ben know where I'll be."

"Thank you."

Jemma returned with her coat only half on as Nate walked away. Hannah finished fastening her buttons, then the two of them headed in the direction of the mudroom. In the kitchen, they met up with the eldest Rolfe brother again. They left the house a few minutes later.

Outside, the icy-cold air felt refreshing. Nate handed her the lantern, then scooped up Jemma, carrying her daughter easily on his shoulders. After entering the barn, they remained near the door, avoiding the people hitching up their horses at the far end of the structure.

Nate put the little girl down and Jemma looked up at him, her bottom lip protruding in a slight pout. He pulled his hat off, plopping it down on her uncovered head. Delight transformed her expression. Giggling, she ran off.

As soon as they were relatively alone, Hannah faced him and asked softly, "What did you mean earlier?"

"Not sure what you're referring to."

"Your comment." Not amused by his stall tactic, she pinned him with her gaze. "About River's Bend."

Nate held her gaze a moment, then looked away. "You told her it wouldn't be a problem."

"Yes, and?"

"You don't understand how that sounds?"

Like no matter what I say, you hear a reason I wouldn't like your homestead. Hannah kept the contentious thought to herself and patiently stated, "Like if I'm ever lucky enough to have you for my own, I'd be proud to live on River's Bend."

His gaze swung back to her. "That's what you meant?"

"Yes."

"Oh." Nate stared at her for a long moment. A smile slowly spread across his face. "Hannah, I—"

"It's time," Ben announced as he walked in.

"I have to go." Nate reached out, touching her fingers gently. "Can we talk tomorrow?"

He'd been about to say something amazing. Hannah was sure of it. She wanted to protest, demanding he stay. But she knew the plan. He and Ben needed to meet up with the sheriff now.

"I'll be waiting." Her whisper was a promise.

Hannah left them to their task, gathering up her daughter, and returning to the house over Jemma's tearful objections. The family planned a traditional Christmas meal a few days after the wedding and hopefully the capture of the rustlers. For tonight, she put together a simple dinner from the leftover reception dishes on a tray and they ate quietly in her bedroom.

283

Once Jemma was down for the night, Hannah returned to the living room. The guests had left. A couple of ranch hands were moving the furniture back in place. Evie had claimed a seat on the couch, with Lily in a wicker basket asleep at her feet. She was entertaining the boys by reading them a story while Alice helped the hired girls clean up.

Hannah rolled up her sleeves and pitched in. Work helped distract her from worry. An hour later, the house was clean, a ranch hand had taken the girls home, and everyone was in bed. She lay awake staring at the ceiling until the early morning hours, hoping all went well and everyone would come home safe. When it started to rain, the soothing sound finally lulled her to sleep.

Hours later, Hannah woke with gritty eyes to a bright room and the sound of people talking. She threw back the covers and rushed through her morning routine. Eager to see Nate and learn what happened, she quickly moved down the hall. She found only the children in the living room. After pausing to drop a kiss on her daughter's head and greet the boys, she went into the other room.

Disappointment filled Hannah when she entered. Only Alice, Evie, and the baby occupied the kitchen. The other women looked as tired as she felt. She swallowed a sigh.

"No word?"

"Not yet." Alice dished a bowl of oatmeal for her with a little cinnamon and sugar sprinkled on it.

Hannah carried her bowl to the table and sat down next to Evie. Her appetite non-existent, she stirred her food without taking a bite. A number of minutes passed in silence, with all eyes trained on the window, waiting. Finally, Claire drove up.

Alice hurried her in. "Is everyone okay?"

"Yes."

"Thank God." Evie slumped in her chair. "Now, why don't you look happy?"

"They caught Lizzie Jane's deliverymen in the process of stealing cattle from the Double J."

Hannah sensed it wasn't all good news. "But?"

"Lizzie Jane got away. She evaded the men Matt had trailing her from here, but Ben spotted her in town right after her men were jailed. Unfortunately, she noticed him as well and ran off into the woods. Nate tracked her for awhile but after it started raining..." Claire shook her head. "She left the bakery a mess, flour everywhere. Sean and Jacob are still looking through the storeroom."

"What for?"

"Matt thinks she was hiding her profits in those heavy sacks. Hopefully, she missed some."

"And Randy?" Hannah wanted to know.

"No evidence tying him to her or the gang, not yet anyway." Evie heaved a tired sigh. "Now what?"

"They're questioning the men and searching her home as well as the bakery, trying to find a clue to where she's gone."

"I bet Randy knows."

"Matt has Ben keeping an eye on him, hoping Randy will do something stupid. That's why most criminals get caught."

"So more waiting?"

"Yeah. Sorry, Evie."

"Pay me no mind. I just want this over and done with."

"I know." Claire went over and gave her friend a hug.

"Maybe you could give me and Lily a ride home?"

"Ben asked if you'd please stay here until he's finished."

"How come I can't go home, but you can drive all over the countryside alone?" The peevish response reflected the new mother's fatigue.

"Because I'm not taking care of a brand-new baby. And, I didn't drive here alone. Pa escorted me from town to the Bar 7's drive."

"Sorry." Evie's cheeks flushed. "I'm ... I don't know what I am ... I'm sorry."

Claire hugged her again. "It's okay. Let me go put up the horse then we'll talk more over a cup of coffee."

"All right."

Feeling restless, Hannah volunteered to help. She grabbed her coat and the two women exited the house, leading the horse and vehicle to the barn. Midway to there a woman stepped out from the shadows of a small shed.

"What are *you* doing here?" The question burst from Hannah without thought and she immediately regretted it.

"Since the sheriff saw fit to steal my family." Lizzie Jane aimed a small, but deadly, six-shooter at them. "I figured I should return the favor."

"You consider your men family, how nice."

Hannah flicked a glance at Claire, puzzled by her inane comment. The other woman's expression didn't offer a clue to what she was thinking. Nervous, she looked back at Lizzie Jane.

"Pa started the gang before I was born, taught my brothers and I everything we know." The woman gestured with her gun for them to get into the buggy. "I always clean up after a job, tie up loose ends, then break them out of jail if needs be."

"Sounds like you get the dirty work."

Lizzie Jane's smile was pure evil. "I enjoy it."

The sight chilled Hannah to the bone. She could hardly breathe as the outlaw climbed in beside her. Three people on a seat made for two was a tight squeeze but she didn't give that discomfort much thought. The end of the muzzle pressed against her ribs had her full attention.

"Head to town."

"But—"

"Claire," Lizzie Jane interrupted impatiently. "Do you want me to pull the trigger now? The bullet will pass through her and then you, killing you both."

"The ranch hands would hear the shot."

"Yes, but you'd be dead and I'd get away."

"Then you wouldn't have hostages."

"Easy enough to gather more from the house during the commotion."

Jemma. Fresh terror washed over Hannah. She turned her head and met Claire's gaze, silently begging her to drive.

"All right. Where in town do you want to go?"

"The mercantile and keep your mouth shut from now on."

Hannah saw Claire's jaw clench but her friend complied. As the miles passed, she prayed they'd run into someone, anyone, to signal for help. But they didn't see another soul. The trip to town was silent, uneventful, and nerve-racking.

Lizzie Jane didn't speak again until Fir Mountain came into view. She then directed Claire to skirt the town, approaching the store from the back. When they pulled up, she motioned for them to get out and walk to the door in front of her.

"Open it. Go in," Lizzie Jane ordered. Inside, as soon as the door swung shut, she called out. "Randy."

"Lizzie?" The shopkeeper entered the room. He stilled, looking alarmed by the sight of her pistol. "What are you doing?"

"Tying up loose ends." She lifted the gun and shot him.

On the sidewalk, yards away, Nate noticed Ben slip into the back of the store. His eyes narrowed. His cousin was supposed to be watching from a distance. He wouldn't risk Randy seeing him without a good reason. As he picked up his pace, a gunshot rang out from inside the building. He sprinted forward, entering the mercantile from the front entrance a moment later.

"Well, well, if it isn't the Recluse himself."

Nate kept his expression a blank mask, covering his shock at the sight greeting him. Claire and Hannah, pale-faced, stood near him, with the only member of the rustling gang not sitting in jail behind them. And she held a revolver.

"Lizzie Jane," Nate called out softly, trying not to alarm her. He didn't want the woman making any rash choices. A board creaked. Out of the corner of his eye, he saw Ben emerge from the back room. He cleared his throat to cover the sound, keeping the outlaw's attention on him. "What brings you out today?"

"Just taking care of business."

"Why don't we talk about it over a cup of coffee?"

Her short bark of laughter held no amusement. "Honestly, sugar, you're not my type."

"Then why all the concern for my poor broken heart?"

"A means to an end."

"A distraction or discrediting me?"

"Men have such egos." Lizzie Jane smiled and the sight put ice in his blood. "It was never about you."

"I don't understand."

"Then I'll speak slower so you can. Step away from the door or I'll blow a hole the size of Texas through your lady friend."

"All right." Nate moved as slowly as he dared while Ben crept up behind the armed woman. "Why the gossip, then?"

Lizzie Jane pressed her gun harder into Hannah's side. "Are you really that simple?"

Comprehension dawned. "Randy."

"A mutual enemy makes for fast friends. He shared every tidbit he overheard, like those the deputy's trusting wife made to his own. Easy to hide cattle when you know where the law is looking."

Lizzie Jane pushed her hostages forward, stopping several feet from the door. A crowd was gathering in front of the big window. She scowled at them as the sheriff stepped inside.

"Give me the gun, Miss Collier, there's nowhere to go."

"Tell them to back off." Lizzie gestured with her weapon toward the crowd. "Including the bastard thinking he's sneaking up on me."

Sheriff Marston shook his head. "It's time to surrender."

"I don't think so, lawman." Her eyes narrowed. "Unless you

want me to shoot your pretty new wife, you'll release my pa and the boys and provide horses for us all. I'll let these ladies go when we're safely away."

"I'm not letting you take her anywhere."

"Then you can watch her die." She shifted her gun, aiming directly at Claire.

Hannah stomped hard on Lizzie Jane's foot, startling the woman. The men seized their opportunity. Matt swept his bride out of danger, pushing her behind a canned-bean display. Nate grabbed Hannah and thrust her behind him to protect her with his body while Ben jumped the outlaw from behind. They wrestled on the floor and another shot rang out. Matt charged forward then, pulling her off his friend.

"You okay?" the sheriff demanded, while he placed a sneering Lizzie Jane in handcuffs.

"No." Blood spread rapidly, staining Ben's shirt as he sat up, with one hand on his wounded shoulder. "Hurts like hell."

"Claire is running for the doctor. For you and Randy."

Randy? Nate glanced at Lizzie Jane, remembering the sound that brought him in here. The woman hadn't been issuing idle threats. She really was willing to shoot someone.

"Good." The wounded man leaned against a pickle barrel.

Nate knelt down beside his cousin with one hand holding Hannah's, unwilling to let her go. "I'll send Sam for Evie."

"She's going to kill me." Ben closed his eyes.

"Why?"

"Because he promised he wouldn't get hurt." Evie entered the store, hurried over, and knelt on her husband's other side. "But I'll forgive you. I always do."

Ben opened his eyes, smiling at her. A second later, he frowned. "Sam couldn't have brought you already. What are you doing here? It still might be dangerous. And where's Lily?"

"Lily is safe with Alice. Hank escorted me here at my insistence so I could tell the sheriff that Hannah and Claire disappeared.

And as for danger, my dear husband, you're the one who has been shot."

"Sorry."

"Well, don't let it happen again." Evie leaned over, gently kissing him.

Claire brought Dr. Wright in a moment later. The doctor glanced at Ben as he strode into the back room, clearly trying to assess which of the wounded needed his attention first. He returned in less than a minute. Nate looked up and saw him shake his head at Matt.

Randy Haze is beyond help. The obnoxious man's death didn't trigger grief but Nate suddenly felt incredibly weary. He stood up slowly, moving aside with Hannah so Dr. Wright could work on Ben. Once the doctor patched his wound enough to slow the blood loss, Sam and Jacob helped their cousin get to his feet. The men then headed off to the doctor's office with Evie trailing behind them.

Nate pulled Hannah to one side of the store and wrapped his arms around her. Unable to speak, he rested his cheek on the top of her head. Sometimes he found it difficult to express what he felt. His mind blanked. Words failed him. Now, one terrifying thought held him hostage. *She could've died.*

Matt stepped up beside them. The sheriff spoke his name in a manner Nate couldn't ignore. He straightened, loosening his embrace, without letting Hannah go.

"Yes?"

"I need your help. I sent for Sean, but I need him to take Lizzie Jane to the jail."

"Of course, but give us a minute first." He waited until Matt moved back near Claire and a sulking, but blessedly quiet, Lizzie Jane then asked, "Are you all right?"

"Shaken but I'm fine. Not a scratch."

"Good." His hands moved to her waist, resting on either side above the generous curves of her hips. "It seems I'm needed here but." He kissed the tip of her nose. "Remember, when I get home, we're going to talk."

Hannah stared up at Nate, holding his gaze for a long moment before nodding. He released her with clear reluctance then moved away to help the sheriff as Sean walked in. While the deputy took Lizzie Jane out through the back and the two men started dispersing the crowd, Claire came over to stand with her. They could hear people already sharing their accounts of the morning's events. Those who had witnessed Ben's bravery proclaimed the man a hero to all who would listen. As they heard citizen after citizen who once viewed Ben with suspicion now sing his praises, the women exchanged pleased smiles.

A number of minutes passed and Hannah's shock started to fade. Although exhausted, she was restless. She wanted to go home, hug her daughter and … try to forget. A glance at Claire found her friend in a similar frame of mind.

Together Hannah and Claire left the store, stopping outside long enough for Matt and Nate to see they were going. Busy, neither man protested. They went to check on Ben straight away and found him stitched up, ready to go home, as well. After a few minutes' discussion, Jacob left. He took Claire's horse and buggy to the livery and from there borrowed a large wagon. Sam helped the injured man into the bed, his wife settled beside him, then everyone without a mount piled in the vehicle for a ride out to the Bar 7 Ranch.

A few hours later, Ben rested comfortably in his own home with Evie and Lily. The ranch hands, along with the younger Rolfe brothers, started catching up on neglected chores. Tired, Hannah and Claire sat quietly and shared several cups of coffee with Alice while watching the children play.

Stars shone in the night sky by the time Matt and Nate rode up to the main house. Alice and the boys had already retired to their cabin. Jemma had long since fallen asleep, unaffected by the drama in town because she didn't know the danger her mother faced. Hannah and Claire were in the living room chatting about nothing, really, when they heard footsteps in the kitchen.

Matt came in alone. "Has anyone seen my bride? I seem to have lost her."

"I'm right here, waiting for you." Claire stood up, turning to face her husband. "Is it over?"

"For us, it's just beginning." Matt grinned. "For Lizzie Jane, I mean Elizabeth Henley, it's—"

"Henley? You caught the Henley gang?"

"With a lot of invaluable assistance, including from my amazing bride, yes, ma'am."

"Oh my." Claire looked at Hannah. "The Henley Gang is wanted for cattle rustling, bank robbery, and murder across several states." She turned back to her husband. "Will we have to delay our honeymoon until you know where they'll go to be tried first?"

Matt shook his head. "Received a wire from a Texas ranger at noon. He'd been out on assignment, just read an old report on the rustling here, and suggested the Henleys. Didn't take long to confirm or for that ranger to act."

"They're going to Texas?" The thought of the woman she'd known as Lizzie Jane being far away brought a measure of peace to Hannah.

"Already have an official wire from the governor. I'm to turn over custody of my prisoners to a group of Texas rangers who are on route to Fir Mountain now."

"So it's over?" Claire asked again.

"For them, sweetheart, yes. Not for us. I know it's too late to reach our hotel tonight, so could I interest you in a night in your new home before starting our honeymoon?"

"As long as you're there." Claire focused on the sheriff as though he was the only person in the world while she walked over to join him. "Anywhere is good." The couple embraced then, lost in each other, turned to leave. Hannah was startled when the other woman stopped and looked back at her. "I completely forgot about Nell Hansel."

"Nell Hansel?"

A floorboard creaked, distracting Hannah. She glanced over at the kitchen doorway and found Nate. Her gaze drank in the sight of him until a soft clearing of the throat brought her attention back to Claire.

"Nell couldn't pay much more than room and board but she desperately needs help on her farm."

"Nell is offering her a job?" Frowning, Nate strode up.

"Nothing definite but it seems promising. Is that great?"

"No."

Her brow furrowed. "Why not?" Matt leaned down, whispering in the other woman's ear. Although Claire scowled up at him, her eyes sparkled. "My husband says we need to go so you can talk."

The newlyweds left after a round of good nights, walking to the barn for their horses. Alone now, Hannah could feel Nate's agitation. She sat down on the couch, inviting him to do the same. He refused, with a jerky shake of his head.

"What's wrong?"

"You can't take that job."

His arrogance put her back up. Hannah stared at him, trying to remain calm. Nate didn't normally act high-handed. *He couldn't have meant it the way it sounded. There has to be a good reason.*

Hannah took a deep breath. "Why not?"

"Because you can't."

His flat statement further ruffled her feathers. Hannah had a harder time keeping her composure. She reached down, smoothing an afghan over her legs. "Please explain."

"It's not necessary."

"Yes, it is." She brought her hand up and rubbed the back of her neck. "I need a job."

"No, you don't."

"Excuse me."

"As Jemma's mother, you're family. We'll take care of you."

"Take care of me?" she echoed.

"Yes."

"Because of Jemma?"

"Of course."

"No." Spine stiff, Hannah made her position clear. "I didn't come here so the Rolfe family could *take care of me*."

Nate waved one hand in an impatient gesture. "Yes, but now that we know everything, we will."

"You will what exactly? Take care of me?"

"And Jemma. Everyone is in agreement."

Emotions on high, she ground out, "Everyone?"

"My brothers. Ben and Evie."

"Jemma is my responsibility."

"She's a Rolfe."

"She's my daughter."

"Your daughter is a Rolfe."

"What do you meant by that? Are you threatening to take her from me?"

"Of course not."

From Nate's visible frustration, Hannah knew he didn't understand why she was upset and that irritated her more. "Look, it's been a long day and—"

"You're probably tired and not thinking straight."

"I'm—" Hannah clamped her mouth shut, shaking her head. She got up and, worried about saying something she'd regret, started walking away.

"Wait." Something in his tone made her pause. "You don't understand."

"Then please, by all means, explain it to me."

Silence stretched. "I don't know if I can."

"Take the night to think about it and try in the morning."

Hannah marched off to her room, hoping when she woke

sense would return to Nate. *What possessed him?* She flopped on the bed, staring up at the ceiling blindly, trying and failing to sort out her emotions. It was a long time before sleep claimed her.

After a long, restless night, Hannah woke up early the next morning stiff and chilled from sleeping fully dressed on top of the covers. She changed her clothes, then took her time brushing her hair before pinning it up. Soon, she started hearing the everyday noises of people moving around. High-pitched voices signaled the boys and Alice had come up to the house. The low murmur of conversation in the next room told her Jemma was awake and playing with her dolls. Slowly she crossed to the door, knowing it was time to face the day.

Hannah picked up her pace, swiftly going through her daughter's morning routine. She then took Jemma to the kitchen and asked Alice to watch over her. Although the older woman clearly didn't understand her rush, she readily agreed.

With a heavy heart, Hannah returned to her room. *Maybe I am putting the cart before the horse.* She went over to the dresser, pulled open a drawer, then stood, staring at the contents. Her trunks were still up in the attic and she didn't have another job yet, only Claire's suggestion for one.

But Alice doesn't need my help here. Frustrated, she closed the drawer with a hard shove and headed to the wardrobe. *And I don't need to be taken care of.*

Without warning, a knock sounded on the door. Hannah opened it to find Nate in the hall, bleary eyed and haggard, looking as if he'd passed a rough night. She took a measure of comfort in knowing he likely hadn't slept any better than she had.

"Come in."

Nate stepped inside. "I don't know what you want me to say."

"How about, I'm sorry?" Hannah closed the door partway to give them some privacy, upholding a measure of propriety by not shutting it completely.

"All I said was that you don't have to go."

Hannah took a deep breath and tried giving him the benefit of the doubt. "Perhaps you're not trying to be offensive-"

"I offended you?"

"Saying I need taken care of implies I can't do so myself. I am not a child in need of a keeper."

"I didn't mean it like that. I meant to ask you."

"You *meant* to ask if you could take care of *me*?"

"Sort of. Not how you're …" Nate shook his head. "I mean I'd like to. No. It's different."

"I don't understand. What are you trying to say?"

"I was thinking you could marry me."

Her heart fluttered. The words were ones Hannah dreamed of but hadn't dared hope to hear from him. Yet they somehow sounded wrong. Emotions flickered through her, indefinable. She rubbed the hard knot of tension between her brows then met his gaze squarely.

"Why?"

His mouth fell open. After a moment, he echoed, "Why?"

Hannah struggled for the words to express what she felt but couldn't. She settled for a nod.

"Then you and Jemma could stay with me."

"You don't have to marry me to see Jemma. I'll make sure to bring her by whenever I can."

"No." Nate shook his head for emphasis. "Not good enough."

"Good enough or not, it'll have to do." Hannah crossed her arms over her chest.

"Marrying me would solve everything."

Hot pride swelled within her. She lifted her chin. "I'm not a problem to be solved."

"I didn't mean it like that."

"Well, then, how do you mean it?"

"I thought proposing is a good thing." Nate raked a hand through his hair.

296

"That depends."

"On what?"

"On what you want. What is it you want, Nate?"

"You."

"What are you saying?"

"I want you." Emotion roughened his voice. "I want to make a family with you."

"Why?"

"I love you."

His unexpected statement caught her off balance. She sank down on the bed. "You do?"

"Of course, why else would I ask you to marry me?"

A whirlwind of emotion swept through her. Hannah was torn between throwing her arms around him and stomping her foot in frustration. "Why didn't you say so at the start?"

"Say what?"

"That you love me."

"I thought it was obvious."

"Not to me."

"I'm not so good with words." With a crooked smile, Nate went down on a bended knee. "Hannah, I love you. I want to be your husband and spend my life with you. I want to be the father of your children, including Jemma. Will you marry me?"

Hannah reached down, framing his face with her hands and kissed him hard. "I love you too."

"Does that mean yes?"

"Yes."

A cheer erupted in the hallway and someone bumped against the door, causing it to fully open. Startled, Hannah glanced over in time to see a small, calico-clad figure race away, yelling at the top of her little lungs. "We're getting married. We're getting married."

Nate stood up, wrapping his arms around Hannah. She could hear other voices responding to her daughter. Soon they wouldn't be alone. He lowered his forehead to touch hers. She could feel the strength of his happiness and knew it matched hers.

"That's right, we're getting married."

Epilogue

River's Bend – June 1, 1892

"May I turn around now?"

"Well …"

Hannah smiled, feeling Alice give the lace cascading down the backside of her skirt yet another tug.

"I'm done." The older woman rose from her chair and walked in front of Hannah. "You-" Boyish laughter followed by the sound of a chase carried through the cabin wall. She glanced at the curtain-covered window. "What are they up to?" With a shake of her head, she hurried over to the door muttering, "I told them to stay clean." She paused before exiting. "You look beautiful."

"Thank you." Alice's heartfelt sincerity made Hannah misty-eyed. For a few seconds, she stood, staring at the closed door.

Something old.

Hannah went to the dresser and picked up her mother's bible from the top. With the tattered book in hand, she walked over by the window and peeked outside. The afternoon sun shone bright in the clear blue sky. Various trees adorned with leaves in shades of green or pine needles ringed the yard, providing shade. Between their trunks, she could see glimpses of the mighty Santiam River that rounded her soon-to-be home. And standing with his brothers near the split-log benches arranged on the grass, was her groom.

I wish you were here, Ma. Tears threatened again. *You would've liked Nate.*

A child's excited shout drew Hannah's attention to an old tree on the left side of the yard. Ben was pushing her daughter on a swing hanging from the alder's lowest branch. Both man and child wore ear-to-ear grins.

Jemma smiles all the time now. Her gaze settled on Ben for a moment. Taking a bullet subduing Elizabeth Henley had given him a hero's status in their community. A few doubters remained, muttering something ugly on occasion, but those whispers died quickly.

Thanks to her. A wagon with Faith Haze, her son, sister and the minister wheeled up to the yard. With dignity, Randy's widow simply tolerated no gossip in the mercantile or her presence in general. Rumors about one member or another of the Rolfe family no longer dominated Fir Mountain society. *I doubt we'll ever be friends, Ma, but I appreciate her efforts.*

Rowdy stepped up to the wagon and lifted his arms. Hannah smiled when Mercy ignored his offer of assistance and climbed down on her own. *She's not making it easy for him.* Undeterred, Nate's brother followed the young woman to the benches, sitting on the one directly behind her. *But I've seen how she looks at him when he's not aware. There will be another Rolfe bride soon.*

Her gaze wandered to the right and found Evie on another bench, holding a chubby six-month-old Lillian. A couple Hannah didn't recognize, the woman holding a baby of her own, shared the seat. *Henry and his wife?* She'd heard that Evie's long-lost brother and his little family had turned up unexpectedly a few days ago but hadn't met them yet.

Nate's parents strolled past Evie's bench, holding hands like a courting couple. Warmth filled Hannah's heart. Mary and Jeremiah returned from Ireland only a few months ago but she felt close to them already. *You would've liked them too.*

Something new.

Hannah glanced at the mirror across the room. Her wedding dress, a gift from Nate's parents, was made of a printed green fabric. The tailored bodice narrowed at her waist, fastening with tiny buttons up the front. Black lace, sewn along its hem, draped over her hips and accented the full skirt. It was the finest thing she'd ever worn. *And I think they like me too.*

Two sharp raps interrupted Hannah's thoughts. "Come in."

The door swung open and Claire walked inside. *More like waddled.* Nate's affectionate teasing from a few weeks ago ran through her mind. Although his cousin was only about five months along, the petite woman appeared much closer to giving birth.

Claire stopped beside the bed and held up a paper-wrapped package. "I brought—"

Something borrowed.

"Becca hasn't come to do your hair yet?"

"Sorry." Rebecca apologized as she entered, pulling the door shut behind her. "I lost track of time."

Clad in a stylish blue dress, with her dark hair smoothed into a bun at the back of her head, the tall, slender woman was the picture of reserved beauty. A smile tugged at Hannah's lips when she moved closer. *Except for the paint smudge on her left cheek.*

"It's all right," Hannah assured Nate's sister, joining the other women by the bed. "Oh my."

Claire had opened the package, revealing the delicate lace veil she'd worn at her wedding. "My grandmother made this for my mother and Aunt Mary wore it when she married Uncle Miah. Would you like to make it a family tradition?"

Hannah hugged her as tight as she dared. "I'd be honored."

"Okay." Claire pulled back, wearing a pleased smile. "Now finish getting ready, everyone's waiting."

Rebecca walked Hannah over to a chair sitting in front of the dresser as the other woman left the room. "Nervous?"

"A little. Mostly excited."

"Good."

Silence fell while Becca concentrated on weaving Hannah's hair into an elegant crown. *You'd like her as well, Ma. She's comfortable being quiet … like Nate.*

"What do you think?" Becca asked, stepping in front of her.

"I love it, thank you."

"You're welcome. Now for the veil."

Aged lace covered Hannah's bright hair and gently framed her face moments later. Someone knocked before she could thank Becca again. She stood but the younger woman motioned her to stay and answered the summons.

"Is it time?"

"If the bride is ready."

Hannah smiled at the sound of Jed's voice. He'd walked up to the Bar 7 in February, rail-thin and ragged, but sober and determined to make things right. The man had worked hard on the ranch and at rebuilding trust. Today, she was pleased he'd agreed to give her away.

Jed stepped just inside the door, handing a bundle of Mock Orange stems covered in pretty white flowers to Becca. "I brought her bouquet."

"Her bouquet. I forgot to get it from Nate." She gave Hannah a contrite look then addressed Jed again. "Thank you, that was very thoughtful."

"Not so much, Bessie, I needed to come here anyway."

Oh my. Hannah headed over to the pair.

"My name," the young woman responded without heat although she gave each word emphasis, "is Rebecca."

Bessie. Becca. Similar names. Two very different women.

The tips of Jed's ears reddened. "Sorry."

Rebecca nodded then turned to Hannah, handing her the ribbon-bound blossoms. "Need anything else?"

"I don't think so." She placed the stems against the bible in order to hold both in one hand. "Thanks for all your help."

"You're welcome." Nate's sister then quietly left.

"I've been trying to work on that."

"I know."

"But today …" Jed shook his head. "Bessie's on my mind."

Like my ma. Hannah gently touched his arm. "I understand."

"She would've loved to be here. And I thought." He pulled a handkerchief out of his pants pocket. "Maybe you'd like to carry something of hers."

Something blue.

"I'd love to." Hannah sniffed, trying not to cry. As he tucked the bit of linen between the bible and bouquet, she kissed him on the cheek. "Thank you."

"You're welcome." Jed held out his arm. "Ready?"

"I am."

A hush fell over the people waiting as Hannah crossed the yard. Anticipation quickened her heartbeat. In his white dress shirt and black jacket, Nate looked especially handsome. The love and pride in his expression was captivating. Her gaze never wandered from her groom while Jed escorted her down the aisle formed by the two rows of benches.

On the seat directly in front of Nate, Jemma sat with his parents. When they reached that point, the little girl stood up and took Jed's place. Hannah walked the last two steps with her daughter.

Nate held out his hand. Solemnly, Jemma put Hannah's hand on his but didn't release her mother as planned. Instead, she directed a triumphant look at Jed's boys.

"I told you we were getting married."

Laughter erupted. The response seemed to stun Jemma. She froze in place, staring wide-eyed at the amused guests.

"Yes." Nate swooped the little girl up into his arms and reassured her with a smile. "We are."

Feeling blessed, Hannah accepted the hand Nate offered and together they faced the minister.

"Dearly beloved, we are gathered here today to witness this man and woman join together in holy matrimony."

Author Note

Thank you for taking time to read *The Cowboy of River Bend*. If you enjoyed it, please consider telling your friends or posting a short review. Word of mouth is an author's best friend and much appreciated.